Praise for Tequila

"Lots of intrigue, treachery and a wealth of secrets. A wonderful debut that definitely takes a wild ride on the perilous side."

—Steve Berry, *New York Times* and #1 internationally bestselling author

"Tim Reuben fearlessly forges new territory, while masterfully mining old, in his relentlessly entertaining debut thriller, *Tequila*. Not since John Grisham's *The Firm* has a legal backdrop been employed across a broad canvas of crime, corruption, and murder to fashion the ultimate David versus Goliath tale. Reuben's ambition is exceeded only by his storytelling prowess in crafting an epic tale where the tequila of the title becomes a metaphor for the eternal battle between justice and greed. A smashing success right out of the box that is not to be missed."

—Jon Land, *New York Times* and *USA Today* bestselling author

"A family saga with a woman at the heart of the matter is always appealing. That Tim Reuben, in his novel *Tequila*, offers us a love story, legal drama, and surprising plot twists, makes it all the better. His lead female character, Maria Ramirez, as CEO of RAM, a luxury spirits powerhouse, is unforgettable. We root for her from the start as she fights for justice in a world of untruths, cruelty, and cartels."

—Susan Shapiro Barash, author of *Estranged: How Strained Female Friendships Are Mended or Ended*

"What an astonishing debut novel! Tim Reuben masterfully tells an epic story spanning several generations about love, betrayal, and deadly dangers as a family builds their multibillion-dollar international tequila business against all odds. Reuben is an exciting new voice in thriller fiction."

—R.G. Belsky, author of the Clare Carlson mystery series

"This book has it all: immersive scenes, a gripping plot, and a thoughtful exploration of the things that people do for power, even to their own kin. Evoking the Genesis story of Cain and Abel, Reuben has spun an exquisite saga about sibling rivalry, the secrets we keep, the ties that bind, and the urgency of telling the truth, even when there's much to lose. Taking readers from agave farms to boardrooms to far-flung cities with glittering lights, this is a sweeping tale of modern life — and its ancient heart. I was entranced from the first to the last page."

—Otho Eskin, Amazon bestselling author
of the Marko Zorn thriller series

TEQUILA

TIM REUBEN

TEQUILA

A STORY OF SUCCESS, LOVE, AND VIOLENCE

MERIDIAN EDITIONS

WESTPORT, CONNECTICUT

MERIDIAN | EDITIONS

ISBN (paperback): 978-1-959170-27-3
ISBN (hardcover): 978-1-959170-26-6
ISBN (eBook): 978-1-959170-28-0

Cover design by Bill Teitelbaum
Book design by John Lotte

Manufactured in the United States of America

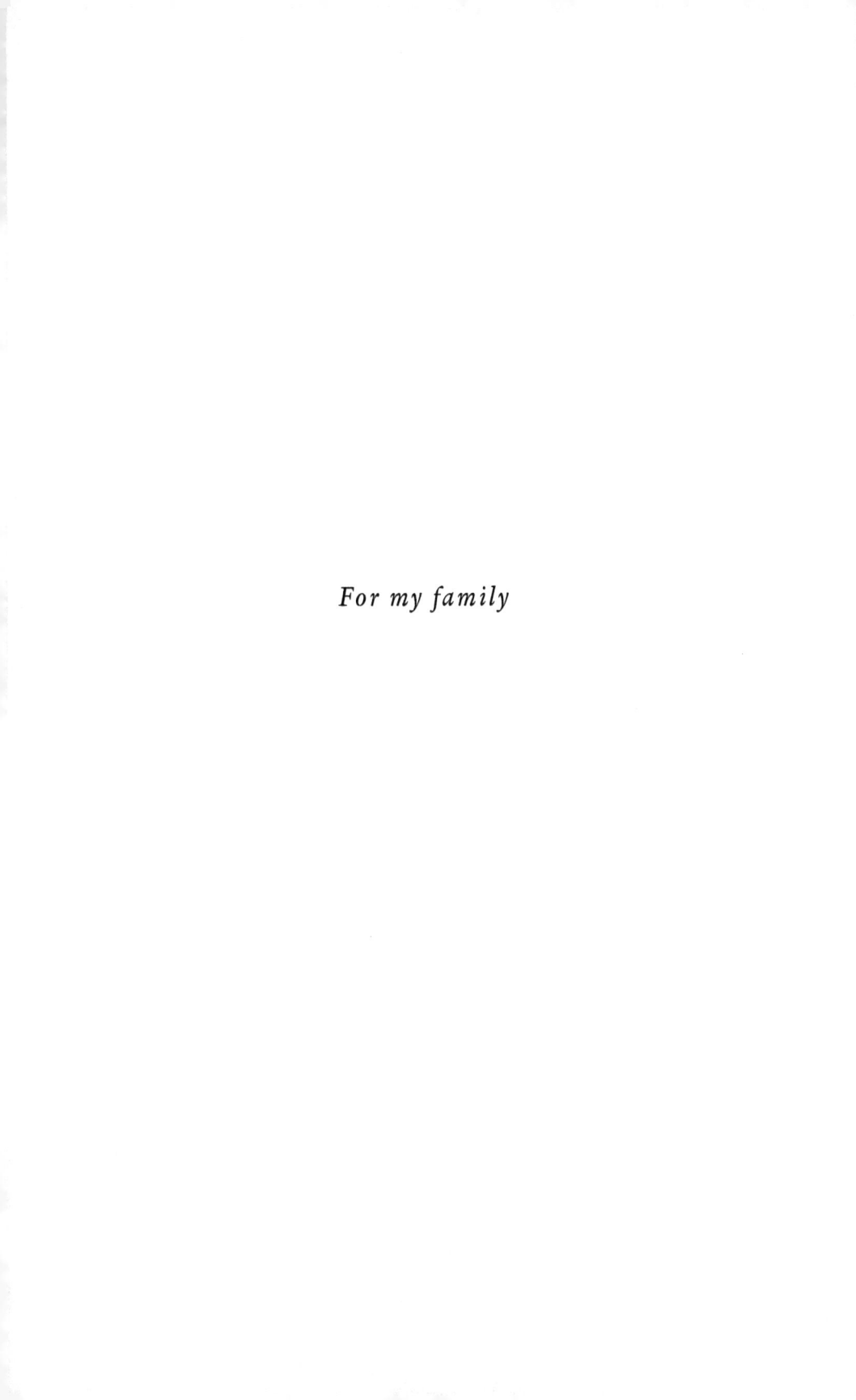

For my family

… Now Abel kept flocks, and Cain worked the soil.

In the course of time Cain brought some of the fruits of the soil as an offering to the Lord.

And Abel also brought an offering —fat portions from some of the firstborn of his flock. The Lord looked with favor on Abel and his offering, but on Cain and his offering he did not look with favor. So Cain was very angry, and his face was downcast.

Then the Lord said to Cain, "Why are you angry? Why is your face downcast? If you do what is right, will you not be accepted? But if you do not do what is right, sin is crouching at your door; it desires to have you, but you must rule over it."

Now Cain said to his brother Abel, "Let's go out to the field." While they were in the field, Cain attacked his brother Abel and killed him.

Genesis 4:2–8
New International Version

TEQUILA

Prologue

1950

T HE SUN WAS HOT at midday over the fields in the Jaliscan Highlands of Mexico. Sotero Ramirez wiped his brow as he worked and then redonned his sombrero. It was September and almost time to harvest the beautiful plants he had nurtured with his sweat and love. He had pruned the sharp stalks, the *quiotes*, and had even hired extra men to help him, the *jimadores*. And they had fought off all the killing insects and worms hungry for the blue Weber agave.

These plants were ten years old—he had worked that long for this harvest, and he had big plans. Soon he would take the hearts and slowly bake them in his large brick oven, then crush them with his stone wheel, extracting the pungent juice inside. Next would come the intense long days to produce the magic liquid that his father had taught him how to make. First the fermentation—he had a special kind of yeast for this—and, second, distilling the fermented liquid, the *mosto*, twice, which itself would take ten days. Finally, he would age the tequila in barrels before bottling.

Sotero had produced his biggest agave crop ever. This year, he planned to make not just the white, the *blanco*, but also the rested, the *reposado*, and the old, the *añejo*. A third he would bottle right away, while the rest went into white oak barrels, one third for three months and the other third for a full year.

Barrels were expensive, but Sotero had decided to make the investment, taking a huge leap of faith that his guess would pay off. Over the shrill objections of Xiomara, he had taken out a loan using his farm as collateral. The interest and terms had been oppressive—at first the Mexican banker had not agreed to loan Sotero the funds.

"Why do you need to make a different, more expensive product?" the banker asked.

"It's my only way forward," had been Sotero's answer. "The white I can sell, but everyone is making white, so I barely break even. If I make the *reposado* and *añejo*, I have almost no competition. No one else is doing it. And it is so wonderful to sip—you don't just drink it all in one quick gulp. The oak enriches the flavor—it is wonderful, so smooth. I think I will be able to sell the *reposado* for twice, maybe three times the price of the *blanco*. And with the *añejo*, maybe even more."

The banker shook his head. "I don't think so. You think the cowboys and peasants will be interested in sipping tequila? Nonsense. They just want to get drunk as fast as possible. And the rich folks will look down their noses at your tequila, thinking it is low-end. They still just want their whisky Manhattans or gin martinis. And when it all fails, I will have to take your land from you—are you *loco*? Do you want to risk losing a property that has been in the Ramirez family for generations? Even with pieces sold off to pay for its upkeep, it is still the largest single farm in our region. Sotero, go home and give up this pipe dream."

But Sotero did not go home; instead, he begged and pleaded and cajoled until the banker relented. Sotero Ramirez got his loan, bought the barrels, and started working harder than ever. At first, he had not planned on making any *blanco*, but Xiomara had insisted. "How are we to pay for food? Or for clothes? Or for all the other costs of keeping up this infernal place?" she had demanded.

"We can use some money from the loan to get us by," Sotero explained.

"You idiot!" Xiomara cried. "We can't take that much of a risk. Have you forgotten your children? Pedro is almost six, but he is growing like a weed, so we need to keep getting more clothes for him. And Marta, she is so smart, even at seven she is reading so many books and needs constant stimulation. And when was the last time I had a new dress? All you think about is tequila and your dreams of making it big with your father's old recipes. Well, you cannot take everything from us. You must make the *blanco* and sell the silver tequila in town like all the other producers so we have enough money to get by. Not negotiable!"

Sotero could not stand the wrath of Xiomara, and after all, she had a point. She was already pregnant with their third child, and *Dios mío*, children were expensive. He wondered why he had been so willing to start a family in the first place. But then, he knew why. Xiomara with her dark eyes and long black hair and deep brown skin—she had a temper like a tornado, but she so excited him even with her angry looks. He adored her. He had wooed her for months until she finally relented and agreed to marry him.

"Why should I be interested in you?" she asked him. "You are just a farmer. You will always have dirty fingernails."

"Maybe so," Sotero answered, "but you will never go hungry. It is a big farm. Besides, don't you think I wash up before coming into the house? And our *hacienda* is old, but it is large, big enough for a big family."

She had looked at him with those piercing eyes, both condescending and not completely trusting. But finally, she succumbed to his logic—and also to his patience and persistence.

"But you must promise me," she said, "that my children will be educated. I don't want them to be farmers. They shouldn't have dirty hands all the time."

Sotero promised and proposed. They were married in a church a few miles outside of the town of Tequila. After the priest pronounced them man and wife and he took her home, he found he could not have her enough. But she would tease him and make him wait and then require him to profess his deepest devotion to her before she would let him seduce her. He was completely devoted—the couple enjoyed that passion of lovers in their twenties, when they have no need for sleep and can make love for hours upon end. Xiomara kept getting pregnant. Sotero was almost thirty and would have three children by then, with more to come if their habits continued. That was part of his reason for seeking bigger returns—his love for Xiomara and the certainty of a huge family to raise and pay for.

After he had harvested and baked and fermented and distilled and aged and bottled, he brought his bottles of *reposado* into town to show the distributors. The *reposado* had a fancier label—another investment of his. He told the distributors that this was a very special tequila that commanded twice the price.

"Why should we pay so much for this batch?" they asked, and so he opened a bottle and offered them all a taste. To his delight, they became very excited and began competing with one another to purchase his product and distribute it. He sold his entire stock of *reposado* on the first day, and it yielded such a profit that he was able to pay off his loan in its entirety.

"*Ay caramba*," exclaimed the banker. "I guess you were right all along. Perhaps you can send me a bottle of that stuff since I was good enough to loan you the money." But Sotero just smiled.

Xiomara was ecstatic. "How much did you end up with?" she asked excitedly.

"Well, after I paid off the loan, there is not much left," he explained.

"What?" she almost screamed at him. "How much did those distributors make off of you? All they do is just ship your bottles. You do all the real work."

"I think they mark up the tequila by 250 percent—two and a half times what they pay us," Sotero said. "But that is the way it has always been done. And we can sell the *añejo* at a higher price to them, and all of that will be profit. They can make their money—it will be okay."

"Aaaah!" she cried out. "We need to do that ourselves. We can distribute our own product as easily as they can."

"But I have always just sold my product to them—I haven't done that before."

"Well," she said, "we are going to start."

"If we do that, the distributors in town will be very angry.

We will be taking away their livelihood. There may be trouble," he said.

"Why should we worry about them? They have been taking advantage of us for years. We will do what is best for us."

"Okay, but we had better be ready." A shadow of concern crossed Sotero's face.

But Xiomara could not be deterred. Despite this warning, she began to focus on the business side of selling and distributing tequila. She wrote to liquor stores in California and investigated how to ship the product from Mexico to the United States, how to deal with customs, and how to rent trucks to move their product. She worked in the office at the *hacienda* while her children played in the yard—except Marta, who wanted to be near her mother all the time. Xiomara discovered as time went on that Marta was very good at math. Marta would check her mother's calculations and catch any error. Xiomara worked late in the evenings when the younger children were asleep. Marta would curl up on the couch and stay with her mother.

After a year, Xiomara had set up her small distribution network, and Sotero no longer sold his tequila to the distributors in Guadalajara; instead, rented trucks transported his product up to California. And their profits increased threefold. After a couple of years, Xiomara realized she hated to pay anyone else to move the product, so she bought one truck, then two, and hired some of her relatives to drive the product to America, deal with customs, and sell it based on the agreement she had made from her home in Mexico. They now had a family business, with only family members involved, totally integrated from production to distribution. Soon, other producers were asking Sotero if Xiomara could arrange to distribute their tequila. Xiomara agreed, charging a much smaller fee than the distributors in town, much less than the other tequila producers had ever had to pay.

The timing was auspicious, since America was in a period of post-World War II boom. Unemployment was low, personal income was doubling, factories were shifting from wartime equipment to consumer products, and the "buy now, pay later" mentality became popular. People wanted to forget the traumas of war and enjoy life, so cocktail parties and drinking at lunch became common. And the Ramirez family operation grew even larger and more profitable.

"We are getting bigger," Sotero said to Xiomara one day while she was working in her study with Marta. "Maybe we ought to have a name for our company. What do you think?"

Xiomara looked thoughtful. "We are a family company," she answered. "No one must ever forget that. We are the Ramirez Family Company. Isn't that good enough?"

"It is a bit long," said Sotero. "Can't we make it catchier? And shorter? We could put the name on all our trucks and maybe it will help sales. The word 'family' makes us look so small and unimportant. Everyone wants to appear bigger than they really are, so why shouldn't we? People are impressed with size today. No one cares about some family from Mexico."

Xiomara thought about this. She knew he was right.

"What about just calling it Ram?" Marta suddenly interrupted. "That is short, but everyone in Tequila, Mexico, will know that it stands for our family. And you know, a ram is a male sheep in English. It also means hitting something hard, like a ram would ram into you if he was mad. So it would sound strong to Americans."

The two parents looked at their young daughter, then at each other.

"Ram," said Sotero.

"Ram," said Xiomara. And they both hugged Marta and kissed her cheeks.

"We could also paint a picture of a ram on our trucks," suggested Marta, smiling at her parents. "It would be like a symbol of how strong our family is."

Sotero looked at his daughter, then at Xiomara. "It could be an angry ram, snorting and pawing, ready to charge and ram into something. Or someone," he said thoughtfully.

"That could suggest that the drink is strong and virile, and the company is strong and virile too," added Xiomara. She hugged her daughter again. "You are a genius, my sweet. We have a name and a mark, and it is all about our family!"

Sotero reached his arms around both of them in a group hug.

The name "RAM" with a picture of a raging ram began to appear on all their bottles, on their trucks, and everywhere else they could think to put it. Their brand became familiar in the industry, and their sales continued to grow, as did their profits.

One evening while her mother was working and Sotero was out in the distillery, Marta, now age twelve, heard the sound of a truck coming up the roadway to the *hacienda*. No one was expected, so she looked out of the window and saw a vehicle she did not recognize enter the round drive in the front of the *hacienda*, and four men jumped out. Each man carried a bat or a club of some kind and had a grim look.

"Mama," Marta cried out. "Some men are here and I am scared."

Xiomara rushed over to the window and saw the men approaching. "These men are here for no good. Run as fast as you can and get your father. Tell him what is happening."

"But Mama, what about you?"

"Don't worry. I will be fine. Now run!"

Marta ran—out the back and the hundred yards or so to the distillery where her father was working. Meanwhile, Xiomara went boldly to the front door planning to confront the intruders, who she saw carried clubs as well as torches that they were now lighting. She burst through the front door angrily, screaming, "How dare you? How dare you come to our home? Get out! Get out!"

"Papa, Papa, men are here and I am afraid they are going to hurt Mama," Marta cried out breathlessly as she ran up to the distillery.

Sotero did not answer her, but he ran to a closet and took out a twelve-gauge double-barrel shotgun and a bag of extra shells. "Stay here," he ordered her and began sprinting back to the house.

But Marta did not stay. She followed him, although she could not run as fast as he. She could hear yelling and screaming in the distance and a crash of glass as she approached their *hacienda*. And then she smelled it. She ran faster, straight to the back door of the house, in the door, up to the bedrooms.

"Wake up! Wake up!" she screamed at her brothers, Pedro and Carlos, as she grabbed her baby sister, Francesca, from her crib. She led them all out of the back door and away from the growing smell of smoke. They hurried toward the distillery, but then Marta stopped and handed the baby to her little brother Pedro. "Stay here!" she ordered. They were

all crying, but she had no time to console them. She began
to run to the front, but before she could get there, she heard
two big booms that made her stop running. Marta looked
up and saw flames on the roof of her home growing bigger
and bigger very quickly. And then she heard two more big
booms. The flames seemed to be all over her home.

She rounded the corner of the burning building and saw
it: Her father had shot four men and they lay bleeding on
the ground, two of them writhing, two not moving. Then
she saw her mother on the ground, with her father kneeling
by her. She watched Sotero rise from Xiomara, reload his
shotgun, and walk over to the men who were on the ground.
Then she watched as he shot each one of them again in the
head, even the ones no longer moving. He tossed aside the
gun, walked back to Xiomara, picked her up, and carried
her away from the flames.

When morning came, the *hacienda* had burned to the
ground, and Marta no longer had a home or a mother.

Chapter One

Houston — Present Day

THE BLACK LIMOUSINE sat parked in front of the spa waiting for its passenger. This was the most expensive spa in town, and it only catered to the very rich. The Temple of Bliss spa rewarded its customers with the highest prices, topping even spas in Manhattan or Beverly Hills, but its wealthy clientele raved about the treatments and affirmed it was well worth the ridiculous price. Dmitri sat patiently in the driver's seat, properly attired in a black suit and tie, listening to Russian radio that he was able to pick up on his system and at the same time focusing on the screen of his phone. He knew this was an easy ticket, a simple drive to the airport and a big tip. It was five p.m. and he was early, but he had the time and was more than happy to listen to the news of his homeland.

A second black limousine pulled up behind him. Dmitri glanced up and then went back to his phone. Other drivers with other fares were to be expected at this place. But a moment later, he looked up to a tap on his driver's side window. A Hispanic fellow in a similar type of black suit was signaling him to lower his window. Dmitri was annoyed.

"What the fuck do you want?" he growled, lowering his window.

"Hey man," said the Hispanic. "You don't need to be here anymore. Your ride has been cancelled. I got it."

"No fucking way," Dmitri shot back. "This is my fare."

"Hey, I get it. It's a big fare. What is it? Two hundred fifty dollars? Three hundred dollars? But you see, this woman's husband has a special surprise for her that he has arranged, so we are taking her there when she comes out. It's a surprise, get it? So she doesn't even know about it. And that's the way he wants it. He's a big shot in Los Angeles and he wants to do something big for her. We will take it from here."

"I haven't heard that my job was cancelled."

"And you won't, see, because this is a surprise so she wouldn't cancel."

"What about my fare? I am not going anywhere, man."

"No problem. Here." And the Hispanic ripped out four crisp hundred-dollar bills and passed them to Dmitri.

This was even more than he had expected on this trip, and now Dmitri did not even have to share it with his boss. But he was still not ready to give up. "I don't know," he said, at which point the man lifted his jacket to show a .357 Magnum pistol in his belt.

"Don't make this harder than it has to be, man. Just take your money and drive off."

Dmitri did not think about it anymore. He drove off immediately, heading for his favorite bar to have a bottle of their best vodka. He sent a text to his boss that the client cancelled at the last minute.

The new black limousine pulled forward to take its place, and a second car, a white van with two more Hispanic men sitting in the front seats, pulled up behind it.

Nora Ramirez sauntered up to the checkout desk inside the spa. The two young girls behind the counter both smiled at her.

"We hope you have enjoyed your stay, Mrs. Ramirez," said one.

"Why, Lisa, it was just marvelous," Nora replied. "And you have such lovely new things in your shop—I had myself a good old time. Now be sure to email that bill to my husband, Tomaso Ramirez. It's gonna be a big one and his getting that is icing on the cake for me. In fact, I just think I'll take another peek in your gift shop—maybe there is something I missed."

Nora smiled in delight, thinking about how Tomaso would groan. She virtually floated out of the spa fifteen minutes later, feeling rejuvenated and totally happy. A box was to be shipped from the pricey store directly back to Los Angeles with not one, not two, but three different cover-ups, since she simply could not make up her mind. She had just spent a fortune, a massive bill that she would make sure her husband saw. She had also purchased a chic new sweatsuit and sandals at the spa's expensive shop, and she wore her comfy new outfit with relish for her trip home. Her large yellow Goyard tote bag, embossed in blue with her initials, NMR, hung over her shoulder. She almost skipped out to the waiting limousine, and the attentive Hispanic driver politely opened the door for her to enter. She breezed in.

"What a day, what a time, what a life! I just love Texas," she said to no one as she sprawled in the back of the vehicle. The limousine moved off with the white van trailing close behind. Nora looked out the window as the buildings passed by. It was a cool autumn day but clear, and the sun shone brightly. The car moved through town as Nora continued to bask in her many recent spa experiences. She thought that just maybe she would give one of those coverups to her teenage daughter Jocelyn. Or perhaps not; she could decide after trying them on again when back in LA.

When the city was left behind, the limousine made a sudden turn into a cul-de-sac to a location that was hidden from the main road. The white van followed. Nora had been lounging but sat up, accidentally knocking her yellow Goyard purse onto the car floor. Some items spilled out of it.

"What are you doing?" said Nora annoyedly to the driver.

"Sorry, Señora, I have to check on something." He quickly stepped out of the car.

"What?" she said. But suddenly both back doors of the limo opened, and two burly men grabbed Nora from both sides. She screamed, but there was no one to hear her. She kicked but the men were quite strong and held her firmly. The driver produced some zip ties, and soon Nora's hands and feet were tied and her mouth was gagged. The men carried her from the limousine and carelessly threw her in the back of the van like a sack of potatoes. Her yellow Goyard bag was left behind in the back of the limousine. The limo driver pulled Nora's cell phone out of the bag, smashed it on the ground, and then drove in the opposite direction while the van left the city.

Nora was bruised and confused, stunned and terrified, and she kept kicking with her bound legs at the side of the van. The men ignored her. After twenty minutes, the van stopped, and the men pulled Nora out of the back of the van. She looked around and realized she was in a heliport. By this time, it was dusk turning to dark, and the men had parked the van on the side of the building, so it was mostly out of sight from anyone around the heliport. The area was deserted anyway, but the men had opted to take no chances that they would be seen. They stuffed Nora into a large burlap sack, hog-tied and gagged, and then carried her to a nearby helicopter and pushed the flopping sack into the middle of a passenger seat. They jumped into the helicopter on either side of her. The pilot was already in the cockpit and had been waiting for them. The helicopter took off and began its flight to the south with only the pilot, the two men, and the sack.

"*Señora*," one of the men yelled to the sack, loudly enough to be heard above the sound of the rotors. "We are going to take you out of there so you can sit up, but only if you don't struggle or kick or fight with us."

"We are high above the ground now," said the other kidnapper, "so if you make any trouble, we can just push you out of here, but I don't think you would like that."

The men untied the sack, pulled Nora out of it, and sat her between them. They also took her gag out of her mouth. She immediately started screaming.

"What are you doing? Why have you taken me? Please don't hurt me! My family will pay for me, anything you ask,"

Nora pleaded. The men ignored her, and the sound of the flight was so loud, it was easy to do. "I'm thirsty. Can I have some water?" They still ignored her. "Please, please," she persisted, and finally one of the men gave her a bottle.

They flew for hours and then landed. The pilot turned off the engines and jumped out, but the men on either side of Nora did not move. Nora realized that the helicopter was refueling. She thought about trying to attract some attention, but looking at her two captors, she gave up the idea. Soon the pilot was back and the helicopter quickly took off again. It was already dark, and Nora had no idea what was happening or where she was going. Her wrists and legs hurt, her head ached, and her bladder was uncomfortably full, but there was nothing she could do.

Soon she realized they were over the ocean, and they flew on for a long time. Hours later, she saw the lights of a ship in the distance, and the helicopter began to lower. It flew to the ship and landed on a helipad at the front, but the pilot did not turn off its engines. Instead, a large black man, lowering his head to avoid the propeller, approached the door of the helicopter, and the two kidnappers slid open the door and pushed Nora out of the cockpit to the black man, who carried her as if she weighed nothing. He moved out of range of the blades with Nora slung over his shoulder. The helicopter took off immediately, and the sound of it soon faded. Nora began to wriggle and yell, but the man held her tightly.

"Who are you?" she cried. "My family will pay for me. Please put me down."

But the man carried his whimpering cargo to the stern of the boat. He flopped her down on a bench and she cried out in pain. She was sprawled on her side, but the man sat her up, and then tied her to the seat so she could not get up or move. Although completely traumatized, Nora struggled to get her bearings and calm her spirits for whatever was to come next. The large man sat on a bench across from her and began to whittle with a pocketknife. She was about to try to speak with him again when another man came up from below the deck, walked over to her, and shined a flash-light in her eyes.

"Well, Nora, so good to see you!" he said. "Welcome to the Caribbean. I hope you enjoyed your trip." He smiled at her with a wicked grin.

Her heart filled with dread when she realized who he was.

Chapter Two

Los Angeles — Two Weeks Earlier

THE STANLEY MOSK COURTHOUSE is located on the top of Bunker Hill in downtown Los Angeles. It was constructed in 1958 with a hundred courtrooms, and it is in desperate need of an upgrade, if not just total demolition. The building is an ugly structure—not like the majestic federal courthouse or the historic state courthouses of Santa Barbara or Riverside County. A dirty, nondescript beige, the odd structure has nine floors, although a portion of the building rises to only six stories, and the rest hops up another three floors—who knows why the architect concocted such nonsense? In fact, the great irony is that the seat of justice for LA County has been in violation of numerous building codes for decades and is a very dangerous place to be in the event of a major earthquake.

But its long almost endless halls were just like the comfort of home for attorney Brian Youngman, who had spent the past twenty years frequenting many of the courtrooms throughout the structure. A graduate of Berkeley Law School, Brian had wanted to begin his career in public service, so he started as a deputy district attorney, choosing to represent the state and put bad guys in jail rather than represent the bad guys and get them a pass on jail so they could commit another crime. But after only a few years, he grew cynical about the policies and politics of the Los Angeles District Attorney and realistic about the controversies in both the LAPD and the LA County Sheriff's office. He met a lot of good cops and also a lot of smart and dedicated DAs, but he saw some bad ones too, and he didn't like the way the unions always defended those bad ones like they were heroes.

Brian Youngman had learned he was not interested in big corporate law when he was a law clerk, although he had a few offers from some of the most prestigious firms. He worked during his summers in law school at a couple of those places and had a bird's-eye view of what life was like as a young associate attorney. That life meant a big salary to do a lot of meaningless churning. The big firms all required annual billable hours in voluminous amounts, so the young lawyers were often given assignments that would take a lot of time and lead to large bills but no benefit for their clients.

So on leaving the DA's office, Brian did what almost no one in his law school class had done: He hung out a shingle and opened up his own shop. His prior job as a prosecutor with plenty of trial experience made him attractive to many clients, particularly because his billing rate was low compared to the big firms. As a solo, he was able to keep his overhead low, could take any type of case, and did not have to report to anyone. Those were the days when his wife had helped him, supported him even. She had been his billing clerk and office manager and accountant—his key team member. But of course, that was before the divorce.

"I'm not surprised," his Jewish mother, Irene, had said to him when he told her that his short marriage was already over. "Judith was never really your type. If you had asked me, I would have told you. But you didn't ask."

"Mom, I am not about to ask my mother who I should marry," Brian had responded with annoyance.

Irene continued, not taking any note of her son's response. "At least it wasn't a big wedding, such an expense." Irene was an accountant, although she had worked most of her life with Brian's father, who ran a small real estate management company. Irene had been doing the books of the business for most of their marriage, and she counted the pennies.

Brian heard his mother's tone and focus on money and felt like a child again when she chided him for being reckless with spending. Of course, he had never been that reckless—just helped out a friend or two when they were in a bind, but they always seemed to forget to pay him back. He had been loath to press his friends for repayment. He noted that none of those "friends" were his buddies these days.

"Well, Mom," Brian had responded, "at least we didn't have children. Then we would have all the mess of child support and custody."

"That's the one thing you could have done for me—given me a grandchild." Brian was an only child, and his parents had both been encouraging him from the moment he was married to start a family.

"Well, it's good I didn't," Brian responded, trying in vain to ignore the guilt trip. "We only need to divide up our assets, which is pretty much nothing. And neither of us need or deserve any support, so it will be an easy split."

"You still need a lawyer," his mother had responded. "And as you know, they ain't cheap."

That had focused Brian on family law. He had handled all types of real estate, business, and personal injury matters, even some will and trust disputes. But he had thought family law was beneath him—that is, until he had to learn family law for his own divorce. When he saw the fees that divorce lawyers got away with charging—with the express support of the judges themselves—and looked at the huge debt he was in post-divorce, he decided that representing spouses who were fighting over dishes and generating substantial fees was starting to look a lot better. And so, he became an expert in all areas of family law—domestic violence, child support and alimony, property disputes—you name it. With all his courtroom experience, Brian found he was good, very good—in fact, better than most.

Brian learned something else about the divorce practice—sometimes he could actually make a positive difference in people's lives. That satisfied his longing to be a do-gooder in the world—at least that is what he told himself: Make some real money, pay off those debts, and occasionally guide a parent to do a better job with his or her child or convince a wife to stop drinking or a husband to take anger management classes. As he practiced, his cases got bigger and bigger.

Today he found himself comfortably in Department 13, a dedicated family law courtroom, before Judge Elliot Grazer, arguing for attorneys' fees and discovery in a brand-new divorce case representing a woman who had just two days before wired $100,000 into his trust account. He had not even met her and did not know what she looked like, but she signed his retainer agreement and sent the money, so he was ready to appear. Hearing the clerk call his case, Brian promptly stepped past the bar and up to the lawyers' conference table before the judge's upraised bench.

"Good morning, Your Honor. Brian Youngman for the petitioner, Ms. Nora Ramirez."

"Good morning, Mr. Youngman," Judge Grazer responded gruffly. "Please take a seat."

As Brian did so, he saw another figure step to the table on his right.

"Your Honor, Sam Callahan of Johnson, O'Reilly & Callahan for Mr. Ramirez." Johnson, O'Reilly & Callahan was the largest and most expensive divorce firm in Los Angeles. Brian had not known who his opposing counsel was going to be until that moment, and he inwardly groaned. He had gone up against Callahan once or twice before, and it had always been unnecessarily contentious—no courtesies or cooperation, just World War III.

"So, this is a new matter, I see. Hold on for a few moments, sit down, and let me look at the file," said the judge as he examined his computer screen. Both lawyers took seats since it was obvious Judge Grazer had not bothered to review the case before it was called. *Another long day in court*, Brian thought. He had often seen judges be completely unprepared and read the case file for the first time while everyone waited and the lawyers' clocks kept ticking.

Many of his colleagues were perfectly happy with this ineffi-
ciency; they billed by the hour, so it just increased their fees.
But Brian chafed to see even his wealthiest clients have fees
double because a judge would not take the time to do even
the most cursory preparation before taking the bench and
calling the case.

Suddenly, another attorney stepped up to the lectern
that divided the two conference tables in front of the court.
Brian looked with surprise at the new arrival, obviously an
attorney, immaculately dressed in an Armani suit, Gucci
shoes, and a Versace tie with matching pocket square.

"Bill Simmons of Findley & Goodwin, appearing specially for RAM Industries Inc." Findley & Goodwin was a
multinational law firm, based in New York but with a huge
LA office that handled every type of complex corporate
matter. Simmons had pronounced the firm name loudly
and clearly so that its status could be emphasized.

Judge Grazer looked up. "Okay, counsel, so what are you
doing here, Mr. ... uh ..."

"Simmons, Your Honor. Of Findley & Goodwin." Again,
he emphasized his famous firm's name.

"Mr. Simmons," the judge started, "this is a divorce case,
and RAM Industries or whomever you represent is not a
party. Not unless corporations can marry—which hasn't
happened yet. And as far as I know, your firm doesn't even
handle divorce. Isn't this a bit out of your orbit?"

"Well, normally true, Your Honor," Simmons responded.
"But we filed a special appearance this morning—we are
intervening in this case."

"They can't do that," Brian interrupted, not even standing up.

But Simmons continued. "You should see our papers in

your computer at the very top. We are representing RAM Industries, which has an agreement with Nora Ramirez regarding the matter before you. Specifically, there is a prenuptial agreement between my client and Mrs. Ramirez, and there is also a prenup between Mr. Ramirez and RAM. We filed these documents along with declarations from the CEO of RAM this morning as well."

"We join with Mr. Simmons on his requests," Callahan immediately commented, even though Simmons had not made any requests.

"Your Honor, I object!" Brian exclaimed, jumping to his feet. "This is nonsense. A company cannot have a prenuptial agreement. I have received no motion to intervene or any of these other filings. We are here on this newly filed divorce petition, and we need orders for legal fees and also for discovery."

"Your Honor, that is exactly why we intervened," Simmons quickly countered. "Mrs. Ramirez expressly waived these rights in her agreement. You can see that in the papers we filed."

"No way," Brian piped in, but Simmons was not to be diverted from his plea.

"There is a sixty-four-page agreement, every page initialed by Mrs. Ramirez. Her signature is notarized, and she was represented by competent counsel. There is even a transcript of the signing ceremony that proves the process was both fair and voluntary. Mrs. Ramirez was paid a substantial sum in exchange for her agreement that she had no rights in RAM and that in the event of a divorce she would have no right to obtain any information about RAM."

"I object," Brian said vehemently. "That's against public policy even if a corporation can enter into a prenuptial agreement, and it can't. My client has a right to learn everything about her husband's interests in RAM and also what the value of her community interest is. And to the extent Mr. Ramirez contends his interest is not part of the community, we would need to do discovery to investigate that. As we understand it, RAM has vast ownership interests in numerous liquor and other beverage brands as well as other products and businesses—we don't know to what extent because it is a private company. We are entitled to find out everything about RAM—that is the law."

"Your Honor," came Simmons's nasal response. "We have provided numerous authorities in our briefs supporting the legitimacy of RAM's agreement with Mrs. Ramirez. And these were all served by email on her counsel this morning. We also brought him a hard copy as a courtesy, which we will provide him right now." A young man carrying a large box stood up from the audience and came over to Brian. The box was placed on the table, and Brian could see it was full of papers and briefs that would take him days to go through.

"Your Honor, this is trial by ambush," Brian complained. "I can't be expected to read all these documents now."

"Nor can I, Mr. Youngman, nor can I," offered Judge Grazer with a sour look. "And while Mr. Simmons's position may be unorthodox, I am not prepared to say one way or another whether his claim has merit. It will take me some time to go through all of this, and I will need to ask for one of the county law clerks to help research all these cases. And I certainly will give you a full opportunity to oppose their position. So, I have no option but to continue this matter to another day."

"That is fine with us, Your Honor," responded Simmons.

"We want Mr. Youngman to have all the time he needs to respond to our arguments. We will file the appropriate replies, and Your Honor will need time to digest all this material. I suggest we reschedule for six to eight months from now."

"We agree with that, Your Honor," Callahan quickly stuck in. He could not agree with Simmons fast enough. It was obvious to Brian that Simmons controlled the purse strings in this matter.

"Six months? That is way too long. How about next week?" said Brian.

"That will not give anyone enough time," answered Simmons condescendingly. "And, Your Honor, this matter deserves your careful attention. I do want to inform the court that our client has authorized us to file both a writ and an appeal in the unlikely event that Your Honor does not agree with our position, although I am sure you will."

Judge Grazer scowled. "Well, six months does seem like too long. I will continue this matter for ninety days. Mr. Youngman, your client should respond forty-five days before the next hearing, and all replies should be filed thirty days prior. If I need more time, I will let you know. In the meantime, the matter is otherwise stayed, but of course the ATROS remains in effect. That is the automatic temporary restraining orders, for your benefit, Mr. Simmons. Go read them. Mr. Ramirez is not to dispose of any assets or in any way encumber or transfer them. Remember that. Thank you. Next case."

Brian shook his head as he left the courtroom, struggling to carry both his briefcase and the heavy box of motion papers. Simmons followed him out.

"What kind of bullshit move was that?" Brian snapped at him. "You sure know how NOT to make friends."

Simmons looked at Brian with contempt. "I would expect no other comment from a low-class divorce lawyer," he replied smugly and strode off, followed by two associates.

Callahan came out into the hall a moment later, as Brian put down the box of RAM's extensive papers on a stone bench in the hallway. "Hey, you're in the big leagues now, Youngman," he called out with a smirk. "Just think of all the fees you'll make as you try to win against us. Tons of stuff for you to read and research. You should be ecstatic. I'm certainly going to read every word of it over the next few weeks—at nine hundred dollars per hour." And he walked off with a smile. Brian sat down on the hard bench.

"What happened in there?" came a woman's voice with a slight Texas drawl. Brian recognized the voice and looked up. Nora Ramirez was a beautiful woman, dressed in the most expensive dress, diamonds dripping from her neck and ears, in Jimmy Choo high-heeled shoes. Standing at a model's height of almost six feet in heels, she was fortyish, blonde, slim, and adorned as if the courtroom was a fashion show. It appeared that she had her hair and makeup professionally done. Brian had only spoken with her on the phone and had not had time to discuss much of anything with her before the hearing. He had not even looked back in the gallery to see who was there, so he had not seen her enter the courtroom. He shook his head.

"Gameplaying. Your husband has gotten his company into this to try to delay everything and increase the expense."

"Well, that sure is no surprise to me. He always runs to

his sister whenever he has a problem and she just always fixes it for him. But she couldn't fix me. She tried, but I am done with all this. That Ramirez family was really never my cup of tea. I don't know how I got through the past seventeen years. It was mostly awful. But you're going to help me get away from them. And I'm definitely going to have some fun with all this."

"Divorce is not really any fun for anyone," Brian commented.

"Well, it will be for me. And it is finally going to let me be free of him. And from his creepy brother. From his sister too, and that old mother of his. From that whole damn family. His sister really controls everything."

Brian looked at her with confusion. "Who's his sister?"

For the first time, a smile left Nora's face and she scowled. "Maria Ramirez. She's the CEO of RAM. She's smart too. Maria is in charge of everything and everyone, including that useless husband of mine. You're probably going to meet her before this whole thing is over."

Brian looked thoughtful. "Actually, I'll probably depose her. I doubt she'll care much for that."

A smile immediately reappeared on Nora's face. "Wonderful! That will be fun. Can I watch?"

Brian rolled his eyes. *Another vindictive divorce client*, he thought.

Chapter Three

New York

MARIA LOOKED OUT at the Hudson River from her fiftieth-floor office in the Freedom Tower in downtown Manhattan. It was a lovely autumn day, and the leaves had begun to change colors, making the view even more spectacular. She always loved the views of New York—they had inspired her ever since her mother first moved there with her.

She had sometimes wondered if she should have rented that office near Trump Tower so she could look out at Central Park—what a tough choice that had been. She had even looked on the other side of the river in New Jersey, which was far less expensive, since she knew her current view of Hoboken could not rival the view she would have had *from* Hoboken of the magnificent Manhattan skyline. But she had to be in the city, had to be in the Financial District, had to be in the Freedom Tower, the great feat of construction that New York had erected in response to the attack of 9/11. She was proud to be an American, proud to be in this building, and especially proud of the family business she had worked so tirelessly to expand both in America and throughout the world.

Her brother Miguel had only wanted to be in Miami, which was fine because then he did not get in her way or embarrass her among the New York elite. She had gladly allowed him to manage the rum business in Florida and the Caribbean, which was only a small, limited, and discrete part of the company. She kept him away from the farms and producers in Mexico, the international distribution network, the distillery in Scotland, and the newly acquired hotel and casino in Puerto Rico, although she knew Miguel sometimes had extravagant stays there at company expense. No matter, let him have his fun as long as he did not ruin the company. He was so rash, so *loco* sometimes, and he had a mean streak that she had seen and it scared her.

She had always wanted to conduct company operations in a safe and legal manner—as aggressively as possible, yet not over the line—but she knew Miguel did not concern himself at all with legalities. He had already put them at risk with his Caymans game playing, importing rum surreptitiously without paying the duty. If he got much worse, she feared she would not be able to control him at all. She worried that Miguel would do something to destroy RAM.

Maria had slowly built the air fleet, acquiring planes one by one. She had also seen and jumped at the opportunity to buy a hotel and casino in Puerto Rico at a discount price. It was Miguel who had started the rum business, and she had allowed him to use the small air fleet to import rum into the country. But soon after, he had surprised her by buying several ships, taking out a huge loan to do so without her knowledge, and forging her signature. At first, Maria had been livid and was going to try to cancel the transaction, but she had to admit that using company-owned ships for transport was going to be less costly than importing through the air. If only Miguel had not borrowed so much money and handled the matter so poorly, she might have made her peace with his conduct and even given him credit. But when she examined the loan documents, she saw he had foolishly agreed to oppressive terms, including a variable interest rate with no cap—it could go as high as the market might take it.

Maria had concluded she did not want Miguel in the business at all, but she could not get rid of him. Under the Family Master Trust, which dictated who controlled the family business and how it was to be managed, Maria did not have the right to just toss Miguel or her other brother, Tomaso, out of the company. Her hands were tied, but she figured she could mitigate the problems those two created. Tomaso had a big title, RAM Industries President of West Coast Operations, but she made sure he was just a figurehead, relegated to taking business associates golfing or drinking and dining. He knew how to do that. And before now, the worst problem Tomaso had caused the company was being too drunk to meet a business associate for dinner. But Miguel was another story. She had moved him to Miami and limited him to rum, but he was still dangerous.

Colleen Stevens entered the open door of Maria's office carrying a file. She was a fifty-five-year-old black woman who had graduated from Yale Law School and now was general counsel to RAM Industries Inc. and all its various affiliates, subsidiaries, and parents. She was not just highly educated and well connected, but she was as street smart as they come, having grown up in one of the poorer areas of Philadelphia. Making sure she had perfect grades in high school and acing standardized tests, Colleen had been accepted into the University of Pennsylvania, qualifying for a full scholarship. Her hard work and dogged determination got her into Yale Law School and then a position in the mega-firm of Findley & Goodwin, which had no other black associates and was delighted to hire someone who was both black and a woman and even a Yale graduate. While there, she had done some corporate work for RAM and happened to meet its young Latina CEO during one closing. Maria had made Colleen an offer the next day, and she had been working for RAM ever since. Indeed, Colleen had been the architect of the complex structure of entities created to avoid tax, take advantage of import laws, shield the owners (all Ramirez family members), and maintain privacy.

"I just heard from Simmons, and he got the whole thing postponed and bumped for three months," Colleen reported.

Maria smiled at her. "Good. That will give us time to deal with Ms. Houston Texas as well as my idiot brother," she quipped. "Now let's get those two bozos on Zoom, assuming we can find them, and Tomaso is not either on the golf course or drunk. Or both."

"Miguel is at his home in Miami. I got an email from him this morning about a new contract he has with a potential rum supplier in the Caymans."

"And Tomaso?"

"As to him, your guess is probably correct, but we can try." Colleen gave directions to Susanna, Maria's assistant.

Susanna was much more than a secretary; she accompanied Maria everywhere and handled virtually everything in her life.

"I have Miguel," Susanna called into the office. "I will put him on your screen."

Maria moved over to her large oak desk. She had opted for old-fashioned office furniture, not the newer sleek and modern styles. It was part of her recognition of the history of the company. She always wanted to remember that her current exalted status was the result of the sacrifices and hard challenges that her family had suffered and overcome and that she was beholden to the past. Her grandmother had died trying to defend the old family home at the original agave farm, but her grandfather, with the help of her mother, who was so young at the time, had struggled on. They had done things the old-fashioned way, not always legal, often taking matters into their own hands. Miguel was like that, perhaps more so than anyone, but not in a good way.

Today, it was not Miguel's nefarious actions that she was focused on; it was the youngest sibling, Tomaso, who had created such a mess with his abomination of a marriage. She had despised that woman from the moment she laid eyes on her, when Tomaso giddily introduced his Texas whore to the family. Nora was so obviously a gold digger, a few years older than Tomaso and on the hunt. Why could Tomaso not see that? He could have just had some fun time with her, satisfying his various physical needs before any wedding and then ditching her to find another Texas whore or whatever and do it again. But no, he was so naive and stupid, and Nora had used her significantly greater experience to bewitch the younger man. She had gotten pregnant and convinced him that he had to marry her. And she had taken their last name. How humiliating!

Nora—Maria shuddered even when she thought about her—had quickly gotten pregnant two more times. Three children! All of them were incredibly spoiled and, although enrolled in an expensive private school in Los Angeles, so far unremarkable. Apparently, Tomaso's DNA was so watered down by that Texas *puta* that Maria's niece and two nephews were simply rich, lazy, entitled teenagers who lacked both ambition and talent. And of course, they had their issues: One, Justin, was already a drug abuser like his father with alcohol, while the other son, Billy, had been diagnosed as autistic and at times had required full hospitalization until the psychotropic medications could moderate his illness. Meanwhile, her niece, Jocelyn, had food issues and was bulimic. Maria wondered if she also wandered into drugs, which were apparently quite available in the private school system in Los Angeles.

Now with the ill-fated marriage finally on the rocks, Maria knew the California court would ultimately allow Nora's lawyers to obtain very private information about RAM. She could not allow that to happen. It was inevitable that any competent forensic hired by Nora would see things that no one must see. And that could be very bad for the company, indeed disastrous for her family, resulting in disgrace, bankruptcy, possibly even jail.

Miguel came on Maria's screen, while Colleen stood behind, always present so that the attorney/client privilege would cloak their discussions and make them undiscoverable. Miguel was shirtless. He might have been naked, but the screen only showed his hairless golden-brown chest. He had long black hair and a large diamond in one ear. He was quite handsome in a sinister sort of way. And his smooth and clean-shaven face made him look young and just a bit feminine. Even his gestures suggested an ambiguous but dynamic sexuality.

"Well, the lawyers in Los Angeles delayed things for a few months," Maria began.

"That is only a very temporary solution," Miguel hissed. "We need to deal with this woman in a way that is more permanent."

"No, Miguel," Maria quickly responded. "She is the mother of our nephews and niece. Like it or not, she is family. We will just have to pay her. A lot. And before the lawyers can get started. And we need to keep any of our dirty laundry buried." Colleen was shaking her head, trying not to imagine what Miguel had in mind.

Miguel continued. "Perhaps so. But she had better not ask for too much. I will hold back for now, but I do have some ideas that would work quite well if you cannot accomplish the goal of shutting her down. Reasonably. I am a reasonable man after all." He smiled, and his white teeth showed. "Just let me know how it is going. I will be interested to hear everything."

"Maybe we can use those three kids as a lever against her—I mean legally, Miguel. Nothing evil or wrong, just that we can try to take them away from her and get the court to give them to Tomaso."

"That is just a joke." Miguel now grimaced. "Our idiot of a brother cannot take care of himself, much less three teenagers. He will just drink more—if that is possible."

"Maybe we can help him get on a better path," said Maria hopefully.

Miguel laughed derisively. "I think you will be coming back to me and letting me handle this situation. You don't need to know how—you can keep safely in the dark as you have done before."

"I have Tomaso," Susanna interrupted. "Shall I add him into your screen?"

"Yes, do so," said Maria, and the round face of the younger brother appeared. He had a beard and mustache, and his hair was cut short, unlike his brother's. He was unquestionably the least good-looking of the three siblings, which was something the facial hair could not hide. Maria was a classic Mexican beauty, and Miguel while not masculine was quite attractive and in perfect shape. Tomaso by contrast had a large belly and a red nose and always appeared to be inebriated, as drunks often do.

"You fucking moron," Miguel yelled. "Why the fuck did you ever marry that cunt? Just because you were finally getting some pussy. You *stupido*. Now she is putting us all at risk."

"Enough!" cried Maria. "This does no good, Miguel. So, Tommy, your lawyers got some time. But now we need to find out how much we need to pay her to keep her quiet and end this thing. Can you talk to her and find out?"

"I don't think so." Tomaso was glum. "She has told me she is going to put me in the poorhouse. She says she wants to show the family that she is not to be trifled with. I don't know, I just don't know."

"Can we use the kids against her?" Maria suggested.

"Maybe. But those kids have their own minds. I can hardly talk to them. And they are pretty devoted to her—I don't know why."

"You don't know shit," Miguel piped in. "You've hardly

been a father to them, that is why. And your failure as a parent and as a husband is only rivaled by your incompetence in handling our West Coast business."

"We are not getting anywhere with this kind of talk, Miguel," Maria interrupted. "I will call the company lawyers. We will see if they can work something reasonable out with Nora. I will let you know, Tommy. But you will probably need to step up and spend some more time with your children. We will need them to cooperate too." And with that, Maria ended the Zoom. Speaking to Colleen, she said, "You know what to do."

"Do you want me to tell your mother?" Colleen asked.

Maria frowned. Marta would not be pleased. "No, I will tell her. I am going out there tonight. I will have the driver take me, and I can work in the car. Emilio and I have arranged a meeting at her house—neutral ground."

Odd to think of her mother's East Hampton compound as neutral in any way, Maria thought. But it was better for her, since with Marta there hovering, Emilio would likely agree to whatever Maria proposed. Still, Maria could not ignore the reality that Emilio was a loving father, that their son idolized him, and that she was far too engrossed in RAM's many ventures to devote the time to their son that he needed, that he deserved, she thought with remorse. The recent hospital stay had been far too long, and she had started to realize that what was best for Antonio was to get away from that sterile medical environment and start living like a normal kid. His treatment course was tapering. It appeared that some new arrangement should be made.

Guilt over her son oppressed her daily, and even the anticipation of this discussion with Emilio brought on new pangs. Yes, he would agree with her, but the best thing for

Antonio was to be with his non-working and devoted father, not his overworked and absent mother, and she knew it. She was going to allow her son to move to Emilio's home, but she wanted some conditions, including that she could drop in any time to see Antonio and that Emilio would bring him into Manhattan regularly at her request. Even these conditions were not going to assuage her guilt or make her a better mother, but she felt she had no other legitimate or responsible choice. Especially with this new transaction she was putting together, Maria knew she simply could not be present for her son.

She cried for a long time on her way out to the Hamptons to meet her ex.

Chapter Four

Caymans / Miami

AT FIVE A.M., the fishing boat pulled up to the dock at Barcadere Marina northwest of George Town on Grand Cayman, just before the light of day. It had traveled all the way from Miami with its precious cargo. It was to unload here and then proceed to Jamaica to pick up a different type of cargo, then return to Miami. Three white males were waiting for it on the dock, but only one of them was armed with an AK-47 and a machete. The other two were simply responsible for taking the various bags off the boat and putting them onto the waiting truck, then driving them to the plantation where their contents could be verified. Then the bags would be taken to the bank in town.

Compared to other Caribbean islands, Grand Cayman was a relatively safe place with much less corruption, not like Jamaica or Haiti. The Caymans had a large banking community, a sound government, and docile inhabitants, but there was a thriving illegal money laundering business there as well.

The bags from Miami were loaded with U.S. dollars that had to be cleaned. That the plantation on the island purported to have generated such a huge amount of cash was perhaps laughable, but the authorities did not care about this kind of crime and just required that someone sign a piece of paper verifying the income. The plantation claimed to produce sugar and also various exotic and extremely expensive fruits, vegetables, and other plant products for export, but in fact there was only a small amount of farming done on the compound and only enough sugar to produce a modest batch of local rum. The plantation also boasted a distillery, but the size of the production was known only to those on the farm. Once declared as income from a foreign business, the money was both clean and largely immune from U.S. taxes, thanks to some of the loopholes the United States Congress had enacted.

The humble-looking fishing boat also declared income from a remarkable amount of catch, although there were never any fish on the boat except from an occasional line thrown into the water by a bored crew member. After the unloading of the bags of cash, the boat was headed to Jamaica, although sometimes it made its way to Haiti or to other ports that could supply what was wanted and do so quietly.

This entire operation had been designed by Miguel, and he had not told Maria the details about it. For example, Maria did not know that in addition to rum and other alcohol products that were avoiding customs, Miguel was also smuggling both marijuana and cocaine on the boats and selling the drugs to local distributors in Miami, except for what he kept for himself. This little side business was just extra pocket cash for Miguel that he did not comingle with corporate funds, although he was using RAM assets to operate his illegal venture. He had made contact with a Mexican cartel to obtain the illegal drugs and was laundering his ill-gotten gains through the banks in the Caymans.

He had presented Maria with a fait accompli with his purchase of vessels and this shipping venture. She had been angry, but he had argued hard with her about it, and in the end, there was little she could do. Miguel had pointed out how unreasonable the customs officials were, how much time and cost they added to importing the rum, and how it was actually very American to find ways to avoid paying fees and taxes.

"Everybody in the business runs rum into the U.S.," he had pointed out. "And if we want to be competitive, we need to do the same thing. Besides, how will we ever successfully expand our brands if we cannot supply enough to our distributors?"

"How dare you!" Maria had responded. "You had no authority to do this, and you committed fraud."

Miguel was not deterred. "Without sufficient volume, they will drop us and just service the Constellation Brands of the world. I have already bought the boats and hired the crew and purchased the property on the island. Everything is ready to go—actually it is going right now, since I have been doing runs to make sure it worked."

Maria gasped. "You are up and running—importing illegally already?" she responded, outraged.

Miguel had smiled, enjoying his sister's discomfort. "Of course. You agreed to let me handle rum and have Miami as my territory, and so I am doing it. You are dealing with New York and Mexico and all the rest of the world. You won't even let me run the hotel and casino. I deserve to have my area of control. I am a family member the same as you."

Maria had a moment of weakness and, while not agreeing, she also had not actually vetoed Miguel's plan as she had wanted to do. Then, when she saw the loan documents, she knew her hands were tied.

Under her management, the rest of the business had thrived, with RAM producing and supplying more and more brands and new products, more than just tequila and rum, but also Polish vodka and both Japanese and Scotch whisky and Mexican beer. The company had expanded into glassware and other drinking-related items, like cheese plates, nut and snack assortments, and bar implements. These could be manufactured cheaply in Mexico, and like all of their business, Maria made sure that RAM both produced the product and transported it directly to market, just like her mother had taught her and her grandmother had envisioned. Cutting out the middleman meant investment in delivery trucks, which had required taking on debt, but it had been worth it, since they were easily able to undercut their competitors. And Mexico did not have the same job safety requirements or high union-negotiated wages and benefits as in America. More importantly, unlike Miguel's rum-running business, Maria made sure all of these other supply chains followed the rules, both locally and at the border.

She was very unhappy about Miguel's "Bermuda Triangle," as she called it, and she intended to deal with it. After she figured out how to handle all the debt Miguel had taken on, she intended to find a way to shut his Bermuda Triangle down, although she knew Miguel would fight with her about it. But she had been focused on her complex new hotel transaction, and she had not gotten up the energy for the Bermuda Triangle battle. Of course, she had no idea about the cocaine Miguel was bringing in on the company boats or his money laundering.

The drug business was not the only wrongdoing Maria did not know about. Miguel had another very personal use for his Bermuda Triangle, one that would have horrified Maria even more than drug smuggling. That is because Miguel was a sadist. And he was mercilessly cruel. In all the ports their ships visited, Miguel was always able to locate some desperate young man, even a boy, who longed to leave the poverty of the poor island. Miguel would smile and smile and make offers and promises, always with a sly and conspiratorial mien. He offered passage to America and a job in Miami working for his company, as long as he would get full cooperation from the man or boy. Miguel did not hide that he expected sexual services—rather he was quite blunt about it while taking his intended victim to an expensive meal.

"You will need to suck my cock as long and often as I want," Miguel would explain to the startled potential victim while eating his salad. "And I will also fuck you up the ass. You need to agree and do whatever else I want that will satisfy me. And you must show me that you like it. If you are not willing, that is all right. I will find someone else who can accommodate me."

Many refused, stood up, and walked away, but a few, after the initial shock of what Miguel requested, stayed at the meal, hunger keeping them there, and ultimately agreed out of personal desperation. Then Miguel would order a bottle of wine and even take his victim out after dessert to buy him new clothes. The hapless young man or boy would relax and start to believe that this was all going to be a passage to a wonderful new life.

When they boarded the RAM ship, Miguel would celebrate the voyage by offering his new young consort a glass of the company's tequila. But after they headed out to sea into the lawlessness of international waters, Miguel would take the young man or boy below to his private cabin, which Miguel had outfitted as a plush interior stateroom, totally inconsistent with the modest outward appearance of the fishing boat. There Miguel would offer his victim marijuana and sometimes even cocaine, which Miguel himself would snort in copious amounts.

When he was ready, Miguel would produce handcuffs or rope ties and bind the young man or boy. Miguel would start slow, initially just shoving his manhood into his hogtied victim's mouth, harder and harder, making him choke. Then Miguel would go to a small closet and take out some device—a whip, a ruler, a switch, or even a small bat. Then the beating would begin. And the screaming. With the noise of the waves and the engine, no one could hear—or if they did, no member of the crew dared to mention it. Miguel loved the screaming. Any victim who did not scream easily would receive a harsher beating, and even worse, as Miguel would pour hot candle wax all over his victim's back and then on his privates and into his anus. He would ultimately sodomize his victim, continuing the beating while doing so. And when worn out from the joy of all his cruelty, he would push his victim, moaning, bleeding, and in pain, onto the cold floor, while Miguel either took a nap or went above to watch the waves. Then depending on his mood and the length of the voyage, Miguel might go below and repeat the process. Sometimes he would find an oversized dildo to ram up the rear end of his victim until it was bloody.

When the boat arrived in Miami, there was no job for the victim. Rather, Miguel would drive him miles outside of the city and drop the bruised and bleeding man or boy on the side of the road. Miguel convinced himself that the free, albeit illegal, passage to America was sufficient payment for the fool that had come on board his boat.

Occasionally, Miguel became so enamored with his victim that he took him home as a sort of male concubine. He had such a boy with him on the morning of Maria's call about Tomaso's divorce. This boy was only seventeen, Haitian, with soft olive skin, which of course had welts on much of it from Miguel's torture. But Miguel found that he did not want to hit this boy as hard—just enough to hear him whimper and scream a bit.

Manuel was his name, and Miguel had started to have some feelings for him. He had even enjoyed fondling Manuel's genitals, which was something he typically was not interested in. He had even considered sucking them himself but had so far rejected the idea, although it did keep reoccurring to him. And he talked to Manuel, even though Manuel usually had no notion of what was being discussed. Manuel would just shake his head and smile, eager to please his master. Today Miguel was thinking about his family.

"She's worried," he said to Manuel, who was sitting on the floor below Miguel like an obedient dog. Miguel had even gotten Manuel a collar and a leash. "That's good. I can use that. Tomaso is an idiot, and Nora is just overconfident, but now I see how they will be useful to me. This whole mess will put Maria in such a pickle that she may have to step down. And then I can take over and force both her and Tomaso out. Actually, the more that I think of it, I am pretty sure I can get rid of Tomaso entirely. That would be nice, wouldn't it, my puppy?"

Manuel just smiled up at his master. Suddenly Miguel reached out and slapped the boy on the face—once, twice, three times. The boy cried out in surprise and pain. Then Miguel grabbed him by the head and shoved him down toward his crotch.

"Let's begin again, shall we?" Miguel smiled an ugly smile. Manuel just whimpered and complied.

Chapter Five

Los Angeles

TOMASO TOOK ANOTHER SIP of his martini. The club made good drinks—nothing was watered down like in so many restaurants, and the portions were substantial. Tomaso could always find an open bar at the club—in the men's locker room or at the main bar or in the dining room, and in the mornings the snack shop served alcohol. Tomaso even had a flask of scotch in his golf bag as well. He figured that regular consumption during his round would loosen him up, allow him to swing the club more easily, let him forget about that bitch he married. Stupidly. He had tried envisioning that the golf ball was her head, but that had only made him tense up and swing too hard, causing a wicked slice that inevitably was a lost ball and an extra penalty.

"Beautiful day to play, Tommy. Are you almost ready?" said Chad Haynes, another member who was a regular at the club. Chad was a solid player, and Tommy often sought him out as a partner in club competitions. But today Tomaso was in a foul mood and needed at least one more strong drink to drown his emotions. He was going to lose to Chad today, he knew, and likely by a lot. And that would make him feel even more frustrated and disheartened.

"I need another half hour," Tommy muttered back. "Let the starter know."

Tomaso turned to the bartender. "Sam, can I get another of these? Three olives." And with that, Tomaso drained his glass.

"Starting heavy, I see," Chad remarked. "Okay with me. I'm going out to the range for twenty minutes. Catch you at the first tee." He wandered off.

"Here you go, Mr. Ramirez." Sam was quick with the drink. "Dry with Bombay Sapphire and three olives. Ice-cold."

Tomaso managed a thankful smile. The lounge at the Riv-aire Country Club in West LA was comfortable—big leather chairs, dark wooden panels on the walls, and a large TV with some sporting event on. Boasting a world-class golf course only a mile or so from the Pacific Ocean, Riv-aire had a majestic clubhouse facility that looked like one of the billionaire mansions in Newport, Rhode Island, only bigger with rooms on the upper floors for guests and celebrities. Unlike some of the equity clubs in town, Riv-aire was more welcoming to people with a Hispanic last name as long as they had the money to pay the incredibly high buy-in fees and monthly dues. The two Jewish golf clubs, Brentwood and Hillcrest, would have accepted him as a member regardless of his Hispanic background, if he had only qualified by giving enough to charity, which was a requirement for membership there.

Tomaso did not give to charity. He had no interest in "wasting" his money, which was strictly controlled by his sister Maria, by donating it to a bunch of fake goodnicks who would spend it on some poor deadbeats like abused single mothers, homeless veterans, or green initiatives. And his substantial salary still could hardly keep up with the wild spending of that cunt of a wife or the whining "needs" of his three children. Oh, he had liked those kids when they were babies, especially since Nora had never been comfortable with him taking care of them by himself. If they cried, he would just leave the room, and if they needed to be fed or changed or whatever, again he would just leave the room.

But now they were all teenagers attached to their phones and completely self-absorbed, so he had no more use for them than they had for him. He would duck out to Riv-aire, where there was always available alcohol.

That was his refuge until he met Rosanna. She had been a waitress at the club, and he began working on her from the moment she started. She was coy and distant at first, but he was persistent. Finally, she agreed to meet him outside of the club for dinner. He took her to a posh restaurant in Santa Monica and got her very drunk on champagne. They ended up in a hotel room on the beach, where he stayed with her for three days. During that time, Tomaso did not even drink much—just wine or champagne with dinner. But they shared their life stories with each other, and Tomaso fell hard for Rosie. She was Guatemalan and had only recently found her way to America. She was poor, as was her family. Her goal was to make enough money to send it back to her parents and her sister, who were all struggling. She hoped someday to bring them to California. Tomaso felt a strong urge to help this lovely woman he was so infatuated with, and he promised her that he would do what he could.

"The rent is so high in my apartment house, and it is in a bad part of town out in East LA. I can hardly afford it, much less pay for the old used car that I need to get me back and forth to work."

"What if you could move to the West Side?" Tomaso said hopefully.

"Oh no, that is so expensive. I am hardly able to pay for what I have."

"Maybe you wouldn't have to."

"I don't know what you mean," she said, and tears came.

"I will get us an apartment right here in Santa Monica. Near the beach. It will be our place, but you won't have to pay anything. I will take care of it. And you don't need to work at the club anymore because I will give you money. All you have to do is enjoy life with me. How does that sound?"

She had looked at him incredulously. "But what about your wife? And your children? You can't just leave them."

"Well, I am going to leave her anyway—it is just about the timing. And my kids are off doing their own thing. They would not even notice if I was gone."

Rosie nodded. "That does sound like a dream come true. But what if you grow tired of me and don't want me anymore? What will I do then? I can't suddenly pay for a Santa Monica apartment on the beach if you decide to leave me."

Tomaso smiled at her. "Ah, you don't completely trust me yet."

She smiled at him. "It's not that, but you know, a girl has to be careful."

"Hmm. I'll tell you what. I will prepay all the rent for a year. Then you know you are secure. What about that?" he said, very pleased with his magnanimity.

"Can you do two years?" she said, looking at him with doe eyes.

Tomaso laughed. "I see you are a clever negotiator. Yes, two years is fine."

"And will you put money in a bank account with just my name on it so I will have enough to pay for food and clothes?"

At this, Tomaso raised his eyebrows. "Well, that is possible. But you will need to make me very, very happy," he said cautiously, now a bit on his guard, wondering what he was getting himself into.

"I will," Rosie cried out, and she jumped on him and kissed him over and over. They made love ferociously then, and Tomaso's circumspection faded away. He was happy—and she would make him happy from now on.

That had been three years ago, and he had paid all that and more ever since. He had even convinced Nora that his job suddenly required him to travel much more, so he had been able to hide this affair. Nora had not cared much that he was gone anyway. She was attached to her two cocker spaniels, and they kept her company. Of course, there were her children, whom she spoiled constantly. Their needs easily kept her distracted, so she paid little attention to the husband she had lost interest in. That is, until she discovered the affair.

Tomaso was drinking his second martini, ruing the day that he had slipped up. His marriage had been insipid and of little significance to him up to then, but at least he pretty much did whatever he pleased, including his frequent visits to Rosie as well as his time on the golf course. But life had gotten pretty miserable since Nora's discovery and all of the abuse she had rained down on him. Nora had even contacted Rosie and scared the living daylights out of her. Nora had gone so far as to rat him out to their children, who now treated him like a pariah. Even after two strong martinis, he found himself raging. He wished she would just disappear from his life.

Suddenly he felt his phone vibrate in his pocket. The club had strict rules about this: Phones had to be on silent, and there was absolutely no talking on the phone in the clubhouse. Tomaso looked at his screen and saw that his older brother was calling him. Miguel had never been particularly nice to Tomaso and had bullied him frequently when they were growing up, until Maria would save him. Miguel had just given him such a hard time on their call for marrying Nora, but he had been right, of course, which further frustrated Tomaso. He had always been afraid of Miguel and would never cross him—he knew Miguel was capable of anything. Tomaso quickly drained his glass, leaving the olives behind, and ran outside and around the corner of the clubhouse to a private place.

"Hello, Miguel," Tomaso said breathlessly after the eighth ring.

"What took you so long?" Miguel responded with annoyance.

"I am at the club and Riv-aire doesn't let us talk inside the clubhouse."

"I don't know why you waste your time playing that stupid game. But whatever. Listen, I have been thinking. That *puta* of a wife of yours, she could get us all into real

trouble. And while you may not give a shit, I am not interested in her bringing this company down, much less landing us in jail."

"I don't think that will happen," Tomaso began, but
Miguel cut him off.

"Oh, you think I am comforted by anything you say, my
moron of a brother? I don't trust lawyers and I don't trust
you. You are just weak and pathetic. And now in your idiocy
you have put me at risk. And I am not okay with that. So I
am going to devise a solution, a permanent solution."

"What do you mean?" Tomaso said, feeling a mix of both
concern and relief.

"The less you know, the better. But I do need some info
from you. That bitch of yours goes to some spa in Texas,
right?"

"Yes, she goes there all the time."

"Good. Find out when she will be there next and let me
know her itinerary."

"What are you going to do?" Tomaso asked.

"I am going to do what I do best: eliminate the problem
in my path. Just get me the info and your life will become
much better. And then you can spend all your time with that
Guatemalan slut that you are paying for. But I need you to
do some things. And to sign some documents. I have them
all prepared. So listen carefully."

And Tomaso listened. He always listened. He had always
been in awe of and, in fact, afraid of his brother, whom he
knew was far smarter than he was. Miguel had also always
been able to convince Tomaso of anything, even if it was obviously not true. He had made a fool of his trusting younger
brother on more than one occasion, in fact many times.

And here again, as the serpent-tongued Miguel began to lay out his plan, Tomaso began to smile. His brother really was quite clever, and the plan seemed so appropriate given what he had suffered at the hands of Nora. She had treated him with such disrespect, made him feel so small and impotent. Now she would come to know that he was not a man to be trifled with. In the end, she would get a scare, nothing more, and finally be forced to become compliant. Tomaso relished the thought. He was going to play a great round of golf and beat that cocky son of a bitch, Chad, and use his winnings to buy Rosie some fresh flowers. Yes, suddenly his problems seemed solvable.

He strode back into the clubhouse ready for battle on the magnificent greens of the Riv-aire golf course.

Chapter Six

New York

MARIA SMILED at her son Antonio. She was visiting him at the clinic, which was located on Long Island.

"They are taking good care of you and you are looking better," she said to him and smiled. She maintained the most positive appearance, but inside she suffered so. *Nothing is worse in life than having a sick child*, she thought.

The eight-year-old boy looked up at his mother and smiled. "Hi, Mama. Can I go home now? I am so tired of being here. I just want to come home with you and Daddy."

"Oh sweetheart, we will go home soon, but I think they have to do a little more treatment first. But I am hoping that will be it. Can you just stay a few more nights?"

Maria knew that it might not be just a few more nights. Antonio had been in and out of this clinic for the past three years, ever since he first contracted leukemia. Most of the treatments they had tried on him had been disappointing failures. This new one was more experimental.

"He has a very rare form of the disease," the doctor had told her. "It just doesn't respond to the usual treatments. But we will keep trying."

This newest approach required Antonio to live at the clinic for weeks—the doctors were not sure how long that would last. He needed daily infusions and a completely sterile environment. Maria had needed to wear a hospital gown and mask each time she visited her son. And he had not continued growing, so although he was almost nine, he still had the body of a five-year-old. And of course, no hair.

"Okay, Mama. I will do it. I am just so bored and tired. I want to play with my video games at home. And I want to see our kitty. I miss her."

Maria had not told Antonio that the doctors had advised her she could no longer have a cat in the house, and she was not about to tell her son that now. Cats generate too much bacteria, they had said, and Antonio needed the most sterile environment, even at home.

"Maybe I can find you a new video game that you can use here," said Maria hopefully.

"Daddy brought me one yesterday, but it already broke. But yes, please."

"Daddy came yesterday?" quizzed Maria.

She had not spoken with Emilio since their meeting at her mother's Hamptons compound when he told her that things must change. They had sat in the living room of the massive home, drinking coffee. It was hard for Maria to talk to him because the conversation was always about Antonio, how he was doing, what were his treatments, what they could do to make him happier, and of course, how likely it was he would ever get better. They were the same dark conversations that they had begun having years before, the darkness that ended the love in their marriage.

She did not blame Emilio for Antonio's illness, and she did not think that he blamed her. But the sadness mixed with anger they both felt had needed an outlet, and they had taken it out on each other. Finally, Emilio had moved out of their Manhattan apartment and bought a place in Brooklyn.

It was an amicable divorce—Emilio was independently wealthy. He did not need anything from Maria, and she did not want anything from him. After all, they were both well-off from inheritance, so money was no issue. Maria had bought the apartment before marriage, and Emilio agreed that Antonio should continue to live there—that is, when he was not hospitalized, which had occurred far too often.

But now Emilio was changing his mind about where Antonio should live. He had pointed out that Maria was so engrossed with RAM and its many moving parts that she was rarely home. Maria could hardly disagree. Emilio on the other hand dabbled in investments with his fortune, which he could easily do on his computer at home and still be there with Antonio. And the father and son were more and more connected, while she was less and less so. She had finally agreed, but she felt miserable about it. She looked at her son, who was due for a trip home in a few days. That trip would be to Emilio's Brooklyn home.

"Yes, Daddy was here and he stayed all morning. We played Monopoly and I won." Antonio was smiling, obviously pleased with himself. "I always beat him at games."

Maria had to admit, Emilio was a caring father. Maybe she was wrong to rush the divorce through so fast. No, she did not feel love for Emilio right now, but she was not sure she could feel anything except for love mixed with sadness and guilt for her boy.

"You are just so good at games. Shall we play one now?"

Maria knew she did not have time to play with her son—there were a million items that needed her attention at the office. But she could not think of leaving him, so she spent the rest of the day with him. *Nothing is more important,* she thought. She knew she would sacrifice anything for her son, give up the family business, whatever. She wished she could take his cancer herself, leaving him healthy and strong. But all she could do at this point was try to make him smile.

She stayed with him until he fell asleep that night, and then, dog-tired, she dragged herself home to her Fifth Avenue apartment alone. She thought about all the work on her desk that she had not gotten to that day because she had spent the time with her son. She realized that with all her responsibilities at RAM, she wasn't able to be the mother she wanted to be, that she never could be. Guilt overwhelmed her, particularly because she felt so helpless. She also realized that her time with her sick son was just not fun, that she had to work so hard to keep a smile on her face. *Emilio is better at that than I am,* she thought ruefully. *I just don't have the stamina, and I can't stand that there is nothing I can do.* The fact that she did not enjoy her visits with her son made her feel even more guilty. She realized that while she was a whiz at work, she just did not have the skills to tend to a sick child. *Emilio needs to take him away from that hospital,* she thought. Emilio did not work. It was the best solution, she knew.

Maria recognized that her mother, Marta, would not be in favor of that decision, but Marta would ultimately understand that it was the right one. RAM needed Maria's full attention, with all the plans and expansion and also because of the issues created by her two brothers. Maria fell asleep, having made the decision to let Emilio take Antonio, but guilt still plagued her, and she dreamed she was in a courtroom and that she was the defendant accused of failing as a human being, being a terrible mother, and letting down her only child. The judge and the jurors all stared at her with disdain, and the prosecutor pointed to her, insisting on her guilt and asking the court to sentence her to eternal damnation. And she had no defense.

She was guilty and deserved severe punishment.

Chapter Seven

Los Angeles

BRIAN YOUNGMAN'S LAW OFFICE was in a modest four-story building on Pico Boulevard, east of Beverly Glen. It was just close enough to the posh high-rise buildings in Century City that allowed him to describe it as "Century City area," although it was quite a different feel than in the midst of one of the most prestigious business areas in the world. But his rent was reasonable, and he was close enough to Beverly Hills, Bel Air, and Westwood so his occasional high-end clients did not have to drive too far. The office still cost more than Brian wanted to spend, but he placated himself with the rationalization that it justified a higher billing rate than if he was in some mediocre building in the Mid-Wilshire area.

His wife—now ex—had found it when he opened his practice and had furnished it by hunting through used furniture places both on the West Side and even in East Los Angeles, where the lower prices were particularly attractive. Brian was quite comfortable there—he had slept in his office more than once. He used to keep a small bar, but soon learned it was too much of a temptation. Brian knew plenty of lawyers who drank heavily, but he found he could not function if he had a scotch in the middle of the day. When he met clients or potential clients, he had to present an air of competence mixed with heartfelt sympathy for their predicament.

Today, he was looking forward to making that impression on his newest client, since he felt he had not looked his best in court last week when her matter was continued for ninety days. They had made this appointment at the time, and questions swirled in his mind about her case. This was to be his initial interview—something he typically did before he took on a matter. He knew he was a bit behind.

Nora Ramirez showed up half an hour late for her appointment. When Brian's secretary showed her into his office, she made no apology or acknowledgment of her tardiness. He was just a servant, after all, Brian realized. Nora was dressed in a free-flowing, airy dress and Gucci slip-ons, which Brian recognized cost more than his entire outfit. She wore gold jewelry around her neck and on each wrist, which Brian knew cost significantly more than he earned in a year. This woman spent money, lots of it, whenever she felt like it, in whatever amounts without a care. Brian needed to wait for things to go on sale to update his wardrobe.

"A pleasure to see you again," Brian began. "Can I get you something? Coffee, tea, water?"

She smiled at him carelessly. "Why, the pleasure is mine," came the Texas drawl. "And no coffee—I might take something stronger if you have it. And I sure do hope this is a better day for my case."

"No, we don't have alcohol here, and yes, the court system is certainly frustrating for everyone, and divorce puts a lot of pressure on people. I can understand that all of this must be hard on you. And your children."

"Oh no, darlin', not at all. I have never been so delighted. I feel free—finally. And that son of a bitch I married does look mighty miserable. And that makes it even better. Now we need to see if we can really get to him. We need to ask him about his business. And his girlfriend, that little whore of his."

Brian was nonplussed. "Well, the business is important, but the girlfriend probably not. California is a state that doesn't really care about infidelity. Before we get to his business, I know you told me a little about your background, but I do need some further information so we can map out a divorce plan. Let's start with the kids. You have three children, all in their teens?"

Nora frowned. "Yes, and aren't teenagers just awful? Jocelyn is the oldest—my daughter—and she has that nasty issue about throwing up all the time."

Brian tried to look sympathetic, although he found it hard to have much sympathy for Nora. She had first-world problems, and her children's issues were likely to be the common ones among the rich in West LA.

"Bulimia. Has she been treated? Is she under the care of a psychiatrist?" Brian began writing notes on his legal pad. He hated using a computer for that.

"Oh God, yes—some miserable fellow that she sees once a week. But it's going nowhere as far as I can tell. She is very smart—actually she's a smart aleck. Or Alice. She is givin' me lip all the time. Like she knows better about everything. I do try to be a good mother and tell her what clothes will make her look nice and take her to the salon to make her hair pretty for the boys and get her nails done right. I tell her she should smile and look quickly at them and flip her hair and always put on a show of bein' hard to get."

"She's seventeen, almost eighteen," Brian noted. "Just starting her senior year. So another year of high school—then college?"

"Yeah, I guess so—she says she wants to go. Actually, she says she wants to get away from me so she can't wait until college. I don't know that she really needs it though. I did go for a couple of years but only so I could be in a sorority and go to all those parties. But she just goes and pukes her guts out. I tell her that will give her the worst breath and nobody is going to want to kiss her."

Brian continued to try to look sympathetic, but it was getting harder for him. "As to college, California law does not require parents to pay for that, so I will put that down as a deal point when we talk settlement with your husband. Maybe we can get him to agree to pay. But for now, we will need to make sure we address your daughter's medical needs in any settlement agreement."

"Settlement! I don't want to talk settlement with that jackass. I want to go to a public trial with him and invite all the newspapers. I want everyone to hear about him—his drinking and whoring and farting and stealing. I want everyone to know how he does nothin' for the company and just gets everything because his sister pays him—to do nothin'."

Brian was taken aback. "Well, in these cases it is always best for everyone, especially the kids, to make a cooperative settlement. You have two other children, Justin and William, and those boys are fourteen and sixteen, so you will have a lot of time—at least four more years—that you and your husband will need to co-parent. And even after high school, it is wise if you can work together cordially for the best interests of the children. As I understand it, both those boys have some issues too." Nora clearly wasn't listening to him. He saw her fuming.

"No settlement. I said no and I mean no. You can dangle it out there for them if you want." She smiled at the thought. "That might be fun, just for him to see it and want it and get excited and then just pull it away. We could do that a bunch of times. I would love to see his face every time he thinks it will work out and then we tell him no."

"But the children …"

Now Nora frowned. "Forget them. Oh, I don't really mean that. I certainly love my three sweet little things. But they will just have to take it. They can suffer a little through this mess—I am sure their Auntie Maria or Grandma Marta will give them a nice little trust fund. Don't you worry about them. Now let's talk about me."

Brian shook his head, disgusted. "In a minute, but first, I need to finish this paperwork. You have a daughter named Jocelyn who is a senior at Brentroads School. Two sons also at Brentroads. I see all the children are at that private school, right? And they are all teenagers, fourteen, sixteen, and seventeen. Jocelyn will be eighteen soon and graduating." He was scribbling notes.

"Yes, yes, but can we get back to me?" Nora responded impatiently.

Brian looked up at her. She was like many clients he had represented, not too concerned with the children who would suffer through the process. He always wanted to focus on the children's best interests, but his clients often insisted on talking about how they could obtain the most money. And how to make their soon-to-be exes miserable in the process. He decided, since he was just a paid lackey, he would humor her. However, Brian vowed to get back to the topic of how these three kids were going to handle the process and what could be done to help them.

"Okay, let's talk about your lifestyle," he said. "I need to know what you spend money on, how much, and how often."

"Well, now we are gettin' somewhere. I have the best private shopper down at Saks. And another one at Neiman's too. Let's talk about them."

Brian maintained his poker face while inwardly groaning. "You do get to estimate a monthly budget for clothing as well as all your regular activities."

"And we can talk about vacations too. I just love St. Bart's. Do you love St. Bart's? I go there whenever I can and it is wild. And I love spas—there's one in Houston that is my favorite. I'm going there this weekend for a little me time."

Brian tried to look attentive, but she continued, not even noticing his disinterest.

"Have you ever been to Houston? I just love it there. Maybe we could have our meetings out of town, at vacation spots, all at the expense of my husband. Wouldn't that be fun?"

Chapter Eight

Los Angeles

JOCELYN looked at herself in the mirror critically. She thought she was fat. In fact, she was not at all fat, although she did have a buxom figure. Of course, that was the problem. She was not a skinny blonde who could pass for a model like her mother, and that is what she wanted to be. Instead, her hair was dark and her figure voluptuous, her cheeks and lips full, her breasts large, and her hips wide. No matter how often she made herself throw up, she simply could not change this. Of course, she had begged her mother for surgery: a breast reduction, fat taken out of her hips and stomach and buttocks, facial reconstruction. But Nora had always refused.

"You are beautiful," Nora had told Jocelyn. "You need to be happy with what God gave you. Trust me, those skinny minis will not look so good to the boys later on. And they will want a woman like you to cuddle up to, like they say in that popular song, about the bass or something. Remember?"

Jocelyn had screamed at her mother and then closed herself in her room again. She hated her parents. She hated her life. Her mother was on some "medication" most of the time to keep herself happy, and her father was a drunk and clueless. She almost never spoke to him. Her two brothers, Justin and Billy, were just annoying. They had been cute once, but now she thought they both just smelled bad, especially Justin. Billy was still somewhat tolerable, and she did feel sorry for him, but he had so many issues that he was hard to be around.

They all attended the Brentroads School. She knew the boys did not belong there—they were both hardly able to pass their courses. But once she had been enrolled, her brothers, as siblings, were admitted without question, and the large donations made by their Grandma Marta had also been a factor. Now the school was doing what it could to help both brothers not flunk out, since those contributions kept coming. Indeed, Grandma Marta had even pledged to fund a new gymnasium when and if her grandchildren received their diplomas. The school also wanted to keep the family because as children of a Mexican father, they were considered "students of color," although none of them looked particularly Hispanic. But with the Ramirez name, the school could count all three in their DEI statistics, as the prestigious and expensive school pursued its currently fashionable quest to claim diversity, which was not easy since the surrounding neighborhoods of Brentwood, Bel Air, and Westwood were mostly white and significantly Jewish.

So, the school provided tutors for Justin in math and English, at no small added cost, while Billy, although good in math, struggled with human interaction. Billy was quite bright, but he was autistic and thus medicated, so he still needed tutors as well as social support and an educational therapist.

Jocelyn, on the other hand, needed no tutors and was achieving excellent grades in honors classes. But she was not a happy girl. Boys liked her, but she was not interested in them. Her depression led the school to recommend therapy, so Jocelyn was required to see a psychiatrist for medication and a psychologist for "talk therapy." Jocelyn liked taking the antidepressants. However, Jocelyn had also discovered cocaine, and that did not mix well with her medication. Instead, the combination made her even more hostile to just about everyone and everything. Except for the dogs.

She sat in her room petting the two cocker spaniels, Nate and Al. She and her mother had agreed to name them based on the famous Beverly Hills Jewish deli that Nora would sometimes take the children to.

"But it's Jewish," Tomaso had commented. "We have to do business with those people, but why eat their food?"

"You are such a bigot," Nora had responded with disgust. "Don't you even get that most of your children's friends are Jewish? And besides, I think the names are cute."

"Well, I suppose the names fit them," Tomaso had replied. "They have long noses like the Jews." And he laughed at his own joke. Nora ignored him, and Jocelyn loved the names, so they stuck.

The dogs lay down docilely, enjoying Jocelyn's attention. A knock on the door brought a frown to her face.

"Go away!" she called out.

"No," Justin yelled back. "Now that Dad's gone and they're getting divorced, I am the man around here, and you need to listen to me."

"Fuck off" was her response. Jocelyn was happy they were getting divorced. She liked her mother sometimes, but she had totally lost any feeling for her father, whom she considered a dumb, boring oaf.

"Hey," came back her brother's reply on the other side of her locked door. "At least can I see the schedule for next week? Don't you have a copy of it? I think there's something happening."

"Yeah, it's an assembly. But just look on your own computer, you moron. It's all there. And leave me alone."

She heard her brother leave. Her mother was out of town, and with her father having moved out, she was supposed to look after her brothers, but what did she care? They were just annoying, would not listen to her, and did not need her anyway. Jocelyn thought about trying to stick her finger down her throat again but realized there was really nothing in her stomach. She groaned and thought about her fat. *I am going to turn out just like my mother,* she thought, *married and doing nothing in life. Except she's not fat, and I will always be fat.*

Justin went back to his room, his efforts to self-aggrandize with his sister a failure. He was sixteen, just fifteen months younger than Jocelyn, with a frame that was becoming more like his father's, a paunch already forming, a bad complexion, and a pronounced nose. He was not on any sports teams, nor did he play an instrument, and his grades were barely passing. Most of his spare time was spent on video games, and at this he was only somewhat capable. His father did not care much for him these days—Justin knew his father drank all the time, so he tried to avoid him. When he was little, his father was not drinking so much, and Justin would try to be near Tomaso, which made Tomaso fond of him. But when Justin started middle school, things had changed, and his father paid him little mind for several years. His mother was okay, but she always seemed to look at him with disappointment, a feeling he'd had since he was a small boy. He did not really miss his mother—she did not make him feel good about himself—but just figured that her leaving the family and going on some trip was part of the whole divorce game and that she would suddenly reappear.

That was fine with Justin, since he didn't want his parents nosing around his business. That business, as it turned out, had started to become quite profitable, which was helpful since his parents barely gave him any cash. Returning to his room, he pulled out a suitcase from under the bed and opened it to inspect its contents. He also needed a little something to cheer him up, since pretty much nothing else did.

The individual bags of marijuana were well organized on one side of the suitcase, ready to be delivered to any of his classmates who had the money and the desire. He also had a supply of edibles for sale, just gummies, nothing fancy. Justin was not interested in these today. It was that bag of white powder, cocaine, which occupied his attention, and also several bottles of pills of different colors. These pills, he decided, were what he needed today: rainbow fentanyl. It was this hit that he had come to crave. He could just take a single pill and after that, lose himself in his favorite video game, *Fortnight*. Tomorrow, he would make deliveries of much of what was in his suitcase, both at his own private school and at the nearby public school. He would be flush. Then he would have to restock, which meant he would need to go to Venice where he would meet that Hispanic kid who gave him drugs to sell.

Justin hadn't always been dealing. He fell into it when he was in Venice looking to score some pot for himself, which is where he met Bernardo, or Bernie, as he called himself. At first, Justin was just a regular customer, but after he bragged to Bernie about the circles he ran in, Bernie had suggested they become partners. Justin was so pleased and flattered. No one had ever indicated that they wanted to be involved with him on anything before. He had always been the last one picked for games on the playground, and most of the boys at school had never wanted to hang with him. That is, until now that he had a partnership with Bernie. Yes, now Justin found himself sought out by some of the popular kids at school, even a few of the girls. That was a new experience for him. He found he genuinely liked having the status of dealer. It made him feel important, relevant, even popular himself for once.

Billy started knocking at the door. "Let me in," he said in a monotone.

"Go away!" yelled Justin. Unlike Jocelyn, he was not sympathetic to Billy. He just found Billy annoying and very embarrassing at school.

Billy knocked again. "Let me in," he said again in monotone. He always spoke in that fashion, and it irked Justin, who just wanted to get high and stare at the wall for a while before getting back to his video game.

"I'll kick you down the stairs if you knock again," he screamed. Billy went away without another word. Justin was placated and looked at his stash with satisfaction, popped a pill, closed the case, and carefully pushed it back under his bed.

Tomorrow is going to be a good day, he thought.

Chapter Nine

A Boat on the Gulf of Mexico

NORA HAD BEEN AFRAID of Miguel since she first met him. He was far more handsome than Tomaso, although not as tall or broad. But he had a perfect physique, and unlike Tomaso's somewhat mottled complexion, Miguel's smooth brown skin was flawless. Tomaso was showing signs of premature balding, while Miguel's thick black hair was well groomed and had a slightly windblown look. But his smile, while bright, always looked more like a sneer to her, and he exuded an ambiguous vibe, so one could never quite tell what he was thinking, but whatever it was had to be bad.

After her wedding, she only saw her brother-in-law at large obligatory family events that occurred annually, and she had always managed to avoid him. He had shown absolutely no interest in her and often spent more time talking to waiters or servers at the high-priced restaurants where these events were always held. She had tried to interact with Maria who was always cooly polite, but Nora knew that the big sister did not much care for her. And that was fine with Nora, who always made some excuse about her children and left early. She would escape to her home when the events were in Los Angeles or to her minibar in New York or Miami.

She had always been able to keep up with Tomaso when he was drinking, which was pretty much all the time since she first met him and had realized he was a perfect long-term meal ticket. But after the wedding, it had soon become boring to be with him, and the doctors insisted that she stop drinking when she was pregnant, which basically ended their relationship. Nora stopped back then, but Tomaso certainly did not. After the children were born, she had started drinking again, but not with him. Instead, she preferred to do so alone. And then the doctors had prescribed those wonderful pills, which worked even better when washed down with white wine or even a gin fizz. Soon she had found it was the only thing that made her happy, the only way she could escape her life. And three little children, even with her two nannies, were just such a burden. She saw them every day but could only be with the noise and commotion for short bits of time. Tomaso could not stand it at all and would rush off to the golf course almost as soon as he woke up.

Those years were miserable. But things had gotten better as the children got older because they spent more time in school, and their aunt had insisted they learn Spanish and play soccer and attend cotillion classes at the club that taught which fork to use for the salad and other such nonsense that Nora could care less about.

Then when she learned about Tomaso's whore—which did not surprise her because she and Tomaso had stopped being intimate long before—it was like a new hobby for her. She could torture her husband whenever they were together, forcing him into a sullen silence. And then she would just continue to abuse him for his various faults and limitations—not just his unfaithfulness, but his drinking and smoking and complete lack of value.

"So that whore likes a man who smells bad, I guess," Nora would say to Tomaso. "And who is fat—you have become so fat. I bet you can't even see your penis when you go to the bathroom with that gut. But you don't care because you are drunk all the time. You are just disgusting."

And she would go on, repeating the same abuse. It gave her a feeling of value, humiliating and humbling her idiot husband.

But now she was afraid, more afraid than she had ever felt. More afraid than when she was in the helicopter between two beefy Mexican toughs. More afraid than when the big black hoodlum had thrown her over his shoulders. Because she realized that she had not been kidnapped by pirates or the Mexican mob who just wanted ransom money. She had been taken by her own brother-in-law.

Miguel looked at her with that evil sneer of a grin, his ultra-white teeth gleaming like an animal's. Nora figured her best bet was to put on a brave front.

"Miguel, how dare you!" she yelled. "What do you think you are doin'? You think Maria would approve of this? Or Tomaso? Untie me now. Right now."

Miguel continued to smile at her. "Tomaso? You ask about your loving husband?" he said. "But you don't know. He has signed and notarized papers about you. Legal papers. They are in both English and Spanish. And we have verified they will work in many countries—Mexico, Costa Rica, Barbados—wherever. And do you know what those papers say, you Texas whore? Do you know what they do?" Miguel smiled again.

"What are you talking about?" Nora said nervously. "We're getting a divorce. He doesn't have power over me."

"Well, the laws are different in other countries," Miguel responded. "He is still your husband and he has signed papers committing you. Legally, he is in charge of you, as long as you are not in America. And you are no longer in America. Tomaso is in charge of you, and there are medical documents here that confirm the diagnosis—you are very sick with all those pills you take."

"Nonsense. Not true," Nora said quietly.

"These papers also confirm that you are a very dangerous woman. So you must be put somewhere safe and away. Tomaso thinks you need care. And isolation. And medication that will make you sleep a lot—won't that be nice? Somewhere far away. Doesn't that sound good to you?"

Nora shook her head and summoned all her energy. "No," she screamed fiercely. "You cannot do that. You have no right. He has no right. I have a lawyer and he will come after you and Tomaso. You need to let me go. Now!"

"A lawyer?" Miguel laughed. "Really?" He rolled his eyes. "I am sure he is very good. But first he has to find you. And he won't be able to."

"Oh yes he will." Nora felt Miguel was taking a step back, so she pressed her point, hoping to persuade her captor. "He will go to court and get an order and he will force Tomaso to own up to this farce."

"Oh, really?" Miguel said doubtfully.

"Yes he will. He is a good lawyer, a really good lawyer. And he cares. I told him all about the family and the company and Marta and Maria and you. I told him I was going to that spa in Houston and when I would be back. We have a meeting scheduled for after. And when I don't show up, he will know there is a problem, and he is going to try to find me."

"You think so?"

"I know so. He will find out what happened and find any asylum or shithole in any country that you put me in. Then, when he finds me, the whole Los Angeles court system will be after Tomaso and you." Nora's confidence was growing.

The smile had disappeared from Miguel's face. "Tomaso, yes, they will be after Tomaso. He signed the papers. He is your husband that you are trying to divorce. He is the one that you make miserable all the time. He is the one who you are asking the court to order to pay you lots of money. He is the one that your lawyer will look at. Tomaso is the one everyone will look at. But why do you say me?"

Nora began to feel less comfortable. "I will tell them about you."

"You will, won't you?"

"Of course. And besides, you're the one who has all these papers. If you're taking me somewhere, you are involved. You are committing serious crimes. My lawyer will find out and then the feds will come for you and you'll be ruined. You shouldn't be involved with our divorce."

Miguel looked up to the sky, then started to nod at her. Inwardly he cursed. He had been foolish to show himself to her. He frowned for the first time, annoyed with himself.

"Why are you doing this?" Nora said, puzzled. But Miguel suddenly smiled again, more cruelly it seemed. She suddenly realized that nothing she was saying concerned him—he was actually enjoying all of this.

"I don't think you will be telling them anything, Nora."

"Oh yes, Miguel. And my lawyer ..."

Miguel interrupted her. "Well, you scum from Texas, you say your lawyer will be coming for me as well as Tommy, and I should be frightened? You think now I am in too deep and I have lots of risk? And that your lawyer will try to find you and when he does, I will be in big trouble, eh?"

"Y'all will be in the shitter. Your company will be ruined. There is no place that will hold me long." Nora paused again. "Where are you taking me? You should just let me go. I won't say anything about you if you do. I will just blame Tomaso."

"But you said I am in too deep now. Isn't that so? You will talk and your lawyer will be coming for me? I think you are right. When they find you in some *loco* house, you will tell them about me." Miguel suddenly turned, walked away from her, and disappeared below deck.

"I will not," she called after him. "I promise I won't if you just let me go. So untie me. Just let me go now." Nora became quiet. She saw the big black man now returning. He had a heavy-looking bag over his shoulder now, and in his hand was a large metal bucket. Miguel came back too.

"I think you are right, Nora," said Miguel softly. "I am afraid of your lawyer and the feds and the court system. I do think they will find you somehow or you will get loose if I commit you in Mexico or Barbados or the Caymans or anywhere. And I am sure you will accuse me as well as your husband."

"I won't, I promise, if you just let me go."

Miguel continued. "Everything is in Tomaso's name, and

his signatures are all over this. He is the one who is on the contract that rented the limo for you, he is the one whose name is on the helicopter manifest. He signed the papers committing you and there are copies that can be found by your lawyer. Yes, it does look like it is all him, and he has a good reason to want to get rid of his unpleasant wife."

"That bastard," murmured Nora.

"But if I commit you somewhere, you will ultimately talk and make sure I am also ruined. And if I just let you go, you will make sure I am ruined. So, this is a problem for me. What should be my solution?" And then Miguel smiled at her again. Speaking now to the black man, he said, "Ricardo, *por favor, aquí.*" Miguel pointed down by Nora's feet, and then Ricardo put the metal bucket on the deck right next to Nora. Then, Ricardo put the heavy sack next to Nora on the other side. Nora stared at the bucket.

"What are you doing?" she screamed. She now had lost any feeling of confidence or calm and was simply terrified.

"You make a good case, a very good case. I am in trouble if I let you go or if I commit you. Of course, everyone will blame Tomaso, since he has a motive to put you in an institution, and he also wants you out of Los Angeles where you are making trouble for him. His name is on all these documents. He has a motive. Your lawyer will focus on him. But my name is on nothing. I am only the older brother who lives far away in Miami. No one will focus on me. Only you can tell everyone about me."

"Not just me," Nora screamed. "What about that pilot and those Mexican gangsters who got me here?" And then she realized how foolish this sounded.

"Oh, I am not too worried about any of them. None of them saw me anyway. No, only Ricardo here, who does not speak any English, has seen my face and knows we are here. Ricardo is from Panama. He is a good boat captain and he likes working for me. He knows how to keep his mouth shut and he never sets foot in the USA."

Nora shuddered, now terrified. "I won't tell," she said, but she saw that Miguel ignored her response.

"By the way, Ricardo thinks you are the girlfriend of one of the rebels in his country, so he has no particular love for you."

Ricardo had now grabbed Nora's legs and forced them into the metal bucket. Nora looked at the bucket with confusion.

"Miguel," she pleaded. "What are you doing?" She saw that Ricardo had now pulled out a long knife. He cut open the bag, picked it up, and began pouring the contents into the metal bucket, over Nora's tied-up legs and feet. She was still wearing her expensive new sandals, but soon she could no longer see them.

"Why, Nora, you have told me so persuasively about my problem, I am just trying to take care of it in the best way I know how." Ricardo had fully covered Nora's feet and calves with the dry, sandy product from the bag and now went over to obtain a spray hose that had been lying nearby. Nora looked on in horror as Ricardo began spraying water into the metal bucket, and as he did so, the contents turned into a mushy mess. Ricardo put his hand into the bucket and began mixing it, the water and the powdery cement. After a few moments, he stopped and walked away. He grabbed a rag and began wiping the residue off his hands.

Nora looked down at her legs in the bucket covered with cement and felt it slowly begin to harden. "Oh my God, Miguel, don't do this. I have children, your niece and nephews. Oh my God, no." And Nora began to cry. "No, no, no, no, no," she begged. "Please, no. I will do anything you say. Please, no."

But Miguel was genuinely enjoying her predicament. He looked at her. "You thought you were so smart, catching my brother. So obvious to everyone but him. And you have lived the high life, doing whatever you wanted, using our money, my money, wasting it on your obnoxious lifestyle and those brats you call children. And you dare threaten me with your fucking lawyer. You are so, so stupid. You are just scum that I knew we would have to deal with someday, and that day has come." Miguel laughed again.

The cement was almost dry now, and Ricardo came over to Nora with his big knife. She screamed, but Ricardo just cut away the rope that had held Nora to the bench. Then, he stood her up. She was unsteady and tried to sit back down, but he held her up with his strong arms and started pulling her toward the stern of the ship. She struggled but was no match for him. Miguel went behind her, bent down, put his hands on the metal bucket, and began pushing. The bucket slid along the deck, making an unpleasant sound with every move forward. Nora was screaming and crying uncontrollably now, and they pushed her slowly toward the back of the boat with her legs encased in dense cement.

"No, please don't," she kept crying, but the two men were quiet as they struggled with the heavy bucket and the writhing, screaming woman. Since they could only move her a foot at a time with each push, the whole process took longer and required more effort than the men expected. Finally, they had her at the very edge of the boat's stern. She stood unsteadily there, weeping and begging.

Miguel looked at her. At his command Ricardo left and

went below so that it was just Nora and Miguel. The night air was balmy. The boat swayed in the water, which was mostly calm. The moon was full and shone brightly, and the light shimmered off the warm waters of the Gulf of Mexico. It was a beautiful night. And the woman continued to cry and scream and plead for her life.

Miguel looked up at the sky, then down at his watch. He walked back to a table and picked up a bottle. It was the family's best, most expensive tequila, Selection Suprema. Miguel opened the bottle and took a long swig. He then pulled a small vial of white powder from his pocket, poured its contents onto his hand, and snorted all of it at once. He looked at the moon and smiled. He took another drink from the bottle and let out a long sigh.

"I have enjoyed this, *puta*," he said to her. "But all good things must come to an end."

"No, no, no," she screamed.

But Miguel just smiled at her. Then with a sudden movement, he kicked at the bucket with all his might. Nora screamed again as the bucket moved to the very edge of the boat, then suddenly slid over the side and down into the sea. Miguel watched as Nora disappeared into the deep.

Then all was quiet.

Chapter Ten

Jalisco Highlands — 1960

THE THREE MEN ran quietly in the dark along the fence line of the Ramirez property. Each man carried a loaded shotgun and wore a belt with extra cartridges. Suddenly the first man held up his hand and stopped, quickly crouching down. The other two followed suit.

"Listen," whispered Sotero. And in the distance not twenty yards away, the men could hear it: the sound of wire cutters snapping the metal fence. "Get ready," Sotero ordered the other two. "Train your aim on whoever comes through the hole they are making. And shoot for their bodies, not their legs or heads. With the spray of the shotgun, you won't miss."

"I know, Papa," replied one of the two followers. "You have told me many times." Pedro was only sixteen, and although he was skinny, he was already taller than his father and looked to grow another couple of inches. His uncle Eduardo, Xiomara's younger brother, was the other man crouching and aiming his gun. The stars and the moon cast a dim light as they watched. The clipping sounds stopped, and they heard the sound of a piece of fence being pulled away.

"Wait until they come on our land," Sotero whispered. "We can shoot them then as trespassers." Pedro did not answer, but his father had also said this many times, and he did not know why Sotero always felt the need to repeat himself. All three watched as four figures crept through the hole in the fence, then stood up.

"Now!" cried Sotero, and all three men shot at the figures. Immediately two of the figures cried out and fell. "Reload," ordered Sotero, although both Pedro and Eduardo were already pulling out bullets from their belts and opening their guns to slide them into the chamber. But when they again took aim and went to shoot at the figures, they saw nothing. They could hear the cries of pain from where they had shot, but no intruders were still standing.

"We got them, we got them all," cried Eduardo jubilantly. "Ha ha! Pretty good." And he began to stand up.

"Keep down," yelled Sotero, but it was too late. Shots rang out from where the figures had been, and Eduardo fell to the ground.

"Aayee," he cried out.

Sotero, staying low, crawled over to Eduardo, and he did not like what he saw. Eduardo was bleeding from his right shoulder and his left thigh. He was writhing in pain. Sotero ripped off his shirt and tore it in two, wrapping half of it around Eduardo's shoulder and the other half around his leg. He was so focused on helping his brother-in-law that he did not realize his son had left him and was advancing toward the area where the four men had been standing. A shot rang out, and another man cried out in agony. Sotero looked up and saw his son was standing up and swinging the butt of his rifle savagely at one of the intruders. He heard the sound of metal on bone, and the other man fell. Pedro immediately launched forward, and wielding his gun like a club, he swung down again and again and again. Sotero jumped up and ran over to his son, who was still swinging the shotgun and hitting whoever was on the ground. Four bloody corpses lay strewn about Pedro as he kept smashing at each one.

"Pedro, Pedro, enough. Stop. They are done."

Pedro was breathing hard, a wild look on his face. "These bastards came on our land. They came to fight and kill. They came to ruin our crop and force us from our own land, just like when they killed Mama," Pedro screamed.

"Yes, yes, but relax now, son. They have failed. You made sure they failed. You were brave and you defended what is ours. Because you are my family, and this is our family's home. But now we must hurry to help Eduardo because he is terribly hurt."

They left the four dead men without trying to see who they were and where they came from, knowing they would have to come back and deal with the bodies. Eduardo was no longer screaming but only moaning when they got back to him, in shock because of blood loss.

"Go back to the barn and bring a horse and a gurney, and we will get him back to the house," Sotero said. "And bring a can of gasoline. I will stay with Eduardo and tend to him."

Pedro ran. Twenty minutes later, he returned with the horse dragging a small gurney and a gas can. He found his father praying. Tears were in his eyes.

"He bled out. He is gone. Why did he have to stand up?

It is my fault. First Xiomara, now Eduardo. They all die because of me."

"No, Papa," responded Pedro. "They both died defending our home and our family."

Sotero looked at his son. Then he walked over to examine the four corpses. It was a grim sight, but Sotero was unmoved. He kneeled down to inspect them. They were all men in their twenties or thirties. Two of them were unrecognizable, since Pedro had smashed their faces in so badly. But Sotero could see the other two men's faces, and he knew who they were.

"These men are part of a local gang of hoodlums," Sotero said to his son. "They were up to no good when they came, but they are not the ones who have any interest in our business or our tequila. They were hired by someone to make trouble for us. And killing them was necessary, but it will not end here. It will just bring us more trouble."

"We will be ready for them, Papa." Pedro put on a brave face and stood up straight. "I will be ready. I will protect our home and our farm."

"Yes, my son, I believe you. But you are just one man, and a young one at that. And while you are brave, that is not enough. And I could not stand to lose you. Even if we hire more people to stand guard, there will only be more bloodshed. This is not the answer. But we must make sure that no one can ever take what is ours away from our family. I vow it."

The two of them dragged the bodies into a pile, poured gasoline on them, and added some dried brush from around the area. They lit a fire and watched it burn. The smell was awful, but it dissipated quickly. Sotero stared into the flames. He knew what he had to do now. And he was not looking forward to it. They lifted Eduardo's body onto the gurney and dragged him back to the *hacienda*.

His funeral was held at the Catholic church where Sotero had married and later buried Xiomara. Eduardo was her only brother and had no children. He was buried in the church graveyard, next to his older sister. Eduardo's parents were inconsolable. Sotero attended with three of his children, Pedro, Carlos, and Francesca. Marta, his oldest, was away at school. Very few others attended the funeral since it was widely talked about how Eduardo had died. No one wanted trouble from whatever gang had lost four men on the Ramirez farm.

Sotero knelt by the two graves and prayed while fresh tears came from his eyes. He knew he must make some arrangement to keep his family and his business safe. He also realized that his family needed to grow, that he could only trust blood. However, he did not want to take another wife and start a new family. He already had four children. And he knew he could never love another as he had loved Xiomara. He simply did not want to replace her in his heart. Sotero also knew his children would never accept any new wife. *They will all just have to marry and have children for our family to grow, but all that will take some time to happen,* he thought. In the meantime, he had to protect them.

A week after the funeral, Sotero drove his truck into Guadalajara. He knew where he had to go. On the outskirts of town, there was a large *hacienda,* and he headed for that property. At the gate, there were two men standing as guards, both of whom had guns.

"I need to see your boss," he told them.

"What do you want? Go away," said one of the guards.

"Tell your boss that Sotero Ramirez is here to see him,

and that I have come to make an arrangement. He will understand. Go tell him. I will wait."

One of the guards raised his weapon, but the other stopped him.

"Wait here," said the senior guard, and he went inside the gate. The younger guard who had raised his gun just looked at Sotero. Sotero waited. Twenty minutes later the senior guard came out.

"Are you armed?" he said. "Do you have any weapons on you?"

"No," Sotero replied and held up his arms to show he had nothing.

The senior guard came over to him and patted him down anyway. "Okay, follow me." The guard led Sotero through the gate and up to the large sprawling home. Sotero passed others as he walked to the *hacienda*, young men lolling about, playing gambling games, cleaning firearms, or whittling with long knives. He also saw gardeners manicuring beautiful flower gardens. When Sotero arrived at the front door, a woman greeted him.

"You can go now," she said, speaking to the guard. "Come in," she said to Sotero in a warm tone. "Follow me, *Señor* Ramirez." She did not offer her name, so Sotero just followed her through the opulent front hallway to a room off to the left. "Go in," she said. "I will bring you some coffee." Sotero entered a large office and looked at a magnificent oak desk. At the desk sat Hector Aguillara.

"Come in, Sotero, and have a seat," said Hector. "I am glad you came to see me. It is about time." Sotero moved into the room and sat on one of the plush leather chairs in front of Hector. "I heard you had some bad things happen out there at your place. I am sorry. So terrible."

"*Sí*, Don Aguillara. *Muy, muy malo.* So very bad, so sad for me."

"Call me Hector. We are friends. Yes, this was bad business for you. It wasn't us, you know."

The woman who had greeted Sotero entered the room with a tray and two cups of coffee. The men stopped speaking. She served each of them a cup, and Sotero thanked her and took a sip. Hector nodded at her but ignored the cup that was placed on his desk and beckoned her to go away. When she left and closed the door, Sotero spoke again.

"I know it wasn't your people. I know who it was," he said. "But I lost my brother-in-law, the only brother of my wife. And I lost her years ago and it has been hard. I cannot stand any more loss."

"Sotero, I am so sorry for you. I wish you had come to see me sooner. Maybe this wouldn't have happened."

"It has got to stop. And now it won't. There will be revenge now, retribution. And I cannot have that risk to my family and my business."

Hector smiled broadly now. "You have developed quite a business, Sotero. Everyone around knows it. You are very respected for all you have done here. But it is true some people are jealous and others are angry that you have cut into their operations."

"I know, I know. So I need protection. I need my family to be safe. And I know you can help me."

Now Hector looked serious and began shaking his head. "Well, I don't think so. That will be very hard. And very expensive. There are different groups and they would all need to be controlled. That will not be easy."

"*Por favor*, please, Hector. I know you can do this. You are the only one."

Hector looked thoughtful. "I can perhaps try. But in order for this to work for me, I must share in your business. I need a stake that will make sense to me. I have my own needs. I am sure you understand."

Sotero looked glum. He had expected to pay a high price, a set fee. He had not wanted to share his business with this local gang boss. That was dangerous too. He knew he had to be careful in this negotiation.

"What exactly did you have in mind?" Sotero queried.

Now Hector broke into a broad smile. "I would own twenty-five percent of your tequila business. I like that idea. What do you think?"

Sotero groaned inwardly. "I think that would not be so good for you," he replied. "You must understand that we are constantly under the eyes of the authorities, not just here but also in the United States where we ship all our product. We have to disclose anyone who has an ownership interest. I don't think it would be good for you at all to be named as an owner of our operation."

Hector frowned. "Perhaps you are right, Sotero." He started stroking his beard, thinking.

"I do have an idea though. I will pay you ten percent of the profits we make. That will be perfect for you. You will have a silent interest in our company that no one will know except our family. We will pay you every month based on our profit calculation. You have no risk, no responsibility, only money."

Hector looked at Sotero with growing interest. "I like this idea. I like it a lot. But we would need to make sure you are paying us our fair share. I am sure you understand. It is not that I don't trust you Sotero, but we have to make sure. And it must be twenty percent." They haggled a bit more and finally agreed on fifteen percent. Hector stood up and walked Sotero to the front of his home.

"We will not meet again in person about this," he told Sotero. "All dealings about our arrangement including payment will be done directly with our local chief of police, Captain Moreno. You will pay all funds to him each month. He will come to your place to collect. He also may choose to look at your books from time to time if he wants to do so, and you must let him. And I will be checking on him as well, so I or a member of my group may call you to confirm how much you gave him, just to make sure he is not helping himself to some of the money. You must not tell him I am doing this. Do you understand?"

Sotero nodded. "You can trust me, Hector. I do not begrudge you your percentage. I cannot have my family or business at risk anymore. As long as we have no more attacks and I do not have to worry, you will always get your percentage."

Hector smiled at Sotero. He was very pleased with this new deal. With this extra flow of funds, Hector knew he could expand his own territory, hire more soldiers, and drive out some of his competitors. Hector had big plans, and his deal with Sotero would help accomplish them.

After that, no more attacks occurred. In fact, Hector influenced others to do business with Sotero. Soon all the producers in the area that had not used the Ramirez distribution network switched over, so Sotero had a monopoly on local tequila distribution. Some of the producers also offered to sell their farms to Sotero at very low prices, and his operation expanded as did his profits.

Sotero slept more easily now. He made sure that the

money was ready for Captain Moreno to collect. It did not surprise Sotero that the police chief was in the pocket of the local mob. But Sotero knew he needed to do more to protect his business long term than just this local security deal. He never wanted anyone to be able to take his farm away from his family. He thought, *I need to make a family pact, some kind of agreement, so that our land and company will never be sold or lost, and we will all stand together and work as a family. But we need more of us, more members of the Ramirez family.*

Three months later, Sotero took a trip to San Francisco to visit his daughter, Marta, at Stanford University. He had made sure that he honored Xiomara's insistence that her children be educated, and Marta had been the first in his family to attend college. She was smart, he knew, and she could make her way forward even in the United States.

It was an auspicious time to be in America. President Eisenhower had just signed the Civil Rights Act of 1960, and Hawaii had recently been admitted as a state in 1959, so a new U.S. flag had been designed. A charismatic Catholic from a wealthy family in Massachusetts was running for president, and the first televised presidential debates occurred. Martin Luther King, Jr., was actively promoting civil rights and was even arrested in Atlanta for staging a peaceful sit-in at a restaurant. The Vietnam War was just beginning, and the Cold War still raged on, energizing the youth of America. San Francisco was a hotbed of counterculture activity, where the City Lights Bookstore in Haight-Ashbury had promoted the literature of the Beat Generation. It was the beginning of the sixties, where much of the youth of America was looking to "tune in, turn on, drop out." At Stanford, students were boldly confronting political and environmental issues, famously having staged a demonstration against nuclear testing in 1959 on the lawn in front of the library.

Energy was in the air, and while it invigorated Marta as a freshman, she had no intention of spending any time being an activist on American social issues. Marta planned to devote herself to work and study. She needed to learn everything she could and attain a college degree for the honor of her family. Besides, she knew her very existence, a Mexican woman at Stanford, was symbolic enough of the progress that was taking place.

Sotero was excited to travel to see his daughter. But he also planned on having some meetings in the city. He was not comfortable with these new ideas and political movements and just wanted to return as soon as he could to his farm. But he needed to venture into the city—he had to find a sophisticated lawyer to do what he planned, and Sotero knew he could not trust anyone in Mexico. His family needed a strong legal document that would control the future of their business, the land, and his family. But first, he donned his best suit, as American as anyone else's, and went to the college to take his daughter to dinner. He was overwhelmed with pride, knowing that Xiomara would have very much approved.

"So what are you learning, my love?" Sotero said, thinking how much Marta resembled her mother, Xiomara.

"Economics, Papa. I love it. There is plenty of math, and I know that I can use it to help you someday."

"You are a good girl." He smiled at her. "I know you will be a big help to me."

"I will," she promised.

Chapter Eleven

New York — Present Day

MARTA looked at her daughter with concern. Maria was clearly not herself. They sat together in the opulent kitchen of Marta's seaside home talking about the next acquisition for RAM, following the plan that they had developed over the years. Susanna was there with them, as she frequently was, along with their in-house lawyer, Colleen. These four women had formed a kind of kitchen cabinet of the company, the think tank for RAM, and all the plans for its growth and success had come out of their collective and cooperative work and wisdom. Sometimes Marta would cook while they talked; other times the women sat around the large wooden table in plush chairs and sipped tequila. Often, Spanish guitar music played softly in the background.

Although she was in her late seventies, Marta was still sharp as a tack. Skinny, wiry even, she kept a disciplined personal schedule, rising each morning by six a.m. and walking two miles, rain or shine, snow or wind. When she returned home, she had a meager breakfast of one soft-boiled egg, a single corn tortilla, fresh squeezed grapefruit juice, and black coffee, while reading the *Wall Street Journal* from front to back. Then she went to her own private chapel, which she had built separately from the house, and spent half an hour praying. By eight a.m. she was already on her computer, checking the stock market, the bond market, the currency markets, and various accounts that each of the related Ramirez entities maintained. At noon, she had a lunch of either tortilla or *albondigas* soup and some fruit. She spent each afternoon reading and researching, then corresponding or meeting with her daughter and various other employees of the Ramirez empire around the world. Marta always watched the news at six p.m. while she had dinner of black beans, rice, and chicken breast, then went back to her chapel to read some part of the Bible and to pray. Finally, she would retire by nine-thirty. Each night, just before she went to bed, Marta drank one shot of *añejo* or *reposado* tequila. And when she did so, she thought of her mother and her father and all they had done so that her family could produce and sell this marvelous drink.

This afternoon the four women were sitting at Marta's kitchen table and talking about another expansion of the company. This was the biggest they had ever contemplated. RAM was near the end of negotiations to buy a hotel chain. This was an ambitious and expensive idea but potentially extremely lucrative.

"The only way to do this," Colleen was saying, "is to

borrow at least seventy-five percent or more of the purchase price. We will need several levels of debt—the initial loan, mezzanine debt, partner commitments. And we should be buying the entire chain, which means ten hotels, all in different markets. We can't just buy one or even two—the seller is not interested, and if we try, they will charge a huge premium."

"I hate debt," said Marta, shaking her head.

Colleen continued. "I know that the history of the company is to start slowly. When we purchased refrigerated trucks, we only bought a few at a time, but the company was just moving its own product. To get credibility in the market, you cannot do it that way. If you are a hotel operator and want to make this move and focus on this business instead of tequila and all the other products, you have to become a big enough player. We already bought the one hotel in Puerto Rico, but that does not really put us on the map. We need a chain."

"That amount of debt just scares me," said Marta.

Colleen nodded. "I know. It does mean that we have to take on a lot of debt. And one concern is that we already went eighty million in debt for those ships and plantation that Miguel bought. I know it wasn't sanctioned, but since we did not seek to cancel those loans and return the boats, we have now implicitly ratified his purchase and accepted the loans. If we add to the debt with ten luxury hotels, that is just a whole lot more borrowing. And it will take at least six to ten months before the cash flow from that business will start covering the payments, so we will have to struggle for at least half a year before things stabilize. So maybe we should hold off."

"Perhaps that is prudent," offered Susanna. "But the

research I pulled up for you on this shows that the opportunity to break into the market is now. There is a lot of pent-up demand nationwide. If we don't jump in now, we may not be able to do so later. And the interest rates are reasonable right now."

"We never needed to borrow before." Marta had a worried expression on her face. "It concerns me. This is hundreds of millions of dollars." She looked at her daughter, who was clearly not paying attention to this conversation. "Maria, you are the one who found the hotel in Puerto Rico and convinced us to buy it. That turned out to be a big winner, although largely because of the casino. But these hotels have no gambling. This was always your idea—you want us to move away from liquor and diversify—but with this debt that we would take on, what do you think about all this? Isn't it too much risk?"

Frowning, Maria looked at her mother. "Do you think I should try to reconcile with Emilio?" she suddenly asked, as if the discussion about the huge debt and the ten hotels had not happened. "Did I make a mistake?"

Marta looked at her daughter with a grimace. "You know I am against divorce—it goes against my faith. Your father and I did separate, but we never divorced under the church's law. But no, you did not make a mistake, and you absolutely should not go back to him. You got out of that marriage because it was loveless. And that is a good reason. Love will not just magically reappear. You are still young, younger than I was when I had Tomaso. And now you can find someone that you can stay with and have more children with."

"More children," said Maria with exasperation. "I don't know if I should ever do that. I wouldn't want another child to suffer like Antonio has."

Marta, who was sitting next to her daughter, reached over and stroked her hair. "I am glad you had Antonio. He is so sweet. I love my grandchild. And having him meant you avoided the impact of the Family Master Trust. Remember that my father wanted the Ramirez family to grow in size, and if you have no children, you cannot have a major role in RAM. That would be terrible. We need you as a CEO. Thankfully, at least one of my children ended up being competent to run our company."

"I love Antonio so much, but more children? I don't know. I wonder if Emilio would even consider reconciling."

Marta immediately shook her head vehemently. "No. Remember, if you go back to Emilio and remarry, you will have to stay married or the trust provisions will ruin you. Two divorces mean you're too unstable to be CEO. So no, you don't go back."

"I think your mother is right on this," Susanna piped up. "I have never seen you happy when you were with Emilio."

"Oh, I don't know," Maria responded. "He has a lot of good qualities."

"He is a very proper Latin gentleman from a good family, he is a good father, and he has money," offered Colleen. "You could do a lot worse."

"Enough of this," said Marta with authority. "You do need to find someone to marry. You do need to have more children. But Emilio is out of the question. Forget about him. Are you dating at all? You haven't mentioned anyone."

"She never goes on dates," Susanna said. "I have tried to get her on some sites. But she has no interest."

"I cannot do this, not with Antonio, not until he is well."

"Well, my dear," said her mother, standing up and continuing to stroke Maria's hair, then rubbing her shoulders, "you are not getting any younger. You do a great job running our company and I am very proud of you. But you need to think about growing your family. Tomaso already has three children. I worry that because of that, they could gain control of RAM, and they could just ruin it. I wish my father had not created that damn Trust."

Maria looked down at the elaborate Spanish tile of her mother's kitchen floor. Then she stood up and looked at each of them. The deal was an extensive expansion of RAM that she had been putting together for some time, but it made sense to her. They could market their own brand of alcohol in their own hotels, and Maria had always wanted to move RAM to a more real-estate-based business. She also wanted to have a company that did more than peddle liquor.

I can do this, she thought, *as long as I stay focused and work like I have never worked before. And I am going to forget about Emilio. He is a great father, better than me as a mother, but I don't love him and don't think I ever did. My time will be devoted to this, to RAM, to my family's legacy.*

She smiled, a smile which her mother had not seen in a long time, a smile of confidence and determination. Maria was resolute.

"We are going for it. We will take on the debt," Maria suddenly insisted with authority. "We are not going to let Tomaso's divorce or Miguel's peccadilloes stop our company from moving into the future."

She poured each of them a shot of tequila, and they toasted to the future of RAM.

Chapter Twelve

Los Angeles

BRIAN looked at the clock on his desk. His appointment was late again. And there was a lot to do. He looked over at the box of briefs and exhibits that RAM's lawyers had dumped on him and groaned. He had already started to do the work on his opposition, but he needed his client's help. Tomaso's attorney had also sent him discovery requests, so he needed to obtain information from Nora about her kids and her life. He also had to fill out an income and expense declaration and have her sign it—they had started it, but there was much more to do. Most important, he needed her guidance on how to unravel the complex corporate structure and assets of RAM itself. He knew that this was where the millions were—in fact he suspected billions. But because the company was private and its website told very little about its structure, he needed Nora to point him in the right direction.

He looked at his watch. She was over forty-five minutes late now. He decided to call her cell.

"The mailbox for this customer is full," was all he got. He had never called her home line before, worried that the husband or one of the children would answer. That was always awkward for a divorce lawyer. He hesitated for a moment—then decided to go for it. Now she was almost an hour late. The phone rang.

"Hello," came an older female voice.

Brian knew this had to be the maid and blessed his good fortune. "May I speak with Nora Ramirez, please?"

"Who is calling?" The maid said this with some alarm.

"Brian Youngman. I am her lawyer. And this is an important personal matter. Is she there? We had an appointment today."

"You had an appointment? Have you heard from her? Do you know where she is?" the maid said, obvious concern in her voice.

"Uh, no. Why? Has she not been home?"

"She never came home from Texas. We are all terribly worried about her. We have not heard from her for days now."

Brian was stunned. "What?" he queried. "Are you sure?"

"Of course we are sure. She apparently never boarded the flight back from Houston. We have contacted the authorities, but so far, we have heard nothing."

Brian shook his head in disbelief. He had seen situations in divorces before where a spouse took off, but usually it was with money or to be somewhere with a lover. This made no sense. Nora did not have to run away or embezzle money. And if she had a secret lover, Brian knew nothing about it. He forced his attention back to the maid. He needed information.

"Do you have a contact number for the authorities who are looking for her? I'm her lawyer. I need to find out all about this." The maid gave Brian a phone number for a contact in the Houston Police Department, which he promptly called.

"Police. Detective White speaking," came the response.

"Hello, officer. My name is Brian Youngman. I'm an attorney and I represent Ms. Nora Ramirez. I've just learned that she may have disappeared and I was given your name and number by the family as the contact who is handling her case."

"Youngman did you say?"

"Yes. I'm Nora's divorce lawyer. I'm calling you from Los Angeles."

"Okay, Mr. Youngman, can you send me some form of identification? Sorry to be so formal, but we just can't give out this information to anyone. You are not a member of the family or anything."

"Of course, detective. What is your email address?"

The officer quickly responded. Brian asked White to hold for a minute and emailed him a copy of the divorce petition, a link to Brian's business website, and also his correspondence with the court clerk about the upcoming hearing. "Did you get my email, detective?"

"Yes, yes, just looking at it now. Very interesting. Hmm. So, you are a divorce lawyer and Mrs. Ramirez is getting divorced?"

"That's right."

"And now she is missing."

"That is what I've heard. Do you have any information you can share?"

"Well, three days ago, she was at the Temple of Bliss spa here in Houston. She checked out at about five in the afternoon, paid her bill, and left the building. She was scheduled on a seven p.m. American Airlines flight to Los Angeles, and she had checked in for the flight that morning. But she never got on the plane, and as far as we have learned, she never even arrived at the airport. The call about her disappearance came in yesterday, from her husband, a Tomaso Ramirez. That was a bit unusual that the husband waited so long to report her disappearance, but maybe that is because he wasn't around, you know, due to the divorce and all. At this point, we are investigating what happened between the spa and the airport."

"What are you doing next?" asked Brian.

"We don't know how she was getting to the airport. Neither does the husband, according to his interview. He was in LA at the time, that has been verified. He didn't pick her up. We don't know if she called a cab, was taking a limousine service, or a friend was picking her up. The spa does not seem to know either."

"Detective White, this woman would not just take a cab. In fact, I know this, because I advised her not to do anything other than conduct her affairs in the most upscale and frankly, expensive way."

"Why would you do that Mr., uh, Youngman?"

"Ever been divorced, officer?"

"Never had the pleasure."

"Lifestyle. She needs to maintain the highest end lifestyle. That becomes important when we ask the husband to pay for that lifestyle. She gets to keep it. If she's suddenly taking cabs, that means she's lowering her lifestyle. And she is not supposed to do that."

"Sounds crazy," replied the cop. "But I hear you. The Temple of Bliss spa is the most expensive in Houston, and we looked at her bill. It would take a year of my salary to pay for what she charged. So okay, we will concentrate on limo services."

"High-end ones. Call me if you learn anything. I'm going to court and will need to tell the judge something."

Brian knew he needed to delay the proceedings, which of course is what the other side wanted anyway. But he also knew he couldn't mount a case while his client was missing.

He was befuddled and simply did not know what to do.

Chapter Thirteen

George Town, Grand Cayman

MIGUEL stood in the luxurious living room of the RAM plantation in the Caymans and looked at the three women who had been delivered for his inspection. They were all Hispanic, very young, and quite beautiful. They also came from families that were extremely poor. One was from Mexico, another from Costa Rica, and the third from El Salvador. Each of them wore a simple smock, but they all wore makeup and had their long hair down. And each one had an anxious look upon her face.

They had all been trafficked onto the island by a contact Miguel was using in the Mexican cartel named Javier. He provided no last name and it was unclear if this was really his name or what exactly Javier's role in the cartel was. But Miguel found himself using this contact more and more often since Miguel had begun a small but growing drug operation. He was smart enough not to run afoul of the cartel in operating his cocaine experiment, so he had made contact and asked permission. So far, things had gone smoothly. They had supplied product, and he had laundered money for them as well as for himself. But this was the first time he had asked for this type of service. As it turned out, Javier was happy to oblige.

"I think I need to see them without clothes," Miguel commented.

Manuel was with him and frowned at this display, apparently somewhat jealous of the situation. "They won't do what I do for you," he sneered.

"Take your clothes off, all of you," commanded Javier.

The three women stood obediently and disrobed. They stood naked before Miguel. He began his inspection, prodding each one, asking them to bend over, inspecting their teeth, their labia, their breasts, their anuses. He made them move in different ways, squatting, going up on tiptoes, twisting, all the while keenly observing each of them.

"What do you know about them?" Miguel asked Javier.

"Not so much, except they all have experience."

Miguel frowned. He went over to the girl from Mexico. She was just a teenager. All three were. "What is your name?" he demanded.

Although the girl had not appeared at all embarrassed when being inspected, she suddenly became shy. "My name is Trini," she said, looking down.

"Where do you come from? Where is your family?"

"I come from Sinaloa, and that is where my family is."

"And what do you do? Did you go to school? Do you work?" Miguel demanded.

"I did not go to school, but I learned how to please men in a house in Tijuana," she replied softly.

"Ugh," responded Miguel. "She is a whore. Are they all whores?" he asked of Javier.

"*Sí*, but of course, *Señor*. What did you expect? I found three beautiful whores for you to pick from. You can buy them all if you want. They all have experience."

"I am sure they have their share of diseases too. Take them all back." Manuel grinned broadly from ear to ear. "I need a pure girl, a virgin. And someone from a good family. Someone who has had some education. Someone who could be a good mother."

Javier shook his head. "How can I find that?" he said. "I brought you experienced girls who know how to do things and will comply with any wish. But what you are asking for, I cannot just steal some man's young virgin daughter and bring her here to sell you."

"Then I will have to find someone else to help me." Miguel turned to the women. "Put your clothes back on and get out." Now Manuel broke into a shrill laughter. Miguel turned to him and slapped him on the face. "Quiet, you dog." Manuel whimpered and slid away. The three quickly put on their clothes.

"Well," said Javier, "if you don't want them, I need a favor. These girls will fetch a very high price in Texas. I need to get them into the United States without trouble and bring them to the right place. So I need you to let me take them on one of your boats. I saw one mooring in the harbor when I got in today. That would be perfect."

Miguel looked at Javier. "What? Now you want me to be a trafficker and spirit women in illegally for prostitution?

On my company's boat? That is a serious crime. I don't think so. Find your own way in."

Javier, who had been jovial and friendly during this entire encounter, suddenly changed his demeanor. He gave a dark look to Miguel. "Listen to me. We let you do your little cocaine business on your boat. And we look the other way because it is so small. But we don't have to. Don't be telling me you are protecting your company's rum business here. You already use your boat for smuggling. It is not pure. You want me to help you, right? You need to be friendly too. And I need this help. It is not optional."

Miguel looked back at Javier and thought about getting a gun from the closet in his kitchen and shooting him right then and there. But then he thought better of it. "Just this once," he said.

Javier's face turned back into a friendly smile. "I knew you would understand. It is good to be my friend."

"But just this once," repeated Miguel.

"Of course, of course. Say, why do you want a virgin? And an educated one at that? Such a girl will never satisfy you or do the things these girls will do."

Miguel smiled. "Because I need someone to have my baby. And raise it."

Javier looked at Miguel with astonishment. "Why would you need such a thing? Why would you want such a thing?"

"It's a family matter. Actually, a family requirement. Something my crazy grandfather cooked up—annoyingly. It's supposedly in that Family Master Trust that my mother keeps so secret. But without a child of my own, I am limited in the family business. It is ridiculous, but that is what the stupid document says. So let me know if you can help me."

Javier shook his head. "For this, you are on your own. Just don't steal the wrong girl. Try to find one that the father won't come looking for you with a big machete."

"I am not worried about any father or any big machete," responded Miguel. "I have my own weapons that are ready if I get any trouble." He stood facing Javier. "You would be wise to remember that."

Javier spat right onto the Oriental carpet in the living room. "You would be wise to remember who I am."

Chapter Fourteen

New York

COLLEEN burst into Maria's office. "Nora is missing!" she exclaimed.

Maria, who was sitting at the computer reviewing the final agreements for the new hotel deal, looked up sharply. Susanna was next to Maria, collating the loan documents.

"What? Missing? Really? How could that happen?"

"Tomaso has apparently known for a few days but did not tell us. He says he doesn't know where she is. He says she left for some kind of health care visit and never came back home. He thinks she checked herself into a clinic somewhere, maybe in Arizona or New Mexico."

"That is so strange. It sure doesn't sound like Nora to check herself in to a program—even a high-end one. She never seems to think that there is anything wrong with her—just everyone else. What is really going on? Is Tommy up to something?"

The closing on the hotel deal was set for the next day. Maria took another look at the dense contracts on her computer and the photographs of each of the ten hotels she wanted RAM to buy, and then stood up and walked over to her floor-to-ceiling window to look at the Hudson River.

"Yes, it is really weird," Colleen replied. "And her lawyer is coming into court to ask for directions since he can't get hold of his client and doesn't know where she is."

"Interesting. Actually, that could be a benefit to us—a delay in everything and no chance for that lawyer to be looking into our business." Maria smiled. "Maybe Nora is at some alcohol or pill clinic or even someplace that uses psychedelics for therapy. I guess we don't care, as long as it paralyzes her case. Whatever, I assume she is just fine. Maybe she really is on a bender somewhere."

"Or she has a secret lover that we didn't know about," suggested Susanna.

"We can find out what's happening in court in about five minutes," announced Colleen as she walked over to Maria's computer and oversized screen. "They are doing an ex parte Zoom hearing that we can watch. Simmons, our lawyer at Findley & Goodwin, sent me the log-in credentials. We will be able to see the whole proceeding." Colleen exited the hotel documents with an "ugh" and started typing on Maria's computer.

Susanna stood up behind Maria to get a good view. "This should be interesting. I have never been in a California divorce court before," she said. "Just a really shoddy one in New Jersey. But California is the high-end divorce place—all those movie stars and rock stars get their divorces there. Maybe they have special luxury rooms for the celebrities to hang out."

"Divorce courts are not much fun, no matter where they are," commented Maria.

The three women huddled around the screen, waiting to be joined into the hearing. Moments later, the screen lit up, and a gallery of four separate boxes, each with a person, was in front of them. Because the women were only interested-party observers, they were not pictured and were muted. Colleen pointed to one of the boxes. "That's our lawyer, Simmons," she said, noting that he had two associates behind him also watching and most certainly billing RAM.

"He looks pretty unimpressive to me," commented Maria. "Just a stuck-up old windbag." In a second screen was Sam Callahan.

"That's Tommy's lawyer," said Colleen, pointing again.

"Such a swagger in that guy," noted Susanna. "He must cost a bundle."

Colleen pointed to the third person in the gallery. "That's Nora's lawyer. His name is Brian Youngman. He's supposed to be pretty smart and a good courtroom guy. I'm pretty sure he's Jewish."

Maria looked at Brian. He was dressed in a simple blue suit, white shirt, and striped tie.

"Aren't all the best lawyers Jewish?" queried Susanna, laughing. "Oh, and he is rather good looking, don't you think? I would like him as my lawyer except I might just fall in love with him and that might not be the best idea."

"No surprise that Nora would pick a handsome guy to represent her," responded Colleen. Maria said nothing, but she just looked at Brian. The fourth box on the screen was blank for the moment, but suddenly it changed, and the judge in a black robe appeared.

"Good morning, Your Honor," Brian immediately started. "Brian Youngman for Ms. Ramirez, the moving party this morning." Maria noticed his voice was strong, clear, and confident.

"Sam Callahan for Mr. Ramirez." This voice sounded haughty to Maria.

"And I am Bill Simmons, Findley & Goodwin, for RAM Industries Inc." Maria winced.

"Yuck!" said Susanna. "I'm sorry, Maria, I know I am supposed to like our attorney, but just yuck."

"Well, maybe someone like that is okay for this purpose," Maria responded.

Judge Grazer looked up from his spectacles. "Well, Mr. Simmons," he began, "I am still not sure you should even be here, but we won't address that today. So, what is going on, Mr. Youngman? You can't find your client?"

"Your Honor, I am quite frankly at a loss. My client was scheduled to meet with me to review the allegations made by the RAM company's papers, to sign verifications relating to discovery, and also to confirm an income and expense declaration. She did not appear at our meeting, and I made a number of attempts to reach her."

"He is so well-spoken," Susanna mooned. "I think I am in love."

"I finally spoke with her maid, who told me she went on a trip and did not return. Her cell phone is apparently dead and is taking no messages. So I am unable to proceed with either opposition to RAM's contentions or discovery.

I would like to stay this matter until we can make contact with Ms. Ramirez."

"Yes, he is good," Colleen acknowledged. "He will be a challenge if we actually have to go against him." Maria said nothing.

"What do you have to say about all this, Mr. Callahan?" Judge Grazer said, turning to Callahan. "Does your client know where his wife is?"

"Your Honor, uh, Mr. Ramirez is completely in the dark," Callahan responded. "He thinks maybe his soon-to-be ex-wife, who is very troubled and has alcohol and drug issues, may have realized how ill she was and checked herself into a clinic somewhere."

"That seems unlikely, Your Honor," Brian piped in. "First, Mr. Callahan's attempt to disparage my client and prejudice the court is totally improper. Those comments should be ignored. He has no basis to make them. But what is concerning is that Mr. Ramirez apparently claims to have no actual knowledge of his wife's whereabouts."

"Well, Your Honor," Simmons said drily, "regardless of who knows what, with the petitioner who brought this proceeding in absentia, the matter clearly cannot go forward. I request that you dismiss it."

"There is no reason at this point for Your Honor to do any such thing, and Mr. Simmons has no basis even to request it since he has no standing here," declared Brian. "I am sure there must be a legitimate explanation for Ms. Ramirez's unavailability. However, currently we will need to continue the hearing regarding RAM's claims about a prenuptial agreement for at least another sixty days to allow me to determine the status of my client."

"That is fine with us, Your Honor," responded Calahan.

Brian continued. "I do think, however, that in the meantime, RAM can respond to the discovery that I have served on the company. The enterprise is quite complex, has many different business interests, and owns enormous assets. It will take us time to review all that information, so the sooner we get it, the sooner we can provide the court with our position on Ms. Ramirez's interests and entitlements. She likely has a right to one-sixth of a multibillion-dollar company."

Colleen frowned. "Interests and entitlements? This guy doesn't quit," she said. "His client goes missing and he still wants to press forward on her behalf."

"He's obviously a dedicated professional, which is what he's supposed to be," Maria said softly, speaking for the first time.

"A cute one too," added Susanna.

Simmons began to speak again. "Um, Your Honor, in my opinion, which I have given great thought to, I don't think it should be allowed that ..."

"Enough, Mr. Simmons," interrupted Judge Grazer. "While I am sure you have lots to say, I don't have the time right now to hear it. And I continue to question your participation in this matter. That said, Mr. Youngman, I will grant you the additional sixty days, but you must report back to the court about your efforts to find your client and explain this mysterious disappearance by her."

"Yes, Your Honor."

"And Mr. Youngman, I will also grant your request to stay any requirement that you provide any discovery."

"Thank you, Your Honor."

"But in light of the RAM company's filing, I will not stay

their production of information. So, I am ordering RAM to fully produce all the documents and files you have requested. And there is no reason that they need any more time to do so. I expect it to be done promptly, Mr. Simmons. You have plenty of lawyers at your big firm. You should have no problem getting the manpower to do all these things."

Simmons looked dismayed. "But Your Honor, that is so burdensome, and ..."

But the judge interrupted him again. "I am sure your multibillion-dollar corporate client has the necessary manpower, and I don't want to hear any more about it."

"Thank you, Your Honor," Brian said.

Judge Grazer turned his attention to Brian. "And Mr. Youngman, I suggest you find your client. And soon. Otherwise, I will have to consider dismissing this case."

"Yes, Your Honor. I understand," Brian responded. And the screens went blank.

"We sure lost that round," Colleen quipped. "So much for high-priced lawyers from big firms."

"Nora's guy was good," Susanna commented. "What was his name? Brian what?"

"Brian Youngman," replied Maria. She looked thoughtful. "I am starting to get a little suspicious about all this. Let's get Tommy on the line. I can't believe he knows nothing."

"Got it," said Susanna as she raced out of the office.

Maria turned to Colleen. "That deal will put us in serious debt with a number of different financial institutions," she said with concern. "Do you think we can handle it? It is enough to put us out of business entirely. You know how it works—if a single payment is not made and one bank declares a default, every other one follows suit and all the loans become immediately due in full. Mr. Youngman may be touting us as a multibillion-dollar company, but if that happens, we sure can't pay back all that debt. And with that stupid loan that Miguel put us into to buy his ships for his Bermuda Triangle plus the debt on our Puerto Rico hotel and our Scottish distillery, if there is a problem in the first year, this whole company goes down."

"Based on projected cash flow analysis, after the first year, we should be good," responded Colleen. "The big risk is only at the very front end. We should be able to get through that first six months. The closing is tomorrow, all the contracts are done, and the loan documents are signed. If you're having second thoughts, we can postpone it. Otherwise, by this time tomorrow RAM will be the proud owner of ten new hotels."

"No, no delay." Maria was shaking her head. "We've worked hard on this deal. I so want to bring RAM into the future, to be more than just a liquor company. Besides, I don't want to have to explain any delay to my mother. She will think I am indecisive. We're going forward."

"Tommy is on the line," Susanna called in.

"Colleen, stay for this, please. We may need to keep it privileged, and if you're here as our lawyer, it may be safer."

"Agree," said Colleen.

Maria hit the speaker button. "Tommy, where is Nora? Don't bullshit me. Colleen is here, so all this is protected under RAM's attorney/client privilege. What's going on?"

"Well," Tommy's voice sounded gravelly, "I don't technically know. But she's supposed to be at a clinic out of the country. I guess that's where she is."

"What? What did you do?"

"I just arranged as her husband to have her committed for a while. Teach her a lesson. That's all. It's time she learned it."

Maria looked at Colleen with utter astonishment, and they both shook their heads.

"You are a first-class idiot," Maria yelled into the phone. "What is wrong with you? You don't do that to someone. She's not your minor child or your slave or some piece of meat. She is a U.S. citizen. What makes you think you have any right to do that to anyone? Especially in the middle of a divorce proceeding. That lawyer is going to find out, and we are going to be in major trouble. You have put us at serious risk. You could even go to jail for this."

"Calm down. It was legal. I signed a bunch of documents, and she was out of the country at the time so different laws apply."

"How would you know that?" Colleen said quickly, and even she had now raised her voice. "And just because you sign some documents and send them to a foreign country does not mean the California courts don't have jurisdiction. And there are federal courts too. She's a U.S. citizen, for goodness' sake. And that you did this and you also lied to the court when you had your lawyer say you don't know what happened—oh boy. When this comes out, you are toast."

"And what's worse," Maria continued, "is that you have compromised the company in the process."

"Yes, you did, for sure," added Colleen. "You put RAM at risk. You think that judge will favor our side when all this comes out?"

"Okay, okay, I'll get her back. She might be in the Cayman Islands at this point. I'll see what I can do. And she won't tell people about it—it would be too humiliating for her."

"Get her back now," Maria screamed. "And don't do anything more without talking to us. You moron." She hung up the phone in disgust. "Why is my brother so stupid?"

"It's worse than that," Colleen responded. "Clearly, he has committed a crime. Likely multiple felonies." She stopped for a minute. "That could mean the end of his rights in RAM. And he really could end up in jail."

"I don't want him in jail, but I do want him out of the company. He is a liability we can't afford, especially now." And Maria began to think more about this. "Doesn't the Family Master Trust say something about this—getting convicted of a crime means you get disinherited, or something like that?"

"Your mother has only let me look at a few parts of that document, so I can't say for sure," Colleen answered. "I asked her for a copy, but it's something she is just not willing to share. She claims that it's not supposed to be shared by the senior member of the family—there's something about that in the Trust requirements—to maintain its confidentiality. I don't really understand it, but apparently it's something that your grandfather wanted—all about keeping the tequila business always in the family and making sure whoever is in charge can pass it on to the next generation. And there's something about the business never falling into the hands of criminals. It's bit strange, and I don't know if it would hold up in court, but Marta believes it should be followed."

Maria looked thoughtful. "So if Tommy goes to jail over this, he loses his inheritance and he's out of the company, right? And his kids lose out too?"

"So maybe that is not so bad," commented Susanna.

Chapter Fifteen

Los Angeles / Houston

Los Angeles boasts a significant Japanese population, and many live in the Sawtelle area in West LA. That
area is host to a number of restaurants offering sushi and
other Japanese cuisine as well as some shops where classic Japanese garments are sold. There are also a few dojos
where the Japanese martial art of judo is practiced.

Brian had sought out one of these dojos after law school,
since he had grown up taking judo lessons and had himself
competed at the college level in *randoris*, or judo competitions. He had been quite successful in his college judo club,
often scoring an *ippon* or point and winning the match.
Points are scored by successful throws or by holds on the
mat that force the opponent to concede with two taps.
Judo does not involve striking the other judoka, but rather

focuses on successfully executing a judo throw while physically holding the opponent's *gi* or judo outfit. Brian found it more elegant than a karate match where the contestants try to kick or punch one another. In judo, Brian relished the art of using the opponents' force or strength against them. A throw would usually only be successful by sensing the direction or movement of one's adversary. Brian could use and even encourage that action and then take advantage of it by sweeping out a leg or propelling the opponent's body over his shoulder.

When Brian found a dojo in the Sawtelle district, he was warmly welcomed by the Japanese *sensei*, or master, to practice, and he began to do so regularly. At first, he proudly wore his *Sankyu* brown belt but discovered that most of the others in the dojo had first or second *dan* black belts. He also was badly bested in his first six months by just about everyone in the dojo, getting thrown over and over. During that time, he would limp sorely into the office the next morning, smarting from the evening sessions. But as time passed and he stuck with it, his skills improved. Brian felt it was a terrific workout and kept him both in shape and respectful, and in time he too was awarded a black belt. Even into his forties, he continued the regimen of regular practice, and along with bike riding on the beach, it kept him fit and strong.

But this evening at judo he was distracted and so found himself frequently on the ground, having been beaten by others.

"Not on your game tonight, eh?" commented Hanagi after putting Brian on his back a third time.

Brian shook his hand, which was stinging from the slap of his fall. "It's work," he said. "Something is not right.

I have a funny feeling about this case, and I think I'm going to have to do more than just sit on my butt and wait."

"Well, you're on your butt now," laughed Hanagi. "I suggest you get off it and try to keep me from putting you back on it."

Brian popped up, grabbed Hanagi's *gi*, and with a leap forward performed a perfect *osoto gari* throw, landing Hanagi flat.

"See how things go when I'm focused?" Brian teased. But then he frowned. "I've got to go. I think I'm getting on a plane tomorrow and have to pack."

"You think?" said Hanagi, who had already jumped back to his feet. "Don't think. Just do. And know what you are doing." He grabbed Brian's lapel, and the two began again, attacking and countering for another half hour. Brian was dripping with sweat at the end of their session.

"You are right, Hanagi. I will not hesitate. I'm going, and I will find out just what happened to my client. I am off to Texas in the morning."

"Texas? Well, don't forget your cowboy hat," said Hanagi. "Or your six-shooter."

Brian laughed. "I'm not one for guns," he said. "They just hurt people."

He left the dojo and hurried home to shower and pack. He booked a flight to Houston, Texas, for the next morning and sent an email to the detective he had spoken to on the Houston Police Department saying he would be there the next day to go over Nora's case. He knew that only by being the squeaky wheel would anything get done on this investigation.

Brian's flight was early in the morning, but with the

time change, he did not arrive at the police station until the afternoon. Fortunately, the detective assigned to finding Nora was at the station. Brian shook the hand of Nathan White, or Nate, as he told Brian to call him. Nate motioned to a small conference room, and the two men sat down on shabby chairs at a shabby table in a shabby room with Styrofoam cups of mediocre coffee. Nate was dressed in plain clothes—a stained white shirt with a cheap tie hanging loosely. Brian wore a polo shirt and jeans and looked more like a tourist than a lawyer.

"So far, not much. Looks like this lady vanished into thin air after a facial, a wax, and a massage," Nate told Brian. "I'm sorry. Kind of surprised to see you, just her lawyer, instead of her husband."

"Well, they were getting divorced."

"Still," Nate continued, "even with that going on, it's the kind of thing that usually brings a guy here to find out what happened. This guy—Tomaso Ramirez—just doesn't seem concerned. I don't get it."

"Could he have been involved?"

"We wondered about that. You know the old line—it's always the spouse. No evidence though. We also think it quite possible that this rich lady went off on a lark. You know—a wild spree like she's a free woman who wants to light up the world with her money. I've been thinking that's a high probability. Putting aside the husband, who would want to kidnap her? I bet he had nothing to do with it but is probably delighted she's gone—that is, unless he has to pay her credit card bill."

"Did you find the limo driver yet?" Brian asked.

"No—well, let me see." Nate began looking at his file.

"I guess we haven't checked every limo company. There are just too many."

"Have you asked people at the spa who their patrons typically use?"

"Yes, the manager did not know. He wasn't very helpful. He didn't want to talk for long."

"How about the staff?" Brian pressed.

Nate shook his head. "That's an idea. But I don't know who to get on the phone."

"Have you gone out there?"

"No, didn't seem worth it," Nate said.

"Well, you know the old saying—always go visit the scene of the crime. Want to take a ride with me?" Brian asked. "Better to go out there than try to find a witness with a phone call."

"Hmm. Why not? I could use the change of scenery. I'll drive."

The two men drove in Nate's old gray Honda sedan out to the Temple of Bliss spa.

"How long have you been a detective?" asked Brian, thinking it might be useful to develop some rapport.

"Too long. I'm hoping to retire next year," Nate said. "I'm getting too old for this job. Don't quite have the mojo anymore."

Brian thought that was obvious since he had to come from Los Angeles to encourage Nate to leave his desk to interview potential witnesses. But Brian kept these thoughts to himself.

The entrance to the spa was ornate, promising a luxurious pampering to those who could afford to enter. Brian and Nate entered a large perfumed room filled with all sorts of items to purchase: robes and pajamas, ladies' blouses and sweatsuits and underwear, soaps and creams of all types. There was even a small men's section with larger robes and hats and sandals. A long front desk stood at the far end of the room where two young women sat behind computer screens. A women's entrance was to the right, and a men's entrance was to the left of the desk. Brian in his polo and jeans looked like a potential customer, but Nate appeared entirely out of place. The two men wove their way through the overpriced wares for sale and walked up to the desk. One of the girls looked up.

"Checking in?" she inquired.

"Not today," said Nate. "I'm Nathan White, Houston police." He produced a badge. The girl's welcoming smile quickly changed to one of concern, and the other girl who had been on her phone looked up with alarm.

"May I have your name, please?" Nate said in a serious police demeanor.

"I'm Sally ... Sally Floro. Is there something wrong, officer?" the first girl said meekly.

"We're investigating the disappearance of one of your customers, um, a Nora Ramirez. She was at the spa eight days ago, and since checking out from here, she has not been seen since then. Did you happen to be working eight days ago, at this desk, Ms. Floro?"

"Well, no sir, I was just hired this week. I'm new." She turned to the second girl, who was staring at Nate. "Were you here, Lisa?"

"Yes, I heard something about this. That lady hasn't been found yet?"

Nate and Brian turned their attention to her.

"No, ma'am, she is still missing. You were here then?" said Nate. "Do you remember her?" Brian looked at Lisa intently.

"I really don't know, officer," Lisa responded. "I just check people in and out. I'm not a technician or anything. I don't really pay that much attention to the customers."

"This is really important," Brian spoke up. "I'm Nora's lawyer and she has been missing for days. She has three children, her daughter is about your age, and the whole family is desperate. Anything you can tell us would be helpful. Please try."

"Okay, let me think about it." Lisa looked thoughtful. "She was being picked up, I think. She was pretty happy. She bought some things."

"Was there a limo for her?" Brian pressed. "Is there a service that typically comes here to take people to the airport?"

"I have seen a few companies. There is Universal Limo and City Limo. And there is some company that has a bunch of Russian drivers—can't remember their name."

Nate was taking notes at this point. Brian took out his cell phone and began looking up limo services in Houston.

"I see Universal and City listed," he said. He began looking at other names. "There is Handy Limo, Limos, Inc., Luxury Limo."

"That's it," Lisa said. "Luxury Limo is the one with the Russian drivers. I remember them because they sometimes come in here and flirt with us."

Brian and Nate talked with the two receptionists a few moments longer, but they had no more information. The two men returned to Nate's car and began calling the three limo services. Both Universal and City were dead ends, but when Nate reached Luxury Limo and identified himself as an officer with the Houston Police Department, the Russian-accented man who answered asked Nate to hold. He came back on after a few moments. Nate put his phone on speaker so Brian could hear.

"We did have an order to pick up a Nora Ramirez at the Temple of Bliss Spa that day and to drive her to the airport, but it was cancelled. We even sent a driver out there, but it was a waste of time. We were going to charge her credit card anyway, but I guess we decided not to."

"You sent someone out to the spa to pick her up, is that correct?" asked Brian.

"Yes, Dmitri, I think, was there."

"Is Dmitri at your office now?" asked Nate.

"He is out on a job, but I think he is just finishing up. He has his papers. He is completely legal." The man on the phone began to sound nervous. "We run a legitimate business here. Sure, we help some guys who are coming into the U.S., but everything is aboveboard. We like the police. We want to be good citizens."

"We just need to talk to him. Don't worry, he's not in any trouble," Brian said.

"He will be in trouble though if he does not cooperate with us," added Nate.

"Okay, okay, I will have him report back. He should be here in twenty minutes."

"Then we will see you in twenty minutes." Nate hung up. "Strange," he said. "They were supposed to pick her up and even sent out a driver but then got cancelled? Doesn't make any sense."

"Sounds to me like whoever cancelled is the one who

may know what happened to Nora," said Brian. "I am afraid my client has been the victim of a terrible scheme."

"Maybe so. And right now, the only one we know who might have a motive is the husband."

"Yes," said Brian. "He was likely going to have to pay her an awful lot of money in this divorce. A lot of money."

"Sounds like the old saying is right: First thing, look at the spouse," commented Nate, as he started the car.

The gray Honda moved away from the spa and toward the home office of Luxury Limo.

Chapter Sixteen

Miami

MIGUEL set down his phone, smiled, and triumphantly drained his glass of tequila. He poured himself another. Maria had just called him to discuss her concern that Nora was missing and that Tomaso appeared to be responsible. He was, after all, the obvious suspect. Miguel was quite pleased with how he had set Tomaso up, having put all the documents regarding the limo and the helicopter in Tomaso's name. Tomaso had been foolish enough to sign documents committing Nora to an institution. Those documents would be easily found by any competent investigator. The truth was only one person knew that Miguel had been involved in Nora's murder—and Ricardo, that Panamanian seaman, was loyal to him. Whether he needed to eliminate that fellow did cross Miguel's mind, but he dismissed it for now.

Pinning Nora's disappearance on Tomaso was only the

first part of his plan. Miguel hoped that Tomaso would go to jail for a long time. Although Miguel had never seen the RAM Family Master Trust document, he knew it prohibited any family member who had been convicted of a crime from ever owning or managing RAM.

Once Tomaso was cut off, so were his children and his entire line. Tomaso would simply be fired and all the company benefits and accoutrements taken away from him and his family.

Miguel relished the thought of seeing Tomaso's pathetic children having to fend for themselves, their father penniless and in jail and, of course, no mother at all. He had despised Tomaso since the day he was born. Why he had hated his younger brother from birth was never something Miguel thought about. He was not prone to introspection, did not engage in self-reflection, never questioned why he enjoyed causing pain to others. Miguel's freedom from any kind of self-doubt made him more effective in achieving his goals. And while he was not the smartest of the three siblings, he was certainly the cleverest.

He did not have the same enmity toward Maria as he did Tomaso, but he deeply resented her and her status as the CEO of the company. He hated that he had to defer to his older sister's judgment, beholden to what she allowed him to do. And while she had given him his own realm to work in, she still kept an eye on his activities, and he was required to report to her. He had kept his small drug smuggling operation secret so far, but he knew if she discovered it, she would dismantle it and could even turn him in. Of course, that would damage RAM. However, he had been avoiding customs with much of the rum he was bringing into the country, and he had already confessed that to her. She was so protective of RAM that Miguel figured she would never risk reporting him to the authorities.

So no, he felt he was likely protected from Maria—she knew about the rum-running and did not stop it, so she was guilty now too. But she could put a halt to his operation and demote him or fire him, which she apparently had the power to do under the Trust if she learned about the cocaine. The rum-running was illegal, but Miguel knew RAM could just pay a nasty fine on top of the back duties that were due to avoid any real trouble.

However, the drug-running was a different story and could sink the company completely, putting all the executives in jail, causing the banks to call all the loans, permanently damaging the brand. Miguel risked all this, plus he had made a connection with the Mexican cartel, and he even knew that someday such a connection could come back to bite him. And yet Miguel, undeterred, brazenly risked all to wantonly satisfy whatever he happened to desire. He was programmed to be utterly reckless.

What Miguel planned was to oust both his siblings and take over RAM. For that, he not only had to destroy Tomaso, but also to dethrone Maria, and that would be far more challenging. His mother, Marta, had long ago appointed Maria to be her successor as CEO, explaining to Miguel that she was the oldest and she had attended both college and business school. Miguel knew Marta did not trust him, knew his true character, and had counselled Maria to send Miguel to Miami. That had worked out well for both of them, since Maria wanted the status and respectability of Manhattan, while Miami was a perfect location for Miguel to participate in all his nefarious activities. After all, what better place than Miami to engage in all forms of licentious behavior?

Miguel looked out of his large picture window at the Biscayne Bay. He had a modern style house on the water with a dock and a boat, all on a large property on Bridge Road, located on Star Island, just off the MacArthur Causeway. His home office on the second story of his posh multimillion-dollar estate sported a spectacular view of the Bay. He picked up the phone and called his cartel contact in Mexico. Javier answered.

"*Hola*, Javier," Miguel began. "I need a bit more help from you."

"*Hola*, *hombre*, glad you called. Needed to talk to you."

"Oh, what about?"

"I've been told you need to start kicking some of your catch back to us. Turns out when they looked at it, they decided that they can't make an exception. Then others will think we will just let anyone start their own little operation. And we can't have that. So even though you are pretty small, you are going to have start giving us our due. It's a matter of principle."

"Whoa, man. No way. You said I could start doing this and no problem as long as I kept it small and quiet."

"Well, things change." Javier spoke calmly. "That's the way of it. You've got to pay."

"How much?"

"Fifty percent."

Miguel was taken aback. "What? No way. That is way too much. C'mon, man, you've got to be kidding."

"Hey, I had to argue with them to keep it that low. So, either give it up or pay. Actually, they don't want you to give it up, just pay. And it's fifty percent now. No promises it won't go up in the future. It won't go down."

"I don't know," said Miguel, trying to think of some way out of this.

"I do know," said Javier sharply. "And don't get cute with our cut. We will check your accounting. And bad things happen to anyone who cheats us on that. You don't even want to think about that."

"This is just highway robbery."

Javier laughed. "Hey man, it's the drug business. Did you think you got a free ride forever? And one more thing. We want your help cleaning it. We know you are doing that in the Caymans. We want in."

Miguel began to sweat. "I don't know if that is possible," he said, becoming desperate.

"Figure it out. Nobody here likes to hear no for an answer. They just don't take that very well. So, what did you want? You called me."

Miguel had forgotten that he'd called Javier to ask for a favor.

He shook himself free from the shock of these demands. "The girl I am looking for. I told you what I want. Can you help me?"

"Oh yes, you want a sweet little virgin. I think you are *loco*. But I will ask around. It's not something we usually do. But I do have an idea that may help you. See? You work with us and we work with you. Everyone's happy. And Miguel—that money needs to be paid monthly. I will be sending someone to George Town to pick up what you owe the first of each month. It will be a regular thing. I will arrange for a pickup in two days."

Miguel hung up and threw his glass of tequila across the room, and it shattered in the corner.

Chapter Seventeen

Houston

BRIAN sat in the Houston police station sipping cold coffee, having trouble believing his predicament. It had become more and more clear that his client had been abducted and her husband was the culprit. What was still a complete mystery is where Nora actually was at this time. He had no client and was under court order to report back to the judge, and if he had no good answers, the case could be dismissed.

Brian started to think about Nora. Was he more concerned about losing his case than what might have happened to his client? He shook himself and wondered what was wrong with him. Sure, he had only met Nora a few times and did not particularly like her; she was so entitled and had enjoyed the finest things in life without working a single day—or at least not since marrying a rich heir to a massive fortune. Brian mentally slapped himself. He needed to care. He was going to care. This poor lady had been taken somewhere against her will. That was never going to be okay with him.

He and Detective White had found the Russian limo driver, who was at first not very cooperative. Brian pressed the man hard and talked about chatting with immigration authorities. The driver, Dmitri, was evasive at first since he had not split the money he received with his boss. When the truth finally came out, it was hard to reach any conclusion other than Tomaso Ramirez had his wife abducted. There had been another driver, who told Dmitri that Nora's husband had arranged something "special" and demanded Dmitri leave. When Dmitri had resisted, the other driver had shown him a gun. He had also paid Dmitri far more than the value of the fare to get rid of him. And since then, Nora had just disappeared. Brian still couldn't believe it. Just then, Nate came into the conference room. Brian put down his cup.

"Well, we've been talking with the LAPD. They're getting a search warrant and going out to the Ramirez place and will likely place the guy under arrest. Maybe he'll be so scared he'll start talking and tell us where his wife is. Guys like him usually give it up pretty quickly. Unless he lawyers up and they tell him to shut his mouth like they always do."

Brian nodded. "Tell me about it. I used to be a DA. That is standard operating procedure. I guess we won't know for a while."

"Right. I assume you'll be getting yourself back to LA. Nothing more you can do here."

"Yep. I already found a flight. Leaves in a couple of hours. Probably should get going."

"Safe travels. And thanks for coming. You got me off my ass. I was so sure the lady had gone off on her own just for fun I was pretty unmotivated. Seems I was wrong."

"You made a reasonable assumption," Brian acknowledged. "I think in your shoes I might have concluded the same thing." He stood up and started to grab his bag.

"By the way, one more thing before you go."

"Yes?"

"You said you had been studying up on this big company of theirs because of all the divorce stuff. And I get that it's a big thing, so maybe this means nothing. But do you know if they have some office or property or something in the Cayman Islands?"

Brian reacted, looking up immediately at Nate. "She told me there was some Cayman connection, and I did see in the list of properties a farm or distillery or something in George Town," he said slowly. "Why?"

"Well, we did a full search of all the airfields and passenger manifests in the Houston area, and we also went farther out to anything within a hundred miles. We checked bus stations and train stations and rental cars. We're still looking into those and specifically if anyone rented a limo in the area. But when we looked at the records at the time shortly after this lady disappeared, there was one kind of weird helicopter run that was out of the ordinary and didn't quite make any sense to us."

"A helicopter?"

"Yep. When we checked into it, seems the pilot put in George Town as their destination. It was a private flight, not some regular thing. It stopped again to refuel and then took off. But the thing is, Grand Cayman is just over one thousand miles away from the Texas coast. And with a full tank, a chopper can only go about four hundred miles. Even if it could refuel somewhere, I don't know why anyone would take a helicopter all that way."

"Grand Cayman?" Brian said. He stood up. "George Town? Nate, I'm going to the airport now, but would you please call me as soon as you hear anything from the LAPD?"

Brian shook hands and walked out, thinking about the Cayman Islands.

Chapter Eighteen

Los Angeles

TOMASO contemplated his predicament as he sat in his twelve-million-dollar Bel Air home on a rich leather chair drinking a Highland Park eighteen-year-old single malt scotch from a crystal tumbler neat. He had moved out after Nora filed for divorce and been staying at a swanky beach hotel in Santa Monica but returned to his house now that Nora was missing. Maria had told him to take care of his children, and even Miguel had encouraged him, pointing out that he had to appear to be a caring and concerned father. Tomaso was planning to see his girlfriend later this evening and was very much looking forward to it. But he knew he had to stay around the house this Saturday afternoon because his three children were home. He tried to think of himself as a devoted father who was taking up the slack for his missing wife.

At the thought of Nora, he smiled. Tomaso pictured her in a facility in the Caymans with locked doors undergoing "therapy," which included tranquilizers. *She must be going nuts*, he thought. Tomaso had not immediately jumped on a plane when Maria demanded that he bring Nora back. He planned to fly out there in a couple of days and "rescue" her, but of course only if she promised to stop making trouble for him and his family.

Miguel had come up with a clever idea to have her committed, and apparently the Caymans had intelligent laws—not like the United States—where a husband's status and control over his wife were properly enforced. She would learn not to have such big britches now. She would gain a new respect for him—yes, even fear him. That is what he wanted. And then she could take care of his spoiled kids while he enjoyed time with his mistress at his leisure. She would learn her lesson, not to cross him, a man of wealth and power. He was feeling the warmth from the liquor and starting to be quite pleased with himself. Just then, his daughter came into the room.

"Dad," said Jocelyn, "the police are at the door. They said they want to talk to you."

Tomaso was annoyed. He had spent plenty of time talking with the LAPD already. When Nora did not return home from the Temple of Bliss spa in Houston, as of course he had expected, he had known he could not just ignore her absence, especially because at a minimum his three kids would notice. Even Miguel had encouraged him to report that she was missing and make sure he demonstrated worry. So he had talked with Detective Samuels, who was assigned to the case, and conveyed that he was totally at a loss. He did not like talking to cops, but he put up a false front of confidence and entitlement. After all, wasn't their job to protect and serve people like him, the rich ones with status and money?

"I'll be along in a minute but tell them to wait outside."

There was no reason for him to hurry, so Tomaso first downed the rest of his scotch and then went off to the bathroom to relieve himself and comb the few locks of hair on his head. He ambled up to the door and saw Detective Samuels, the fellow who had taken down his statement, standing outside with two uniformed police officers.

"Hello, detective," Tomaso began, trying to adopt a concerned tone. "Is there some news? Perhaps a break in the case?"

"Hello, Mr. Ramirez. Yes, possibly there is." The detective looked somberly at Tomaso. "Would you mind coming down to the station with us and answering some more questions? I think there may be some things that you can clear up."

Tomaso inwardly groaned. "Well, I certainly want to help any way I can," he responded, "but now is not a convenient time for me to be leaving. You see, my three children are home and they are awfully worried about their mother, as am I. I really need to be here with them, for them, to do what I can to keep them calm and hopeful." Tomaso was actually thinking that he sure did not want to miss that date with his girlfriend later in the day. He was even hoping to get in nine holes of golf first. "Can't we just chat here? I have already told you pretty much everything I know, which is not very much. But if you have a break in the case, I sure am eager to hear about it."

"Well, sir, that just won't work. We really need you to come with us and discuss what we have learned."

Tomaso began to show his annoyance. "Listen, detective. I think it is a little unreasonable for you to show up here out of the blue, no notice at all, and just ask for that. I mean, it is a Saturday, and I have a family. So I think I am going to decline that request. Just tell me what you want to know."

"I was hoping we could do this the easy way," said the detective.

"Easy way? What do you mean?" Now Tomaso became worried. "Maybe I should just have one of my lawyers call you."

"You can do that, sir. In fact, you will probably need to do that. Tomaso Ramirez, you are under arrest. You have the right to remain silent ..." The detective continued reading Tomaso his rights while the two uniformed officers handcuffed him right there on the front porch of his luxury mansion. The police then put him into a patrol car and drove him to the West Los Angeles police station.

The initial charge was obstruction of justice, but that was only the beginning. Based on the communications from the Houston Police Department, the LAPD knew Tomaso had not told the truth about his wife's disappearance. They had the Russian limo driver's testimony fingering the husband, and of course the soon-to-be-divorced Tomaso had an obvious motive. The Houston police had also recovered a yellow purse with Nora's initials on it, so she clearly had been taken against her will. Moreover, kidnapping was a federal felony, and the likely charge involved an interstate crime, so after being booked for lying to the LAPD, the federal authorities had been notified of evidence that Tomaso was directly involved with his wife's disappearance from Houston, at least as a co-conspirator but more likely as the mastermind.

The LAPD had hoped to get Tomaso talking and thereby further incriminate himself, but they did not want to ruin their own bust by pushing the issue too far. After the arrest, the cops knew the rich man would hire an expensive lawyer and the negotiations would begin, and their hope was that with the right amount of pressure, Tomaso would crack and give up the location of his wife. Detective Samuels had been looking forward to arresting this fat cat.

Needless to say, Tomaso did not play golf and missed his date with his girlfriend that evening. In fact, despite the best efforts of his lawyers, he ended up in jail, waiting for a bail bondsman to show up and post a million-dollar bond. The cell he sat in was small and smelled like a sewer.

There definitely was no single-malt scotch in a crystal glass served neat.

Chapter Nineteen

Grand Cayman

MARIA STEPPED OFF the RAM company jet into the balmy warmth of the Caribbean. She was angry.

The flight, although long, had been pleasant enough, so her ire had nothing to do with the trip itself. She knew that despite her direct order to Tomaso to bring Nora back immediately, he had been delaying. After closing the complex multibillion-dollar transaction where RAM acquired ten operating hotels and went deeply into debt, she decided she had to fly south and see for herself what kind of mischief Tomaso had initiated. She also guessed that somehow Miguel had instigated this ridiculousness, since not only did it involve the Caymans, but it was the kind of mean, crafty antic that Miguel would concoct. She knew that Tomaso, while mean, was neither clever nor particularly proactive—it was always a chore to get him to actually do anything but play golf.

Maria also realized she had never been to the company property in George Town. She had planned to inspect
it ever since Miguel had acquired it, but something had
always come up. The truth was, she had no desire to be
down here—ever. This little rum operation that Miguel put
together had been small but profitable, so there was never
any compelling need to investigate a problem, and Maria
had kept putting this trip off. But with Tomaso admitting
to kidnapping and institutionalizing his own wife, who was
trying to divorce him, she saw the serious risk he had created for the company as well as for himself. And she knew
she could not rely on what she was told by either of her
brothers. Plus, this topic was too sensitive and potentially
explosive to send someone else down here.

Maria had planned on spending this time with Antonio
after finally closing the hotel deal. She so longed to hold
her son and comfort him. The doctors had indicated they
saw the potential for a breakthrough in his treatment. She
dreamt of the day he could stop going to the hospital and
return to the path of a normal child, going to school, playing soccer, taking piano lessons, and just watching TV in
his own home. This forced absence from her son added to
the huge amount of guilt she was already feeling, and this
guilt turned to rage that she had to waste her time over her
brothers' misconduct instead of being with her son.

Still, as she looked around after leaving the plane, she
was reminded of the lush beauty of the islands. As angry
as she was, she could not help the feeling of relaxation that
rushed over her. A Mercedes S-class drove up to the private
jet, and she walked toward it.

"Hello, *Señora* Ramirez," the driver called. He stopped
the car, jumped out, and grabbed Maria's bag. "My name is

Ernesto. We welcome you to George Town. All of the people at the farm are looking forward to meeting you. Thank you for coming." He smiled at her. He was black and dressed comfortably in shorts and a T-shirt. Maria looked at him and forced a smile.

"Hello, Ernesto," she replied, masking her anger. "It's a pleasure to be here and to meet you."

After all, it was not his fault that her brothers were such troublemakers. And she was the CEO of the company, so she was always careful to remember that even an unkind look from her to an employee could hurt quite a lot. She knew she was lucky to be so wealthy and successful and recognized so much of that success was due to the efforts of her subordinates. She had followed the rule of always being respectful of everyone in the company, and that approach had paid off. Most everyone genuinely appreciated her humility and worked even harder because their CEO treated them politely and kindly.

"How far is it to the farm?" she asked.

"Only thirty minutes as long as we don't get caught up in one of our island traffic jams." Ernesto chuckled warmly. "I will get you there in no time. *Señor* Miguel is also expected to arrive soon. It will be quite lovely there for both of you."

"Oh," Maria said with surprise. "I thought he was in Miami."

"No, ma'am. He is flying down here right now." He opened the back door of the Mercedes.

"Ernesto, let me ride in the front with you. That way we can talk, and I will be better able to see your lovely island."

They drove off with Maria in the passenger seat. During the trip to the RAM plantation, Maria was able to get a nice view of some of the island. She was entranced by the lush tropical beauty and wondered if she ought to visit more often. At Maria's urging and due to her receptive countenance, Ernesto was put at ease and prattled on about all the local news on the island, adopting the status of a host and amateur tour guide, which Maria continued to encourage. They drove along the coast, and Maria marveled at the luminescent blue water.

When they arrived at the plantation, Maria was impressed with the large house and the beauty of the property, but she also noticed that most of the land was not being farmed, and there were no extensive sugar cane fields, which would have been needed to produce the amount of rum that the property was supposedly generating.

"Ernesto, please give me a tour of the property before we go into the home," she said, starting to realize that all was not exactly as she had been told.

"Why, delighted to, ma'am," responded Ernesto with a wide smile. He was quite enjoying attending to the company's CEO and felt quite proud and important. Maria smiled back at him. He first drove over to a small building behind the big house. "This is the distillery. Shall we look inside?"

"Absolutely," Maria replied. She wondered why it was so small. Inside, her first reaction was confirmed. She knew that this small facility could not possibly produce the amount of rum that was being reported. "How many bottles are we getting out of here each month?" she quizzed Ernesto.

"Well, we can put out about three hundred bottles a month." Maria nodded at him but was thinking this was a small fraction of what she had been told by her brother. The distillery was clean and workmanlike, but it looked to Maria more like a personal home project than a major production facility creating rum for a large liquor distributor.

"Show me the grounds," she said.

Ernesto led Maria on a lovely hike around the property to the sugar cane fields as well as to the fruit and vegetable gardens. Everywhere she inspected was well groomed and in fact quite lovely, but small, far smaller than she had expected based on Miguel's reports.

"Thanks, Ernesto, it is all quite amazing for me to see," she said. "Let's go into the house."

He led her into the large structure where she was immediately greeted by half a dozen locals who worked at the farm, the maid, the cook, two gardeners, one mechanic, and a distiller. They were all deferential and very friendly, and she thanked them. It was obvious to Maria they felt quite grateful to RAM for giving them a good life. Ernesto was clearly in charge, and he took her through the house, with eight guest bedrooms, a master suite, and servants' quarters where most of the staff lived.

"Is there an office?" she asked.

Ernesto looked very serious. "Oh yes, ma'am, but it is locked, and we are not allowed to go into it."

"Well, perhaps you are not, but I can assure you that I am."

Ernesto looked doubtful. "Better you wait for *Señor* Miguel to come, ma'am," he suggested.

Now Maria frowned for the first time. "No, Ernesto. I am the CEO of this company and I have authority over Miguel and everyone else. Now go get the key and let me in."

"But I am worried that I will be in trouble with *Señor* Miguel. And that is a bad place to be."

"Nonsense," she said firmly. "You will be in a much worse place if you don't get me that key right now."

Ernesto looked scared, and she felt sorry for him. But she needed to get into the office and see what Miguel had been up to, so she was not about to back down for Ernesto's comfort. Off he went slowly, but he returned with the key and led her to the office where he opened the locked door. Maria saw a large desk with lots of documents on it, a computer, and a filing cabinet.

"Thank you, Ernesto. Now I will be in here a while, so please have someone send up some tea and water."

He left, and Maria walked over to the desk and sat down. Piles of paper were strewn about the office, and the computer was accessible.

She opened every drawer in the desk and also the filing cabinet and took out every item and put them on the desk next to the computer. And then she began to read. And as she read, she became angrier and angrier.

"That reckless fool," she said out loud. "He has put us all into incredible danger."

And she cursed her brother.

Chapter Twenty

George Town

BRIAN'S COMMERCIAL FLIGHT to George Town landed at seven p.m. in the evening. As he deplaned, he smelled the soft, moist air of the island, and despite the seriousness of his mission, he could not help but smile and feel the relaxation of the tropics, just as Maria had. *It is a romantic place,* he thought, as he gazed at the ocean on his cab ride to the hotel, and he noted to himself that he currently had no romance in his life.

He had called ahead from the Houston airport and booked a room—a cheap one for Grand Cayman—but Brian thought it was significantly overpriced when he arrived. The room was small but at least appeared reasonably clean, and the place had internet service. Brian quickly got online to see if there was a message from his new friend, Detective Nate White of the Houston Police Department.

And he was not disappointed. White had emailed him about the arrest of Tomaso, indicating that the LAPD was questioning him already.

Brian hoped to hear more news in the morning, so with nothing more to do, he found an inexpensive local place for dinner. The catch of the day was snapper, which he greedily consumed and washed down with rum from a local distillery. He asked the waiter if he could examine the bottle. Looking at it, he saw an angry ram's head and realized it was made and distributed by RAM.

"Does RAM have a rum distillery here on the island?" he quizzed.

"Oh yessir," said the friendly server. "They have a big plantation and they brew the rum right on their place. We get all our house rum from there."

Brian decided to have another glass, after which he felt quite woozy. He paid and stumbled back to his modest hotel room and fell into a deep sleep. The next morning, he woke quite late with a slight headache and a very dry mouth. The sun was high overhead, and the temperature and humidity hit him as he opened the window. He called down to the front for coffee and jumped into the shower to wake himself up. The coffee arrived conveniently after he had dried and dressed, and he drank a cup before he opened his computer. There was another email from Nate.

> Brian—Tomaso lawyered up right away
> and his lawyer is trying to negotiate
> a deal. The guy apparently claims
> that his wife checked herself into an
> institution and is allegedly getting
> needed psychiatric help in George Town.

He doesn't know the name of the
facility. Maybe you can check this out.
Get back to me. — Nate.

P.S. We found Nora's purse at a local
pawn shop.

Brian was excited. He had been right to book a flight
here. Now he could investigate any institution on the island
and hopefully find his client. He opened his laptop and
googled hospitals, mental health centers, even spas with
so-called mental health programs. His search turned up a
dozen different facilities. Brian pulled out his phone and
began to go through the list, dialing each location and each
time asking for Nora Ramirez. Ten spas advertised mental
health programs, but each one had the same answer—no
Nora. One of the spas suggested that Brian should book an
appointment for himself, while another turned out to be a
front for prostitution and urged him to come by to have any
of his sexual fantasies satisfied. Finally, Brian tried the hospitals, but none of them had a patient named Nora Ramirez.

There was one psychiatric residential treatment center
on the list, but that facility refused to divulge the names of
any of the "residents" who were being treated. Brian realized that this must be where Nora was—Nate had said
Tomaso claimed Nora was in an institution that provided
psychiatric help. And these tended to be locked facilities
where patients could not just walk out of—rather they were
at the mercy of whomever had committed them. If Tomaso
had in fact committed Nora, this is likely the only place on
the island where she could not leave of her own free will.

Brian realized there was no way he would get any information over the phone—in fact, he might not learn anything by visiting the place either, but he had to try. He scribbled the address on a piece of paper and almost ran down the stairs to the front desk. Hurriedly, he showed the concierge the address and asked how he could get there. The concierge looked oddly at Brian but called him a cab, which did not arrive for twenty minutes. Brian paced the entire time in anticipation. Finally, the lazy cab puttered up in front of the hotel, and Brian jumped in, giving the cabby the piece of paper with the address.

The ride to Happy Health Center took another twenty minutes, so it was getting close to the lunch hour. But Brian could not think about food. He knew he was about to get some answers. He also knew he had to be clever if he wanted to get past the privacy barrier. The cab pulled up in front of a dull gray building with a sign on the front door bearing the name Happy Health Center, a facility for adults.

Brian entered a small receiving area, much like a cozy albeit somewhat dilapidated living room. No one was there. There were some closed doors at the end of the room, and by one of them there was a call button with a speaker above it. Brian walked over, pushed the button, and heard a soft bell sound coming from the speaker. He waited. There was no response. After a moment, Brian pressed again. This time someone came over the speaker.

"Yes," came the tinny, somewhat surreal voice.

"Hello, I am here to see Nora Ramirez," Brian answered.

"And what is your relation to the patient?" came the response.

That made Brian hopeful. Maybe she was here. "I'm her attorney, Brian Youngman, and I have urgent legal matters that she must attend to right away," he responded.

"Did you say Nora Ramirez?" the voice said, now sounding somewhat sharp.

"Yes, and it's extremely important that I meet with her."

"You are sure it is Nora Ramirez?"

"Yes, I'm sure."

"Just a moment. Someone will be out to discuss this with you."

Brian waited and began to pace again. He was excited. He thought he had found Nora and was going to get her out of this awful place. After a few minutes, a door opened, and a black man in a white shirt and tie came out of one of the doors.

"Hello," he said. "I am Dr. Sidney Johnson, and I manage this facility. Did you say you were the lawyer of Nora Ramirez?" A quizzical look was on his face.

"Yes, I am Brian Youngman, Ms. Ramirez's lawyer, and I must see her right away."

"Are you sure her name is Nora Ramirez? Could she be called by any other name? Are you sure her first name is Nora?"

That took Brian back a step. "Yes, I am quite sure. Nora. Nora Ramirez."

Dr. Johnson shook his head. "Well, we don't currently have anyone by that name here," he said. Brian was crestfallen and started to turn to leave, but Dr. Johnson went on. "I think you better come with me to my office so we can clear something up." He gestured for Brian to enter, and the two walked down a putty-colored hall. Dr. Johnson turned into a room, and Brian followed him into a small, shabby office with a desk and two chairs. In one of the chairs sat a well-dressed, attractive woman Brian did not recognize. She looked up at him and an astonished expression crossed her face. It was clear to Brian that this woman recognized him.

Dr. Johnson spoke first. "Madam, this is a gentleman who says he is the lawyer of a Nora Ramirez. Mr. Youngman, please meet Mrs. Ramirez. Is she the client you are looking for?"

"I am not," said the woman. She rose. "Mr. Youngman, nice to meet you. I am Maria Ramirez, the president and CEO of RAM Industries and the sister of Tomaso Ramirez. Nora, as you must know, is my sister-in-law."

Brian was dumbfounded.

Chapter Twenty-One

George Town

"IT APPEARS we are both looking for Nora Ramirez," Maria continued. She saw the astonishment on Brian's face. "And we both came to the same place. But she is not here."

"That's right," added Dr. Johnson. "We did have a communication that she might be checking in and we even received papers indicating that Mr. Ramirez, that is Mr. Tomaso Ramirez, was her legal conservator and had the legal right and power to commit her to our care regardless of whether she was agreeable or not. But she never arrived. She is not here, and I can be of no service to either of you."

Brian tried to collect his thoughts. "Let me understand something," he began slowly. "Did you say that you were told that Tomaso was the legal conservator of Nora Ramirez, his wife?"

"Yes, indeed. Otherwise, we could not have admitted her here against her will. Of course, I don't know whether or not she would have refused to take treatment here, but Mr. Ramirez was clear in his communications that she might be resistant, and we were told she might have delusions that her husband was unfaithful or does not love her, that she was divorcing him. We certainly have seen this kind of thing before."

"Well, she is divorcing him and I'm her divorce lawyer, and what you were told wasn't true," said Brian firmly. "Did you say he gave instructions? And did he show you any documents to support what he was telling you?"

"We were just getting to that," Maria piped in. She turned to Dr. Johnson. "This man is Nora Ramirez's divorce attorney. He is her legal counsel and has a right to see any materials about her." Maria turned to Brian. "Dr. Johnson was giving me the runaround and refusing to show me anything. He claimed it was all quite private and that without Tomaso's permission, he could give me nothing." She turned to Dr. Johnson. "I am her sister-in-law and here is her lawyer and representative. He certainly has the right to see anything about Nora. I demand that you provide these items immediately or there will be consequences." Maria looked at the psychiatrist sternly.

Brian, who was still trying to get his bearings, was impressed with her air of authority, her commanding tone. But he shook himself away from her and turned back to Dr. Johnson, who looked dubious.

"Look," Brian began. He opened his briefcase. "Here is my card, and here is a copy of the legal agreement where Nora hired me." Brian shoved documents on the table.

"Here also is a copy of the stamped and filed divorce petition." He pointed to the document. "See my name on it. See Nora's signature. This shows that I am her legal representative and that you were lied to. This woman is missing. You admit that Nora Ramirez was supposed to come to your facility, but she did not. She is missing, and her husband is under arrest in California."

At this, Maria reacted. "What? Tommy was arrested?" She became ashen.

But Brian persisted with Dr. Johnson. "I need to see everything you have about Nora Ramirez. And if you don't cooperate with us right now, I will be going to court and naming you as a co-conspirator. This whole facility could be shut down, and you could be extradited to the United States, tried as a kidnapper, and spend the rest of your life in prison."

Now, Dr. Johnson's face became ashen. Slowly, he rose and went to an old looking cabinet in the corner of his office. He pulled out a file and threw it onto his desk toward Brian, who immediately grabbed it and opened it.

"Please tell me what you know about Tomaso," Maria said quietly.

"He's currently under arrest for obstruction, but I am sure that is just the beginning of the charges against him. I guess he spent some time in jail before his lawyers could get him out. It all just happened." Brian spoke without looking at Maria, as he was thumbing through the file. Still not looking up, he said to Dr. Johnson: "You should know that Mr. Ramirez is absolutely not the conservator of Nora Ramirez." Brian continued to look through the file. "My God," he uttered. He looked up. "These are clearly forged documents. Someone went online and obtained some of the forms from the LA probate court and doctored up a completely fraudulent order and letters appointing Tomaso as conservator of his wife. But I can see these are not legitimate—the stamp on the documents is not the stamp that is affixed by the courts. And the judge's signature—that is just bogus."

"But how could I know that?" Dr. Johnson responded. "You are a lawyer, an experienced attorney. I am no accomplice. There was no reason to question any of this."

"Someone went to a lot of trouble to do this," Brian commented, still perusing the file.

"But it doesn't make sense," interjected Maria. "Why would anyone go to the trouble of setting all this up, forging court documents, contacting this hospital all the way out here in the Caymans, and then not have Nora brought here, even against her will?"

Brian looked up from the file at Maria. Her dark eyes looked troubled, but he could not stop being affected by her presence, her power, her magnetism.

"You're right," he said, shaking his head. "If she had somehow avoided being brought here, she would have surfaced somewhere and called me. And she has children—she would have let them know she's all right. And I'm starting to think that maybe she's not." He looked grim.

"I need to talk to Tommy—Tomaso," Maria said, looking up at the ceiling. "He'd better be able to explain this."

Dr. Johnson, standing in the corner, was now forgotten by them.

"Oh, I don't think so," said Brian. "His lawyers will have told him to talk to no one, even his family, even you. That is standard in the criminal defense business—shut your client up and keep him that way." He took out his cell phone and began taking photos of the file.

"What are you doing?" Dr. Johnson suddenly spoke up. "That's confidential. You can't take the file."

"Oh, don't worry," said Brian, without looking up or stopping his picture taking. "I intend to leave it right here with you. You'll ultimately get a subpoena for it, since it is evidence and I don't want it out of your possession. But I don't want it to be changed or lost or somehow disappear. It will be admitted into the court someday. It will be relevant to the prosecutor in Los Angeles, since it proves a variety of crimes committed by Tomaso Ramirez. And I certainly intend to share them right away with the police."

Maria looked at Brian darkly. "You don't know who did this," she said. "You don't know if this was Tomaso. These things are forged—you said it yourself. It isn't clear what has happened."

"You're correct, of course," Brian responded but continued photographing. "There will be some exhaustive investigation, though, and it will all come out. It always does. And your brother's fingers appear all over this mess. Who else had a motive to do something to Nora? Only Tomaso. He stood to lose a bundle in this divorce."

"Nonsense," Maria responded. "Yes, it would be expensive but we—RAM that is—could afford to settle their divorce. There is plenty of money—neither Nora nor Tomaso would ever have a financial care, nor would their children."

Brian looked up at her. "Interesting. I suppose the owners of the company all have a motive, don't they? And that would include you, wouldn't it?" Maria stared at him with such ire that Brian almost stopped. But he pushed himself to continue. "You hired a lawyer to stick his nose into the divorce and made all kinds of efforts to prevent me from learning about the company. There must be something very secret and perhaps very dirty that you are hiding." Brian saw that Maria now looked even angrier, which he had not thought was possible. But he kept going. "Nora wanted to expose something about the company, and clearly you couldn't have that."

"Just stop right there," Maria almost screamed. "I came here looking for Nora. Why would I have done that if I was involved in sending her here?"

"Good point," Brian said. "But how did you know to come here? I think the jury is out about what role, if any, you played in all this."

She glared at him, but he had finished his photo job. "How dare you?" she hissed.

But he had a point. She only began looking for Nora because her brother had confessed to having her abducted and, despite her demands, had not brought her back to Los Angeles. Maria had researched possible facilities on the island and discovered this one was the only likely place Nora might be. She had been outraged when she learned what Tomaso had done, but she had not, after all, gone to the police or reported the fact to anyone else. The Ramirez family never trusted the police and always preferred to handle any issues in-house. That was family history and practice. So, despite her anger, she experienced a pang of guilt for not reporting what she knew to the authorities. Then again, how could she turn in her own brother?

Brian, on the other hand, seemed not to be bothered by Maria's anger. "I think I am done here, Dr. Johnson. Please maintain these records and be prepared to be contacted by the appropriate authorities for a statement."

The psychiatrist looked pale. "But I had nothing to do with this," he began.

Brian held up his hand. "Don't bother to explain. Save it for the next guy." He began to walk out.

"Wait," Maria spoke up.

Brian turned. "For what?" He looked at her and was once again almost breathless in awe of her beauty.

"Maybe we can help each other."

"I don't know how. I represent your sister-in-law, soon to be ex, and you are the head of the company that is trying to intervene in the divorce action. Technically, you are represented by counsel and I shouldn't even be talking to you—it's an ethical violation. Plus, based on what I have seen here today, I think your brother, Tomaso, should be in jail. And now I am more worried than ever that something may have happened to my client, Nora Ramirez, something very bad. I think she may have come to harm."

"But don't you see, I need to find Nora too—and know what has happened to her. Whatever may be, she is part of my family. And if Tomaso has in fact done something wrong, he will need to leave the company—I will force him out. And his children are supposed to be part of RAM someday. I think I have more of an interest than you do of learning what has happened. You are just a lawyer and will move on to your next case, forgetting about this one. But whatever the facts, I will have to deal with this mess, both now and for years. So, I need to investigate. I need to know. On this point, we are aligned."

She was pleading with Brian, and her begging made her look even more attractive, seductive even. He found it hard to think clearly, impossible to resist her. "We're on the same team, eh?"

"Yes." Maria nodded. "Yes. We are on the same team." She was earnest and looked at him with piercing dark eyes that took Brian's breath away for a moment. He felt he could not say no. He was smitten.

"Okay. So, what do you suggest we do now?"

"I have a car outside," she said. "Come with me back to RAM's plantation and we can figure it out."

Brian nodded. "I'm happy to drive," he offered.

"Perfect. I'll navigate."

And they left together, now on the same team.

Chapter Twenty-Two

Tequila — 1970

PEDRO SAT BY THE GRAVE of his father Sotero look-ing grim. Marta sat next to him, quietly sobbing. Their other brother, Carlos, and their little sister, Francesca, were standing behind them. It had been a quiet funeral. Surpris-ingly few of the many who knew Sotero had come to pay their respects. They were all afraid, fearful of being identi-fied by the local gang, knowing that anyone who showed up for the Ramirez family could have a target on his back.

The arrangement with the gang run by Hector Aguill-lara had worked reasonably well for almost ten years, and the family business thrived. So had Hector's gang, rich off the profit participation from tequila, which was added to the returns from his growing business in cocaine. This had been a big change, since for years Hector had only trafficked in marijuana; but the cocaine trade was growing and had become far more profitable. That of course had been Hector's downfall. The money was so plentiful that a war broke out among the gangs for control of the Guadalajara cocaine trade. And there was foreign competition from Central America, so men had come to Mexico to seize control of the trade.

There had been much bloodshed, as well as new truces, amalgamation, deception, more bloodshed, and more amalgamation. Hector had thought he had won the war, only to have his throat slit in the middle of the night by a Columbian prostitute. His death created a temporary vacuum, and several gangs sought to take over the area. It was not a time to be out at night in Guadalajara.

When Hector was murdered, Sotero stopped making any payments. He figured there was no one to pay and also no one to protect his farm anymore so no reason to pay. The gangs were so busy fighting with one another that Sotero and his business were ignored for a time. But ultimately, one gang won out, and soon thereafter, three men made a visit to Sotero's farm. The property had been substantially transformed. A large Spanish-style mansion had been erected where the former *hacienda* had burned down. A massive distillery had been created, along with facilities for trucks and a separate structure just for bottling. The farm had become a small industrial complex.

The three men drove onto the property in a yellow Cadillac and parked in front of the house. The driver jumped out of the car and opened the back door. Out stepped a small man dressed in a dark Italian suit, white linen shirt, and narrow silk tie, in stark contrast to the two others who could have passed for cowhands. The three walked up to the front door and rang. A maid quickly answered.

"*Buenos días, Señora,*" said the well-dressed man politely. "I am Don Victor Gonzalez. I am here to speak with Sotero Ramirez. Is he available?"

The maid looked at him, then at the two ruffians behind him, then at the yellow Cadillac. "Please come in, *Señor,*" she said with a nervous glance.

Victor entered, but she quickly closed the door behind him before the two ruffians could follow, almost slamming it in their faces. She looked at Victor meekly. "We do not let rough men in the main house," she explained quietly.

Victor looked at her at first, frowning, then broke into a loud laugh. "*Sí, Señora, comprendo,*" he responded, still laughing. "We have the same rule at our home. I don't need them. Now where can I find Sotero?"

"This way," she said and beckoned him through the foyer, which was richly decorated with Spanish tiles and a magnificent Persian carpet. A grand stairwell led from the entrance to the upstairs bedchambers, and brightly colored original art decorated the walls. She led him under the stairwell down a hallway, which was also adorned with an elaborate Persian carpet and more paintings, this time portraits of Mexican leaders.

Victor found himself slowing to admire the works. "Sotero clearly likes to decorate," he commented.

"*Señor* Ramirez supports local craftsmen and buys all his art from them," she responded proudly. "He is dedicated to our community. One of these was painted by my own daughter—this one." She pointed to a portrait of a military general looking over fields at a battle below.

"Quite nice," Victor told her. "You must be proud to have such a fine artist as a daughter."

They could hear voices from a room at the end of the

hallway. The maid entered first, and Victor followed. The office was again richly furnished with ornate wooden furniture, pillows and cushions for comfort, a massive desk, and bookcases filled with notebooks, maps, and various artifacts. Behind the desk sat Sotero, now well into his fifties. Carlos and Pedro were there as well, one on a chair by his father and the other on a couch at the side of the room.

"Excuse me, *Señor*," the maid said on entering. "You have a visitor—*Señor* Victor Gonzalez." Victor gave a short bow. The maid stood there, not knowing what she should do.

"*Buenas tardes, Señor Ramirez. Mucho gusto*," Victor began. "I am ..."

"I know who you are," responded Sotero, looking troubled.

"Ah, then you know why I am here," Victor responded and smiled. He confidently walked up to the other chair in front of Sotero's desk and sat down. "These two sturdy-looking young men must be your sons." He pointed to Pedro and Carlos.

"They are." Sotero was quiet and said nothing more.

"Perhaps we can talk privately. We have business to discuss."

Sotero looked at Victor and slowly nodded. This was bound to be most unpleasant. "That will be all," he told the maid. "We don't need anything right now." Sotero turned to his two sons. "You both go on and check on the inventory we were talking about. I am fine, I don't need you to be part of this."

Pedro, who was sitting across from his father and next to Victor, looked hesitant. Carlos had an angry expression on his face.

"But Padre," said Pedro. "We should become familiar

with all aspects of our family business. You have said so many times. We will be quiet if you let us stay. We need to know about such things."

"Pedro's right," chimed in Carlos. "We need to know what is going on."

But Sotero was shaking his head and was not about to change his mind. He knew he was dealing with a criminal—a monster in fact—and while he found it detestable, he also knew he had no choice. He had to make an agreement with the new gang in charge. But he did not want his sons to see him bargaining with this snake of a man. It was just too humiliating.

"Out with you both. Now," he commanded, pointing his finger at the door.

Victor laughed, enjoying this display. Pedro and Carlos rose slowly, unwillingly, but they were not about to disobey their father. He had always been stalwart and stern, raising them without any mother, yet he had always been there for them, and they both loved him fiercely.

"As I said, go check the stock—and shut the door as you leave." When they had left, he turned to Victor. "I guess your side won the war."

Victor sneered, then turned and spat on the lush rug that was next to his chair. "Those scum all got what they deserved, and you better take a lesson from them. Anyone who goes against us will suffer the same fate or worse."

Sotero looked angrily at Victor, outraged by his offense. "Now see here, do not spit in my home," he snapped. "This is a dignified house, built on the hard work of my family. Do not disrespect it."

Victor laughed loudly. "Why should I give you any respect? Since you made nice with those dead cockroaches and were in business with them for years? Don't tell me you deserve anything from us. You were in bed with those shit eaters, and you ate shit with them. You are just shit to me. That is all." Victor spat again on the expensive carpet.

Sotero stood up angrily. "Get out! Get out of my house. I assumed you came to talk business, not defile my home. Get out!"

Victor did not move but only gave Sotero a smug look. "You want to talk business, eh, you filthy insect?" he hissed. "Well, from now on, we will take eighty percent of your profits. Got that? Eighty percent, or you and your family and your business will be burned to the ground. You will watch your children die, just like you watched your wife die because you were too weak and pathetic to protect her. And we will post our men here. You will provide for them—whatever they want. Your days of high living are over. You belong to us."

Sotero was turning redder and redder as Victor spoke. He knew he was bigger and stronger than the little drug criminal in front of him, and all he wanted to do was throttle him. But he was even more worried than angry. He knew his family was exposed. He knew he needed to buy time, to figure out how to deal with this animal and his masters. Perhaps he needed another ally. Sotero sat down. He decided to negotiate for now. He looked out of his window at the waning day. The sun was casting long shadows, and brilliant colors began to appear on the horizon.

"Eighty percent is too much, far more than we paid your predecessor for protection. I will pay you more than them, but I have to have greater protection. I will pay twenty-five percent. That is high as it is. And we cannot have your men here, interrupting our business. We work all the time. They would be a nuisance."

Victor started laughing again. "You think I am a gringo, you can negotiate me down?" He spat once again on the Persian rug. "I said eighty percent. That is it."

"I told you we cannot do that. It is just unreasonable." Sotero shook his head. "We won't survive. I might as well retire and stop making tequila with that deal. The absolute maximum I can give you, and I am not even sure I can, is fifty percent. That is it. No more. Otherwise, I will stop doing this. And that will mean you get nothing."

Victor shrugged his shoulders and held up his hands. "I think I can get a better deal from your kids," Victor said. "Those two ugly weaklings that you just sent away like a couple of lowly servants."

"Then our business today is done," Sotero replied, standing up again. "I want to talk with your boss. I am sure he will understand and be more reasonable." He looked down at the small well-dressed man who continued to sit. "So out with you. I am done with you."

"And I am done with you," answered Victor, who put his hand into his jacket. He took out a small revolver and shot Sotero three times in the face in rapid succession. Blood spurted out from Sotero as he fell forward onto his ornate mahogany desk. Victor stood up and shot him three more times. Then, he threw his empty gun onto the floor, turned around, and walked out of the office and back down the hallway. On the way, he took off the wall the painting of the soldier that the maid had told him was done by her daughter.

As he left the house, he saw with satisfaction that Pedro and Carlos were sitting on the ground with their hands tied behind their backs, while his two men had their guns trained upon their prisoners.

"I just made a deal with your father," Victor said, smiling

at them. "He agreed that you will pay us ninety percent of the profits of your business. He also agreed that he would retire and you would run the business for us. But *lo siento*, I am afraid he is dead, and you will need first to clean up the mess in your house. We will give you seven days to do what you need to do to mourn your father, and then we will come back." He walked toward the yellow Cadillac and beckoned to his two men to follow.

They drove away, as Sotero's two sons looked on in shock, tied up, not able to say anything.

Chapter Twenty-Three

Los Angeles — Present Day

TOMASO took an extra-long shower that morning. He had showered the day before when he returned to his Bel Air home, the one his children lived in, the one his wife used to live in, the one he had been arrested in a few days before. He had smelled so bad that he took a shower and then soaked in his tub for thirty minutes. But even today, he still smelled that horrible odor from the jail cell. It certainly was not what he was accustomed to—being stripped and photographed and thrown into a holding tank and then transferred to a cell with the most unsavory cellmates by unsympathetic officers. It was horrible, but Tomaso kept thinking that prison would be so much worse. He would be brutalized and ostracized—things were looking grim.

His lawyers had finally gotten him released on bail, but he'd had to post a five-million-dollar bond, and the bondsmen had taken a deed of trust on this house. His sister was out of the country, and she would not even take his calls. Miguel refused to take Tomaso's calls—now his brother was nowhere to be found. Fortunately, that awful woman lawyer that Maria had hired as in-house counsel did answer her phone and had found a top criminal attorney to help him—Tomaso had a meeting with him this morning. But now he had to reckon with the fact that he had no idea where Nora was. And Miguel had gone missing and was no help—this had all been his idea. He had set this up. It was Miguel's fault, and now he'd just disappeared.

Tomaso sprayed Yves Saint Laurent cologne all over himself and dressed in a hand-tailored suit, an Hermès tie, and a white silk shirt. He was going to look like a titan, someone to be respected by the defense lawyer, not like some common criminal. The suit was a bit tight, he noticed, but he was able to get into it. He couldn't button the jacket, and the pants were annoyingly snug, but he figured he would just unbutton them when he was sitting in his car on the way to the attorney's office.

How did he get into this situation? Miguel. And Nora. Why had she not been more cooperative? Why had she ridden him so much, made so many nasty threats at the company? And where was she? He had no idea but hoped she would turn up soon. Then he could get her to recant any charges, make all this go away. It would be expensive, and Maria would hate him even more for it, but at least he would not be in prison. He would even agree to give up his job, as long as the company paid off Nora, and, of course, continued to support him, pay for his golf club, and give him some reasonable allowance.

Tomaso took the 405 to the 10 to drive downtown to

the attorney's office in the First Century Tower in the heart of LA's business district. He hoped this meeting would be quick, so he could drive back to his Santa Monica apartment and have the afternoon with his mistress, Rosie. He hadn't seen her for days now, and he desperately needed some love and care. And a whole lot of alcohol.

Tomaso gave his car to the valet, noting that parking was forty dollars, and took the elevator up to the thirtieth floor. As he stepped off the elevator, he was greeted by a dramatic vista of Los Angeles, and since it was a clear day, he could even see the ocean. The reception area was grand, all marble and brilliantly decorated. A desk stood by the side so as not to block the view. The couches and chairs were perfectly coordinated. The attorneys' office was truly magnificent, and even Tomaso was impressed as he walked up to the receptionist. He wondered how much this law firm was charging RAM to defend him. He also realized he had never really thought about how expensive his lifestyle was before; he'd always had anything he wanted. He started to think about how he could get by if he suddenly did not have RAM behind him.

"Tomaso Ramirez to see Mark Martin. I have an appointment. I am his client," Tomaso said.

The young woman at reception smiled at him. "Of course, Mr. Ramirez. Please have a seat. Someone will be right out."

Tomaso sat down on the plush couch and stared out the window at the expansive vista of Los Angeles. Perched in the sky above all the people below him, he felt his confidence growing. He was, after all, the son of Marta, and while he was the youngest, there was no reason why the company did not belong to him equally with his siblings.

And RAM hired the best lawyers in town—they would have no problem solving this little squabble with his wife. He also figured that Nora would show up eventually—she was probably on some bender, enjoying herself in St. Barts or some such place. Thinking of that, Tomaso realized that he really wanted—no, needed—a drink. He was about to ask the receptionist if they had some scotch or bourbon or something, anything alcoholic, when a young man approached him holding some papers.

"Excuse me, sir," began the man. "I am Jeffrey Stein, an associate attorney working with Mark Martin. You are Mr. Ramirez? Mr. Tomaso Ramirez?"

Tomaso shook himself and sat up. "Yes, of course. Where is Mr. Martin? I need to see him."

"I understand," the well-dressed young man said. "But we need you to sign some paperwork first. Let me show it to you—here it is." He handed Tomaso the document and a pen. There was a green tab at the end of the papers indicating a signature line and date. "This is a disclosure of a conflict and a waiver by you of that conflict."

Tomaso looked confused. "What?" he said. "I don't understand. Why do I have to sign anything? What is this all about?"

The young man maintained a serious expression. "Our firm represents the company, RAM Industries Inc. RAM also pays our bills, including any fee that we charge on your behalf. But since you have been accused of a crime, we can only represent you if we disclose that there may be a conflict of interest between the company and you, and you agree to waive that conflict."

"How can this be?" said Tomaso with growing concern. "I am part of the company, part of the family that owns

RAM." He started to get irritated with this obnoxious fellow.

"I'm so sorry, sir, but there is a conflict, certainly a potential one, and there may be an actual conflict. You see, if you're convicted or even plead guilty to a felony, the company may terminate you from RAM."

"What?" Now Tomaso was mad and started yelling. "They cannot do that. I'm one of the heirs, one of the owners."

The young lawyer was slightly taken aback, but he quickly recovered and went on. "Well, not technically. RAM is owned by a Trust, and that Trust has certain provisions. According to its terms, you could be disinherited as well as fired from the company. Your mother is currently the managing trustee, and her siblings are co-trustees. They're required to force you out if you are convicted of a serious crime. It's all explained in that document, so please read it because until you agree to waive the conflict, we cannot act any further on your behalf. After you review it, you can ask me any questions about it. Or if you want to, you can hire another lawyer to advise you about it—or even represent you in this criminal case, if you prefer not to waive the conflict."

"I don't prefer. Mark Martin is supposed to be the best criminal defense lawyer in town. I need him." Tomaso frowned, looking at the document in his hand.

The associate stepped away. "I will let you read that then. I will come back in half an hour to check on you and answer any questions."

Tomaso was steaming. "No," he again yelled. He saw that the receptionist was looking at him with concern. She picked up a phone and began talking to someone in a hushed tone.

Tomaso did not care. "I will sign it," he said, and he grabbed the pen and hurriedly signed by the green tab.

"Sir," said Jeffrey Stein, whose tone was now curt. "We need you to actually read the disclosure and waiver. It must be a knowing waiver. It has legal implications. For example, it states that if we deem the conflict too serious, we have the right to withdraw and continue representing RAM. It also states that RAM can at any time stop paying your legal fees and even seek reimbursement from you personally, in which case we would also withdraw from your representation. I appreciate that you signed it, but I must insist that you read it. I will be back."

With that, the young lawyer turned and walked away. Tomaso fumed but said nothing. He had half a mind to walk right out of that office. He noticed that a uniformed security guard came into the lobby and sat on a chair by the receptionist. That further irritated Tomaso, but he decided he would try to look at the papers in his hand. He began reading, but it all sounded like legal mumbo jumbo to him. Skimming the papers, he saw that Mark Martin could stop representing him for any number of reasons, and that if that happened, the law firm could still represent RAM. And he saw that there was a waiver of the attorney/client privilege between him and the company. Essentially, anything he told the lawyer, RAM would get to know. That meant his sister would find out everything he and Miguel had planned. But only if he told the lawyer that. He realized he had to be careful what he said to this attorney. Tomaso knew he had to make a decision. He calmed himself. He really needed a drink, but he promised to attend to that later. He tried to compose himself, stood up, and walked slowly across the room. He even tried to put on a friendly smile.

"Miss," he said, adopting a contrite tone and addressing the receptionist, who had been eyeing him with concern. The security guard also looked at him, but not in a friendly way. "Please let them know I have read and signed the document. I understand it and agree to it."

She picked up the phone and made a call, and soon Jeffrey Stein came out to him. Tomaso handed him the waiver document. "I have read it and agree," he said.

"Please come this way," said the associate, taking the document. Tomaso was annoyed, but what was he to do? His choices were non-existent.

He stood up and followed the lawyer with his head hung low.

Chapter Twenty-Four

George Town

MARIA LOOKED AT BRIAN from the passenger seat of the rented car as he drove. *He is quite handsome,* she thought. She had noticed it immediately when she first saw him on the Zoom screen in the courtroom, but she realized he was even more attractive in person. He was obviously extremely bright and dedicated, even intense, and genuine. They were adversaries, of course, she knew that, but for now they were on the same quest, the same team, to find Nora. She thought she could let down her guard a bit.

"Turn here," she said.

Brian turned at the gate to RAM's George Town property and came to a stop. A large sign over the gate had a picture of a ram's head snorting ferociously, under which read RAM CARIBBEAN HEADQUARTERS. He rolled down the window and pressed the button on the gate receiver.

"Yes, who is it?" a tinny sounding voice squeaked out.

"This is Maria Ramirez," she said loudly and with authority, before Brian could answer. "Please open the gate immediately."

"Yes, ma'am," the voice responded quickly and more clearly, and the high metal gate began to swing open.

Brian looked at Maria. "I see your people hop to it when you speak," he said, grinning. She smiled back. *She is so beautiful,* Brian thought, feeling a bit uncomfortable with his attraction to her. He was, after all, violating his duty of loyalty, fraternizing with the enemy. *No,* he corrected himself, *she is not my adversary. Her company may be, and her brother certainly is, but not her.* And as long as they maintained nothing more than a cordial dynamic while pursuing a common goal, he felt he was still on solid ground, even if she had an almost magnetic countenance.

"I hope so," she said. "I like to think I run my company with a firm but kind hand." She winked at him. *Why did I do that?* she thought. *I should not be flirting with him. He is dangerous.* But she also felt she was not crossing any lines, at least not yet.

He drove past the gate and saw the lush grounds, the well-manicured hedges, and palm trees that lined the drive, which went on for almost half a mile. Brian could see farm fields off in the distance with sugar cane growing high. *What a massive property,* he thought as he drove slowly along the road.

"It's really lovely here, isn't it?" Maria said, noting how Brian was marveling. "This is actually my first trip down here. I had never seen it myself. I think I'll have to come back sometime with my son."

"You have a son? How old?" Brian asked, finding he had a sudden feeling of disappointment.

"He's almost nine now. He is such a sweet boy. My ex and I share custody in New York. A trip down here would do his health some good." Maria stopped speaking. *Why did I tell him I had an ex? He is not my friend, remember?* she cautioned herself. *But relax, you are not doing anything wrong. Being friendly with him may just come in handy if we end up negotiating. You are just creating a positive rapport that can be used later.*

"That is a great age," Brian commented, finding himself relieved having heard the word "ex." *She's divorced*, he thought. But then his attention was turned to the big house when it came into view. "Wow, nice digs!" he said.

"Yes, it is quite a place. And I am hoping my brother Miguel is here now. Maybe he knows something about Nora. I have not been able to reach him since he has been en route here." She shook her head and began to frown. Brian noticed the change in attitude when talking about Miguel but said nothing. He parked the car, and as he opened the door, a handsome man dressed in khaki shorts and a polo opened the front door, smiling and waving.

"Welcome back, Ms. Ramirez," Ernesto called out. He walked quickly toward the car to escort her in. Maria was already out of the vehicle and walking toward him.

"Hello, Ernesto. Thank you."

"Your brother *Señor* Miguel is here," Ernesto said, suddenly serious. "He waits for you in his office."

"Good," Maria responded curtly. "I have some issues to take up with him."

"Who is your guest, ma'am?" Ernesto asked, looking at Brian, who had delayed but now was walking up behind her.

"Ernesto, this is Brian Youngman. He is a lawyer from the United States, California actually." Maria looked back at Brian, and her stern look was replaced by a playful expression. "He and I have some mutual interests, and I just happened to run into him in town. He was gracious enough to drive me back here, and I wanted to show him our plantation and facilities." She turned back to Ernesto. "Would you offer him some refreshment and show him around the place while I speak with Miguel?" She turned to Brian. "Do you mind if I talk with my brother alone first? We can chat with him together after. Okay?"

"Sure," Brian said, thinking the tour would offer him some free and unfettered investigation into RAM's assets. He wondered about the value of this property. "I would love to look around. It's quite beautiful here."

"Great. I won't be long." Maria went into the house, while Ernesto walked toward Brian, who held out his hand. The men shook.

"Let's start at the distillery, shall we?" Ernesto said with a large smile, showing his brilliant white teeth. "Maybe you can have a small taste and see how delicious our rum is." He turned, and Brian followed him.

"How much product do you make each season?" Brian quizzed.

"Not too much," answered Ernesto easily. "Enough to supply everywhere on the island with our rum and to send out maybe a few thousand bottles to Miami. They go by sea now that *Señor* Miguel has purchased some boats to transport them."

"Boats? How many of those do you have?"

"Oh, I think we have five. But for shipping only three.

Perhaps we can show you those down at the harbor. It's a short drive. We can go in a golf cart."

"I would like that," said Brian. *More easy discovery into RAM's assets*, he thought.

They walked toward the distillery and entered the facility. Brian had never been in a building dedicated to making any kind of liquor. The sweet aroma immediately hit his nostrils. Ernesto smiled and led him to a large vat.

"The rum is stored in here, but later it is moved to be bottled over there," he told Brian. "Let's go have a taste."

"Sounds great," said Brian, and he began to follow Ernesto when the man suddenly stopped to answer his phone.

"Yes, sir. I understand," he said. Hanging up, he turned to Brian. "Slight change of plans. We can come back for a tasting and to see the fields a bit later. We are to meet *Señora* Ramirez and *Señor* Miguel at the docks. We were talking about going there anyway, so this is just a reorganization of your tour. We will inspect the boats with them, and then come back and finish up here."

"Why the change?" asked Brian, feeling that this detour was somewhat odd. He had half a mind to protest and perhaps just leave. It did not appear that any progress at finding Nora Ramirez was likely to be made by looking at boats, although he did want to inspect any RAM assets.

Ernesto smiled at him as he pointed the way to the parked golf cart. "*Señor*," he responded. "I am just a worker here. *Señor* Miguel rarely explains his reasons to me. He just tells me what to do."

Brian grudgingly followed, deciding not to make any waves, yet he had an instinctive feeling that this deviation made no sense and could be a bad idea. On the other hand, he did not want to just leave without seeing Maria again. He wondered why he felt this way. He began to realize that he was very attracted to her. And that fact made him uncomfortable.

"Okay, let's go."

Chapter Twenty-Five

Tequila — 1970

PEDRO AND CARLOS crawled on their bellies in the dark toward the *hacienda*, shielding themselves from view by moving near low shrubs and ground cover. They both had double-barrel shotguns strapped to their backs and fully loaded pistols stuck in the back of their pants. Pedro also had a long hunting knife in his belt, and he had sharpened it just this afternoon in anticipation of his plan.

So far, all had gone well. Marta and Francesca had performed their tasks perfectly, beckoning the three gang members stationed at their property into the house with a promise of tequila and *mole*. Music played in the background as the guards confidently entered, hoping for a home-cooked meal, special tequila, and perhaps more from the smiling, coquettish young women. The three men sat at the table where a Mexican feast lay upon it, their guns at their sides. Marta and Francesca both poured the delicious amber-colored tequila, *añejo*, they said, a special batch, and the guards had greedily gulped down the delightful liquid, unaware it was laced with arsenic.

Soon the men were so ill they could not move, and Marta promptly clubbed each one on the head with a large *molcajete*. It was still full of guacamole when she did so, and the spilled green dip mixed with the blood from their bodies. But Marta did not care, so enraged was she, and the fact that she had pretended to like these awful gang members fueled her intensity. Pedro and Carlos had come in to find the mess, with Francesca somewhat taken aback at her sister's furiosity. But the men were all dead, and so Pedro and Carlos collected their shotguns for the next stage of their plan.

"These corpses are so messy that we are going to have a hard time using them," Pedro remarked, although he was secretly pleased to see how they had been brutally bludgeoned. "We need to wrap their heads for the ride and try to keep some of the blood in them."

The four of them worked together, wrapping the dead in cellophane and carting them outside to the waiting pickup truck. Each man had had a shotgun and a pistol, so Marta took one shotgun while Francesca handled the pistol. All of them had been taught to shoot long ago by their father. Sotero had made it his mission to prepare his children for possible violence, so despite the girls' lack of interest, he had forced them to practice with all manner of firearms. Marta was quite good with a rifle, while Francesca favored a pistol and turned out to be a crack shot with it, better than all four of them. They knew that their skills would be necessary that night.

Nerves started to get to all of them as they piled into the pickup truck and drove to the gang's headquarters. It was dark, but Marta knew the roads well, so they drove without headlights. They arrived after ten p.m., and when they were about a hundred yards away from the one-level structure the gang used as its headquarters, Marta maneuvered the truck off the road. Everyone in town knew where the gang's house was; they made no secret of it. They were so sure of their invincibility—besides, who would try to attack them? They knew the community was in terror of them. Marta drove the pickup truck into the rough terrain for about fifty feet and stopped. The four of them slid out as quietly as possible and pulled the three corpses out of the back. Slowly, quietly, they dragged the dead men toward the *hacienda* until they reached some rocks about twenty yards from the front door of the structure. They lay the three men on their stomachs and propped them up as best as they could so their arms and heads were on the rocks but their knees were on the ground. Marta ripped off the cellophane from each head, balled the messy plastic up, and put it into her pocket. Blood oozed from the corpses onto the stone where their heads lay. She looked at the surreal image of the dead kneeling on the rock and shook her head.

"I hope this works," she muttered.

"It has to," Francesca whispered. "Otherwise, we are all dead."

The two sisters sat behind the rocks and watched and waited as Pedro and Carlos went into a low run, circling around to the other side of the *hacienda*.

"I know," Marta responded. "It will be hard enough if there are only six of them in the *casa*." She had been spying on the *hacienda* all week, counting gang members, trying to estimate the likely number. "But there could be more. We shall see."

When Pedro and Carlos had reached the other side of the property, although still twenty yards away, they began to crawl toward the building where a light shone out of an open window. They could hear voices and laughter inside.

When they reached the exterior wall under the window, Pedro motioned for Carlos to stay low while he slowly raised up to peek inside. He smiled as he saw their good fortune. This window opened to what appeared to be the kitchen, and three gang members were sitting at a table drinking beer. Pedro motioned to his brother to stand and showed him three fingers. Carlos then drew his pistol, as did Pedro, and the two of them angled their pistols inside the room, aiming at a different man, Carlos focusing on the right and Pedro on the left. They both fired. Then fired again. Blood spurted out of two of the men as they fell from their chairs to the floor. The third was so surprised he did not even stand before being shot by both Carlos and Pedro almost simultaneously.

Not waiting to celebrate, the brothers dropped the two pistols by the window, pulled the shotguns from their backs, and began to sprint around the house, rounding it on the side that was away from their sisters, who were sitting by the dead gang members. They reached the front door from the other side in seconds and crouched on the ground, behind bushes, waiting. A moment later, two men burst out of the front door onto the front porch, each with guns and flashlights in hand, looking wildly around, shining lights here and there. Two gunshots rang out. One man spun around, mortally struck in the chest and fell dead. The other was hit in the shoulder, which caused him to drop the gun that he held in his right hand while his other still held the flashlight. Carlos stood up at that moment, leveled his shotgun, and pulled the trigger on each barrel. The man who had been holding the light came apart, pieces of him exploding everywhere, as he fell off the porch.

Carlos jumped up onto the porch, warily looking for any other gang members. "I think it's clear," he said.

Pedro stood up and started to climb up onto the porch when he heard another gunshot. Spinning around, he saw a gang member behind him lying on the ground. The man had apparently come out the back, was rounding the house, and was about to shoot him, but Francesca saw him and fired first. Pedro knew his sister had just saved his life. The downed man was still alive, though shot in the leg, trying to crawl, reaching for his pistol on the ground.

Pedro walked up to the fallen gang member, aimed his shotgun, and pulled a single trigger, completely eviscerating him and putting an end to any danger.

"That's six," Pedro called out. "We've gotten all six."

Marta, on hearing this, stood up. She was thankful Francesca was such a terrific shot and had not wavered. Pointing her shotgun at the heads of the three corpses, she pulled the triggers, obliterating any sign that their heads had been battered by a *molcajete*. "There, that looks like they were shot in a gunfight by their own," she said, placing her shotgun by the men to make it look as if they had been using it before they were shot. She turned to her sister, but she saw Francesca was sitting there trembling. Pulling her up, Marta hugged her tightly. Francesca was still holding her pistol, so Marta gently took it out of her hand and again placed it near the three corpses. She held her sister up as they walked toward the *hacienda*, where Carlos watched from the porch.

"Great shooting, *Señoritas!*" he called out, smiling and waving.

Just as he did so, a shot rang out from inside the house. Carlos fell. The sisters dove to the ground and lay on their stomachs. The door opened and Victor emerged, still dressed in a suit and tie. He walked over to Carlos, who was lying face down on the porch, and shot him again, this time in the back of the head.

"Your brother is dead now," Victor called out to the women. "And soon you will be too." He raised his gun to aim at the sisters.

At that moment, Pedro came around the corner and pulled the second trigger of his shotgun. The blast took Victor square in the back, and the force of the shot knocked him off the porch. Pedro dropped the gun and ran over to his brother, but Carlos was dead. Pedro heard the sound of Victor groaning, so he pulled out his hunting knife, leapt upon the prone gangster, and stabbed him over and over.

"Pedro, stop," said Marta, who had run up to him. "Enough." She jumped onto the porch where Carlos lay. "Carlos, Carlos, Carlos," she cried out in anger and pain. Pedro came up beside her, openly weeping. "We need to get him out of here. Francesca," Marta said, turning to her sister, who had come up to the porch and was also crying. "Take some of these guns and put them out by the rocks—I only left the two. They would have had more guns. Pedro, you and I will take Carlos."

Marta took out of her pocket the balled-up cellophane and unwrapped it. The clear plastic was still messy with the blood of the gang members. She paid no mind to that, but carefully wound it around the head of her own brother to stop blood from oozing out. Then, with Francesca at their side, she and Pedro carried Carlos back to the pickup truck, loaded his body, and drove back to their home. They cleaned him as much as they could and wrapped him in a white sheet. And they cried and cried and cried.

The next day, the town was abuzz with news of a bloody gang fight where some of the members must have quarreled with the others, and they all killed each other. People were jubilant. But Pedro, Francesca, and Marta just mourned. They had to keep their brother's death a secret for the time being. They would make up a story later, that he was accidently killed by a barrel falling in the distillery.

They quietly buried him in the middle of the next night near their father's grave with no headstone or ceremony or fanfare, just endless tears.

Chapter Twenty-Six

George Town — Present Day

MARIA ENTERED THE office where she had been directed to find Miguel and saw him sitting behind the large desk. As she walked into the room scowling, she was surprised to find another man sitting on one of the chairs. He was wearing a dark T-shirt and running shoes. Neither was talking, but rather they seemed to be waiting for her.

"Miguel, hello," she started. "We need to talk alone. Who is this gentleman?"

The man laughed gruffly in response. "Very few people call me a gentleman," he said.

"Maria, his name is Javier." Miguel spoke with eyes like slits. "He is here to help us. To partner with us."

Maria frowned. "What nonsense is this? Javier who? We don't take on partners. And even if we did, we certainly would not do so without my express approval. You know that."

"Just Javier. That is all. And we need his help."

Maria was taken aback. This did not sound like Miguel, to claim he needed help. "We can deal with this later," she said, shaking her head. "We need to talk about Nora. Privately. Do you know her lawyer, Brian Youngman, is here on the island looking for her?"

"Yes, I know about Mr. Youngman. That is rather unfortunate, rather awkward. I am afraid we have to deal with him in some way."

"What do you mean? This is about Nora. Do you know where she is? Do you know about what Tommy did? Were you in on it?"

"Tommy had a problem. But how he decided to handle it, I really don't know."

"You know nothing?"

"Correct. I wasn't involved." Miguel shrugged his shoulders with his hands out.

"Well, I find that hard to believe," said Maria. "Also, I have been through the books down here. You have been laundering money and skimming money and God knows what else. It is terrible. You have put us all at risk—but mostly yourself. I actually have to decide whether to turn you in. The company cannot tolerate what you have done. It all has to stop immediately, and we have to come clean and report everything and make it right. I am not running any illegal operations."

"Well, this is where Javier comes in. He is going to make things go away in a manner that will be final, so you won't need to worry about this again."

Maria looked over at Javier, who smiled a toothy smile at her. "I am glad to be of service," he said.

"None of this is making any sense," Maria almost barked at her brother.

Her rage made Miguel react, at first with a frown of resentment, then with a smirk. "This will be better explained if we show you how things will be resolved," he said. "First, I must apologize to you, my dear sister. I was wrong to borrow all that money and buy those boats. And that is where Javier comes in. The people he represents down here are prepared to buy those boats from us and take us out of debt, so I can make things right. RAM will be better for it and there will be no more rum-running. I really am sorry."

Maria looked at him with surprise, thinking it a bit strange. Miguel was not prone to apologize for anything, much less to acknowledge an error and offer to fix it.

"You've made an agreement to sell our ships? Again, without consulting me or involving me in any way?" she asked angrily. "And exactly who does this man represent?"

"I represent a consortium of rich individuals in Mexico," Javier said smoothly, unruffled by Maria's ire. "We have been looking for such an opportunity to help us transport various products. We need ships like these and are hoping to buy them from RAM. I am glad we can do business together."

Javier smiled at her, but Maria felt an unpleasant tickle go down her spine. She wondered what kind of "products" this fellow was talking about.

"I thought this is what you wanted, that this would make you happy," said Miguel. "Remember, you were so unhappy with me when I told you I had borrowed money to buy these vessels? Well, you were right. So now I am fixing things. Javier's group will buy these boats, and we will fully pay back the loan. No more debt. All will be right again."

Maria began to calm slightly. The thought of less debt on the RAM company books was something she certainly wanted to achieve. And she did not want to ship rum any-where illegally, so without the boats, this practice would cease.

"We were just finalizing some of the points, and so it is good you are here," said Miguel. "You are the CEO so you can review the transaction and approve it if you agree." He smiled at his sister, but it looked like a leer to her.

"One of the issues is the condition of the boats, and I need to look at them," said Javier. "They are used and may have some wear and tear that could affect the price. Perhaps you could accompany us."

"Yes," concurred Miguel. "Let's go down to the dock and allow Javier to inspect the boats. You will be able to see everything too, and we can discuss the terms. Then you can examine the documents and decide if you approve." He stood up, as did Javier.

"But what about Nora?" pressed Maria.

"I have told you that I know nothing, so there is not much to discuss. But we can talk about this messy Tomaso business after we have finished our deal with Javier. Let's get that out of the way first."

"I do have a schedule to keep," added Javier.

"Please, Maria," urged Miguel. "We have asked Ernesto to bring Mr. Youngman to the dock as well."

At the mention of Brian, Maria's anger changed to con-cern. "What? You are going to show Nora's lawyer the boats, which you used to conduct your illegal activities?" she queried. "Why? He is not to be trifled with. If he finds out what you have been doing, he could easily go to the authorities. Leave him out of this."

"Look, he is just going to see a few boats. He won't know about anything more. He wanted to know about all our assets, so this is good. He will see that the boats are leaving RAM." Miguel gave Maria an innocent look. "Besides, Maria, you said you want to come clean, so isn't it good to start by being open with Nora's lawyer? He has been wanting information. You will feel better if we are candid with him. I am sure that if we cooperate with him and show him everything, it will be easier to resolve our issues. Isn't that what you want?"

By now, Miguel had come around the desk and put his hands on Maria's arm to help her up. She was thinking about being honest with Brian and what that would mean. She did not want him to think she had sanctioned illegal activity, and she certainly did not want any wrongful conduct by the RAM corporation to ever come to light. But just looking at some ships wouldn't necessarily indict anyone, so there would be no harm in him inspecting the boats.

"Perhaps," she said.

"There is a vehicle waiting to take us to meet him. He may already be there."

Maria's first reaction was to refuse to go with Miguel, but then she thought about Brian. Miguel had presented her with another fait accompli by having Brian brought to the dock, so now she felt she had no choice but to join him there. She wanted to reunite with him, although she was not sure why she felt that so strongly. She stood up and let Miguel lead her out of the building and into a waiting car, with Javier following and getting in the back seat.

The afternoon was warm and humid, there was no wind, and the sky was cloudless. It felt to Maria like the kind of day when bad things happen; the heat and stillness sat heavily upon her, and her discomfort made her anxious. Miguel drove them to the harbor in silence. Javier also was quiet. Maria felt she had to assert her authority.

"Miguel, you cannot make deals of this size without getting my approval first," she said, breaking the silence.

"I told you I was sorry. What more do you want?"

"You are getting a pretty good price from me," offered Javier from the back seat. "These boats are used, so they probably have lost a lot of value. I'm sure I'm overpaying. You should thank me."

"Javier's people are taking RAM out of debt, so you should be happy about that, especially since you borrowed so much for those hotels," Miguel added.

He pulled into Barcadere marina and drove up to a dock with three boats moored on it. Maria saw Brian standing by a golf cart near the dock next to Ernesto. He had a serious expression while looking at his cell phone and appeared to be texting or emailing someone. But just the sight of him made her oddly excited; again she did not understand why. When Miguel stopped, she jumped out of the car.

"I see we are back together," she called out to Brian, trying to sound in control. Miguel exited the car as did Javier.

"Ernesto, you can return to the farm now," Miguel directed. "We have no more need of you."

"Yes, sir," said Ernesto, and he hopped into the golf cart and drove away.

"Mr. Youngman, a pleasure to meet you," Miguel began. He rushed by Brian, not waiting to shake hands. "I am

Miguel, Tommy's brother," he said, calling back. "And this is my associate, Javier. Please come this way. I wish to show you our little fleet of boats." Miguel and Javier began walking down the dock toward the last boat.

Brian walked over to Maria. "Wait a second," he said. "I don't understand. Why are we here? Explain." Brian looked at Maria, then at Miguel and Javier who continued walking and did not respond. Brian turned back to Maria. "What is this all about?"

"Apparently, Miguel is selling RAM's fleet of boats to some group this fellow represents. But honestly, I am a bit surprised. I did not know about it," she responded, still feeling the premonition that all this was leading to something unpleasant. "I am really angry about all this. And I am sorry. If you don't want to go and look at these vessels, I totally understand. But I am CEO and have to monitor what he is doing, since he's talking about a multimillion-dollar deal that will eliminate a large outstanding debt. I have to decide if I approve. But you don't have to be here. You can go back to your hotel. I can call Ernesto to take you back. Again, I'm sorry. This is all just so bizarre."

Maria put her hand on his shoulder, which sent an electric pulse through him. He placed his hand on her hand, which sent a similar pulse through her.

"I think I need to go with you," he said. "This is all sounding so odd. Maybe we both should leave. I don't like the way this is happening. And who is that thug with Miguel? He looks like a character out of central casting."

"Yes, he gives me the creeps too. I don't know. He says he represents a consortium of very wealthy Mexicans."

"Sounds like he represents a bunch of drug lords. Let's leave."

Brian looked down the dock at the two men. They had reached the boat at the end and were boarding it. They had not looked back. Just then, Miguel turned and beckoned to them to come. He turned and walked up the gangplank onto the ship and went below deck. Javier also had moved out of sight.

Maria looked toward the boat at the end of the dock, and then at Brian. "No, I have to. I can't trust him. I need to see what this is all about and make sure it is right for RAM."

Brian frowned. "But is it dangerous?" he asked.

Now Maria smiled. "Well, Miguel and I are certainly not close. We never have been, and we're frequently adverse. And now based on what I'm seeing I may have to change his status at the company and maybe take away some of his authority so he can't do this kind of thing again. But he is my brother. I would not expect anything to be dangerous. So, it's okay, you just go on back to your hotel. I will call you after I get done with all of this. We can have dinner."

Now Brian smiled. "Dinner would be nice." He had started to worry, to feel protective of Maria. "But if you have to go, then I'll go with you. I just don't like the look of that other guy." He squeezed her hand. "Come on, let's get this over with."

The two of them walked down the dock toward the boat. They saw two smaller vessels tied up on the dock, each one labeled with the words RAM INDUSTRIES INC. with its insignia, a ram snorting smoke. The third boat was much bigger, about seventy feet in length, also with a ram painted on its bow. It did not look luxurious at all, more like a cargo vessel. The boat had a high bridge where the controls were housed and a small helipad on the foredeck, which made the working craft look quite odd. They walked to the gangplank at the rear of the vessel and saw that the aft deck was ringed with buoys and life preservers in the gunwales. Round inner tubes were affixed to the sides at various locations. A toolbox sat in the corner next to some metal pails and what appeared to be two bags of cement. A doorway in the middle of the deck just below the bridge led to the lower compartments.

On reaching the entrance, Brian stepped aboard first and held out his hand to Maria. Miguel came back up on deck through the doorway from the lower compartments just as Maria was getting onto the boat.

"Well, I see you two have become quite comfortable with one another," Miguel commented. "You almost look like a couple, instead of a couple of adversaries."

"Enough, Miguel," Maria responded sternly, frowning at him. "So, this is one of our ships that has put the company into so much debt?" She pointed at the other two boats. "Can we really get enough to pay off that ridiculous loan that you took without my knowledge or approval? Now, my patience is really at an end. Do you want to give us a tour of the ship?"

Miguel just smiled a wicked grin at her.

Just then, a large black man emerged from below the deck. He said nothing but proceeded to cast off the lines holding the boat to the dock.

"What are you doing?" cried out Maria.

"He is apparently planning on taking us for a ride," said Brian, now starting to move toward Miguel. "Why is he doing that, Miguel? What's this all about? Where are we going?"

Miguel continued to smile. "You should be interested, Lawyer Youngman," he said, quickly moving around Brian.

"You were here to look for Nora, true? I suppose we are going out to sea to look for signs of Nora. I know she is out there."

Miguel headed toward the gangway they had used to board, which was still attached to the dock. Maria, on hearing Miguel mention Nora, was taken aback, and she suddenly had a sickly feeling in the pit of her stomach as she realized Miguel was involved with Nora's disappearance.

Brian, on hearing Nora's name, reacted even more physically, like someone had struck him. "What?" He spoke sharply, turning toward the retreating Miguel. "You know something about Nora and where she is? Where? Out in the open sea? I think not. I think we are not going anywhere. And I think you need to explain yourself because it sounds like something happened to Nora and you know what. You may need a lawyer yourself."

"Is this true?" Maria demanded, turning to look at Miguel, who had hustled off the boat and down the gangplank onto the dock. "You need to stop right now and answer me."

But Miguel ignored her and instead quickly unhooked the entry bridge between the boat and the dock. However, instead of hopping back onto the boat, he turned and began walking at a fast pace down the dock toward land. Maria and Brian stood there for a moment in shock, watching Miguel making a sudden speedy exit. The large man had finished untying the boat, which began to float away from the pier. He bounded up the stairs to the bridge and turned on the engines, which made a low growling sound.

"Miguel, where are you going?" Maria cried out after him. Miguel did not turn or respond but continued almost jogging down the dock toward the car. The man on the bridge gave gas to each of the engines, maneuvering the craft away from the dock and out to sea.

"Your brother won't be coming with us," came a voice from behind Brian, and when he turned, he saw that Javier had emerged from below. In his hand, he held a Colt .45 pistol with the business end pointed toward Brian and Maria. "So why don't the two of you sit down and relax while we get underway? We are taking a little boat ride."

Javier smiled, but Brian and Maria did not notice, since they were both looking at the gun aimed directly at them.

Chapter Twenty-Seven

Los Angeles

Tomaso opened the front door of his Bel Air house. A messenger stood there with a letter in his hand.

"Are you Tomaso Ramirez?" said the young man.

"Yes, what is this about?" responded Tomaso.

"This is for you." The messenger handed Tomaso the letter, turned around immediately, and quickly left. Tomaso ripped open the letter. It was on the letterhead of his criminal defense lawyer, Mark Martin. It read:

> Effective immediately, we are required to
> withdraw from any further representation of you.
> An unwaivable conflict of interest has developed
> between you and RAM Industries Inc. Thus, as
> referenced in the conflict waiver that you signed,
> we will no longer represent you, but we will

continue to represent RAM Industries Inc. We
strongly urge you to promptly seek new counsel,
as events in your matter have taken a serious turn,
and you will need immediate representation.

Tomaso groaned. He retreated to his living room and
called RAM's in-house counsel, Colleen Stevens.

"What the hell is going on?" Tomaso demanded when
Colleen got on the line. "I just got fired by my lawyer. Did
you do that? Did you forget I am a member of the family
that runs this company too?"

"I am sorry, Tomaso, but we had no choice. Didn't the
lawyers tell you what was going on?"

"No," Tomaso screamed. "They just told me to get a new
fucking lawyer. What the hell?"

Colleen was not ruffled but proceeded calmly. "Nora's
lawyer has been investigating the matter and went all the
way to the Cayman Islands looking for Nora. What he
found was that there are documents that you signed committing her to an insane asylum there. He contacted the
Houston police, and copies of documents were emailed to
the authorities." Tomaso, on hearing this, started to feel
sick to his stomach. Colleen went on. "But Nora was not at
the asylum and no one knows where she is. However, the
documents apparently show that you personally had something to do with abducting Nora and making her disappear.
I think you better get a lawyer fast because I suspect there
will be new indictments issued against you—this time on
both the state and the federal level."

"Oh my God ..." Tomaso groaned. He had turned ashen
and now was quite ill.

"And pursuant to the terms of the Ramirez Family Master Trust, in light of all these facts, you are suspended from any position in RAM Industries Inc. You no longer run any part of RAM, and your access to any RAM facilities, emails, computers has been terminated. As of now, you and RAM are adverse, and no RAM assets are at your disposal. You will receive written confirmation of this. If you fail to defeat the criminal charges against you, pursuant to the Trust, you will be completely disinherited." Colleen waited to hear any response. None was forthcoming. "Tommy, you are officially on your own now, and I can no longer help you or even communicate with you any longer. But I would get a new lawyer as fast as you can. This is our last direct conversation because from now on you will be dealing with our outside counsel." And with that, Colleen hung up the phone.

Tomaso sat down on the floor of his plush and expensively decorated living room. Nora had spent a fortune on the interior design of their home, much to his chagrin, but the result was extraordinary. The elaborate wallpaper matched perfectly with the drapes, and all the furnishings were artistic pieces, extravagant but perfectly coordinated. It was a warm and inviting room, with a cozy designer sofa, comfortable chairs, soft lighting, and inspiring art on the walls.

But Tomaso was utterly miserable at this moment in this elegant setting. He cursed Colleen, then he cursed Maria, and finally he cursed Miguel. He had only wanted to soften Nora up so she would not be so difficult to negotiate with and would make a reasonable deal. He did not understand how he had gotten himself into such an impossible situation. He wondered where she was and why he had not heard anything about her. It still did not occur to him that something truly tragic could have befallen her. As he wallowed in his misery, moaning and rocking back and forth, he realized he desperately needed a drink. No, not one drink, but many drinks. He needed to get drunker than he ever remembered being, to escape from his predicament. Tomaso wanted to escape.

He roused himself and returned to his study to find his favorite bourbon, the one over one hundred proof. He was ready to drink it all from the bottle, but then the doorbell rang again, followed by a loud rapping on the door. He groaned and decided he did not want to accept any more messenger deliveries with unpleasant letters containing unpleasant news. Tomaso ignored the door and went over to his bar, which was richly supplied. He did not want tequila—that would just remind him of his family and his lost position at RAM—but he was going for that strong bourbon.

Suddenly, he heard a loud bang at the door as something crashed through it. Sounds of men entering and yelling his name were cacophonous to his ears. He placed both his hands over them, then sat down on the floor again. He had gotten close to his whisky bottle, but now he sat paralyzed when three men burst into his study. They were federal officers, he could see, and they approached him and shouted his name.

One man came over to him, kneeled down to his eye level, and said, "Tomaso Ramirez, you are under arrest for international kidnapping of Nora Ramirez. You have the right to remain silent."

And Tomaso did remain silent through the remainder of the recitation of his rights. Then two of the officers grabbed him roughly by the arms and stood him up, while another placed handcuffs on him, right there in his own study, before he was able to reach his whisky. And off he went, mostly dragged, by two of the federal police officers outside toward a waiting patrol car, which had its lights blazing. When he got outside, he saw his daughter, Jocelyn, who had just come home from school and had parked her car in the driveway. She was looking at him, shackled, being hustled into a police car by three beefy cops. He gave her a pathetic look as she stared with horrified eyes. Just before he was muscled into the police vehicle, she cried out to him.

"I hate you, Daddy. I hate you. Where is my mother? What did you do? I hate you!"

Chapter Twenty-Eight

Caribbean Sea

THE WATER WAS CALM AT FIRST, but it became rough as they continued on, farther and farther from land. The late afternoon started to wane, and twilight came upon them. They had been traveling for over two hours, and now there was no land in sight. The sun had set, but there was still the dull light of dusk. Soon it would be dark.

Brian and Maria sat together on the starboard side of the aft deck. Javier had taken the rope off of one of the buoys and tied Brian's hands together. He had not bothered to do so with Maria since he figured she was no threat. The buoy lay on the deck next to them, next to an inner tube. The man who had been driving the boat never spoke to them, while Javier simply sat opposite the couple, hardly paying attention to them, but always with his gun held loosely in his hand.

"What happens now?" Brian asked, but Javier ignored him. Instead, he called up to the bridge. Brian had a good idea what might be happening next. Maria had been totally silent. Brian had tried to encourage her, to keep up her spirits with hopeful statements, but these had fallen hollow.

"Ricardo, *ahora, quanto tiempo?*" Javier called out.

"*Trente minutos,*" Ricardo responded.

"Only half an hour more, not long," Javier said to Brian and Maria, smiling.

"So, your friend up there is named Ricardo," said Brian. "Does he know what you're planning?"

Javier laughed. "What do you think I am planning, my friend?"

"Nothing good," answered Brian.

"On the contrary, we are going to search for Nora. Isn't that what you both wish?" Javier laughed again, then turned to go below deck, take a leak, and grab a beer. "Now don't be going anywhere," he called out.

Brian whispered to Maria. "See that toolbox?" he queried, looking seriously at her to try to get her attention.

She appeared to have fallen into a trance, but then she spoke. "I just can't believe how foolish I've been. How blind. I always knew Miguel was bad news, but he was part of the family, and he had rights. My mother knew he was trouble, but I think she was just not willing to act against her own son. We thought he would be out of trouble down here and just get high all the time, but we were wrong. Oh, what have I done?" Maria began to sob.

"Look," said Brian. "We all make mistakes, especially when it comes to family. But can you please focus? See what's in that toolbox and maybe you can cut my hands loose."

Maria looked back at him mournfully for a moment but then suddenly sprang into action, moving faster than Brian thought she was capable of. Opening the toolbox and scanning it, she grabbed a screwdriver and rushed back to him. He was impressed with how quickly she transitioned to action and could not help thinking how beautiful she was.

"Turn around," she said. "Maybe this will work." He complied. Maria worked the tip of the tool into the knots of the rope.

"Ow," Brian reacted as Maria worked, but soon she had unloosened the bonds. "Hold on to it, maybe we'll need it," he said, and she pushed the screwdriver into the back of her pants so it was out of sight. She could feel the cold metal against her skin, but she paid it no mind. "Be ready to follow my lead," Brian said. "I assume you can swim." Maria nodded. "We may have to act fast."

He moved the buoy and the life preservers closer to him and resumed his earlier position, leaning against the starboard side of the ship with his hands behind him. He wrapped the rope around his wrists to make it appear as if they were still secure, just as Javier reemerged from below deck, a bottle in his hand and the gun in his belt.

"It's getting pretty dark," said Brian. "Don't you want to turn some lights on?"

Javier sneered. "Afraid of the dark, lawyer?" And he called up to Ricardo. "*Aqui*, Ricardo, *aqui es bueno. Finito.*"

Ricardo complied and cut the engines rather suddenly. The boat stopped moving through the waves and began to drift. Javier turned back to Brian and Maria. "I think we will need to look for Nora now."

The two captives watched as Ricardo came down on deck and began to open one of the bags of cement. This time Maria called out to Javier. "That cement is the property of RAM. So is this boat. I am the CEO. I order you to take us back."

Javier looked at her and laughed. "But don't you want to see Nora? I think she is down there somewhere."

Brian nudged Maria and whispered, "Get ready."

Maria nodded and then spoke loudly to Javier. "So are you admitting to me that you used RAM assets, RAM equipment to murder Nora out here in the middle of the ocean?"

Javier smiled again. He was enjoying this conversation.

"Me? No, *Señora*. Not me. I missed those festivities. That was Miguel, your loving brother. But Ricardo here, he was there. In fact, he mixed cement for Nora too."

Javier took a final swig of his beer and turned to the port side to toss his bottle into the ocean. Ricardo had his back to the couple, working on pouring cement into a pail. Just as Javier began his throw, Brian leaped to his feet, surprising Maria with his speed, and grabbed the buoy, two life preservers, and an inner tube. Holding all these items in his arms, with a free hand, he pulled Maria up from her sitting position. When Javier turned back around, he watched with surprise as the couple climbed onto the edge of the boat and then leaped into the sea. Ricardo looked up to see the two of them gone. He walked over to the edge of the boat to look. Javier tried to run across the deck to the starboard side but tripped on the way, sprawling onto the hard surface. Grunting, he pulled himself up.

"What the fuck? Where are they? *Donde estan ellos?*" Javier yelled.

Ricardo pointed into what was now darkness. Javier saw forms in the water moving away from them. He drew his gun, pointed it at the forms, and began to fire. One, two, three, four shots. He heard a muffled cry of pain over the sound of the ocean, which made him smile. He had hit one of them, he hoped fatally. But he stopped shooting. He only had a couple of bullets left, and it was becoming even more difficult to see anything. He leaned over the side of the boat, struggling to make out the figures he had shot at, trying to take better aim.

"We need to follow them. *Necessito* ..." but Javier did not finish his sentence. Instead, to his astonishment, he felt himself roughly grabbed. "What?" he started to say, but before he could utter another word, Ricardo threw Javier over the side and into the ocean. Splashing down into the warm sea, Javier immediately felt himself sinking, weighed down by his now soaked clothing with no flotation device. He dropped the pistol, which was still in his hand, as he fought to break back to the surface to breathe and shed his sodden pants.

The gun sank to the bottom of the sea.

Ricardo, having followed the directions of his boss, quickly climbed back up to the bridge, turned the engines back on, and put the ship into full throttle, quickly sailing away from the desolate spot in the middle of the sea, heading toward Haiti. He figured he was due a bonus. He decided to tell that to his boss, Miguel, whom he had to contact by radio soon. He had followed instructions carefully. Miguel had told him to slowly cruise into the Caribbean for at least three hours, then after he and Javier had disposed of the couple, he was to throw Javier in the water as well and speed away.

For his part, Miguel had arranged for a private plane, so when he left Maria and Brian at the dock, he drove immediately to an airfield close to the harbor where the plane was waiting, and it promptly took off for Miami. Miguel wanted to be far from the Caribbean when the dirty business he had ordered occurred. He landed in Miami and was in a limo on his way back to Star Island with Manuel when his cell phone received the radio call he had been expecting, in fact hoping for. To his delight, it was Ricardo, who spoke to him in Spanish and relayed the events.

Miguel's plan had mostly gone off just fine. He was somewhat disappointed that Brian and Maria had not experienced the same terrifying fear before their deaths that Nora had—that had been so satisfying to Miguel. He had hoped to cause them extreme trauma, and the thought of it had made him excited. But the two had been left in the middle of the ocean, which was good enough for Miguel. He had also planned to rid himself of the demanding Javier, whom Miguel had realized was not someone he wanted around anymore, particularly as he planned on taking over the entire company. Javier would have made further demands when Miguel was in charge of RAM, and Miguel could not have that thorn is his side. Better to get rid of it now. And Miguel wanted it to happen in such a way that Javier knew that Miguel had planned to end his life in a miserable way, out in the middle of the ocean. Miguel knew sharks frequented the area, and he pictured them tearing Maria, Brian, and Javier to pieces, the vision of which particularly delighted him.

But it was good enough to hear from Ricardo how clearly shocked Javier was when Ricardo catapulted him into the water. Miguel smiled at the thought. So, when Ricardo called from somewhere in the middle of the sea and gave his report, Miguel was in ecstasy. He even enjoyed that Ricardo was asking for more money, which Miguel immediately told Ricardo he deserved and would certainly receive. In Spanish he asked Ricardo, "Do you have your cell phone with you?"

"*Sí Señor, esta aqui.*"

Miguel told Ricardo that he had to send an SOS signal since there were three people overboard. It would make no sense to the authorities if Ricardo showed up at some port without these three—they would obviously be missed. One was a Los Angeles lawyer, another was CEO of RAM, and the third was a member of a Mexican cartel. People would ask questions, which could lead somehow back to Miguel, and he was not going to let that happen. Miguel explained to the slow-witted Ricardo that the SOS signal would make it appear that a terrible accident had occurred and the people who fell overboard in the dark needed help.

"So right after you hang up this call, you just need to press SOS on your phone, and that will be our cover for what happened," Miguel said in Spanish. "Just do it and call me back afterwards to confirm you did so. I need to be sure this happens."

"*Sí, bale,*" responded Ricardo and then hung up. He looked down at his phone, but it had no service. This confused him. He wondered why he would use his phone to do this when he had a radio that could accomplish the same thing. He radioed back to Miguel to make sure that he was supposed to use his cell even though it had no service.

"*Esta bien,*" Miguel explained. "The police will look at your phone. You need to show you tried. Call me right back after you do that. I need to hear from you right away and confirm that you put the SOS on your cell phone."

Ricardo said he understood, ended the radio call, and picked up his cell to press SOS. When he did so, the phone did not connect with any coast guard or other agency that would help, but it did send a signal below. Wired to the engine were three kilos of C-4 explosives, which could be activated by sending a wireless signal from any phone. Miguel had realized he needed a fail-safe plan in case Javier or Ricardo screwed things up. The signal went to the explosive device, triggering the process, and a massive explosion erupted, destroying the hull, engines, the entire vessel. No one heard the sound, but the ship blew into a million pieces, along with Ricardo.

No one was ever going to come back from that trip, and no one was going to be able to explain what happened. Miguel even planned on collecting from the insurance company for the lost ship. There would be no evidence of the explosion, and he was rid of all witnesses and the only people who could foil his plot. He waited for another return call from Ricardo, but it never came. He started to laugh. Then he looked at his own phone and decided that it must also be destroyed, which he promptly did.

Miguel thought that he needed an upgrade anyway, now that he was going to be the new CEO of RAM.

Chapter Twenty-Nine

Tequila — 1973

MARTA could hardly believe that she was going to be married. She did not really want to marry—she had avoided doing so for years—but she knew it was her duty to marry, to have children, to grow the family and keep its name alive.

Fernando, her husband-to-be, was certainly handsome enough. He also came from a well-respected local family, although they did not have much money. Marta knew her family's wealth was the primary reason Fernando had sought her hand, but she did not mind that. After all, he was a means to an end. And he was not ambitious and had no interest in running the family business. Rather, like a member of the English royal family, he was content to live a luxurious life accomplishing little or nothing but going to popular events and parties. He was even agreeable to one of the provisions of the Family Master Trust, which required all children to keep the Ramirez name. And of course, he was more than happy to regularly sample the tequila they were producing, to have long talks with the tequila makers about their techniques, how they would age the *añejo* and the extra *añejo*.

She was fine with that too, since with enough drink, he would fall asleep and then sleep late into the morning, which worked for her because he would be too drunk to have sex with her. She really did not look forward to sleeping with him, but she had complied because she needed children. She was already pregnant on her wedding day, so she saw no need for any more coitus until after she had the baby and was ready to start another. Of course, he had asked for other things, like oral sex, but she had refused, and he had accepted that. After all, he was content not to have to work and still to live a rich and entitled life. He did not need intercourse with his wife too frequently. There were others who could satisfy his needs.

They were married in the same small church where her mother, father, and brother were buried. It was a Catholic ceremony, but a very small one. Afterwards, he went off with his friends to drink, and she had returned to her father's office to work. She still thought of it as her father's office. She thought of him whenever she entered it.

Marta grew and grew over the ensuing months, and when Maria was finally born, Fernando did not even come to the hospital. Marta was okay with that. She did not need him to help with her baby, actually did not want him there. She would need him later, but for now she found that her life had purpose. Maria's birth sparked in Marta a fierce and powerful love coupled with ambition, and she vowed that her daughter would have a better life, escape the violence the family had suffered, and live in America.

Her plan to move RAM to New York City began to form. New York was where the money was, she knew, and although Los Angeles was closer to home, it did not have the same status, unless of course one wanted to make movies. Marta wanted no part of the entertainment industry with its glitz and fanfare.

Fernando did not want to move to New York, but Marta told him not to worry. He could stay at their property in Tequila and mind the production. She knew he would do little beyond sampling the product and having sex with local girls, but she also knew she could control RAM from New York. Pedro was still working in the distillery, and he was always reliable. He had taken on a wife, but for some reason, they had not been able to have children. He was reasonably happy, it seemed, and had not suffered emotional harm from the violence.

Not like Francesca. She'd had trouble forgetting about all the trauma they had suffered. The only way for her to live without fear was for her to leave Tequila, leave the family home, leave the business entirely, and create a new life for herself that carried no reminders of her past. Francesca had moved to London and started taking courses in the garment industry. Marta stayed in touch with her little sister, and she seemed happy. London was, after all, a center of ideas and art and music. The Beatles, the Rolling Stones, Herman's Hermits—so many bands and so much happening. It was a different world from the lawless and base cruelty that she had suffered in Mexico. Francesca was dark and pretty and slim, so she was sought after by many an English suitor. She dated and danced and enjoyed life with an intensity that helped her forget her past. And that was fine with Marta.

New York immediately felt like home to Marta, and with Maria in an apartment on the upper east side, Marta was quite happy. She preferred for her daughter to grow up "Americanized," speaking English almost exclusively and with no Spanish accent. Maria went to private schools in Manhattan, starting in kindergarten, and grew up like every other New York rich kid. For her part, Marta spent her time devoted to expanding RAM and solidifying its financial standing as well as attending to her daughter. As to Mexico, Marta never wanted to return and only did so when she absolutely had to. So, it was a bit of a surprise to Fernando when Marta told him she was pregnant again.

"How did that happen?" he queried, speaking over the phone.

"It was on my last visit, silly," Marta responded. "I guess it did not mean anything to you. You'd had so much tequila that you were almost too drunk to do anything. But you did, and then fell right asleep." This seemed to satisfy Fernando, and he was not interested in pursuing the matter further. It could have happened that way, so he decided that he did remember their coupling just as Marta described it.

But of course it was completely untrue. Little Maria had one day asked her mommy why she did not have a little brother. Marta realized that she needed to have more children, if for no other reason than it would benefit her under the Family Master Trust her father had created. Pedro was having none, Carlos was dead, and Francesca was partying her life away. But spending more time in Tequila, Mexico, away from her beloved Manhattan apartment just to have

Fernando try to impregnate her was not something she was willing to do.

Then she hit upon it: artificial insemination. She found a sperm bank and signed up. Picking the donor was tricky business because there was not a lot of information about whose sperm was available. And Marta was limited—she could not pick some Harvard professor's sperm. She knew she had to have a Mexican donor. The problem was that there was only one such option at the sperm bank, and there was almost nothing else she could learn about this particular donor. Crossing herself (she still went to Catholic church every Sunday) and hoping for the best, she took a chance and accepted what was offered. After several attempts, she succeeded, and Miguel was born the following year.

But Miguel was not an easy baby like Maria had been. Marta was sick throughout the pregnancy, and the baby refused to come out naturally, so she was forced to have a C-section. Miguel was fussy and needed constant attention. As he got older, things did not get better, and he learned to throw loud tantrums. It seemed he had a destructive instinct, pulling apart stuffed animals and dolls or purposely breaking toys. Marta assumed all boys were the same, but when she found him at the age of five torturing a cat, Marta knew she had a problem. By that time, she was pregnant again. Recognizing that her son Miguel was unnaturally cruel, she almost committed blasphemy and had an abortion. But she did not, since the pregnancy was not by artificial insemination this time, but by Jose. And she cared about Jose.

It had started off almost by accident. Jose was one of the doormen of her co-op. He was from Mexico City and had found his way to New York after illegally crossing the Texas border. Because he was desperate for any work, the building's board of directors had been able to hire him for under minimum wage. He kept their secret and they kept his.

Marta found him both helpful and quite personable, and she enjoyed chatting with him in Spanish. More importantly to Marta, he was so warm and friendly to Maria, who seemed to love him. After school Maria would sit in the lobby with Jose and read or color or play a game. Jose also taught Maria some Spanish, which Marta particularly appreciated. Maria was living as an American kid and was only speaking English, but Marta knew Maria had to become fluent in Spanish if she was going to run RAM someday.

Marta began inviting Jose to dinner up in her apartment, which he could do if his shift ended early enough. Jose was a simple fellow, full of cheer but straightforward and down-to-earth. He had grown up on a farm himself. Marta realized it was healthier for Maria to have family time with more than just herself, and while not her father, Jose was a man, and she wanted Maria to be comfortable with men. Marta also enjoyed Jose's company—there was no pressure with him, no issues, and he was just a pleasant and friendly face. Then one day Marta received a disturbing call from Fernando—he wanted a divorce. He had developed a relationship with a young woman and had promised to marry her. He also wanted money.

"You have abandoned our marriage anyway," he told her. "And I have not gotten in your way. Now you must not get in my way. I will let you keep our daughter—I would not know how to raise a girl anyway. But you must send our son back to Mexico so I can raise him to be a man. You don't know how to do that, that's for sure. He is five years old—so it is time he started to learn. I don't want him growing up like a girl. And you must also pay me for all the time you have spent away from me."

"Can you wait a year?" she asked him.

"No, but I can wait two months."

Marta realized that this turn of events was to her advantage for the most part. She found it more and more difficult to handle Miguel, and for some reason she did not have the connection with him that she expected she would have as a mother. But she had decided she needed one more child, and since the experience with Miguel had not turned out so well, this baby would have to be conceived in the normal way.

"I will come down there in a month and we can talk about all this, work it all out. And I will bring Miguel," she had told him.

"I won't be changing my mind, but come," he had replied. "And bring the girl too. It has been a while since I have seen her."

That very day, Maria asked Jose up for dinner and gave him some of her best tequila with the meal. Jose, who had not been one to drink, found himself quickly inebriated. After Maria went to bed, Marta asked him to stay and watch a video with her. She sat on the couch next to Jose, and before he even realized what was happening, she was snuggling against him, touching him, kissing him, undressing him, on top of him in a wild heat. Next time he came to her apartment, no tequila was necessary, and each night thereafter, they made love over and over after Maria was asleep, staying up most of the night, becoming more passionate as time went on. In two weeks, Marta was pregnant for the third time. But she found that she did not want to stop with Jose. And she did not stop—that is, until she went back to Tequila, Mexico.

When Fernando asked for a divorce, Marta was not unhappy, but it did put her in a quandary. She did not want to have her third child out of wedlock. Divorce was frowned upon by the Catholic Church, so she would insist they remain married in the eyes of God and under church law, even if they were divorced by a court order. Fernando also had to be convinced to wait for a year, so that it would appear that this baby was a product of the marriage, albeit the final product. She decided that when she returned to Mexico, she had to quickly seduce Fernando, and then try to delay him. Perhaps she could even change his mind. She knew she would have to be very seductive to coax Fernando into her bed, but that was her plan. Marta hated to leave Jose, but she thought she would be gone only for a couple of weeks. As it turned out, she was gone from New York much longer, so long that when she returned, Maria had become fluent in Spanish.

And when she returned to New York, Jose was gone.

Chapter Thirty

Somewhere in the Caribbean —
Present Day

THE DARKNESS was all around them. Blood oozed from Brian's left shoulder where the bullet had pierced him. The salt water had cleansed it, and he had been applying pressure to the wound, although he needed Maria's help since the bullet had passed through, so he had both an entry and an exit perforation. Miraculously, he realized, although he was in significant pain, the bullet had missed his artery and his bone since he was still able to move his arm, and he had not bled out. Lucky? He was floating in the middle of the Caribbean with only some small flotation devices and a gunshot wound, so maybe not so lucky.

"Does it hurt?" Maria gasped, as she pressed one hand against Brian's back while clinging to the buoy with her other arm.

"Like hell," moaned Brian. He did not feel like talking at this point.

"I am so sorry, so sorry. This is all my fault. I got you into this." She was sobbing.

"Don't cry," said Brian weakly. "It's not your fault that your brothers are assholes. And I guess now we know what must have happened to Nora."

That made Maria cry harder. "Oh my God, I never liked her, but she did not deserve this. I feel so guilty."

"Well, don't. Forget about that. We need to figure out how to find help. Or land. Or a boat. Or something. Ouch," he reacted as the pain suddenly got worse. He grimaced, and it subsided a bit. Maria stopped crying. Brian could feel her strengthening, becoming resolved.

"They are not going to get away with this," she began. "I am not going to let them. We are going to figure out how to survive. And they are both going to pay." Maria started to think.

"Well, that sounds good to ..." Brian's response was interrupted by a large hand that grabbed his good shoulder and pulled hard. He cried out as Javier lunged out of the water and tried to wrestle the two life preservers away from Brian. But Brian's right arm was hooked around the circular tubes, so Javier's effort simply pulled Brian away from Maria, who had been pressing on Brian's wound.

"Give them to me, you gringo," screamed Javier, as he pulled and pulled, panicking and wildly thrashing. He tried to pummel Brian, letting go of the preservers, but Brian kicked away, trying to get back to Maria. But Javier kept coming.

"Give them to me or I will kill you."

Brian almost laughed. "You already tried to do that and

you failed." He continued to kick away, his injured shoulder forgotten. But Javier came on, swimming forward and once again grabbing the preservers, again trying to pull them from Brian.

"Stop it!" Maria cried out. "Get away from us!"

"Shut up, you *puta*," responded Javier, pulling even harder and shaking the preservers, trying to loosen Brian's grip. Maria used her one free arm and moved herself around Brian and toward Javier.

"Stop it!" Maria screamed again. "Get away!" But Javier kept thrashing about, alternately shaking the preservers and swinging at Brian, but now connecting, hitting him in the face and head.

"Go fuck yourself," Javier said. "I will finish the job, and when I am done with him, I will take care of you." He hit Brian again, and Brian's grip started to fail.

"Stop!" Maria yelled, and she remembered the screwdriver. Thankfully, it was still there, tucked in the back of her pants. She pulled it out with her free hand. Pausing for a second to get up her will, she screamed again: "Stop!" Simultaneously, she pulled her arm out of the water and with all her strength plunged the screwdriver into Javier's neck. Instantly, a spray of blood hit Maria in her face, and she recoiled. Javier let go of the preservers and reached for his neck. Maria quickly kicked away, grabbing a stunned Brian on the injured left shoulder and pulling him with her. She continued to kick as hard as she could, creating as much distance between them and the thrashing man. She knew she had injured him, but she did not know how badly and worried he might now come after them with the tool after pulling it from himself.

But as it turned out, she did not have to worry about that. She saw Javier continue to thrash and knew he was bleeding badly. Then, Maria saw movement around him in the water.

"Sharks," said Brian weakly, and he also started kicking as they continued to distance themselves from Javier. "They smell the blood. Let's just hope they'll focus on him and not us."

The two of them kept kicking away. But then they heard Javier scream. And scream again. And scream again. And then there was no more screaming, but as they moved away, they could tell there was much churning in the water where they had been. They stopped swimming, dead tired, and just drifted until the dawn.

Chapter Thirty-One

Miami

MIGUEL FLEW BACK to Miami immediately on leaving Brian and Maria to Javier and Ricardo. He was sitting in his living room with Manuel at his feet while Brian and Maria were floating in the sea and a few pieces of Javier lay on the ocean floor, since most of him had been devoured. Miguel did not know what had happened but figured he had to appear to have been nowhere near it. He had planned to get rid of all of them—Ricardo too. With Maria gone and Tomaso in jail, he was going to be able to control all of RAM. And with Javier gone, he was done with his connection to the Mexican mob.

He had decided to get away from them entirely. With control of RAM, he realized he did not need a side business and could purchase plenty of cocaine whenever he wanted to. He had big plans. He would move the headquarters of RAM down to Miami. Most of the New York staff including that bitch secretary of Maria's and that repulsive lawyer Colleen would be terminated. He would of course still pay homage to Marta, but what could she do? He was going to have a formal wedding to a girl from Mexico he had found, and after that he would impregnate her repeatedly, so he would meet all the requirements of the Trust. Marta would have no choice but to leave everything to him. Then when she was gone and there was no one to stop him, he might just sell everything off, get rid of the wife, and spend all his days debauching. He smiled at this. He did not need to figure all that out yet. But he had to start the process. He called his mother.

"Marta—it's me, Miguel." He never called her "Mother." He had lost any affection for her ever since she left him with his father, who decided to make a man of him. That meant a lot of beatings and whippings. In Mexico, there was no law against severely "punishing" your child. And Fernando did just that, with nothing to stop him.

Nor was there a law against torturing and killing animals, so Miguel appeased his urges and frequently found an animal to murder. Sometimes he would catch a wild animal like a squirrel or a bird, and sometimes he would find a stray cat or dog. But when he killed any of the farm animals, his father would beat him. After a time, Miguel had come to despise Fernando, but he hid his enmity and pretended to respect his father. He found he could usually find some rat or rabbit to slaughter and avoid the cattle or chickens, although he desperately wanted to kill a horse. But Miguel's talent at catching wild animals did not mean that he avoided beatings. Fernando would also strike Miguel when the boy was not sufficiently respectful or if he thought Miguel was acting effeminate in any manner. Miguel had learned early on that he was more interested in boys than girls, and when he was ten, he was caught by Fernando getting naked with one of the servant boys. That had been a bad beating, and Miguel was bruised for days. He still cursed his father to this day for that memory.

"I have good news for you," Miguel told his mother. "I am getting married. She is Mexican, which should make you happy. In fact, I am sitting here in my home in Miami making wedding plans." Marta was silent for a moment. Manuel looked at Miguel like a pained dog.

"You're in Miami? I thought you went to George Town. And since when were you interested in getting married?" Marta said suspiciously. "Is this because of the Trust?"

Miguel was annoyed. "Yes, of course," he spat back. "And I will have children." Manuel reacted with a low grunt, and Miguel kicked him.

"You? Oh my goodness, no. You have no business being a father. I think you know that."

Miguel bristled, although he knew what his mother said was true. "I am no worse than your other son, who has pro-duced three—all of whom are defective. And of course, I doubt Maria's kid will survive the year." Miguel smiled inwardly at this.

Marta sighed. "Enough, Miguel. So, who are you marry-ing? And when?"

"Her name is Angela, and soon." Miguel could hear Marta's almost silent hissing on the line.

"Miguel, I know that the Trust requires the trustee and CEO to be married with children, but you know it is Maria who is CEO. You don't need to get married. You are not in line to be trustee or CEO. I certainly have told you that in the past."

Miguel grimaced at first, then he began to smile. "Yes, but it does say that any children I have will become part of the family company if they so choose, right? And besides, what if Maria decides to step down or something? I will be ready to replace her."

"Well, she won't be doing that. Get married, have children. But don't do it if you don't want to, and don't do it for the company."

"Of course." And now Miguel was silently laughing. He added, "Maria went down to tour our facility that I bought in the Caymans. I have not heard from her. Have you? I am wondering what she thought of it. I did not have a chance to get down there to show her around."

"No, but she doesn't always call immediately. I am hoping she is having a bit of a vacation. She needs a break."

Miguel was beginning to enjoy this interchange. "Sure hope she gets what she deserves. I think Tomaso will be getting a long break," he said, deciding to upset his mother. "He also may deserve it, though in a very different way." Miguel could hear his mother sigh unhappily, so he decided to continue, hoping to cause her more pain. "And it is a permanent break from RAM—being a criminal—that's what the Trust says, and you can't change that, right?" To his delight, he heard Marta begin to cry.

"I can't talk about this," she said, openly weeping. "I knew he was no genius, but I cannot believe he would do this. I just cannot believe it. I have to go." And she hung up the phone.

Too bad, Miguel thought, *I was just beginning to enjoy this.*

Wait until she hears about Maria. But he felt frustrated and somewhat uneasy, a feeling he was not used to. In the back of his mind, he had a nagging pang of doubt, some inexplicable sense that there was a flaw in his plan. His smile turned to a frown, so in order to relieve his discomfort, he turned his attention to Manuel, starting off by slapping him across the face. Then he pulled the belt out from his pants.

"I haven't really punished you for some time now," he said to Manuel, who started to look quite frightened, staring at the belt in Miguel's hands. "Clearly you have gotten just a bit too comfortable, speaking up when you should be silent. It's time you experienced some real punishment, just to remind you of your proper place."

And then a serious beating began, one which Manuel would long remember. His screams shattered the silence of the house.

Afterwards, Miguel made his plan for a wedding, which was to be a short ceremony attended by no one other than a priest. He would bring his new bride back to Miami and leave her at his home while he did whatever he wanted. He figured she could clean his house. He would have sex with her a few times at the right time of the month until she was pregnant, then he planned to ignore her. *Maybe Manuel would help with that,* he thought. *I will use him to get me excited and when I am about to burst, I can enter her.*

He began to think of ways Manuel could "participate" in helping him impregnate his new bride.

Chapter Thirty-Two

The Caribbean

THE DAWN OVER THE SEA was brilliant, with vibrant colors of red and orange dancing over the gentle waves of the warm water. It was the kind of morning that promised lazy moments on the beach, plenty of sunscreen, a refreshing ocean dip, and perhaps a fruity cocktail.

But for Brian and Maria, floating with two life preservers lashed to a buoy with the rope that had bound Brian's hands, there was only exhaustion, pain, and a progressive loss of hope. They had survived the night, the sharks, the gunshots, and their contemplated execution, but drowning was still a distinct probability if they did not find a way out of their dire predicament. Brian's shoulder, washed clean by salt water, still ached and oozed, although it was in remarkably good shape for a gunshot wound. The heavy concentration of salt in the Caribbean made their flotation a bit easier, and the warmth of the sea kept them from becoming cold, but all they could do through the seemingly endless night was cling to their makeshift raft and hope when the day came, a ship or plane might notice them helplessly floundering. They did not sleep but kept each other awake with words of support, each trying to keep up the other's spirits, congratulating themselves on their narrow escape and promising that they would find a way to survive.

"Thank you for saving me" and "I am so sorry" and "you were so brave," Maria said to Brian again and again. And he echoed those sentiments, telling her "you are the brave one" and "you saved me" and "you took on that horrible killer and got the best of him." Then they told each other they would both make it, and Maria vowed to deal with her insidious brother Miguel, expel him from RAM, and see that he went to jail. And so, they floated through the darkness.

But as light came, so also did they become aware of the profound thirst—water all around and not a drop to drink. The sun would allow them to see and perhaps be seen, but it would also burn their heads and faces and shoulders. Of course, the salt made their condition worse, so long had they soaked in it, as the sea sucked moisture from their bodies. Quite soon they both silently realized they would die of thirst, that dehydration would sap all that was left of their strength and determination, and they would just sink below the water. And through the morning as the gentle waves pushed them aimlessly and no rescue ships came into sight, their thoughts turned more and more to their impending death. It hurt to speak, so they stopped talking and just held on, sinking deeper into despair.

The Caribbean is filled with more than just swanky island vacation resorts and sugar plantations. The sea is dotted with hundreds of cays, atolls, tiny islets, and reefs, too small for anything but seagulls to land on but worrisome for ships that ignore their indisputable existence. Maria, who was at this point much stronger than the wounded Brian, kept watch, pushing herself up on the buoy to look around every twenty minutes or so, and as luck would have it, she caught sight of a tiny speck of land in the midst of all the blue. She cried out, although it hurt her to do so.

"An island, an island, there, there, there!"

Brian roused himself from his growing depression. "What," he croaked. "Where?"

Maria was pointing. "It's kind of a long ways away," she said. "But I see it. We need to swim toward it, or we'll miss it."

"Ugh," Brian groaned. "I don't know if I can. I can hardly move." He could hardly speak.

"We have to," Maria snapped at him angrily. "We just have to."

Brian recoiled at her sudden harshness. But it woke him up. "Okay, okay. I'll try to kick. You'll need to guide us."

"I'll kick too. We will both kick. Now."

They started swimming, pushing their flotilla, feeling exhaustion and pain, but adrenaline helped ... and hope. Fortunately, the sea was still calm, although the waves made going a challenge. But the two of them kicked and pulled with one hand, while holding onto their float with the other. Only Maria spoke from that point on, and just to give directions. Brian could hardly speak and was so weakened he was amazed he could even help.

The two swam and pushed and panted, taking turns to rest so that at least one of them was propelling forward. Slowly, painfully, the islet came closer, and even Brian could see it, although it seemed impossibly far away to him. There was some greenery on it, vegetation of some kind. The sight of this snippet of land gave him hope, which gave him strength, and so he soldiered on, kicking and pulling, kicking and pulling, then resting while Maria did the kicking and pulling.

After what seemed like forever, and in fact was a couple of hours, they had maneuvered themselves close enough to see their destination. The islet was shaped like a pear, and rocks protruded from the larger side of it, which was what they were swimming toward; however, the other side by what would be the stem of the pear had a sandy beach. Flowering plants grew not far off from the shore, but Maria and Brian could not make out what kind of plants were there. Only a few treelike forms were visible. Still, this bit of terra firma looked like Eden to the couple.

"There," cried Maria weakly, pointing to the sandy shore. "We need to go there. Or we might get hurt on those rocks."

Brian said nothing, too weak to think or talk, so he just obeyed Maria. Ever so slowly, for what seemed like an interminable period, they maneuvered away from the rocks and toward the beach side of the islet. Closer and closer they came until magic happened: Their feet touched the floor of the sea, and they could walk the rest of the way. Trudging through the last steps to get out of the water, Maria started to smile. She was dead tired, thirsty beyond imagination, and starving, but she began to hope. Brian was so weak, he could not even manage a smile.

As they crawled out of the water, he lay down on the sand and could not move any farther. Maria stood and dragged their soggy life preservers and buoy up onto the shore, then sat down and looked out at the ocean, then at Brian, then at the sun. Her shirt was ripped, showing her bra underneath. Her shoes, sunglasses, and hat were all long gone, and her pants and shirt were still soaked. She wanted nothing more than to lie down and not move, but she knew that she could not just sit there. It was a warm, balmy day, so she stripped down to her soggy underwear which she figured would dry quickly, and lay her clothing on the sand. As her body dried, the thirst became overpowering. She had no idea where to get anything to drink. Brian was almost comatose, so Maria knew it was up to her. She rose, turned away from the sea, and dragged herself forward to try to forage.

Not far from the shore were flowers, and she headed toward them, looking for anything that would provide even a drop of water. Then she spied something—the plants had berries, small purple spheres in bunches hanging off the vines. She stumbled toward them and grabbed some with her hand. Squeezing them, she discovered that they had large seeds, almost the size of the fruit itself, but they also had juice, so her hand came away covered with a purple slime. Maria stopped for a moment to think—these could be poisonous. But quickly she realized that they were going to die if they did not get some moisture in their bodies soon. Without hesitation, she stuffed several in her mouth. Small amounts of juice came onto her tongue, and she spit out the large seeds. The liquid was bitter, but it was still liquid, and she quickly grabbed another bunch and stuffed them into her mouth, again spitting out the seeds.

She repeated this multiple times, sucking out the bitter juice, until she started to feel just a bit better, the fluid moistening her dry throat and the sugar immediately entering her bloodstream. She kept at this for a while, eating bunches of berries. Then she sat down on the ground and would have fallen asleep on the spot, if not for Brian. He needed fluid and sugar and to get out of the sun. She knew she had to help him. She dragged herself up and moved back toward the beach where he lay motionless. *Oh no,* she thought, *is he still alive?* She rushed over to him. He looked like death, with his swollen red shoulder, sunburned head, and sodden shorts and shirt.

"Brian, Brian, wake up, Brian," she said to him as she knelt and shook him. He groaned in pain, which Maria considered a positive sign, and she tried to pull him farther away from the water. Then he cried out in pain—more of a croak—and opened his eyes.

"Stop," he begged.

"You need to get up and out of the sun," she insisted. "And there are berries—more like grapes—but they have juice in them. You need to eat them." She tried again to sit him up, and this time he complied.

"I don't think I can stand," he gasped.

"Okay. I'll be right back."

She ran toward the bushes of grapes, ripped a few bunches from the vines, and hurried back to him. Pulling a handful from one of the bunches, she said, "They have big seeds, so you have to just chew on them to get the juice out and then spit out the seeds. And they aren't very tasty."

Brian could only grunt as he let her shove berries into his parched mouth. Slowly, almost painfully as Maria watched, he chewed the bitter fruit. But the foul taste did not bother him, so desperate was he for any moisture. He spit out seeds onto the sand and beckoned her for more. Again, she hand-fed him and again he chewed, thankfully, and again he beckoned over and over again. The slow process of rehydrating and absorbing the small amounts of sugar from the strange berries began to revive him, and he started to move after consuming three bunches, all she had brought. Spittle dribbled down his chin. She looked at him carefully.

"Can you stand?" she asked hopefully.

"Maybe," he answered with much less of a croak.

"Ready?" she said, and he nodded, so she grabbed his uninjured arm—the other hung limply—and pulled. He started to rise, and then fell back to the sand.

"I don't think I can," he muttered.

"You must. We got this far. We escaped those murderers and the sharks, and now we have escaped the sea. You were even shot and we made it here. We are not going to stop now. Come on."

She crouched down to look directly into his face, closely, staring into his barely open eyes with a look of determination. Somehow, she communicated or possibly transferred her will to live, to fight, to survive, and he opened his eyes wider and started to come back.

"Okay, let's try again," she said.

He simply nodded, and with her help pulling on his right arm, he finally stood. She put his right arm over her shoulder and pulled him close. "Now we walk," she said, and they moved forward, slowly but without stopping, away from the beach and toward the greenery. They stopped on reaching the bushes that had berries, and she sat Brian down.

"Ouch," he complained, but he looked up at her and managed a weak smile.

"Let's get that shirt off you, and I need to take a look at the bullet wound. You grab some more of these berries and keep eating."

Brian reached for a bunch as did Maria, and they both

chewed and spat. Then Maria, as carefully as she could, pulled Brian's right arm out of his shirt and over his head. He groaned in pain, but she continued undeterred. The left side of his shirt was stained, but most of the blood had been washed away by the sea. Still, the fabric stuck to the open wound. Maria looked at it.

"I think the salt water actually cleaned your shoulder. But I have to check it, which means I have to pull this shirt off of you. And it is going to hurt a bit. So, okay?"

Brian grimaced at the thought. "Yes, okay, let's get it over with," he said and steeled himself as best he could.

"Ready?"

And she carefully pulled away Brian's shirt. He screamed. She was momentarily startled, but then she focused on business, looking first at the front of his shoulder, then the back. The bullet had gone clean through, and blood oozed from both the front and back, but not too much. The wound in the back looked bigger. She wished she had something to sterilize it, but it did look fairly clean, having been submerged in salt water for almost twenty hours. She did her best to clean around the two openings, then pressed with Brian's shirt on each side of his shoulder, hoping some direct pressure would stop all the bleeding.

"Ahhh!" Brian complained, but soon was quiet while she worked on him. The oozing dissipated, and satisfied she had done all she could, she wrapped his shirt around his shoulder in a manner that covered both wounds and put gentle pressure on them.

"Thanks," Brian said weakly. "Did you have some medical training?"

She smiled at him now, her first real smile since they had left the harbor in Grand Cayman. "Well, not really, but

I am a mother. We need to know something about fixing booboos."

"Lucky for me, although I think it is a bit more than a booboo," he said and returned her smile. "But now, can I have some more of those awful berries or grapes or whatever they are?"

"Let's both have some."

She foraged a bit farther into the shrubs and found several more bunches, which they both greedily consumed, again chewing and spitting, as their spirits started to rise. They still did not know that the bitter fruit was safe, but in fact these wild grapes grew throughout the Caribbean. The juice both hydrated them and gave them sugar, and because they could only consume them slowly, this helped their systems tolerate the bitter fruit. Somewhat more revived, they moved farther from the beach into shade under a stubby tree, and before they knew it, both had fallen fast asleep on the ground, shirtless but dry, next to one another.

And the warm and balmy climate kept them comfortable enough, so they slept soundly, all alone on a deserted cay, far from their homes in Los Angeles and New York.

Chapter Thirty-Three

Los Angeles

TOMASO sat on a metal bench in his orange jumpsuit waiting to be called for visitation. He was desperate to make bail and be released back to his comfortable mansion in Bel Air, but he had not been able to access any funds, so he had been remanded to federal prison. The judge had refused to release him on his own recognizance, finding that there was a genuine risk of flight in light of his connections in Mexico combined with the seriousness of his alleged crimes. Tomaso did not have a lawyer, so he had been represented by a federal public defender at his hearing. All access to RAM accounts had been cut off, and his own personal accounts had also been frozen, so he had no way to provide sufficient funds for any retainer for a private lawyer, much less security to the bondsmen he had contacted to help him get out.

He first tried contacting Rosie. Tomaso had been putting money into an account for her for a couple of years at this point, so he knew she had enough to start the process of getting him freed. After that, he could offer his house as security—RAM could not take that away. He also was hoping he could cut some deal with the federal prosecutor by providing information. He would be happy to plead guilty to some lesser crime, do community service, whatever, as long as he could avoid incarceration. It had already been so terrible for him, even though it was federal prison. He knew that if he was sent back to state prison, it would be much worse. Tomaso did not know if he could survive there. He assumed that Rosie would help him, so he called her first from a pay phone in jail.

"Yes, Tommy," she had said. "I am so sorry for what has happened to you."

Hearing this, he brightened a bit; his darling Rosie, someone who actually cared about him.

"Oh sweetheart, it is so good to hear you. I miss you. I so want to see you. I want things back as they were so badly, spending all my free time with my loving Rosie."

"Well, that would be nice," she answered, somewhat cooly. "But it doesn't look like that's possible now."

"Oh, but it is, my sweet," he had urged. "Soon my divorce will be over and I can be with you all the time. I just need to get out of here, that's all. I will get a new lawyer and he can make some deal with the prosecutor. Then we can go away somewhere, maybe to Mexico."

He tried to sound warm and appealing, but there was an obvious hint of desperation in his voice.

Rosie was silent for a moment. "Is that really possible? And what would you do? Didn't you lose your job?"

"I think I can appeal to my sister and get things back on track," he had said hopefully, although he did not really believe that. "And my brother Miguel, he will need to help me, he got me into this."

"So, call her," Rosie had said simply. "Call her now. Get her to help you."

"Now is not the right moment," Tomaso responded. "I need to be clear of all this before she will even talk to me. I just need a little help from you."

"From me?" had been Rosie's surprised response. "What do you mean? How could I possibly help?"

"I need all that money in your account to hire a lawyer and make bail," explained Tomaso. "I can't access those funds because I put them in your name. But there must be a couple hundred thousand dollars by now."

"You want me to give you my money to spend on lawyers for you? And bail?" Rosie said in genuine astonishment.

"Well, it's not really your money, after all, is it? It's my money that I gave you for safekeeping, for us after all," began Tomaso. "And now I need it, but don't worry. There will be lots more later." Rosie was silent, so Tomaso kept on. "I will likely have to pay about a hundred thousand for the lawyer, then another hundred for bail on top of the lien on my house, and then there will be fines to pay. I'm sure that . . ."

"No," interrupted Rosie, harshly. Tomaso had been taken aback by her tone. She had never sounded like that before. "No," she said again, less fiercely but sounding resolute.

"What?" said Tomaso.

"I earned that money, every penny of it," she said, now quietly. "It's mine, and I am certainly not going to waste it on your lawyers. Find another way."

"But Rosie," Tomaso pleaded, "don't you understand? We can be together again. Now all the time. And I will take care of you. I just need this now. I really need it."

"No," she said again.

Tomaso started to lose his temper. "Listen," he said gruffly. "That money is mine and I need it and you better give it to me." Now he was raising his voice. "Do you understand me? I need it and you better give it to me."

"No," she said again.

"Rosie," he shouted.

He heard a click as she hung up the phone. A guard came over to him and glared.

"Something wrong here, Ramirez? No yelling allowed. You know that."

"Sorry, sorry," answered Tomaso meekly. He tried Rosie's number again, but only reached an answering machine. He tried a third time, but again nothing. Tomaso realized he had lost his girlfriend and all the money he had given to her, and she was never going to lift a finger to help him.

And so, he called on his children, specifically Jocelyn, the oldest, the seventeen-year-old he had mostly ignored during her entire life, the girl who had yelled that she hated him as he was taken away by the federal authorities. Not surprisingly, she was not happy to hear from her father in jail, who had apparently been involved in her mother's disappearance. But he'd begged and begged and denied causing her mother any harm—that this was all just a misunderstanding. He asked her to come visit him and he could explain more—he had already used up all the time and all the quarters he had for the phone. She was reticent but finally relented and promised to visit him.

Today was the day she was coming, and he sat plotting

how he could convince his daughter to raid her own trust fund and get him the money he needed. He sat on that metal bench waiting, hoping, believing that his teenage daughter would save him, since clearly no one else was going to. And finally, he heard what he was waiting for.

"Ramirez, you have a visitor," the guard called out. "You can proceed to the visitation window."

The Los Angeles Metropolitan Detention Center or MDC is located in downtown Los Angeles on Alameda Street just a few blocks from the federal courthouse. The structure rises over ten stories and is an opaque off-white color. An *LA Times* reporter claimed that the building has "more the look of a downtown office building than a prison." The doors have plate glass windows instead of iron bars. The MDC has a population just under one thousand prisoners and holds both male and female inmates prior to and during court proceedings. It even holds some criminals serving short sentences, when the authorities deem it unnecessary to send them to the Terminal Island Correctional Institution. This is where Jocelyn went in order to see her father.

She was not happy about it. Tomaso had moved out when the divorce started, and she had not seen him at all until he moved back into the family home when Nora disappeared. Jocelyn had become convinced her mother was gone for good, that her father had arranged for her death. She couldn't be sure, but it made no sense that Nora would disappear this way, and Tomaso clearly had a motive to get rid of her. She had not been fond of Tomaso for some time, but now she hated him, which is why she was wondering how she had come to make this unpleasant trip to this awful, scary place to see a man she loathed.

But she could not get away from the fact that he was still her father. She felt she had a duty to him on some moral level, even if he was a creep. It was clear he needed help. She would probably help him if she could, even if he'd had her mother killed. But she was not going to just ignore his crime. She planned on confronting him, really confronting him, like she had never done before. The situation was different now, and it made her bold.

To enter a federal prison, a person needs a valid form of identification and must pass through a metal detector. Jocelyn showed her driver's license to the front officer.

"You aren't even eighteen," he said.

"I will be in a few months, though," she replied.

"I don't know," he responded. "You're supposed to be accompanied by a responsible adult."

"Sir," she said. "Please understand, I am here to see my father. I need to see him. And my mother is missing. I think you are holding him here because you suspect my father had something to do with it, like had her killed or something. I am the oldest. I need to see him. And there is not really anybody else. Please."

"Hmmm," mulled the guard, as he looked at her. "Okay, but I am going to put you down as eighteen."

"Thank you, sir," she said with appreciation. She went through their procedure, leaving her cell phone and keys behind in her purse in a secure lockbox. Then she was ushered by another guard into a waiting room adjacent to the visiting room. And she waited.

After what seemed like over an hour, another guard finally called her name. She entered the room and sat down at a metal table on a metal chair that was pointed out to her. After a few minutes, out came her father, escorted by another guard, who placed him in a chair opposite hers. Tomaso looked pale, and Jocelyn noticed he had lost weight. He looked so guilty in his prison garb. She was almost sorry that she'd come. He didn't deserve it.

"Jocelyn," he called out in a pathetic tone. "It is so good to see you." Tomaso was actually very happy to see his daughter, more so than he had ever been. He had never before realized who she was. He tried to smile, although to Jocelyn it looked more like a grimace.

"You don't look so good, Dad." She blinked, tears coming.

"I'm sorry, my dear. This place is not the Ritz."

"Why are you here?" she looked up and asked, staring him straight in the face. "What did you do?"

"We shouldn't talk about that now, Jocelyn. There are ears listening. I can't really talk about it."

"Well, that's not okay. Where is Mom? What did you do? Did you have her killed?"

"Oh no, no. We certainly had our issues, but I would never do such a thing. That's not who I am. Don't you know that?" He tried to look at her with a sincere and trusting countenance, but to her he just looked even more guilty.

"She would be back now if she was okay. And I don't think she ever would have disappeared by herself. I don't think she's coming back. And that is your fault." Jocelyn now had tears coming down her face. She realized it was the first time she had cried. She knew it was because she had actually spoken the words for the first time, and that made it real to her. Her mother was gone forever, and Jocelyn knew it. She went on. "Whatever the truth is, whatever happened, I know you are to blame, at least in part if not all. And I will never forgive you. I want you to know that.

I know you are my father, but I can't look at you without knowing that I will never love you, never care for you, never want anything to do with you."

Tomaso was now starting to tear up. This was not going as he had hoped. He had expected a more agreeable, less emotional meeting. He did not know what to do. He was guilty. Miguel had misled him, but he knew that was no excuse.

"I'm sorry. So sorry." He was silent for just a moment. "I need money."

She looked at him with disgust. "What? Is that why you asked me here?"

Tomaso looked almost sheepish, embarrassed. He was asking for help from his seventeen-year-old daughter. He felt pathetic, but he kept on. "I'm sorry, Joss." He called her by her kid name, a name he had not used in a long time. "But for the moment, I can't access any funds. The government has frozen all my accounts. I'm sure it will only be for a short time. I just need a loan from your trust fund."

She looked at him incredulously. "What about the company? They can loan you whatever you need."

"While this is going on, they've shut me out. I have to fix all this so things can get back to normal, but I can't while I'm in here, and I can't get out without money for bail and a good lawyer."

Jocelyn looked down sadly. "Things will never get back to normal," she almost whispered. She missed her mother. She looked back at her father. She blamed him for her mother's disappearance and hated him for it, hated him for his affair, hated him for never being there, for not being the kind of father she needed, like so many of the girls at school had. He had not coached her soccer games or come to back-to-school nights. Only her mother had been there for her. No, her mother was no saint, and Jocelyn knew she drank too much and took too many pills, but she had been there. Why, she wondered, why should she help this pathetic excuse for a father? She looked back at him. He looked so forlorn and out of place here. "Why should I help you, after how you treated Mom?" she asked him.

He looked away. "I know now I was wrong, Joss, and I am so sorry."

Now he looked down at the hard cement floor. Jocelyn stared at him. He was not the careless, arrogant, thoughtless oaf who acted like he was above everyone for no reason other than his family had money. No, he was still weak, likely always would be, but he was clearly desperate. And scared.

"Two minutes more," called out the guard from the corner of the room. "Your time is almost up, Ramirez. Say your goodbyes."

Tomaso started to panic and began to speak faster. "But I can't make it up to you or your brothers or anyone else if I am stuck in here." He looked back at the guard. "And it's dangerous in here for me. I just need to get out, and when I do I promise you I will turn over a new leaf. I will not be the same person ever again. I know this now. Please, Joss, please. I really need your help. You and the boys are all I've got now. Please."

Jocelyn looked away again. "How much do you need?" she asked haltingly. She was almost sorry she spoke.

"Three hundred thousand dollars," he answered hopefully.

Jocelyn was taken aback. "Three hundred? That is so much money. That is almost a half of the entire trust." She started shaking her head. "And there's not much chance I'm going to get it back," she said looking straight at him. "Because you are guilty and probably going to jail anyway."

"I might be able to get by with two," he said quickly. "A hundred for the bond and another hundred for the lawyer."

"Time's up," the guard called out and started walking toward the cold metal table. "Miss, you'll have to leave. You can come back and visit him another day if you wish." Then to Tomaso, "Get ready to stand up, Ramirez," and the guard bent down to unlock the chains that held Tomaso securely.

Jocelyn rose. "I need to think about it," she said.

"Please, Joss, I need it and soon. Please."

The guard began to lead Tomaso away.

"I will let you know tomorrow."

And with a clang, the heavy metal door closed with her father on the other side, and a guard from behind her stepped up to her to escort her out of that wretched place. She went down the steps of the building and walked to her car parked in a nearby lot. It was not sunny that day; the sky was overcast, which seemed appropriate to her. She had missed school that morning and did not plan on going now. When she reached her vehicle, she could not help herself.

Jocelyn cried and cried, harder than she had since she was a little girl.

Chapter Thirty-Four

Tequila — 1977

MARTA LISTENED TO THE RADIO in the black Cadillac she was driving on the dusty back road behind the vast Ramirez plantation, an extension of the first farm that she had grown up on. A new singer named Elton John was playing on the station. Marta had always loved the music of Mexico, but in New York with Maria, she had become exposed to music from around the world—the Beatles, the Beach Boys, the Kinks, the Rolling Stones, the Temptations, and of course, the Four Seasons. Maria had a passion for all popular music and had insisted since she was a little girl that her mother listen to what was current. Marta did not like it too much, but Maria sat next to her in the car as they bumped along, excited about the music.

"Isn't he wonderful, Mama?" she said excitedly. "I think he is going to be really big."

Marta smiled at her daughter. "We'll see, my dear. I hear your Spanish is really improving. Why do you only speak to me in English?"

Maria smiled back at her mother, that winning smile of hers. "I don't want my English to get rusty. I speak Spanish with everyone else, especially Papa."

At the mention of Fernando, the smile on Marta's face turned to a frown. She had been trying for weeks now and had not been able to seduce him. No matter how sweetly she purred and coaxed, Fernando would just smile at her and tell her she was no longer his woman, that he had someone younger and prettier and a lot more eager and responsive when it came to lovemaking. Marta's plan to make Fernando think he was the father of the child she was carrying appeared to be a failure. All too soon, her belly would be showing, and then it would be too late.

RAM's property now extended as far as the eye could see. Her brother Pedro was an excellent manager of the development and had carefully watched over the distilleries, and now there were four. The result was a massive production of tequila, which continued to gain popularity throughout the States. This was where it had begun for the Ramirez family, and Marta was glad Maria could see it all. Marta wanted much more than to produce and sell tequila. They had already started to import a Mexican beer into the U.S., and Marta hoped to expand product lines further, even worldwide.

Pedro's house had been built on the edge of the original Ramirez property. It was near the location where his uncle was killed by intruders long ago. Pedro had fought bravely, even viciously, beside his father and the intruders had paid with their lives. To Pedro, this was holy ground where he and his father had stood strong against the local gang. He'd erected a small statue of an angry ram in honor of his uncle and ultimately decided to build a home for himself and his wife nearby. Now the old fencing was gone, and the adjacent land had been annexed to the original property, all of which was owned by RAM Industries Inc., so Pedro's home was actually located in the center of the extensive RAM farm.

Marta drove the Cadillac up to the front of his home. She had wanted to spend time with her brother and let Maria get to know her uncle better. The house was classic Spanish style with a beautiful front courtyard, a fountain, flowers, and perfectly manicured bushes and trees. Two dogs began barking as they pulled up to the front door, but Maria quickly jumped out, and the Australian shepherds immediately came to her and began licking her. She giggled as she petted them. Her uncle opened the front door and shouted out.

"They love you so, my little niece. The dogs know a good girl when they smell you." Pedro walked over to Maria and picked her up in a big hug. He was so glad to spend a bit of time with his lovely little niece.

"*Buenos dias, Señor,*" Maria said with her best Spanish accent. "*Como estas?*"

Pedro set Maria down, and she turned her attention back to the dogs. She ran off with them, dancing about, throwing a stick, giggling.

Marta came around the car and hugged her brother, who noticed she was getting a bit thick around the waist.

He smiled at her. "I have some interesting news—maybe it's good news," he said to his older sister.

"What now?" Marta asked, pulling away from his embrace.

"Well, it looks like we have a wedding to attend."

Marta took a step back in surprise. "What? What are you talking about?"

"Our little sister is getting married."

Francesca had been in England for years and had never spoken of any commitment or regular boyfriend. Rather, she had flitted about, going to parties and enjoying single life. That she was serious about anyone was surprising news.

"What? Who? When?"

"He is a new one, a Scottish fellow. They are having the ceremony there, and she is relocating from London to his farm in Scotland."

"This is so sudden. How did this happen?"

Pedro told Marta what he knew, which wasn't much. Francesca had apparently been swept off her feet by a handsome young Scot who was visiting London. He had taken her back to his home near Aberdeen, a large farm passed down through generations. After all these years of flamboyant single life, their little sister had decided to settle down—but in a farm in the north of Scotland? Pedro and Marta could not believe it.

"I hate ever to leave here, but I suppose we will need to attend the wedding," Pedro grimaced. "I have never been outside of Mexico, and I don't want to go now—just for a wedding."

"Why should it be in Scotland? Why can't it be here?" Marta asked.

"Francesca never wants to come back to Mexico, and his family and people are all there. Even her friends, to the extent she really has any, are in London. She never wants to be here, and I never want to leave here. And frankly, if I am gone, I just don't trust that all will be well. Something will happen."

"Well, at least they can do the ceremony in London. Who wants to go up to the tip of Scotland? The weather there is horrendous. We need to talk with her."

Marta looked at her brother and remembered once more how much she loved him. She was now a sophisticated New Yorker, head of a multinational company, negotiating complex agreements and building an empire. Pedro was still a simple farmer who loved the land, was connected to their family property, and focused on the minutiae of everyday agave farming, tequila production and bottling, and maintaining their now grand estate. She counted on him to do what she did not want to do so she could manage all aspects of their land and business, and she never had to worry about meeting her contractual obligations to deliver the best quality product to places not just in the U.S., but now also in Europe.

In fact, she had recently agreed to send their tequilas to London, yet she had never visited the city. Now, with Francesca getting married and the new business relationship, she knew she could not go directly back to New York, back to her affair with Jose, the front doorman. She was growing with the child inside of her, and she'd had no success at seducing Fernando Allicante, the soon-to be-ex-husband. She decided she would make one last try, but then she had to leave her homeland and travel to the United Kingdom, where she would meet her sister's fiancé, do business with her new London distributor, and of course, get fatter. *At least,* she thought, *Maria will see more of the world, although she won't be practicing her Spanish there. One more week here, and then I have to be off.* Marta went to Pedro and hugged him, to his surprise.

"Regardless of what Francesca decides, London or Scotland, you don't have to go," she said to him reassuringly. "We will develop an elaborate excuse for you, but I need you here."

"And I need to be here." He looked relieved. "I wouldn't even recognize her today, I suppose."

Marta shook her head thoughtfully. "Maybe I won't either. She has been living a very different life. But I need to go see what this marriage is all about. I am going to go meet her and this new fellow. I want to make sure she is not being taken advantage of, that this guy is not after the company's money. What's his name?"

"James MacDonald," Pedro answered. "I had her say it three times, and then I wrote it down."

"A Mexican woman and a Scot." Marta smiled. "Won't they have interesting children?"

When Marta arrived in Heathrow airport, having flown nonstop from Mexico City, she was exhausted. Maria, on the other hand, had slept for the entire nine-hour flight and was full of energy. Marta had been unable to sleep as she thought about her last failed effort with Fernando.

She had purchased a new dress, full of vibrant color and even had her hair and makeup done by one of the local professionals. Looking in the mirror, she realized she had never looked better. Not only was she beautifully groomed, but she was in that early stage of pregnancy, before any significant showing, that made her exude life and energy. Having arranged a "meeting" with Fernando, she was ready with the best RAM tequila and had the *hacienda* chef prepare a special *mole* which was her husband's favorite dish. Candles lit the dining room, and Marta had even asked the chef to spike the main course with concentrated marijuana extract, hoping the combination of tequila and THC would make Fernando compliant for a little extracurricular activity, just one last time, with his wife.

Fernando had not lived in the Ramirez mansion for some time, but when they had wed, this had been their abode, and she hoped he still harbored pleasant memories of their time here. She did not blame him for his desire to move on from her—she too had been uninterested in their marriage for years, ever since Maria had been born. He had drifted away, content to be financially supported by the Ramirez fortune but eschewing any real work for RAM other than offering his professional opinion on the various tequilas the company produced. Pedro did not dislike Fernando but only tolerated his opinions of the taste profiles that Pedro strived to achieve.

Since Marta had moved to New York, her marriage had become even more tenuous, and after Miguel was born, it simply stagnated. Miguel certainly did not help. He was a nuisance to everyone, it seemed. He had been living on the Ramirez property tended to primarily by the staff for several years, since Marta had found him too difficult to manage in New York. He was often found torturing some animal, which he ultimately skewered or otherwise disposed of. Recently he'd been running around with some locals he had met. *Thankfully,* Marta thought, *he is not here tonight, out again and likely making trouble,* and Maria also was not at the *hacienda* but was with Pedro and his wife Cassandra for her last two days in Mexico. Cassandra had taken over Spanish lessons for Maria, who had made remarkable progress.

"*Señor* Allicante is here," announced the maid, and in

came Fernando. But to Marta's shock, he was not alone. Instead, his new and much younger future wife walked in.

"Hello, Marta," Fernando said smugly, obviously pleased to see Marta's surprise. "I don't think you have met my fiancée, Felicia." A stunning young woman, dressed in a flowing white dress and with long dark hair, was holding Fernando's hand.

"*Mucho gusto*," said Felicia, bowing slightly.

Marta took a moment to recover. "Yes, a pleasure as well," she finally got out. Then she turned to Fernando. "This is a surprise, my dear. I thought this was to be a private dinner between just us so we could sort things out."

Fernando laughed in response. "Well, I know that is what you had in mind. But nothing is secret from my beautiful Felicia." He turned to her and smiled, then hugged her ostentatiously. "Anything we agree, she must be part of. She is my best new adviser. And besides, she is also my protector, since you have been trying to get me into bed the last few times we saw one another. You do look quite lovely tonight, I see, so perhaps you were hoping for another try, but I am now entirely Felicia's. I will always be faithful to her and only her." He looked back at Felicia and again hugged and also kissed her lightly on the lips.

That was the end of Marta's efforts to try to fool Fernando into thinking he was the father of her unborn child. She would have to figure something else out, likely a bribe, since it looked like Felicia was going to be an expensive choice for him. The meal itself was quite delicious, but Marta had a miserable time, although she kept up a fake smile. The combination of tequila and marijuana clearly worked magic for Felicia and Fernando, and they left urgently, eager to find a convenient place to have sex.

Little was settled, but Fernando expected lifetime support from RAM, and he also wanted Miguel to stay in Mexico. Fernando did not give much time to his son, but he was proud to have him. As to Maria, since she was a girl, Fernando had little interest in her. The evening ended with Marta realizing she had unfinished business with her husband that would need to be sorted out in due course. *Maybe,* she thought, *we can work something out after their wedding.* Marta had told Fernando that they would not be divorced in the eyes of the church, no Catholic wedding was allowed, but she would agree to arrange a divorce with some Mexican lawyers used by RAM; all he would have to do would be to sign some papers. Lifetime compensation was promised, which was to be negotiated over the next few months. The whole business was so disappointing that Marta was depressed for days, and the flight to London made things no better.

"Mama, can we take a tour and see the city? I want to see Big Ben and the castle and all the famous places here," Maria had said excitedly on the taxi ride to the Ritz hotel near Piccadilly.

"We shall, dear, but give me a chance to rest a bit, please," Marta sighed.

When the cabbie dropped them off and they entered the hotel, Marta saw a stately, well-dressed woman heading toward them, and before she knew it, she was being hugged.

"Marta, Marta, it's been so long!" cried Francesca. "And this must be Maria—oh, you are so beautiful. I am so sorry that your *tia* has not been more a part of your life. But that will change now."

Francesca swept Maria into her arms as the girl giggled and hugged back. A tall, red-haired gentleman, also extremely well-dressed, came up behind them and extended his hand to Marta.

"A pleasure to meet you," he said. "I'm James MacDonald, but you can call me Jamey—all my friends and family do." He gave Marta an earnest look as she took his hand. "And I want to marry your sister if it's all right with you."

"My goodness, I heard you were a farmer, but you certainly don't look like you have been in any fields recently," replied Marta.

"Aye, that is so. Just so we're clear, we do have a farm that grows barley, but our main business is whisky. My family has been making it for many years and it is our primary occupation. Perhaps I can offer you a wee taste?"

Marta suddenly understood. "You are in the liquor business, just as we are?" she said.

"Aye, that's true. It is part of what brought us together—like we were kindred souls. We grow the barley, and then we have an old distillery that makes the finest single malt."

"Scotch whisky," said Marta.

"It's the best kind," Jamey answered as he smiled a broad smile.

Chapter Thirty-Five

The Caribbean — Present Day

COCONUTS WERE NOT originally indigenous to the Caribbean; the trees were imported by the Portuguese. But these plants were incredibly well-suited to the climate and soon became ubiquitous throughout the islands, their seeds spread by birds flying from place to place, consuming bits of the plant and then defecating. These trees would produce coconuts in bunches, and some would fall to the ground, ultimately producing more trees. The nuts themselves, depending on their ripeness, are filled with a milky fluid, which has certain medicinal qualities, including antibacterial effects. The meat of the coconut is rich with all kinds of nutrients, including protein and various minerals. Husks from the coconut are typically discarded but are actually highly fibrous and can be woven together to create a kind of stringy, skinny rope. And although it is much easier to open a coconut with a knife, it can be done with a sharp rock, particularly if the rock is applied to what is called the eye of the coconut, a soft place in the shell. If carefully split open, the shell itself, once hollowed of the meat, can be used to make a small bowl, which can catch and hold liquid. Even the leaves of coconut trees are incredibly useful, as they can be fashioned to build roofs or even small huts or structures.

In addition to coconuts and the seagrapes that thrive naturally throughout the islands, other types of edible and even tasty fruits grow wild. The hog plum tree produces a round orange fruit that looks like a small apricot or mango and tastes just like a SweeTART. The noni or "starvation fruit" also grows wild and can be eaten, although it does not smell very nice. Sweetsop is a dark green fruit shaped like a pear with a prickly outer texture, and it also boasts various health benefits.

Maria and Brian did not know anything about the local flora, but necessity is the mother of invention. Both were motivated, talented, productive people, and they worked together to discover ways to survive on this scrap of land surrounded by the sea in the middle of nowhere. For example, they quickly found coconuts on the ground and cracked them open, initially destroying the shells and spilling the milk. Soon they learned by experimentation how to extract the milk, and in addition to drinking it, Maria used it to wash Brian's wound, since the salt water stung him when she tried that. She did not know that the milk was also preventing infection, so Brian's gunshot injury began to heal.

Brian also meshed together the coconut husk fibers to create a kind of line to which he attached a sharp stick that he honed on the rocks. He was not much of a fisherman and at first failed to catch anything, but since he kept at it, finally luck was with him, and most days he was able to snag a local fish or two. They had to eat the fish raw at first because they had not yet been able to make a fire, but one day Maria worked for two hours with some dry wood from a palm tree and finally she succeeded.

They slept on the sand and found a place on the island for a handmade latrine, using leaves for toilet paper. Modesty was gone, and they both wore shorts that had to be washed in the sea until a rainstorm came suddenly, and they used their handmade coconut bowls to capture as much fresh water as they could. They were a good team, and they came to rely comfortably on one another to work for survival. As they slowly but surely mastered living in this idyllic wilderness, they both grew healthy and strong.

And they brainstormed about ways to signal for help. They built structures with rocks on the shores, attempting to make them look like people, and put SOS signals in the sand using sticks and branches. Brian climbed a tree and used a scrap of white cloth from Maria's pant leg as a signal flag, which he attached as high and as visibly as possible. They talked often about what else they could do to try to get rescued. They were both eager to be rescued, and as they became healthier, they also became more impatient and frustrated. Maria was desperate to get back to protecting RAM, knowing Miguel was likely wreaking havoc at the company, and she also missed and worried about her son, Antonio. Brian recognized that his one-man law practice had to be disintegrating, and that he was missing all his appointments and failing to meet his obligations to his clients. But they saw no ships or planes except an occasional jet high in the sky. They would wave and yell at it, all to no avail. And the days passed.

One afternoon, Maria found Brian asleep on the sand under the shelter of dried coconut leaves a few steps away from the small fire they kept burning day and night. There were two fish he had caught lying not far from the embers. Brian had only his shorts on, which were wearing very thin at this point. Maria had on her T-shirt and cutoffs. Neither had worn shoes for some time, but their feet had adapted to the island.

She looked down at the man who had saved her and whom she had saved and who she had worked to survive with, and she knew she loved him. She loved him more than she had ever loved anyone. It had started when she first saw him in court—that was just pure attraction. She had thought him so handsome and confident and intelligent and impressive. Then, when she crossed swords with him at the psychiatric facility, she could hardly contain her feelings, since everything he said created an emotional overreaction, and though angry, she was also excited, even titillated. His demeanor and easy conversation when they decided to work together to learn about Nora made her feel comfortable and at home with him. His bravery and initiative that had gotten them both off the boat had amazed her, and her efforts to save him had triggered a maternal instinct to protect him. Now they had worked together, supported each other, and found ways to survive under the most challenging conditions. That was the most profound connection of all.

She loved him in ways she had never felt before. While working together, making a palm tree hut or foraging for fruit, they had talked about their past, their families, their lives, so in addition to all her experiences with him, she had come to know all about him. He was not proud but instead rather humble and sometimes even self-deprecating. Brian told her about law school, his time as a prosecutor, his failed marriage. He cared about people and was devoted to his legal craft. And he was not all about money; he knew it was only a necessity, a means to an end—but that the end was the important thing.

Brian had become tanned and lean, and as he lay shirtless and asleep, she examined him, every part of him. The heat rose inside of her as she thought about how much she loved him. They had not yet been intimate, at least not physically, but Maria knew that time had come. She shed her shirt and pants and stood in front of him naked in the daylight while he slept. Then, the potent passion that had been restrained came unbridled, and she fell upon him, gently kissing every part of his body, stroking his arms, his legs, his chest, his face, then kissing more. She could not stop, did not want to stop. Brian awoke to the feel of Maria's lips on his chest and neck and knew all at once. He reached his arms around her and held her close, and she kept kissing him, now on his neck, his cheeks, and finally his lips, licking them and kissing them hungrily. Suddenly she pulled away from his embrace and moved lower on his body, her hands grabbing at his shorts, pushing them off of him. He chuckled.

"Be careful," he whispered. "They're the only pants I have."

She giggled like a schoolgirl but kept working to undress him, quickly successful, so he was also completely naked. She kissed him there, moved up his body, then quickly down, and suddenly he was inside her. She moaned.

"Oh, Brian," she purred.

"Yes, my love," he answered throatily.

"I want always to be like this, always to be with you, always to be connected to you, always."

"Always," he answered, holding her close.

And then they did not talk for a while but made love fiercely, savagely, passionately, on the sand on a deserted isle in the middle of the Caribbean Sea, where nothing existed but them and their love, and all they cared about was each other.

Chapter Thirty-Six

New York

MIGUEL HATED NEW YORK CITY. He did not like the cold, and although there were some exciting places to go out late at night, he always felt uncomfortable, like someone was watching him and that he could not get away with his usual predilections. He intended to leave as soon as he could for the warmth and comfort of Miami, with its lazy licentiousness. In fact, he intended to move RAM's headquarters out of New York entirely. He had many plans.

First, he had to convince Marta to make him "temporary" CEO while Maria was missing. He knew she would never be found, but Miguel had to put on a concerned face and continue to orchestrate a fake search effort. Then, when everyone realized further efforts were futile, he would insist his "temporary" status become permanent. After that, he could really start all the changes he planned, like firing that annoying in-house lawyer, Colleen Stevens, and that useless assistant Susanna.

He walked into the high-rise office building in the financial district. The Freedom Tower that replaced the Twin Towers that had been destroyed by the 9/11 terrorist attack was a powerful monument, a symbol of hope and strength. It rose above Manhattan in defiance of the despicable acts committed by the followers of Osama bin Laden.

But Miguel did not care about the building. He understood the mind of the terrorist. *You destroy your enemies so you can increase your power and take from them what you want,* Miguel thought. That's what he was doing. First, he took out Nora, which really was to frame his brother, Tomaso, but also to eliminate her claims on any interest in RAM, since he did not want some California court to interfere—after all, who knows what some family law judge might do?

The elevator took Miguel up to the fiftieth floor, where he knew his mother was waiting for him. He had convinced her to leave her compound in the Hamptons, now that Maria was officially missing and Tomaso was in jail. Miguel smiled at the thought of Maria going to her death at sea, knowing he had set her up. He wondered if Tomaso had even figured out how Miguel had set him up—his younger brother was so stupid.

Marta, he knew, was not stupid. But what choice did she have? Still, Miguel worried about dealing with his mother, since she would likely set up some kind of challenge for him, some hoops he would have to go through, before she would approve his taking charge of the company.

The elevator doors opened, and Miguel stepped into RAM's headquarters. The lobby was not ostentatious but was tastefully adorned with colorful Mexican art. Miguel had not been back to the New York office in years, but he noticed the rich carpet, the plush sofas and chairs, and the beautifully carved mahogany reception desk with Mexican designs. A well-dressed receptionist sat behind it, and when Miguel entered, she stood nervously.

"Welcome, Mr. Ramirez," she said. "Your mother is waiting in the conference room."

Adopting a cocky and proud countenance, Miguel did not respond or even nod to the woman but simply strode past her. She was beneath him and would be fired soon enough, which was his plan for all the employees in this office. They were undoubtedly loyal to Maria, which made them unacceptable to him. He walked down the hall and into the conference room, where he found Marta, Colleen Stevens, and Susanna sitting at the conference room table drinking coffee, an untouched plate of sweetbreads and croissants sitting in the middle of the table.

"Miguel," said Marta as he entered.

"Hello, Miguel," said Susanna somberly.

"Nice to see you," echoed Colleen.

"Mother," answered Miguel, hating to call her that, and he nodded at the two women. Putting on his best effort at sincerity, he began: "So unfortunate that we have to meet at this terrible moment, with Maria missing and presumed dead, and Tomaso, incarcerated, clearly guilty of a horrific crime against his own wife. These are sad times."

Inside, Miguel was laughing, but he worked hard not to show his true self, which was almost impossible. Marta sighed a long sigh.

But Susanna spoke up quickly. "Why do you say presumed dead? We don't really know that, do we?"

Miguel quelled his urge to slap the woman. "I know

it's hard, but we have to face reality now," he said, trying to adopt a mournful tone. "We are doing all we can to find out what happened, but so far nothing has come from our search."

"This is so hard, so horrible," Marta said, almost in tears. "I cannot believe this—how could this happen?"

"As I have told you, Maria wanted to see everything about the Caymans, and that included the boats. So one of the sailors took her out, apparently far out, and they just didn't return. We have radioed and sent out planes and helicopters and ships, but the Caribbean is a big place. I think perhaps the motor blew up and sank the ship, and there would not be much chance of survival if it happened fast. I hate to say it, but I have lost all hope."

"I can't believe this either," commented Colleen with a tinge of anger. "Weren't these ships properly maintained? They certainly cost a lot, and until it is clear what happened, we can't even persuade the insurance carrier, AIG, to pay. First, they have to investigate, but in the meantime, the bank has indicated they may need to call the loan since a big piece of collateral is missing."

"Colleen has a good point," responded Miguel, eager to appear collaborative with the woman he desperately wanted to fire. "RAM has issues and needs a clear leader to navigate out of this trouble. Its CEO is missing, and its West Coast head of operations is in prison. But before I go on," and he looked at Susanna and Colleen, "I think this is a conversation that I need to have just with Marta. Would you two excuse us and give us some privacy? This really is a family matter." Miguel managed a friendly look. The two women looked at Marta.

"I am the in-house counsel," Colleen said. "I need to be

present to give advice—that is my job. Any discussion of leadership needs to include me."

"Well, it doesn't need to include her," Miguel answered sharply, pointing malevolently at Susanna. "She is just an assistant, a secretary. She needs to leave."

Marta sighed. "I'm sorry, Susanna, but would you mind? I think Miguel is being a bit dramatic, but if it makes him more comfortable, there is no harm in your excusing yourself for a bit. But," and Marta turned to Miguel, speaking firmly, "Colleen is right, and she stays. She will have to document things anyway, and she knows the terms of the Family Master Trust, and she is a great adviser."

"It's okay, I'm not offended," said Susanna, looking quite offended, and she rose to leave. Miguel, happy to see her go, thought, *At least it is a minor victory*. He turned back to Marta.

"As I was saying, RAM's CEO is missing. Likely for good. That is why, Mother, you must appoint me CEO immediately. We must show our employees, our banks, our suppliers, the whole world, that RAM is in control, that these terrible setbacks have not derailed the company. You need to act now, and I am clearly the person who should head RAM from this moment forward."

"Miguel," Marta responded sharply. "We don't know for sure that Maria is gone for good. We just don't know. I think it would be premature to assume that and make you or anyone else CEO."

"There isn't anyone else," Miguel shot back, losing some of his self-control. "I am the only one left. Tomaso's kids are teenagers, and maybe they'll even go to college if they don't overdose first. Maria's kid is too young and has serious health problems."

Marta stared at her son now. She wondered if he could be trustworthy and responsible. She wanted to believe it was possible. "I could come back on as CEO," she said simply.

Colleen reacted, smiling hopefully. "The Trust does allow for that," she offered.

Marta continued. "And there is Francesca and her son."

"Mother, that is totally unrealistic. You passed those reins long ago, and frankly you have been out of the day-to-day of the company. And let's not forget your age. And your comfort. Francesca is also too old and has never run anything but the scotch distribution. And I think her son is just a farm boy like his father."

"What makes you think you are up to the task?" queried Marta. "It's a big leap to be in charge of the entire international operation. It's bigger than just Miami. We are a multibillion-dollar company, privately held but with hundreds of employees all over the world and even more independent contractor or partnership relationships with companies and individuals in ten countries. We have offices in New York, Aberdeen, and Tokyo, not to mention multiple offices in Mexico, Los Angeles, and Miami. We own eleven hotels in addition to distributing worldwide tequila, scotch, beer, and Japanese whisky, plus various products. We own trucks, planes, and ships, and maintain licenses of all kinds in multiple markets. And especially with the recent acquisition of the hotels plus your purchase of vessels and our other obligations, we are now highly leveraged with debt at over sixty percent. What makes you think you can just come up here and manage all that? It was a full-time job for Maria, and she was educated at Harvard Business School and learned all the ins and outs of the company from childhood."

Miguel stood up and began to pace. "How about we do

this: Make me temporary CEO, with all CEO powers, but just for six months. You can see how I do. At the end of that period, we should know about Maria, but in the meantime, the company will be stabilized. What could be the harm in that? If Maria thankfully is found, she can resume. If Tomaso miraculously escapes prison, you can consider him. And it will give you time to find out about Francesca's son. Go to Scotland and see him."

Marta looked thoughtful. "I suppose that might be okay," she said.

Colleen just stared at the ceiling.

Miguel continued, still pacing. "But one thing should be clear: I have full powers. You can't revoke them or remove me for six months. That will give me a fair chance. Even if you don't like one of my decisions, you have to let me run RAM for at least that long. Actually, a full year would be better. No interference. See where we are with my leadership and vision and talent, but I don't need to be looking over my shoulder all the time, worried that my mother is about to second-guess me. You may have built this company in your time, but you are older now and it is my time."

Now Colleen spoke up. "A year is a long time, too long, if you want my view. Marta should not give up the ability to change things if the company is going down the wrong path."

Miguel wanted to slit her throat but instead smiled at Colleen and continued. "A year is hardly a long period in a long-term business. But it must be irrevocable. What do you say, Mother?" He turned back to Marta, wishing Colleen would just disappear.

Marta thought for a moment. Her mind went back to her childhood and how her mother Xiomara had built the business almost from nothing. She thought about how her father had struggled and been cruelly murdered and also how she had avenged his death, only to lose Carlos, her youngest brother. And she thought about all she had done to expand the company into a worldwide enterprise. Could her wayward son be expected to handle this responsibility and protect the company her whole family had suffered for? She looked at him, wanting to believe. She knew she had few options.

"The Trust does indicate that a family member should always be CEO, subject to certain conditions," she said. "I guess we could give you a try. Understand, if Maria returns, she immediately resumes her post as CEO. But I think Colleen is correct—a year is too long. Let's agree on six months—that should be enough time to see how you do. If RAM is foundering, I will take back the role or do something else. And you are right that I should go see my nephew Angus in Scotland. I have not been there in years now—maybe he can take on more of a role in the company."

Colleen cursed inwardly and thought she should get her resume in order.

Miguel was jubilant but did not show it. "If you think that is wise," he said solemnly. "And I will do my best."

"Colleen, write it up," Marta said. "And prepare an announcement that can go out to all our employees and associates. I think we have no choice but to do this."

"Yes, Mother," echoed Miguel. "RAM has no choice."

Chapter Thirty-Seven

Los Angeles

JOCELYN CURSED HERSELF as she left the bank. Why was she helping her father? He was a bad man, and she knew it. She was also pretty sure he was responsible for her mother's disappearance and probably her death. She missed her mother, although they hadn't gotten on so well in recent years. And it was his fault she was gone. Yes, she had been a selfish woman and focused on all the wrong things, like whether Jocelyn was popular with the boys and what Jocelyn's figure was like, but at least she was around. Her father had rarely been at the house—especially after the divorce—but even when he was there, he kept to himself and drank and drank and drank. Now was the first time she could remember him showing any interest in her—only because he needed money. *Why should I give him any? Shouldn't he just rot in jail?*

But as bad as he was, he was her only father, and now likely her only living parent. Jocelyn knew her mother had treated him badly. Nora had been no Mother Teresa. But Tomaso had abused her too, so they were both at fault for their mess of a marriage.

Jocelyn had seen one benefit of her father's incarceration: He could not drink. He simply had been forced to dry out, and that was a good thing. She had noticed it when she went back to see him a second time—he was not so red-nosed and his hands did not shake and he seemed to think better. Maybe there was hope for him. But not if she didn't bail him out and help him get a real lawyer.

She looked at the two certified checks in the envelope she was carrying, one made out to the Eveready Bail Bond Company in the amount of $100,000, the other payable to Parker & Israels, attorneys at law. She knew the bail bondsmen would also take another lien out on their house to bond both the federal and the state prosecutions, while Phil Parker was her father's new criminal lawyer and had agreed to handle both prosecutions, federal and state. She just had to deliver these two checks, and her father would be free by the end of the day. He would meet with Parker tomorrow.

The money came from her own trust fund, set up by her Aunt Maria, and Jocelyn was not allowed to access it except in an emergency. Jocelyn had a fairly persuasive argument that this was an emergency, with her mother missing and likely dead and her father in jail for it. But she had still needed to ask for help from RAM's company lawyer, Colleen Stevens, who balked at first but realized it was better for the company anyway that Tomaso was represented and not sitting in prison. Colleen had also taken pity on Jocelyn, recognizing the enormous conflict of accessing her own

funds to help a wayward father who was charged with kidnapping and killing her mother. That was the conflict that
gave Jocelyn pause now. Even her two brothers, Justin and
William, had both been against the idea.

"He doesn't really deserve our help," Justin had
commented.

"I miss Mom and it's his fault," said Billy with tears in his
eyes. "I think he should stay in jail for the rest of his life."

"That may be what ends up happening to him," Jocelyn
answered. "But don't you think we at least owe him this—a
lawyer and some time out of jail? He's not drunk anymore,
and he acts awfully sorry. Maybe he will change for the better."

"I don't really care," Justin responded.

"Me neither. I hate him," echoed Billy.

So Jocelyn was helping Tomaso without much support
from anyone. She walked out to her car, which was parked
on the street in front of her family's Bel Air mansion. She
had to drive downtown to the bail bondsmen's offices first,
then back to the West Side to Parker's office on Wilshire
Boulevard in Westwood. This was going to eat up her whole
day, and she had taken off school to get it done. After fighting through traffic on the 10 Freeway, she found that shoddy
office and delivered her check to a man in a cheap suit who
grinned at her lasciviously. Shuddering, she made her way
back to her vehicle and drove to the lawyer's office, where a
receptionist accepted the second check.

"Is Mr. Parker available? Can I talk to him?"

The receptionist was friendly. "Let me check, sweetie,"
she replied. "Have a seat."

Jocelyn sat on a worn-out couch, and soon a fifty-year-
old fellow with a red-striped tie loosened around the neck

of a wrinkled white button-down shirt came out to the reception area.

The lawyer held out his hand. "Hello, Jocelyn, and thanks for the retainer," he said. "I'm Phil Parker. I'll be representing your father. So sorry that you are having to deal with all of this."

"Can you get him off, Mr. Parker? Or is he going to jail?"

The lawyer sighed. "I can't really talk about the case, and no one usually knows how this is all going to go anyway, but your dad is in real trouble and I will try to help him. That is all I can say."

Tomaso was not released that day, since the bondsman did not get to it as quickly as he could have, but the next morning he was let out of jail with an ankle bracelet, and Jocelyn was there to pick him up, missing another morning at school. She stayed in her car and waited for him, then watched her father walk toward her parked vehicle. He had lost a lot of weight, and while he looked haggard and beaten, oddly enough he looked better to her. Jail combined with the import of what had happened—his lost job at RAM, the desertion by his girlfriend Rosie, the indictments against him in both state and federal court, the disappointment of his children—all that had changed him. He was not just thinner but no longer hooked on alcohol, and he had lost the swagger that had never quite fit him. He had even come to appreciate his children more. Necessity had made Tomaso realize he now had to fight to survive, and even with all his efforts, he might fail anyway. He opened the passenger door.

"Thank you so much, Joss. I don't know what I would have done without you."

"Just remember, Dad, you promised no more drinking. That was a big part of our deal."

"I remember and I won't. I can't be doing that now. I have to figure out how to get myself out of this mess. And it will start with Miguel."

"I think it has to start with the new lawyer. You need to meet with him."

"But this mess was all caused by Miguel, who now doesn't seem to know me. And if your mother is truly gone, I swear to you that I did no such thing, Joss. I never would have. Miguel has to be at the bottom of it. And I am going to prove it."

"How are you planning on doing that, Dad? He's in New York or Miami, and you're not allowed to go there while you are out on bail."

Tomaso shook his head. "I will find a way," he vowed to her as she pulled onto the 10 Freeway and headed toward the Pacific Ocean.

"Okay, but for now, let's go home. You look really tired. Maybe just start with a good night's sleep."

Now Tomaso smiled at his daughter, and she could see him looking at her with her peripheral vision as she drove. "I may have done a lot of things wrong," he said, "but I see that I have quite an amazing daughter. At least there is you. I am very proud of you, Joss."

"Why? Just because I raided my trust fund and bailed you out of jail?" she responded with a frown. "That's not really something to be proud of."

"Your loyalty is. And you did it all, and you did it for me, and I am not so worthy. But when everyone else deserted me, you were there. I'm sorry I have not been the father I should have been. But I am changing. I will be better. I will try to be there for you and the boys now."

"It's kind of late."

"Well, better late than never. You will see. I will prove myself to you."

"We'll see. And to the boys too. They need you. I think Justin is way into drugs. And Billy just needs someone to help him grow up. I don't know what's going to happen with your trial and all, but maybe you could work on those things."

They rode the rest of the way home in silence, with Tomaso brooding over his next steps, especially how he could get to Miguel. Tomaso had long since realized his brother had played him; he had been a fool to trust Miguel and go along with that far-fetched plan to teach Nora a lesson and put her in her place. Tomaso had certainly hated Nora but had never thought she would come to any harm.

He had just wanted her compliant. Now Tomaso knew Nora was gone, he knew that Miguel with his evil streak was capable of such a thing, and he knew that Miguel had set Tomaso up to take the fall for it. Tomaso also knew that Miguel was quite aware that the Family Master Trust had been crafted so that no one with a criminal background could work at RAM and, even worse, they were cut out of any inheritance, as were their children. With his newfound appreciation for his daughter, Tomaso fumed that Miguel had found a way not only to destroy him but also to disenfranchise his three offspring.

I'm going to do something—find a way, he thought to himself. He realized he would need to go to Marta and confess, but also tell her it was all Miguel's doing. Maybe his mother would take pity on him. Maybe she would not believe him and would refuse to help him. But what choice did he have? He began to form a plan of action.

When he got home, however, after hugging both his sons, who were not particularly comfortable with that, he realized how exhausted he was. He went into his study, thinking he would start to plan. He saw all the scotch and tequila had been taken away, but he did not mind it. He fell fast asleep in his study on the big leather couch and slept for twelve hours without waking up.

The next morning, he showered, shaved, and donned his best blue suit with a white shirt and blue tie. The suit did not fit him anymore; it hung loose and he had to use a belt and suspenders to keep up his pants. He planned on visiting a tailor that day, but first, he needed to have that meeting with his new lawyer.

And then Marta, if she would only talk to him. She had not been willing to do so up to now.

Chapter Thirty-Eight

The Caribbean

IT HAD RAINED hard that night, which was a mixed blessing for Maria and Brian. They had almost run out of fresh water before the storm and had been able to collect throughout the night a significant amount in various handmade bowls and pouches they had created. But their makeshift hut was severely damaged, and of course they had gotten almost no sleep. And while Maria and Brian were making love almost constantly, exploring and experimenting, they still needed their rest with all the chores they had to do just to survive. They also found themselves talking constantly, sharing what they wanted and cared about and worried about, baring all and leaving nothing unsaid. Maria opened up to Brian about her first marriage and her son and all the guilt she felt. Brian shared the tale of his broken marriage. Both agreed that staying married requires a variety of actual skills that no one seems to recognize or learn before the vows are taken.

"One thing is just talking to one another," said Maria, as she leaned against the trunk of a palm tree, relaxing in the sun after what had been an active bout of lovemaking. Brian lay on the sand next to her, and she bent over and kissed him lightly on the lips. "That should be obvious, but maybe it's not."

Brian nodded in agreement. "I think that's because people are guarded and don't want to open up before they get married about what they want, how they want to live. I'm just glad I didn't have any kids with Judith before realizing that we were just wrong."

Maria sighed. The sky was blue and it was late afternoon, the calm after the night's storm. The sun was sinking, creating dancing colors reflected off the calm water.

"People just don't think about anything beyond the ceremony."

"And the party," Brian added.

Maria looked at him, realizing he was so in tune with her he could almost finish her sentences. She found that every day she fell even more in love with him. She bent over and kissed him again.

"Right. Then to combat the letdown after the wedding is over, people just have kids without knowing what kind of parent and partner the other person is going to be and how that big adjustment is going to happen because a child just changes everything."

Brian smiled at her, then became serious. "We are in a romantic paradise here, and I almost don't want to be rescued."

Maria's expression changed and tears came to her eyes.

"Oh Brian, I know, it's almost like we're safe here. We don't have to worry about the craziness of the world, about RAM or my family or my son's illness or the horrible things that Miguel has done and is probably still doing. Part of me almost never wants to leave because when we do, things will never be the same. Will we be adversaries again?" she asked.

Brian shook his head. "I don't think so," he said thoughtfully. "I don't have a client anymore, so that case is over. But I guess I would be testifying against your two brothers."

"They both deserve it," Maria commented. "But their going to jail would be bad for RAM. Not that we need them to run the company, but it would hurt the reputation." Then she suddenly stood up. "Oh my God, wait a second." She started pacing. "We could lose some of our licenses, like the license to distribute in the U.S. That would trigger all the loans and they would accelerate and become due. The company would go down." She looked at Brian. "That could be the ultimate disaster."

Brian stood up and went to hug her. She let him but did not hug back. Suddenly, she pushed away.

"What is it?" he asked, startled.

"We need to get back. I need to get back. I have to get back. I miss my son, and I feel so guilty about him, I just haven't been the best mother. And Miguel is probably ruining the company, and with the fallout from what those two did, I need to figure out how to save RAM. You need to understand, I have devoted my life to the family business. I have promised to grow it and nurture it and protect it and leave it to the next generation in better shape than when I became CEO. Now, because I failed to keep my eye on Miguel and recognize his evil, everything is at risk. It's my fault."

"No," said Brian seriously. "You cannot blame yourself for Miguel. How could you know?"

Maria looked at him stone-faced. "We all knew," she said slowly. "It became obvious Miguel had a devil streak in him. I guess I didn't want to believe it, how bad he was, but the truth is, I knew he was capable of anything. We all did. And now things are bad. We have to get back. We just have to."

Now Brian came over to her and held her, then kissed her. "Well, what more can we do?" he queried. "We've set up stone messages and we put a makeshift flag up on that high tree. But I'm not sure what else we can do."

"What about signal fires to try and get someone to notice us? We talked about that," Maria suggested.

"It will be arbitrary. We won't know when to do it or if anyone will see it and figure it out. And we'll need to burn much more fuel, which will deplete our little piece of paradise." Brian was thoughtful. "We'll run out of wood and leaves pretty quickly and then have nothing left to sustain us. That's why we haven't tried using fires."

"What we've done so far just isn't working," said Maria.

Brian could see the desperation on her face. "It's dangerous, but we'll do it. We will keep doing it until someone sees us and rescues us. I promise, we'll try. Maybe we can figure out a way to conserve fuel but still signal with smoke, you know, smoke signals, like the Indians did."

Maria now hugged him tightly and began to sob.

The next few days were spent collecting anything that might become fuel for signal fires and creating smoke, which required wet fuel. This included seaweed, which they swam out and collected, then laid out in the sun until it was dry enough to burn. The couple realized that they would not have enough to keep a large fire going constantly, so they had to be tactical about when they would light their signal fire and send smoke into the sky to alert anyone to their existence. After much discussion, they settled on creating a fire at the most prominent area of their small isle at dawn each morning and keeping it going for at least several hours. There was a small promontory made of rock that was slightly higher than the sand that was the obvious place to build their fire; from that point any ship sailing from almost any direction could likely see the burning and smoke.

Maria became obsessed with searching for anything that could burn and spent hours in the water collecting plants and then more time picking leaves and small debris to pile up on the rock. Brian was left to manage their dietary needs and pretty much anything else that had to be done, but he made sure to spend time foraging for fuel and showing Maria that he was her partner in this endeavor. Days passed, and each morning they made smoke, and then again in the evening the fire burned brightly. They sat around it for hours, feeding it, talking, sometimes dancing, sometimes making love, always hoping. But nothing happened; no boats or planes ever passed by. Maria was hopeful in the first days, but soon she became frustrated, then depressed, and their fire time became punctuated with her sporadic moans and periods of weeping. Brian did his best to comfort her, but she progressively became inconsolable. The days turned into weeks, and no one came for them.

One night when Brian himself was feeling particularly frustrated, he left Maria to her tears and walked to the beach area where they first landed. He needed a moment alone, away from Maria's depression. He sat on the sand and thought about his life—how he had loved being a lawyer, how he had failed at marriage, how he had come to love

Maria. He missed his old life, he realized, where he could practice judo with his Japanese friends each week, ride his bike in the early morning in the LA sun, work whenever he wanted to at his own private office, have a beer with a few of his law school classmates and talk trash about the judges. He wondered how he could return to that life and restart his practice, which by now had to be in shambles.

And then he thought of Maria but could not figure out how she could continue to be in his life. She lived in New York—all the way across the country. Long distance relationships were never likely to last. He knew he was not about to leave LA and take the New York bar. She, on the other hand, had a company to run in New York, and a son and a mother there. She was also unlikely to leave her home. Perhaps this time on the isle was all they would ever have. He could fathom no clear answer to how they could stay in each other's lives. He looked out at the darkness, then back toward the signal fire, and shook his head. Maybe he did not want to be found. Maybe there was no better life than this one. He waffled back and forth, a wishy-washy mindset about what he wanted and what was possible.

He looked back to the sea and the darkness ... and then he saw it. It was far off, but yes, it was a light, and it was becoming clearer. He peered hard into the night and struggled to make it out. Yes, it was there, and he had to tell Maria. He hesitated for a moment, then ran back to the signal fire.

"Maria, Maria, a boat or something. Look out there. Put more fuel on the fire! We need to wave torches, now, before it passes us by," he yelled as he ran.

Maria started screaming and waving and throwing more leaves on the fire and grabbing any stick and lighting it and waving it. And the light in the darkness came closer. And soon it was not one light but several lights. As they waved and screamed, they soon saw the outlines of a ship coming their way. They kept up their efforts, their voices becoming hoarse.

Brian looked at Maria and saw her smiling. He hoped this ship was friendly and that they could radio back to Los Angeles and New York from it. *No matter*, he thought, *there has to be food and water, and they will be going somewhere we can get off and contact everyone*. He started to feel relieved, although he was a bit sad to be leaving the little isle that had spawned their intense feelings for one another. He wondered whether they would still feel the same back in their respective roles in the world.

But he brushed that thought aside and smiled back at Maria as they both continued to shout for help at the top of their lungs.

Chapter Thirty-Nine

New York / Miami

MIGUEL was enjoying himself as he stood watching Susanna, Maria's assistant, put her personal items in a box.

"That's right," he sneered. "Collect your crap and get the hell out of here. You have fifteen minutes more before I have security throw you out."

Susanna looked up at him in tears. "You are going to ruin this company," she yelled at him. "Marta never should have let you be in charge." She turned away from him and continued to sob. "Where are you, Maria?" she said under her breath. "Are you really gone?"

"Hurry up!" Miguel said.

He fired Susanna last and took pleasure in her discomfort. In fact, he'd had fun terminating all the people in the New York office. He particularly had wanted to watch Colleen Stevens clear out her desk and taunt her while she was doing so, but she was too fast for him. The day after the press release about Miguel's ascendancy to CEO of RAM, she had come to the office early in the morning, taken all her personal items from her office, then left a letter of resignation on what used to be Maria's and was now his desk. He had come in that day at noon, so Colleen was long gone by then. But he had a plan in mind. He called Susanna into his office.

"Take a letter," he ordered, and she sat down with a taut face. "This is to our landlord, Westminster Partners. To whom it may concern: RAM Industries, Inc. hereby terminates its tenancy in your building effective immediately."

Susanna looked up at him in shock. "What?" she said in astonishment. "I think we have a long-term lease. I don't think you can just terminate the lease like that. There will be consequences."

"I have no interest in your opinion. Just go type it up and bring it to me for signature. And I want it hand-delivered and emailed today. Go now. Get it done."

Susanna stood and left the office, shaking her head. She returned shortly thereafter with the letter. Miguel snatched it from her hand, signed it, and held it back out to her.

"Get it out now," he ordered. "Confirm to me when it has been delivered."

She left the office, and Miguel began walking around the New York headquarters of RAM with a security guard he had hired the day before. He proceeded to personally fire each and every employee in the entire office, one by one. He did this with a smile, and he had saved Susanna for last. By four o'clock, the office was empty of everyone except for Miguel and the security guard. He had literally eliminated the entire New York operation of RAM.

"Movers are coming tomorrow," he commented to the security guard, "to box up all the records and files. They are also disposing of all the furniture and other items. This place will be empty." He was boasting. He was pleased with himself. He turned to the security guard. "You're fired too. Don't need you either anymore."

Miguel walked out of the office, out of the building, and into a waiting limousine.

"To the airport—JFK," he commanded, as the vehicle edged into Manhattan traffic.

Miguel was going to run RAM from Miami, where he could handpick his employees and they would be loyal only to him. He knew all the New York people had been selected by Maria and her disgusting group of female confidantes, like that repulsive lawyer, Colleen Stevens. They would do all they could to undermine him, and he needed to start with a clean slate, which is what he would tell his mother Marta when she found out about his demolition of the New York office. He knew she would never have approved, so he had decided to confront her with a fait accompli. Now there was nothing she could do about it, so he would ask for forgiveness and tell her she needed to trust him. What choice did she have?

Maria had acquired ten hotels, and he figured he could visit each one and make his mark. It had not occurred to Miguel that it was not Marta who would be his problem but the lenders on the transaction. While Miguel was a clever, manipulative, sneaky, immoral fellow, he was not a man of high finance, nor did he have a business degree. He certainly could make a basic deal and negotiate simple, straightforward terms for the purchase of a house or even a short distribution agreement. But complex loans with their interminable and indecipherable legal mumbo jumbo were beyond his ken and his patience.

Miguel also incorrectly believed that running the international dealings of a conglomerate like RAM had to be easy enough—his sister had done it, so he assumed he was quite up to the task. He smiled with satisfaction as he thought of it on his ride to the airport: Now he was in control of the money. It was a massive ocean of dollars he could dip into at his whim. He would simply need someone to collect the income and pay the bills—all rather straightforward.

During his years of overseeing RAM in Miami, he had developed a few business relationships which he was planning on using, specifically his accountant, Sammy Levine. Yes, he was a Jew, but Miguel assuaged his bias with the knowledge that the Jews get money. Sammy had become his accountant years before, when Miguel bailed him out of a dangerous debt obligation, specifically a significant gambling loss. Sammy had a particular fondness for—some would say dangerous addiction to—gambling on anything, be it horses or sports or just plain poker games. Sammy usually lost—but if he won, he kept "reinvesting" any winnings so that he ultimately lost them as well.

Miguel had found Sammy in a seedy office in a poor part of Miami where he was taking advantage of the locals, charging them unreasonable fees for filing tax returns and overseeing escrows. Only a cheap accountant with questionable ethics was the right person for the way Miguel liked to do his personal accounting. The fees were all charged back to RAM, but Miguel had never wanted to use RAM's accountants, who were conservative and honest and reported to Maria. Sammy had the right kind of kinkiness for Miguel, so he hired him. Shortly after that, he had visited Sammy to go over how he wanted to cheat on his taxes, but Sammy had looked so desperate, sweating like a pig, that Miguel had inquired. He learned that Sammy was about to have his kneecaps broken due to his failure to bring a local bookie current. Miguel saw an opportunity and made Sammy his bitch—Miguel arranged to pay off the bookie with dirty funds from his cocaine business, and put Sammy in his debt.

Now Sammy was about to be elevated to RAM's CFO, but only to pay bills and deposit funds. Miguel made it quite clear to Sammy, who of course couldn't be trusted, that Miguel also knew folks who could break his kneecaps as well as pull his fingernails out and possibly castrate him. Sammy turned white at the thought but was more than happy to move into RAM's new Miami headquarters and leave behind his dilapidated office and poor clients, many of whom were starting to get wise to Sammy's double-talk. Miguel planned on integrating Sammy into RAM's bank affairs immediately, and on the way to the airport, he called Sammy to arrange it.

"Our primary bank is First Midland, and I set you up with a password. But you can't take any money out or sign a check—you just print them and I will sign them. And you make deposits—all the deposits, not just some. Don't fuck with me, Sammy, or someone will definitely fuck with you in a very bad way." Miguel could almost hear Sammy wince on the other end of the line. "And I have all the mail coming to you, so make sure to take care of it."

"Sure thing, Mr. Ramirez, and I hired an assistant today to help out so everything will run smoothly for you, sir."

Miguel smiled, knowing Sammy was always trying to cheat on his wife. Maybe now that he had a new job, he would divorce her. Or she him.

"What's her name?" asked Miguel.

"Gloria. She's Cuban. And she's top notch. You will like her, Mr. Ramirez, I'm sure you will."

Miguel laughed. "Just keep her hands out of the till as well, or she will lose those hands. You can have her keep them on your balls." He hung up.

Everything was falling into place. He slept most of the way. A car picked him up from the airport and brought him to his waterfront abode. He was looking forward to abusing Manuel, but when he called out for him, there was no answer. Instead, his new wife, Angela, came down to greet him. He realized he would need to have sex with her again soon so she could get pregnant. He had been doing it with Manuel's help since he married her, so she could already be with child, but he planned to keep doing it weekly until he was sure she was. Manuel had made it possible so far, since Miguel would start with him first and then before ejaculating, quickly penetrate the woman and plant his seed. Miguel had first considered artificial insemination—that would be easier and quicker and would not involve him having to be intimate with Angela. He didn't want to beat her, which was the only thing that would excite him, because he needed her healthy and uninjured for pregnancy and childbirth. He also did not want her to run away. In the end, using Manuel had solved the problem.

"Where is he?" Miguel asked.

"He's gone," she said.

Miguel was astonished. "What? Where did that little bastard run off to?"

"He didn't tell me anything. He looked pretty bruised and he was limping. And I think he might have taken some things with him. I don't know."

Miguel began to fume. He leaped past Angela and bolted up the stairs to his room, which he kept separately from his wife. He only slept by himself or sometimes with Manuel.

Things did not look right, and after investigating, he discovered several of his watches were gone. Miguel ran to his office and saw things were a mess. It would take time to figure out what was missing. He seethed and swore under his breath. He planned his revenge and wondered how he could track that *puta* down. Miguel knew he needed to do something to make himself feel better, but cocaine was not what he wanted. Instead, he found the best bottle of RAM tequila in his house, located some prescription opiates, and settled himself down for the night.

Angela, seeing his condition, fled into her room and locked the door. He had not beaten her yet, but she had come to know who he was in the short time since their wedding night and realized it was inevitable, particularly if he was completely inebriated. She had seen him beat Manuel and presumed that was why he took off. She had also recognized that Miguel preferred Manuel to her for his pleasures, which was fine with Angela, but it was also clear to her that Manuel was not happy Miguel had gotten married and there was a female in the house. Angela had seen Manuel become moody and dissatisfied with the new situation, so it was no surprise he had deserted Miguel, nor was she surprised he had taken whatever he could easily pawn.

Oh well, she thought, rubbing her midsection, *I am late now, so maybe I am pregnant, and that will be a good thing. Miguel will leave me alone, and I will have a baby, and my baby will grow up strong and be a rich Ramirez family member. And all this suffering with this horrible man will have been worth it.* Angela smiled and patted her tummy where her hopes lay.

She prayed it was a boy.

Chapter Forty

Scotland — 1978

MARIA SHIVERED from the cold wind whipping across the Scottish Highlands as she and Marta watched her aunt's wedding ceremony. It never seemed to fully warm up there, even when the sun was shining and the almost constant breeze died down, which rarely happened anyway, at least while she was there. The warm sun of Mexico was far away, and Maria knew she felt a kinship with the land of her family. Scotland felt foreign, and although the people were kind and the vibrant plaid patterns on their sweaters and scarfs and kilts were magnificent, the hard bread and fatty mutton was not to her taste.

Tortillas are so much better, she thought. Still, she was glad to be here, part of a family event that seemed to make her mother happy. Marta had been quite busy with helping Francesca get ready, which went on for hours. Maria could not understand why they took so long just to put on a dress, but she had watched as the two sisters argued over eye shadow, perfume, and all brands of makeup. Finally, thoroughly bored, Maria had left the castle and gone off for a walk along the Scottish moors.

Maria looked at the savage landscape. She could not understand why her Aunt Francesca wanted to live in this place. The moors here were not dry, grassy, open areas but wet and boggy with patches of peat. The Scots used the peat for fuel, since it was available in abundance, and after drying it, they said peat was as good as dry wood. Jamey's whisky distillery had used this peat for years to fire the family's kiln, and the aromatic smoke flavored the sprouted barley in a unique way. The barley or "bere" fields were several miles away from this area, but all the land was owned by Jamey's family and had been theirs for many years. More barley was grown in Scotland than any other crop. Maria had tasted tequila when visiting Mexico, and it had been sharp on her tongue but easier to drink. When Marta let Maria taste the Scotch whisky distilled on the MacDonald land, she coughed and spit it out, much to the merriment of Jamey and his family.

"A bit too much for you, lassie?" he had chuckled.

He was not a very handsome fellow, but he was big and strong, and he had an air of confidence. Francesca had become enamored with him and his background, and something about the family farm and distilling whisky had appealed to her, made her feel at home. She had never wanted to return home, having worked so hard to forget the tragedies suffered in Mexico. This seemed like a perfect compromise, with the cold and rugged country so different, but the family history so similar. What Francesca did not know was that the family had fallen on hard times and had mortgaged their property repeatedly, so it was on the edge of foreclosure. Jamey had conveniently failed to mention it and instead had paraded her around his family's estate as if he were a well-heeled Scottish lord or "laird." But a week before the wedding, Marta had confronted Jamey about the truth, having hired an English solicitor to investigate who her sister was marrying. She soon discovered the massive debt and the pending foreclosure proceedings.

"You are going to lose everything!" she had yelled at Jamey.

The ruddy smile on Jamey faded. "Aye, it now does look that way, although we are going to ask for more time."

"How will time help? You are just building up more interest expense."

"As long as we are here, we are not leaving," Jamey said stubbornly. "We will fight."

"Then they will just evict you, put you out on the street, humiliate you."

Jamey raised his arms. "What am I to do?" he cried out. "This is my family's land. We have had it for ages. Am I to lose it all?"

And he walked away. Marta realized that he was an unrealistic fool who was taking her sister into disaster, but when she talked to Francesca, her sister would have none of it.

"I love him," Francesca said angrily to Marta. "And you are not going to ruin my happiness. I deserve this. And if you don't like it, you can just get out and go back to Mexico or New York or wherever."

Marta decided to go to the banks that held the mortgage and begin negotiations to purchase the loans. The property was in hock for millions of euros, and the lead bank

was in France. She told Francesca that she had some business a few days before the wedding and flew to Paris, leaving Maria behind in Scotland.

"Don't worry," she had assured both Maria and Francesca. "I will be back in time. This is just something that
came up out of the blue, something about our tequila shipment to Europe," she lied.

It was a short flight and then a longer drive into the
business district. Marta sat with her English solicitor in
the waiting room to speak with the head of the real estate
foreclosure department, and they kept her waiting for two
hours. But Marta used the time well, making phone calls
to her bankers in Mexico and New York. By the time of the
meeting, she had arranged for the French bank to receive a
fax confirming a guaranteed twenty-million-dollar line of
credit. The French banker finally allowed her into his office.
Two younger bank officers sat in the office as well. The
senior man was classically Parisian in appearance, except
for the three-piece black suit he was wearing, which Marta
thought looked English by its tailoring. He held the fax
between his fingers as if it was distasteful.

"This is only for twenty million and that is dollars. After
conversion, it is only about twelve million euros, madame.
And that is short—not enough. We have a debt of over fifteen million euros with accumulated interest." He gave her
a disgusted look.

"You have only the property to foreclose on," began
Marta's solicitor. "What are you going to do with that? Sell
it? Manage it? Are you going into the Scotch whisky business? It was a foolish loan from the start. How will you look
having to foreclose on the property? It will be your alba-
tross. It could be the end of your career. But if you sell us

the loan at a discount, you will have immediately recovered most of your capital. And you will be happy to do that, since no one else is going to give it to you. So think hard about this before you turn it down."

The French banker shook his head. "I cannot go back to my people with such a short pay and no interest, no return. That will be on my head." The banker motioned with his hand at the solicitor, as if brushing away a gnat. "If we have the property, I will hand that off to another department and it will be their problem. I cannot agree to accept less than fourteen million euros. That is our best offer."

"Well, we don't have fourteen million euros," said the solicitor, and he began to stand up. Marta put her hand on his shoulder and sat him back down.

"Look, monsieur," she said. "I don't have a lot of time and I am out of patience. *Comprendez-vous?* So I am going to make one last offer, and if you don't accept it, I am going to court in London and will sue and seek an injunction against your bank. Then I am going into bankruptcy court and that will tie you up for years. So here is what I will do for you."

The Frenchman listened with a glum and condescending look. But two hours later, Marta held the documentation that conveyed to RAM all right and title to the loans on the MacDonald properties.

And she made the wedding.

Chapter Forty-One

Los Angeles — Present Day

TOMASO GRITTED HIS TEETH as he sat beside his attorney, Phil Parker, at the conference table in the U.S. attorney's office, staring across at the three prosecutors looking disdainfully at him, like he was a lower form of life than an amoeba. It was not going particularly well, he could tell that much. These three-piece pinstripe dark suit, white shirt, blue tie lawyers were insisting that he serve jail time in federal prison—not just a short stint, but at least five years. He knew that this negotiation was only to be followed by a second, likely harder one with the Los Angeles Deputy District Attorney since he was being prosecuted by both the state and the feds. His high-priced lawyer had told him that maybe they could obtain a suspended sentence from one office, but likely not both.

"We will point out that you have already served some

time in jail, and that things are not likely going to be easy for you, that you may be a target if put into a maximum-security state institution with the gangs there," Parker had explained. "We will argue hard for house arrest, but it's going to be a challenge. The kids are a big factor there; we'll point out that with their mother missing, you are their only parent, and they need someone at home, even if you won't be able to physically leave the house for a significant period of time. Why should the state pay to house you when you can house yourself? That is an angle as well. But you have an awfully nice home, and the DAs won't like that."

Parker relaxed beside him in the conference room chair wearing a perfectly tailored blue suit. Tomaso was reminded that he had paid for his lawyer with his daughter Jocelyn's college fund, her trust money that was supposed to assure her future. They were dealing with the feds first, since Parker had explained that the state typically allowed the more prestigious and higher-level feds to go first. Then whatever deal was cut, if there was a deal, the County DA might just follow, possibly coterminously—so that every day of time in federal prison also counted against his state court jail time. And minimum security federal prison with white collar criminals was going to be an awful lot better than maximum security state prison.

Tomaso kept holding onto the hope he could maybe avoid both. He did have one card to play, he knew, but was waiting to see what his lawyer could achieve without it, since that card had a high cost. Maybe it would be too high a cost for his family, but Tomaso was desperate. And his family had mostly deserted him. Except for his daughter, and as he thought this, guilt washed over him again. He shook himself back to the present.

His lawyer kept pointing out to the prosecutors that there was an issue of proof since it was unclear what had actually happened to Nora, his wife. There was no body and no witness who could testify to what exactly occurred. She could be on a beach somewhere, happy to escape from her miserable family in Los Angeles. Moreover (Parker liked that word), no one could prove that Tomaso actually prepared the documents that were so incriminating—the ones where he committed Nora to a mental institution, and Tomaso was not acknowledging them. In fact, the feds did have a chain of title problem, which could make those documents inadmissible. Tomaso's attorney kept arguing that the evidence was objectionable and mostly circumstantial, and the prosecutors (moreover) would face a clear question of doubt, which could lead to a not guilty verdict for the federal indictment.

"Where did those documents come from, I ask you?" posed Parker. "From Nora's divorce lawyer who just happened to be in the Caribbean? And who now nobody can reach? Maybe he is off with Nora somewhere."

For their part, the prosecutors pointed to the testimony of the doctor from the Caymans, whom they intended to fly into Los Angeles for trial. They believed the judge would let in the documentary evidence showing Tomaso had signed for Nora to be committed to a locked facility and drugged into a stupor. They also pointed to the limo driver who had been told that the husband had arranged a "surprise" for Nora—and the driver had also seen a gun in the waistband of one of the kidnappers who made off with Nora. The yellow Goyard with her initials had been pawned, but recovered by the Houston detective, Nate White, implicitly proving she had been forcibly abducted.

"She was clearly taken against her will—she left behind her expensive handbag, and her phone was destroyed so it could not be tracked. No juror is going to let Mr. Ramirez off the hook when they see that the guy attempted to commit his wife into an insane asylum when she had filed divorce proceedings and was seeking to obtain financial information through court processes, which she would have ultimately been able to obtain," pointed out the lead U.S. attorney, emphasizing his disdain when referencing Tomaso's name. "That he has three children and yet was secreting away their mother will make him exceptionally unappealing. We are confident we can secure a guilty verdict, and the court will most certainly impose well in excess of fifteen years for kidnapping—and if he is found to be guilty of a felony murder, he could go for life. Five years with a plea to one count of a lesser charge is a gift to your client, and if we turn up any further evidence, that offer will be withdrawn. So the clock is ticking. Tick tock, Tomaso. Tick tock."

Tomaso inwardly groaned but followed his lawyer's orders and kept quiet, trying to show no expression.

At the end of the session, they had come to no terms, since there was no offer better than a plea and five years in federal prison for Tomaso. Parker told the U.S. attorneys that he would discuss the matter thoroughly with his client, and that he might want to reconvene to discuss other issues that might motivate the prosecutors to improve their proposal. He was met with shaking heads. Tomaso walked out of the building with Parker, who seemed in good spirits.

"That is not a bad offer," Parker was saying. "If we can get the state to agree, with good luck, you could be out in four years. That's a whole lot better than life in prison."

The two of them proceeded into the overpriced parking

lot. Jocelyn had dropped off Tomaso, and he had told her he would ask his lawyer for a lift back to the West Side, where she could pick him up at the attorney's office.

"No," Tomaso had said weakly, deathly afraid but still holding onto the hope that somehow he could avoid jail time. "There must be another way."

His lawyer shook his head as they walked. "Don't think so," Parker answered.

The two of them got into the attorney's S-Class white Mercedes. Parker searched for his exit ticket and pulled out his wallet to pay the automated machine. He was remarkably relaxed, while Tomaso could not stop sweating in his expensive retailored suit. The car pulled out into afternoon traffic and they headed for the freeway.

"The offer may get worse if they develop more evidence," Parker continued. "And I'm guessing that may happen. If they're convinced that they can get you for your wife's death, there will be no five-year deal. I'm sure that is a point that the DA will make to us when we meet tomorrow. You need to get serious about this decision."

Tomaso grimaced and perspired even more. His shirt was entirely wet. "What could we do to get a better deal?" he almost whispered. The Mercedes merged onto the 10 Freeway heading west.

"We would have to give them something they want but don't have. Like an accomplice." Parker glanced sideways at his client. "Do you have someone you could give them?"

Up to this point, Tomaso had not wanted to mention his brother, who had in fact been responsible for everything—Nora's abduction, the false documents committing her, her disappearance. Everything. Tomaso had wanted to see what the prosecutors had and were willing to offer.

Not that Tomaso intended to let his brother off the hook. No, he fully intended to seek vengeance on Miguel. But he knew Miguel would deny everything, and he would also have covered his tracks, so any accusation would be almost impossible to prove and inherently suspect. There was no corroborating evidence, nothing to prove Miguel was more responsible than Tomaso, that Miguel had duped him into a scheme that eliminated him and his family from any of the rights or benefits from RAM. Tomaso still had trouble believing his brother had so destroyed his life. Certainly, Miguel had never treated him particularly well, but this? It seemed incomprehensible. Miguel had never respected Tomaso, and he clearly did not fear any retribution from his typically inebriated, inept, ineffective little brother.

But jail time had changed Tomaso, and Miguel did not know that. No longer drunk, having suffered so much loss, slimmer and tougher, Tomaso had a new life goal, which was somehow to deliver to Miguel what he so richly deserved. So now he thought he should explore the option of giving up Miguel—it was time.

"What if there was someone?" he asked Parker, who on hearing this visibly perked up.

"What do you mean by someone?" the lawyer immediately shot back. He chanced a quick glance at his client before turning back to the bumper-to-bumper traffic.

Tomaso was slow to answer. "My older brother," he hissed.

Parker looked back at his client again. His face was serious. "What about him?"

"It was Miguel. It was all Miguel. It was his idea to teach Nora a lesson. It was his idea to commit her at some asylum in the Caribbean. It was his idea all along, and that was all that I ever agreed to. And if she is dead, he was the one who killed her."

The Mercedes picked up speed as the traffic started to break up.

The lawyer was silent for a moment.

"How do we prove that?" he posed, finally breaking the silence.

Tomaso looked grim. "I could tell them what happened, how he had it all engineered."

Parker shook his head. "They're not going to believe you. You have every motive to lie. That you finger your brother for your crimes makes you look pretty low. They are going to need some hard evidence, and unless you can give it to them, that won't play. Do you have any emails or recordings or anything like that?"

"No, I only spoke with him on the phone."

The lawyer looked quickly at Tomaso. "A cell phone?"

"Yes."

"Your cell phone? The one you have on you right now?"

Tomaso looked confused, but the lawyer sounded excited. "Yes."

"I'm going to need that phone, and you're going to have to pay a tech expert."

"What? Why?"

"We need corroborating evidence," said Parker. "Let's see what kind of metadata we can get off that phone. I am going to delay tomorrow's meeting until next week. We need to get this stuff ASAP. Maybe we can find something that will help before that meeting with the DA."

Tomaso did not know what metadata was, but Parker's enthusiasm made him start to have a little hope.

Chapter Forty-Two

The Caribbean

BRIAN CURSED as he sat in the hold of the ship with his hands tied—*again,* he thought. It was dark, and an unpleasant smell permeated the murkiness of the storage hold he was locked in. It was a tight space, and although Brian was not claustrophobic, the closeness of the space accentuated his discomfort. The motion of the ship in that small area was nauseating, and if he had anything substantial in his stomach, he would have thrown it up many times. As it was, he had dry heaved more than once. He was alone and bruised, but he had stopped bleeding. It wasn't his aches and pains that were on his mind, although they were a constant reminder of his dangerous predicament. Rather, his thoughts were on Maria and how she was being treated by the brutal drug smugglers who had "rescued" them from their small island—*Our paradise,* Brian thought.

The contrast was stark. They had so wanted a ship to find them, any ship, until they were subject to the treatment from hardened criminals whose sole interest was to ... what? Who knows? Kill them? They hadn't done that, so he assumed it was not their current plan. What else? Ransom them? *Not many folks out there would pay a ransom for me,* Brian thought ruefully. That was a troubling thought since it was clear that their captors were smugglers, likely transporting illegal drugs. They would not be interested in any witnesses to their illegal conduct. Brian did not have much hope that these cartel-types would have any compunction about putting a bullet in his head.

He and Maria had been so excited, jumping and screaming and crying out for joy when the skiff came out from the larger vessel toward them. But as the small boat came closer, they started to see several hard-looking men, staring at them with cold eyes. Then as the craft hit the sand, they saw the raised guns. The smiles faded from Maria's and Brian's faces, and they looked at each other with dismay. It was definitely not the landing party they had hoped for.

The men quickly tied their hands behind their backs and herded them onto the boat. Brian tried talking to them, but his efforts at communication ended with several fists punching his face, so he quickly realized these men were not interested in anything he had to say. Bloodied and shackled, the couple was pushed on board and presented to a man who must have been the captain or the leader or whatever. He sneered at Brian, and in Spanish he ordered that Brian be taken below to the cargo hold he now sat in. Brian saw the leader look lasciviously at Maria, resulting in Brian's protests, which were met with more beatings and more bleeding. Maria urged Brian not to resist, to comply, assuring him that she would be all right. He didn't believe her but respected her courage. He was roughly shoved below. His last sight was of Maria on deck trying to talk to the blackguard in charge.

By his best estimate, Brian had been down in this wretched room for more than two days, with only water, a few crusts of bread, and an old can to relieve himself in. He had never endured such awful conditions, but he thought not so much of himself, only of Maria. He loved her—he knew for sure now. Were they raping her? Beating her? What kind of humiliations or horrific treatment was she suffering? He thought back on their time together, their first meeting at the psychiatrist's office. She was so strong, always carrying herself with that air of authority. He admired her immediately, unlike any previous adversary, but not truly an adversary since her bearing was so appealing to him from the moment he met her.

Nora had mentioned Tomaso's sister, but only in the most negative of terms, describing her as a control freak who was completely in charge of RAM and who bestowed on Tomaso and his family only what she deemed sufficient. Apparently, both Tomaso and Nora, who did not agree on much, both found Maria to be a tyrant who did not allow her brother all that he deserved based on his birthright. What a contrast from who she really was, a thoughtful, considerate human who was always competent and could under extreme circumstances do what was necessary. Brian recognized that Maria might have been perceived by the spoiled Nora and the lazy Tomaso as overbearing, but he saw that Maria had treated them better than they deserved, better than he would have if he were RAM's CEO.

Of course, he had been tasked with attacking RAM, forcing the company to disclose closely guarded financial and business information, all toward pressuring the largest possible settlement for his client, Nora. That had been his job, so he had been naturally aligned against Maria, who would have had to approve any substantial dollar amount. But he had no client anymore, he was sure of that. And after their initial friction, Maria had been a delight to be with, almost magnetic. Then, of course, when her other evil brother had sent them both to their deaths, they had worked together to escape. She had even saved his life. On the island, they had been an amazing team, working in sync, then making love with wild passion. Brian thought a lot about this. He had never felt that way about love before with anyone—not his first wife, not any other woman he had ever been with. It was totally new to him—this love, this close and joyful intimacy combined with profound respect—and he felt like he had changed fundamentally, finding a version of himself that had never existed, a grand new dimension full of genuine emotion and heart and tenderness. The hardened cynical advocate was a thing of the past. And so, he suffered, missing her, worrying and pacing the few steps he had in his tiny jail. He prayed she was all right.

He looked up suddenly as the door to his cell opened. Two burly ruffians stood there. They motioned for him to exit, and once he did so, each grabbed hold of one of his arms and pushed him along toward the ladder leading up to the deck.

When they had first boarded the ship and Maria had seen Brian bleeding from the abuse and shoved below deck, her heart had cried out in pain. But she stayed silent, stoic, with no expression, realizing she could not show emotion or fear or trauma to these scum that had captured them.

She could not show any weakness. She had to treat these criminals like they were beneath her, as if she viewed them as peasants and of no concern to her. They would revel and be emboldened if she demonstrated the least bit of uncertainty. Maria knew that criminals like these were all basically weak and could be intimidated if she played it just right. If not, she knew that she would likely be mauled and gang raped repeatedly.

"So, I assume you have your price," she had said to the leader in Spanish, exuding confidence that she did not have.

The leader looked back at her with cruel eyes. He was not a large man, and he had scraggly oily black hair and an ugly scar on his sunburnt cheek. His arms and torso were covered with tattoos.

Maria spoke again. "Your price. What is it you charge for your victims? I assume you have done this before. Or is this your first time?" She smiled at him, the coldest, hardest smile she could muster. Still, she knew she needed to keep smiling. The leader looked slightly confused. She pressed him. "Isn't this your business?" she said sharply. "Don't you get money for people you steal?" She gave him a condescending look. "Do I have to explain all this to you?"

A puzzled look crossed the leader's face. Rom was a hardened criminal, but his business was smuggling drugs. These two were not part of his plan, and he was annoyed that they had been taken from the island and not just either left there or shot on sight. The second-in-command had decided to bring them back, likely thinking they could rape the woman and force the man into labor, doing the nasty work like cleaning the ship's head, before murdering them. Rom would not have bothered with this—it was too much of a distraction and it could lead to trouble. He did not need any added uncertainties on this voyage. But now here he was, confronting this aggressive woman—not like the women he was used to. She wasn't timid or scared—she seemed like a boss, like she was in charge. Then when he heard the word money, he started to think that maybe it had been a good idea, that he could make some serious coin if she was worth it.

"That is," Maria continued, "unless you don't need an extra twenty-five thousand dollars in U.S. currency—dollars. I have heard that's the going rate these days amongst you pirates who ransom people." She started the negotiation low but hoped it was the right amount since it was just a guess. When Rom's eyes widened, she knew she had hit pay dirt.

"That is not enough," he said slowly, clearly thinking. "You are very rich and worth much more than that, isn't that so, *Señora*? And your husband, if that's what he is, what is he worth? Or shall we just throw him overboard?" Now Rom smiled broadly.

Inwardly, Maria shuddered, but she maintained her calm mien. "Ha, that is one way to get rid of a husband, but I think I will keep him. Let's say that is another twenty-five thousand dollars. And that is a high price—fifty thousand dollars. But it only works if you deliver both of us—and in one piece." This last point Maria delivered with emphasis and a severe but confident look directly into the cruel eyes of the leader. He laughed, and she worried she had overplayed her hand.

"I think your people will pay more for the both of you, especially if you come back in, as you say, one piece. I think for only fifty thousand dollars, maybe we could keep a few pieces of both of you and send them later. Or feed them to the fish." Rom had clearly started to enjoy this negotiation. He was being paid a good sum to smuggle illegal drugs around the Caribbean, but it was dangerous work, he knew, and his "client" was no understanding entity, but the Mexican cartel that claimed predominance in the region. Any shipment issues, such as a missed handoff or some missing product, even a small amount, could easily mean his head on a spit, and only after horrific torture.

He'd never had a problem except for once, when he caught a couple of his men sampling a shipment. Knowing his own risk, he ruthlessly strung both men up on the deck and in front of the whole crew, cut their eyes out, then their ears off, then their nose, then each one of their fingers and toes. Each time he cut, he cauterized the wound with a fiery hot iron, causing even more agony but preventing too much blood loss, since he did not want them to bleed to death immediately. Rom let them hang like that for two days, blood oozing out, without food or water, before they finally expired. When they made port, the leader personally went in search of replacement product, and when he delivered the shipment, it was fully replenished. No cartel member ever learned of the event, but the whole crew talked of it often, sometimes in fear, other times in awe. Rom was not popular, but no one had touched the product or crossed him ever since. Rom had solidified his status as leader, and no one called him by his first name again. He was just "boss" or "leader."

Maria knew she had to be careful in her negotiations, since this wretched fellow could easily use Brian as a way to significantly up the price. She proposed that perhaps the ransom could go up a bit, but not too much—her people were not that wealthy, so she suggested sixty thousand dollars. Rom scratched his chin and then ordered she be incarcerated in his cabin. He did tell his men that she was not to be touched, though, at least not yet, so she breathed a sigh of relief. Clearly, he was going to make her sweat a bit before resuming negotiations.

She sat in the modest captain's cabin and worried about Brian. She knew his accommodations and treatment were not as good—in fact likely awful. She was hoping he hadn't suffered more beatings.

So, she waited—there was nothing else for her to do—and she thought and thought and planned and planned. She realized she had to figure out how to get funds for a ransom. She and Brian had been missing for weeks now and were likely presumed dead. Miguel was most certainly in control of RAM—that had been his plot all along. She realized it was Miguel who spirited Nora away and not Tomaso, who had been set up to take the fall. Eliminating both siblings meant Marta would have little choice but to empower Miguel at RAM. He would be in control of the financials and likely intercept any plea for money that came to the company, so she knew that was no option.

No, she did not want Miguel to learn she and Brian had escaped. She needed to be back in the U.S. before she dealt with him, and that alone would be tricky. She could make contact with her mother, but that was not the best plan. Marta's phone, cell, and email were all routed through RAM, and Miguel could easily be monitoring Marta's phone; in fact, Maria knew that was likely. If Maria got through to Marta by some different source, she might even mistakenly alert Miguel, not recognizing he was the evil culprit who had orchestrated such horror. Or Marta might act precipitously against Miguel before Maria had returned and could plan the most effective way to deal with him. The terms she had struck with the lenders to close the hotel transaction required that no material change in RAM's structure or leadership occur, and if it did, all debts would become due, with penalties. That would destroy the company. Maria also did not know to what extent Marta had empowered Miguel. She suspected her crafty brother would require some sort of blank check or total control. Maria had to get back first, figure out the status, and then put together a plan to deal with Miguel without hurting RAM.

The next morning, Rom opened the door followed by a mate who carried a tray of porridge, a crust of bread, and an urn of black coffee. He smiled at her but waited for the mate to leave before speaking. Maria realized that the leader had a price now.

"One million dollars," he said. "That is what it will take for both of you to leave in one piece. If it's less, I don't think your husband is going with you."

Maria gasped, then put on a stern face. "That's outrageous," she said in a measured tone. "Too much. That's not possible."

The leader shrugged his shoulders. "That's the number." He sat down at his desk and turned his chair toward her. Maria sat on the cot that was the only other place to sit in the cabin. "I could take a little less, but then your husband will be returning without a few of his parts, maybe your favorite part." The leader leered at her.

Again, Maria kept her composure. "Whatever number we agree on," she began, "how can we trust you? How can we make the exchange?"

The leader laughed. "You can't trust me. I am a criminal. But you have no choice now, do you?"

"Okay, so how do you want the funds? In dollars?"

"Crypto. I don't want phony money. Bitcoin. What's it at now?" Rom pulled out his cell phone. "Trading at 70,000 U.S. per coin today."

"Do you even have an account?" Maria asked, her mind racing.

The leader nodded his head. "Oh yes, of course. How do you think I get paid?"

"So how will you set us free if you get paid?" Maria pressed. She knew the devil was in the details, and that if this pirate had the chance, he would hold on to them and ask for more.

"I can just let you go at the next port. We arrive the day after tomorrow. I have a shipment that needs to be dropped in Jamaica. That is where we will be. I am not dropping it in Kingston Harbour, but we can stop there. I get my million, and the two of you can just walk away. No problem." Rom tried to put on a sincere and genuine expression, but he simply looked like a killer trying to claim innocence.

"I would need to call my contacts to make arrangements," Maria said, looking at the leader's cell phone. "And I see you appear to have service. I need to see what they can raise and if they can get it to you. Will you let me use your phone?" Maria reached out her hand.

"Not so fast, *Señora*. Who would you be calling? Who can get me that kind of money? Not you, I am sure, and not that husband of yours, who by the way is not doing so well. His circumstances," and the leader looked around the cabin, "are not as pleasant as yours and they clearly do not suit him. I hope he will be fine, but I fear maybe not if he is maintained in that way much longer."

Maria tried not to appear concerned, but she could not

help a reaction at the thought of Brian. She loved him. She knew that all too well now. "You are asking for a lot of money," she said slowly. "An unreasonable ransom. I don't have that kind of money, and I can't access any crypto site anyway. I would need to talk with my aunt and uncle. They are overseas in Europe. To do what you are asking, you need to let me contact them right now. Maybe we can set something up. But I need to call them. You do have service, yes?" He nodded. "Hopefully I can get them on the phone." She reached out her hand. Cautiously, the leader handed Maria his cell phone.

"Put the phone on speaker," he ordered. "And do not try anything that I would not like. I think you know what I mean."

"I won't," she replied.

She dialed her aunt Francesca's cell phone number. She had not spoken with her aunt in a few months, and then only in passing to discuss some distributions from RAM to her aunt and uncle. She spoke with Uncle Jamey more frequently, but only about the production and distribution of RAM's premier Scotch whisky.

Maria did not much care for scotch, and the product did not bring in much revenue. The cost of the farm and distillery in Scotland was barely covered by its sales, and some years the gross income was not even enough to do that. Maria had often wondered if her mother had been wise to invest in scotch, but she knew Marta had not been motivated by profit. That RAM distributed a small amount of whisky certainly made sense, just as the company had also sold the rum that Miguel had developed. But neither of these product lines made any real money. Tequila had been their profit source, and now Maria hoped the hotel business would take the place of the liquor business as the leading source of profit for the company. But allowing these smaller, less profitable items had kept the family together in a way; it focused everyone on RAM's success, so Maria had done her best to support the whisky business. It had also kept her in regular contact with Francesca, which had made Marta happy, and now it might make a difference in her freedom from kidnappers. Fortunately, the phone rang only three times before her aunt picked up.

"Hello? Hello? Who is this? You better not be another one of those spammers."

"It's me, Aunt Fran, it's Maria."

"Maria? Maria? Is it you? My God, we thought you were gone forever," Francesca gushed. "Oh my child, how are you? Where are you? Is it really you?"

"Yes, yes, it is your niece, Maria. And I cannot tell you how great it is to hear your voice."

"Oh Maria, but tell me something that you would know, just so I know it is you. Tell me something that no one else would necessarily know. I need to make sure."

"Okay. Remember when my mom bought the loan on Uncle Jamey's family's property? Well, do you recall how angry you were at first, and you started yelling at Marta that she had no right to interfere with your life, and then a moment later you started crying and hugging her because she had saved Jamey's family whisky business and you wanted to stay in Scotland?"

Francesca gasped. "Maria, it is you. That is a pretty powerful memory to bring up, but a good choice. Now I know it is you. But where are you and where have you been? I haven't heard anything from your mother—she is so distraught. Does she even know you are all right?"

Maria looked up from the phone at the leader, who now was grinning. "Well, Aunt Fran, no, I am not entirely all right and I really need your help in a very big way. So please listen. First, you need to know that I have been kidnapped, and the kidnappers are here with me now listening to this phone call." Maria heard her aunt gasp. "I am actually calling on their phone. So please do not say anything that you would not want them to hear. And since you know me, I am sure you will understand what I am saying."

Francesca was aghast, panting, but calmed herself. Maria was going to speak in code, and she had to listen carefully to correctly interpret her meaning.

"Oh my," said Francesca. "This is so terrible. Have they hurt you? Are you okay? What can I do?"

"Marta does not know. You are my first and only call. I cannot contact Marta because this all is because of Miguel. I can explain this part later. But it is important that the people at our company," Maria emphasized these last words, "specifically just the people in charge of the company, must not be told what's happening."

Francesca understood Maria immediately. Miguel should not know, but that did not include others, like the authorities. She realized that Maria had signaled her that the police could and should be contacted.

Maria continued. "I am unhurt and on their boat, it's like a fishing vessel, not too uncomfortable—maybe sixty to seventy feet and with a blue hull. We are heading for Jamaica—Kingston Harbour. We should have someone appropriate there to meet us, just like you, Marta, Carlos, and Pedro did because of Sotero. I know from my mom that you did a very proper job taking care of things then. I am hoping you can do the very same thing for me now."

Again, Francesca understood that Maria was telling her not only how to recognize her captors' ship but also that she was requesting a surprise attack with lethal force. RAM's history had always been not to be taken advantage of and to fight. The family was rarely given any other option, and Maria believed that again there was no choice but to deal with her captors aggressively and by force.

"I need to be properly greeted there," Maria said. "They won't release me without ransom money, and I need your help to get what they need for my safe release."

"Oh no, my dear. Are you all right? Have they hurt you?"

The leader spoke up. "Your niece has not been hurt—at least not yet. And if you want to see her alive along with her husband, you'd better listen to her and be prepared to follow instructions and pay up." He said all this in the most commanding tone he could muster.

Francesca was silent for a moment.

"Her husband?" she said.

"Yes," Maria said quickly. "There are the two of us. We both need to get away from these people. And I cannot go to Marta or Miguel. You are my only hope for the ransom money."

Francesca was quiet again for a moment.

"What do you need?" she asked.

"One million American dollars for the life of your niece and her husband. And all of it in bitcoin," the leader said.

Francesca audibly gasped, then was silent for a moment.

"That is a huge amount of money. And how do I get that to you? And how do I know you will release my niece and her, uh, husband?"

The leader laughed. "You will have to trust me."

"For one million dollars, I will not be trusting you. You

can provide the account number by texting it to me, but I cannot pay until I know they are free."

This haggling continued for a bit, and they finally agreed to terms. The ship was to dock in Jamaica in two days. Francesca needed the two days to arrange for the funds and convert them to crypto currency. When the boat arrived, Maria was to call Francesca on Rom's phone to confirm they were in port. Francesca would then arrange to transfer the first $250,000. Once the transfer was confirmed, Maria would be allowed to walk off the boat, at which point she was to call again, and the next payment of $500,000 would be transferred. Rom was persuaded that Maria would not leave her "husband" behind. The final $250,000 would be transferred after Brian had walked off the boat and was on the pier, accompanied by the leader himself, who would be holding a knife against Brian's ribs. They would stop at the end of the pier, and Maria would greet them and confirm that Brian was safe and on dry land. Once the payment was made, Rom promised that Maria and Brian could just walk away, and the leader would return to his ship and quickly set sail—at least that is what he promised. If the last payment was not made, he'd also promised to put his blade into Brian's ribs, shoot Maria, and toss them both into the water to drown or bleed to death.

When the negotiation was finished, Maria added a final term. "You also need to release my husband now from wherever he is and bring him to me. You can lock us both up in this cabin. But I need to see that he's okay. That is part of the deal, you know."

"What? You need to have sex with your husband?" the leader responded lasciviously. "Have you missed it that much? I can provide that to you, if you would like." Rom laughed derisively, but he relented and agreed to have Brian brought up from his horrible confines and deposited with Maria. Pleased with himself and thinking about the money he was going to receive, he left her to give the orders to his men.

Maria watched as they dragged Brian out of the hold and pushed him up the stairs. Tears came to her eyes. He looked so ragged and tired and spent, and he limped, obviously in pain. His face was cut and bruised.

When he arrived at the door of the cabin, she ran to him, crying, feeling so guilty that this had happened to him and he had suffered so much. It was all her fault—her brothers had brought this about, and she felt responsible for all that Brian had experienced and lost. He was a good man and was just doing his job as a lawyer, but the Ramirez family had caused him so much undeserved harm. It seemed that everyone close to RAM had to suffer in some way. Brian looked at her and smiled weakly, holding out his arms.

They embraced and held each other for a very long time before saying a word.

Chapter Forty-Three

Miami

IGUEL CURSED. He sat in the new offices of RAM at a sleek, modern design desk chair. A teakwood table stood next to him on which sat a tall glass of iced coffee spiked with RAM tequila and also a four-inch statuette of a ram snorting and looking fierce, nostrils ablaze, horns jutting out, ready to charge. He looked out of the floor-to-ceiling windows from the twenty-seventh floor of the office tower that provided an expansive panorama of the Biscayne Bay, Miami Beach, and the Atlantic Ocean beyond. The view was spectacular, but things were not going as smoothly as he had expected.

Miguel had secured these offices well before he had sent Maria and Brian and Ricardo and Javier to their death. He had been so confident that his plan to take over RAM would work, he'd hired a full staff of employees: secretaries, accountants, and salespeople. He had left it to his CFO to interview and make salary arrangements and had taken out another loan to start up his new RAM headquarters before he headed out to the Caymans to hatch his plot. Miguel even paid extra to expedite tenant improvements—he wanted a totally modern look, streamlined desks, hard-scape, almost sterile. The only furniture that was comfort-able in the entire space were the chairs and sofa in his office that only he was allowed to sit on. He wanted everyone else to be uncomfortable.

He looked at his CFO, his old accountant, Sammy Levine, who was wearing a rumpled suit and standing in front of him holding a file full of papers. Miguel did not par-ticularly like Sammy—he was a Jew—but Miguel trusted him, as long as he paid him enough and of course threat-ened him sufficiently. This was important because Miguel did not actually want to work hard or be involved in all the petty decisions in running a business. He just wanted to be the king without any day-to-day responsibilities. Today, however, Sammy was giving Miguel bad news and asking him what to do about it, and this made Miguel start to really dislike Sammy.

"Just call them and tell them they will get paid in due course," Miguel instructed. "All those fuckers care about is their money. Let them know they can't fuck with us—we'll sue them. And we'll accuse them of discrimination. Even though we make their payments, they call our loan because they hate minority-owned businesses, Hispanics particu-larly. Find a lawyer, a Mexican or a Puerto Rican. Make sure he has a Spanish name and is olive-skinned. Those white motherfuckers will quake in their boots when you tell them we are going to sue their bigoted asses. This is Miami and you can't get away with treating Latinos badly here. Tell them we will issue a press release. Hell, it should be good publicity—our sales may just go up."

Miguel took a sip of his spiked drink and patted the ram statue. Sammy looked at him with a deadpan expression and extended the file for Miguel to take, but Miguel ignored him and continued to look out the window.

"Sure, sure," Sammy responded quietly, looking away. "But you need to understand they have the right to do this. We've breached multiple covenants of the loan agreements. We would lose in court. And they may tell me that they have no choice, that directions have come from the top of the bank, their CEO."

"Well, get me his name. We will sue him first and claim he just hates anyone who is not white." Miguel laughed. "This could be fun."

"There's more though," Sammy continued. "We've also received a demand letter from the New York landlord, since we walked out on our lease. They are requiring us to continue paying the full rent, plus they are charging back rent that had been free but suspended. But due to our breach of lease, they claim the free rent is no longer free and is now due on top of everything else. That is a boatload of money."

"That landlord can go screw. Or sue. We will tie him up in court down here for years and years." Miguel kept patting and even rubbing the ram statue.

Sammy was shaking his head. "The lease provides for arbitration in New York, which will be fast and lead to a judgment within months. And once the lenders for the hotel deal declare default and start seizure and foreclosure proceedings, the loan you took out for all the ships will also be breached, and they will come after us too and repossess our vessels. You may recall that you used our planes as added collateral, so they will repo those too. And our trucks. That will stop our imports and exports, all our distribution, so the money will dry up, and we will be in violation of all our agreements with suppliers. Our third-party relationships will go away, and we will lose everything—the hotels, the ships, the planes, the trucks, even the farmland in Mexico. With all that debt due, the banks may even seek a receiver to take over all our operations and throw us out of control of RAM. Then we will have to declare bankruptcy to stop that, and probably the court will appoint some trustee to take over and throw us out anyway."

Miguel looked at Sammy threateningly, then turned back to the view. "That better not happen," he said menacingly. "You better prevent it." Miguel picked up the ram statue and shook it at Sammy with the horns pointed in his direction.

There was a knock at the door, and a small thirty-something Cuban woman walked in carrying a box. "Excuse me," she said, looking down, "but this was just delivered by a process server."

Sammy looked at her with a pale face. "You didn't sign for it, did you?" he asked weakly. Miguel glared at the woman.

"I had no choice," she replied, looking up. "He said he was going to barge in here and drop it on *Señor* Miguel's lap if I did not sign for it." She walked over and placed the box on the table next to Miguel where the ram statue that he was holding had been sitting earlier.

"You idiot!" Miguel screamed at her, now shaking the ram at her. "You good-for-nothing piece of shit. He was bluffing. He has no right to do that. Now you have screwed us over. Get out of here. Now! You are fired."

The woman ran out with a terrified look. Sammy went over to the box to examine its contents. "Probably from the lenders," he said. He opened it and saw multiple complaints. "Oh God," he whispered. "It's not the lenders."

"What now?" Miguel demanded.

Sammy picked up one of the documents and looked at it. "These are lawsuits, a bunch of them, all wrongful termination cases, all against RAM and you personally, from the New York employees you fired."

Miguel ignored him, put the ram down on the table next to the box, and turned back to the windows. "Big deal," he said.

"Miguel, these are serious," said Sammy, looking at one of the complaints. "They say you discriminated and harassed and all kinds of horrible things. They are seeking punitive damages and their fees too. And you won't believe who is representing them all."

Miguel turned back to Sammy. "Who?"

"It's Colleen Stevens. She opened her own law firm immediately after she quit. She is on every lawsuit. And there are over thirty of them." Sammy was horrified. "We're not going to be able to make it out of this," he whispered. "RAM is doomed."

"No, it's not," Miguel said slowly as he turned to look out the window, his mind plotting. "We can bankrupt some of the entities, which will get rid of all those claims, and relocate to the Caymans with a new company. I can run it out of the plantation."

Sammy looked at Miguel with an open mouth. "I can't

go to the Caymans," he said. "And besides, the claims against you are non-dischargeable in bankruptcy."

"What?" said Miguel, looking at Sammy with the first sign of concern.

"Miguel, bankruptcy won't get you out of the fraud and deceit and malice they are suing you for. You're going to be liable for all of that. And this is in federal court—the Caymans will recognize a United States judgment. You would have to go to a different country altogether to avoid all of this. I am not sure where, but somewhere else."

Miguel picked up the statue of the ram and threw it hard at the window, cracking the glass. Then he picked up his iPad and started searching for countries that would not allow extradition to the U.S. He realized he might need to run after all—that his location in the Caymans was just too well known, and that he had to have a backup plan. And he also began to realize that managing a large international company with complex financial dealings was a bit more challenging than he had recognized. *Okay,* he thought, *maybe Maria was better at this than I thought, but so what? I hated her and I hated that Marta favored her and I hated that she was my superior and I hated every one of her employees. And I hated Nora too, and I always hated Tomaso. I don't even like Marta. They all can go to hell.*

Sammy looked at Miguel and knew he had to somehow get away from him.

Chapter Forty-Four

Los Angeles

TOMASO SAT IN HIS STUDY, seething with anger. His leg ached from the ankle bracelet he was wearing that prevented him from leaving the city limits of Los Angeles. He could go to court or to his lawyer's office; in fact, he could go to the grocery store or a restaurant if he wanted. But if he left LA's city limits, the device would be triggered, and he would be in violation of his bail requirements. Then his right to be free pending trial would be revoked, and Tomaso would end up back in jail.

That was someplace he decided he was just not going back to. His daughter had drained her college fund for his freedom and his new lawyer, and he felt horribly guilty about that, but his remorse only fueled his rage at his brother Miguel for setting him up. *I was such a fool,* he thought ruefully, *a pawn in his game to oust me and my family and gain control of the company.*

He had tried calling Miguel again and again, but his efforts were always blocked. He had spoken with Marta many times, so he knew that Maria was missing, and like Nora, he presumed that Miguel was at fault and that she had suffered the same fate as Nora. He had realized that control of RAM was Miguel's plan, and that because of the terms of the Family Master Trust, Tomaso's family was cut out. The removal of Maria had clearly completed Miguel's evil plot—Tomaso knew his brother was bad, but he was truly astonished at how vicious and cruel Miguel was. How had his brother come to such a place, he wondered, but he just became even angrier as he thought about that, realizing how blind he had been to Miguel's perfidy.

He had to do something. Marta was paralyzed, heartbroken over Maria. Besides, Miguel had her sign an irrevocable assignment of all her rights and powers in RAM, and she was powerless to act for six months. There were five months left, but even after that, Marta had few options with Maria gone and him tied up in criminal proceedings.

Tomaso's lawyer had been right about a few things—the state had agreed to let the feds take the lead. The U.S. attorneys had handed his phone over to a top forensic, who in turn had indeed found in metadata what might be corroborating evidence for Tomaso's accusations against Miguel. For example, the scan demonstrated that Miguel had contacted Tomaso, not the other way around, for a twenty-minute phone call a week prior to Nora's disappearance. Several short follow-up calls were also initiated by Miguel to Tomaso. What was not on Tomaso's phone were any calls, texts, or emails to the Caymans, and certainly not to the locked facility where Tomaso had supposedly planned to incarcerate Nora. While the prosecutors knew Tomaso could have used some other phone to communicate, this lack of any contact clearly was consistent with Tomaso's story that he did not arrange to abduct Nora. Of course, the metadata revealed no other nefarious communications with any Mexican mob member or helicopter pilot or limousine service in Texas. Again, this did not prove Tomaso was innocent, but it was consistent with his claim that Miguel had set up everything, that he had only gone along with it and signed some documents Miguel had faxed to his LA office.

What the prosecutors did discover were lots of phone calls to Tomaso's now ex-girlfriend, Rosie, so this was not helpful to Tomaso since it arguably gave him more of a motive to eliminate his wife. While the phone records were a mixed bag, the fact that he willingly surrendered them to the prosecutors and explained what he expected them to find and how the metadata was consistent with his tale of woe did help his case. But only a bit, since the phone calls not only enhanced Tomaso's motive to eliminate Nora, but also proved he had conspired with his brother to commit her. Then there was the felony murder rule—which is simply that if someone dies while a person is in the process of committing a felony, that person is also deemed guilty of murder, even if not planned or intended or wanted.

So, while the prosecutors opened up an investigation into Miguel, they had not lowered their offer much, and Tomaso saw himself doing hard time for years unless he went to trial and his lawyer somehow won, which not only seemed impossible but Tomaso could not afford. His daughter's money had taken him far but would not pay for a full-blown jury trial, and his lawyers were not about to do that without another six-figure retainer.

Tomaso looked ruefully at the ankle bracelet on his right

leg. It was locked on snugly, and a green light pulsated from it, indicating it was working just fine. He was allowed a very limited distance, and if he broke the location restrictions of the device, the green light would turn red, and the device would start beeping transmissions to the police, providing his location and the fact that he was now in violation, likely running. They would swoop down somehow and pick him up and throw him back in jail for good.

Tomaso looked around his study at the sports memorabilia on the walls. He had collected quite a lot of it over the years, attending innumerable fundraising events for his kids' schools and aggressively overbidding at silent auctions on any sports item that caught his eye, whether signed photographs or framed jerseys or autographed baseballs and basketballs. Although he was not much of an athlete himself, he loved to fantasize about himself being a famous superstar. Usually his dreams started with golf, since he actually played that game and was a decent club player. He was renowned in his imagination for his many holes-in-one, and great players like Tiger Woods and Arnold Palmer were his friends. Tomaso's mind would wander, and suddenly he was a Hall of Fame quarterback holding multiple Super Bowl rings, one for each finger, and Tom Brady was his equal. He might then turn to tennis, and John McEnroe was his doubles partner, but Tomaso went on to win singles in both the French Open and Wimbledon. These daydreams could go on for hours and had sometimes included Rosie, along with several of her "friends," all of whom massaged and pleasured him. He would occasionally fall asleep and his fantasies continued, causing him wonderful naps here in his plush study, on his soft leather sofa surrounded by comfy throw pillows.

Now he could not find his way back to any of his wonderful daydreams. Every time he tried, instead of fame and fortune and adulation, his mind turned to failure and prison; he found himself in jail, being repeatedly beaten and raped by black gangs, Mexican gangs, and skinheads. His beautiful fantasies had become nightmares, and he stood up and began ripping his once precious sports memorabilia off the walls and throwing each item to the floor or breaking them to bits. He finally stopped after picking up a baseball signed by Tommy Lasorda and Fernando Valensuela and throwing it so hard at the window that the glass shattered loudly.

His daughter, Jocelyn, burst into the room, followed by his son Justin.

"What are you doing?" she cried out. She looked around the room in dismay. "Dad, you need to hold it together." She shook her head disapprovingly at him, and he looked down sheepishly.

"I'm sorry," he said tearfully.

She gave him a stern look. "Don't do this again," she said forcefully, the child having become the parent. "And clean this up. Justin, help him. I am too disgusted with him to help."

She turned and stalked out of the room. Justin walked in slowly, looking around at the mess. Tomaso sat down on the sofa and held his head in his hands. The bracelet on his ankle continued to blink green. Justin walked over and sat on the sofa next to his father, not too closely but still on the same couch.

"Actually, Dad, there is something I guess I have to tell you," the boy said. "You're going to find out anyway."

Tomaso raised his head, still with a pathetic expression. "What?"

Now the son looked down, not meeting his father's gaze. "Well, today I was expelled—thrown out of school," Justin said meekly.

Tomaso was so consumed by his own desperate circumstances, he had not even thought about his son. For a moment, he forgot about himself.

"What? Why? When? What is this about?"

Justin was silent.

Tomaso looked at him intently. "Come on, out with it."

Justin kept looking down. "They kind of caught me with some drugs. But they weren't mine—they were someone else's, but they happened to be in my locker."

"What do you mean, they weren't yours? And when did this happen?"

"Today. I mean, it happened this afternoon, and they told me that I was expelled, that I could not come back to school ever. It was really unfair. I guess they're sending you a letter and maybe calling you. But I think they were trying to decide whether to report it to the police."

"The police?" Tomaso groaned. He was already in enough trouble.

When Justin said this, like an eerie coincidence, the doorbell rang, followed by a loud knocking. His son looked at him with fear. Tomaso headed to the front door, but Jocelyn was in front of him, and the door was already open by the time he got there. Three policemen stood outside, one of whom was holding a paper in his hand. Jocelyn just stared at them in disbelief. Police at her home again. When the officer holding the paper saw Tomaso, he turned his attention to him.

"Tomaso Ramirez? I am Sergeant Brewer, LAPD. We would like to enter your home and do a search of the premises." The policeman waved the paper. "We do have a search warrant to search the premises, and specifically the room of one Justin Ramirez who resides here. Will you allow us to enter and proceed?"

Police often ask nicely to enter and search, even when they have a search warrant or probable cause. That way, they add another argument to the legitimacy of the search: permission. Probable cause can be debated and there can always be some flaw in obtaining a search warrant, but if the occupants agree to let the police in, then it is very hard for a defense lawyer to argue that the search was illegal. Jocelyn didn't know this and was already shaking her head yes and agreed before Tomaso could speak.

"Certainly, officers. Please come in."

The three police immediately entered the dwelling. Two went upstairs while the other one who was holding the paper headed in the direction of the kitchen. Justin had finally come out of the study and was watching the police as they headed up the stairs. As they did so, he ran out the front door to his Toyota Rav4 parked on the street in front of the mansion near where the police had parked their squad car.

"Justin, where are you going?" Jocelyn called after him.

But Tomaso knew what his son was doing. He was running.

That was something Tomaso was desperate to do himself. "He's gone," Tomaso said slowly to Jocelyn.

"That little jerk," she responded.

From upstairs one of the police called out. "Sergeant, we found it. It's up here."

The sergeant came back out of the kitchen and bounded up the stairs. "Which room is Justin Ramirez's room?" he asked as he passed Tomaso and Jocelyn.

"The blue room on the right," Jocelyn called out.

Soon the officers came back down the stairs holding a large suitcase.

"The blue room with the Grateful Dead poster, that is Justin Ramirez's room?" quizzed the sergeant.

"Yes," Jocelyn spoke up.

The policeman looked at Tomaso. "Is that correct, sir? Is Justin Ramirez's room that blue room with the rock 'n' roll posters?"

Tomaso nodded his head. "Yes, officers."

"And are you familiar with this suitcase?" the sergeant asked.

"No, I have never seen it before," he said. Jocelyn was shaking her head no as well.

"We're taking this suitcase," explained the sergeant. "It's filled with what appear to be illegal substances, drugs of all kinds. But we have to take it back to the lab rats to test it and verify for court."

He began walking to his squad car when the landline phone at the house rang. Jocelyn turned and ran to answer it.

"Dad, it's for you."

Tomaso felt as if he were in a daze, a bad waking dream. He stumbled over to take the phone from his daughter.

"Mr. Ramirez, this is Dean Ronney from the Brentroads School. I am so sorry to have to say this, but as you may already know, your son Justin was expelled from our school today. It has become clear that he has been dealing illegal drugs at school and has been doing so for some time."

Tomaso was shaking his head. Everything was falling apart. The dean continued.

"Several students came forward and informed us, and

then others confessed. With all that substantive information, we felt we had no choice but to open up his locker. We don't like to invade our students' privacy, but for the safety and well-being of other students, we felt we had no choice. His locker was filled with all kinds of illegal drugs. As you know, the school has a no-tolerance policy, and in this case, the gravity of his conduct is truly abhorrent. He is not just a user but is a supplier and encourages other students here to violate the rules and engage in a terrible habit. This is simply way beyond what we could ever accept. At this point, he is not welcome back at school and will be escorted off if found here. And the police have been called. Did you know about his drug habits, sir?"

"Uh, no."

"Well frankly, I encourage you to pay more attention to your children. And as for your daughter and other son, their status at our school is being reviewed. We don't believe that either were involved with the peddling of contraband, but it is hard to believe that neither one knew it was going on. Our honor code requires them to report such improper conduct, even if it is their own brother—in fact, especially if it is a member of their family. We will get back to you about Jocelyn and William, but for now they are both on probation until a decision is made. We will get back to you next week on that. Do you understand? Do you have any questions?"

"Uh, no."

"And be advised, the authorities have been contacted."

"I figured."

The dean curtly hung up. Tomaso put his head in his hands. Everything was going in the wrong direction. He realized he needed to talk to his lawyer. He called Parker and told the receptionist it was an emergency. Parker called back ten minutes later. Tomaso had not moved. He answered the phone and told his lawyer the entire story.

"This is bad," said Parker. "Really bad. I thought I was making some headway with the U.S. attorney—telling him how your kids needed you and how you could help them catch the bigger fish, Miguel. Do you realize they can prosecute you for all those drugs, claiming that you were the one orchestrating the sale of drugs by your kid at school? They were in your house, you were there. And you're not exactly going to be viewed as a model citizen in their eyes. No one is going to think anything other than you are a terrible father—negligent at best, but the drugs were in your house. You are the responsible party. This will blow any chance of arguing for home confinement for sure. They'll think the kids will be better off in a foster home. And I don't believe there's much of a chance for you to get off if you go to trial. You'll be looking at maybe fifteen years, plus drug charges could add more. And it will cost you another two hundred thousand dollars for a trial retainer, and that is non-refundable. And you will most likely lose anyway."

Tomaso hung up the phone. He started to cry. "I am going to do something," he said out loud through his tears. "I can't go to jail for the rest of my life. I just can't." And a plot started to form in his mind, an angry one, a desperate one, a vengeful one.

And for the first time in quite a while, Tomaso began to smile.

Chapter Forty-Five

Jamaica

THE SMUGGLERS' BOAT was moored at the end of the pier in Kingstown. It was two o'clock in the morning and the port area was silent, not a soul in sight. Rom had quietly maneuvered his ship into the harbor after midnight, planning on using the darkness to complete his bargain, get rid of his prisoners, and make his ransom. He hoped it would all work out cleanly, since he did not want to kill Brian anyway—that was just bad karma. His optimism was certainly spurred by the thousands of dollars' worth of bitcoin now sitting in his account. Aunt Fran had seen to it that the first part of the ransom was paid in the manner instructed. Rom was ready to release his first hostage.

He had actually grown to like Maria; she had been so tough, so confident, not like the women he frequently ravaged on his stops around the islands. Those women only showed fear, which excited him, but Maria seemed not to fear him at all, which had kind of intimidated him at first. Later, he grew to respect her—as much as anyone could respect a bossy white woman. Well, she wasn't only white, she was Hispanic, but she talked like one of those entitled American tourists.

He walked her down the gangplank onto the pier, then all the way to land. Maria had placed the first call to Francesca, and the bitcoin had promptly shown up in Rom's account. Now was the time for the second call.

"This is it," he said to her. "You need to get me the rest of my money if you ever want to see your husband again." He offered her his phone.

She placed the call, leaving it on speaker, and again Francesca answered.

"I'm here," she told her aunt. "At the end of the pier. I'm safe." Her aunt assured her the second payment would be coming quickly. Maria hung up, handed the phone back to Rom, and stepped onto land and away from his grasp. That moment gave her a profound sense of relief. She was back to civilization, and no longer a prisoner. Yes, she still had to get Brian free, but after the ordeal of the past month or so, just stepping onto land in this quiet area of Kingston Town was like a change of life, a renewal.

"Hold on," Rom said. "I need to verify." He looked at his phone. After a few minutes, he smiled. "It seems your *tia* wants you back. Now, I need the rest."

"Don't worry, you will get your money," she said to him. "She said it will take a bit more time, but it will happen and I will be here. Just come back with my husband. When he is here, I can call again to confirm and she will make the transfer."

"It better not take long," he said. "I need to be off in two hours, so if the money does not come, you will not be seeing him again. I'll come out when I see the final deposit." Rom smiled, and Maria shuddered.

"No, you must come back in half an hour with Brian and I will call my aunt and then you'll get your money. Just be ready."

Rom turned around and walked back to his ship to retrieve his other prisoner. He was confident now that he would be paid. As soon as she saw he was out of sight, Maria turned and broke into a run. She was making her way to a boathouse she assumed was her rendezvous point. She saw the building ahead of her, but it was dark and looked deserted. However, when she was a few feet away, the door opened. An officer with the Jamaican police force stood there and beckoned her in. Rushing in, she suddenly was being hugged by her Aunt Francesca and her Uncle Jamey.

"Oh, my dear, my dear," was all that Francesca could say.

"We'll get those blokes and teach them not to mess with our clan," her uncle added.

Maria was crying for joy. "How did you figure all this out? How did you both get here?"

"We've been working with the U.S. embassy and the Jamaican police force. Everything is in place. But who is this husband? I did not know that you remarried."

"Not yet," Maria said, and then realized the presumption in her statement. "But he is very special to me."

"Well, he will soon be free and we will be flying you back to the States," promised Francesca. "I think I will go with you. It has been a long time since I saw my sister."

"Good," said Maria, pulling out of her embrace and looking thoughtful. "I'll need you there anyway, if I'm right, because I think all of you need to be present and sign for what I have in mind." Then, realizing what her aunt had done, she said, "Aunt Fran, thank you so much, but how, how did you get that much money in bitcoin so you could pay my ransom?"

Jamey chuckled. "Well, my lassie, this game of ransom and payment by bitcoin is not a new trick by these rascals. We had some help, from some of the folks that I know."

"But to lose so much money!"

"Oh, I don't plan on anyone losing it," commented Jamey with a grim smile. "Except for those scum who took you prisoner." His expression turned angry. "But how did that happen? We could not figure that out. Did they come to the Caymans and steal you away?"

"I will tell you everything, but not now. I have to get back and get Brian."

"Brian's his name, eh?" said Jamey.

Francesca looked at Maria and smiled. "Well, I hope he'll understand that you are saving his life."

"Oh, he will—and it's not the first time for either of us." Maria smiled. "But I have to get back and collect him. Is everything set?"

Francesca nodded and Maria turned to leave.

"When you get hold of him," said the police officer holding the door, "please run away as fast as you both can. There may be some fireworks and we don't want you caught up in them."

Maria ran back to the pier, where she expected to see Brian. When she rounded the corner, she could see two figures in the darkness at the end of the pier. She hurried to them and saw that Rom had a gun aimed directly at Brian's head. Brian had both his hands behind his head.

"Where the hell have you been?" Rom growled suspiciously.

Maria was panting. "I had to use the facilities," she responded.

Rom clearly did not understand. "What?" he hissed, his eyes squinting in the darkness.

"The bathroom. Do I have to spell it out?" Then to Brian: "Are you okay?"

"Yes, my love, now that you're here." His voice was strained.

"Okay, I'm ready to make the call for the last payment. May I use your phone?" Maria extended her hand.

"I'm thinking that I let you both off too easy." Rom cocked the gun, still aimed at Brian's head. "I think I need a bit more. Another two hundred fifty thousand is too low. I think it needs to be five hundred."

Maria was speechless. Brian spoke up. "Hey buddy, you've been paid a lot and all she has to do is make a phone call and you are going to get more. I think you need to keep your end of the deal."

"Shut up!" yelled Rom, and he pistol-whipped Brian, knocking him over, almost into the water. "What's it gonna be, missy?" he said, looking at Maria.

She looked at Brian who lay bleeding on the ground. Rom took this opportunity to kick him in the back. Brian grunted and moaned.

"You animal!" she yelled. "Give me your phone, and I'll see what I can do."

Rom laughed and handed Maria his cell. "Leave it on speaker," he ordered.

Maria dialed her aunt, who was only about fifty yards away. "He wants more money to let us go. And he has a gun."

"It's got to be another five hundred thousand or you don't get to see these two again," Rom threatened.

"I don't know if I can," Francesca responded with concern. "Let me see."

The line went dead. Maria bent down to help Brian, who was trying to stand up, blood dripping from his head.

"Why did you have to do that?" she said angrily to Rom.

He started to wave his gun in the air. "Listen, missy, you are not in charge here. I am in charge." Rom continued ranting, but while doing so, he took his eyes off of Brian, who now saw an opportunity. He grabbed for the arm holding the gun and executed a perfect judo throw, flipping Rom entirely on his back. The gun clattered out of his hand and away, but on the impact, it went off loudly, the bullet directed harmlessly at the ocean. Brian leaped over to it and kicked it into the sea. He grabbed Maria's hand, and the two started running.

Rom had been stunned but quickly recovered. He drew a long knife and started after them, calling out to his crew on board. "Mateys, I need you."

Three men from the ship who had been watching ran down the gangplank, up the pier, and onto land. All were armed with pistols. Although Maria and Brian were running as fast as they could, Brian's injuries were slowing them down, as he was hobbling and bleeding, so Rom gained on them. He got closer and closer and raised his long knife, planning on plunging it into Brian's back. Just as he was about to strike, a single shot rang out, and a look of shock and surprise crossed Rom's face. He felt himself falling. He let go of the knife. Behind him the three mates who had been running slowed down.

"Police!" cried out the officer who had held the door for

Maria. Four officers emerged from the shed, guns drawn. The three mates turned and started to run back to the ship. Suddenly, a bright light shone upon them as a police cruiser that had been quietly moored nearby, camouflaged by other boats, came to life. Another police cruiser came around the bend and moved up next to the smugglers' ship. The men stopped in their tracks. Soon they were in custody, and Brian was in the shed with his injuries being attended to.

"Brian, are you okay?" Maria said nervously.

He smiled at her. "Nothing that a few stitches, a hot bath, and a good night's sleep won't cure. Well, maybe a few nights' sleep."

"So, who is this brave fellow?" Jamey asked. "That was some move back there, lad. You must have some training."

"Brian," said Maria, "I want to introduce you to my Uncle Jamey and my Aunt Francesca. They came all the way from Scotland to save us."

And the group hugged.

Chapter Forty-Six

Los Angeles/Mexico

GUILT was all Tomaso felt at this moment. The enthusiasm mixed with anger had left him now, and he realized what he was doing was unfair to his three children. He had come to terms with that unfairness, though, recognizing that he was not a good father and never would be, that he had failed them long ago. He would only be a further burden on them if he went through with the trial and the inevitable incarceration. He reasoned they were better off without him in their lives. There was little he could do for them. But just maybe he could get to Miguel.

He drove in a beat-up brown Ford pickup truck along the highway just outside of Tijuana. His ankle hurt where the bracelet had been. He was glad to be rid of that. As miserable as his experience in jail had been, he had certainly learned a few things, most of which he thought he would never need to know, but in retrospect, one never knew what type of information might come in useful one day.

Escaping from prison was a regular topic amongst the inmates he had come in contact with, and a few had dreamed up elaborate schemes. Most included crossing the California border into Mexico, then traveling into Central America. That was not where Tomaso was going. Others had discussed how to hike across the border from San Diego County into Tijuana. There they could buy cheap used vehicles with Mexican tags for cash. One inmate had mentioned that an ankle bracelet or handcuffs or leg irons could be cut off in one of the chop shops near the border, again for the right price in cash.

Tomaso had kept an emergency stash of money at his home. It was only twelve thousand dollars, but he believed it would be enough to do what he needed, and he hoped he could add to that amount by selling his own car at a ridiculously low price, so low that no used car dealer would refuse. Of course, Tomaso had to set up the sale beforehand in a perfectly timed way. He also had to arrange for a guide to help him hike across the border. Once there, he would need to find a chop shop and then buy a vehicle. At first the whole plan seemed insurmountable, but as Tomaso researched online, he found he was able to slowly put the pieces together.

First, he found information online to obtain a fake ID. There were even multiple vendors that promised fast service and quality fraudulent driver's licenses from multiple states. Information on which state license was easiest to copy and which to stay away from was also available with just a quick internet search. Tomaso was amazed—he had no idea it was this simple for underage people to obtain convincing false documents. But he had little time to contemplate the many methods of the underhanded; he needed an ID with a different name quickly, and as luck would have it, California licenses were deemed the easiest to forge. He ordered one immediately, changing his name to Juan Ramos and using the address of a vacant lot near his home. He paid extra for expedited shipping and handling so he could receive the fake license the following day. He used his credit card—he knew this would ultimately be found by any competent investigator, but in light of his intentions, that would be too late to matter.

Next, he contacted a used car shop located as close to the Mexican border as he could find. Again, an online search was all he needed. He explained to the manager that he wanted to sell his car, but he needed to meet first thing in the morning to make the transaction fit his other personal plans.

"We normally don't open until ten a.m.," responded the manager.

"I understand," said Tomaso, "but I need to do this promptly at six because I have various plans. Is it possible? I also need cash—it has to be a cash transaction."

"That's a lot to ask for. What kind of car is it?"

"It's a Mercedes E station wagon, 2022, and it is in perfect condition. It's white and has only ten thousand miles on it. The blue book on it is $65,000, but I will sell it to you for only $17,000 cash—it must be in cash—and you must meet my time requirements."

This had been Nora's car, which she had used to pick up kids from school or to drive to Beverly Hills for lunch and shopping, so it had an extremely low odometer reading. The vehicle had been in his garage unused since her disappearance. Jocelyn and Justin each had a car, and Tomaso drove a red 2020 Porsche 911, but he didn't want to take his kids' cars, and the Porsche could attract too much attention. Besides, even though he was leaving it behind, he could not conceive of selling his hot ride to some scummy used car dealer.

The manager was no fool and realized something was not right in this proposal, but Tomaso texted him the title document and a few photos of the vehicle as well as the odometer reading. The potential profit to the manager was too much to pass up, even though Tomaso's demands were so unusual that the whole transaction was suspicious. But after all, he was a used car dealer, not a saint, so he ultimately agreed. He figured the less he knew and the less he raised questions or doubts, the better.

Tomaso then found online a San Diego cab company that would send someone to pick him up at the dealer early in the morning and take him close to the border. He was even able to learn through the internet about potential trails that ran from the southern border of San Diego County into Mexico. Locating chop shops and cheap used car dealers near the border was also pretty straightforward, and he printed out a list with maps and locations. He figured he would need to hike five to seven miles just to cross into Mexico and then another five miles to get to the closest chop shop. One of the inmates had commented that guides frequented these trails looking to pick up a few dollars from desperate people trying to navigate a surreptitious border crossing. He was also certain that for the right price he could obtain a ride to one of the car lots to buy a modest vehicle that would blend in and not arouse suspicion.

As Tomaso worked through all these details, he became

impressed with himself. He realized that when confronted with necessity, he really could research and develop a plan. Indeed, this might have been the first time he had actually done something this elaborate. It was a relief from the heat of furor and humiliation that he felt most of the time, when he thought about how Miguel had set him up. This dramatic change—a sense of self-pride—acted as further motivation, convincing Tomaso he could achieve his task.

The most difficult part of his plan was masking the signal from his ankle bracelet. None of the inmates had given him a clue how to do this. Tomaso figured he could leave in the middle of the night, say at three a.m., and be at the used car lot by the border at six a.m. The bracelet would let the police know he was on the run shortly after he headed south on the 405 Freeway. It would take a bit of time for the authorities to mobilize to locate him and pick him up—this was the big risk. A three-hour window, even in the middle of the night, was likely enough time for them to catch him before he crossed the border. Tomaso knew he had to do something to muffle the signal, but he was not able to figure out online how to disable an ankle bracelet. Ultimately, based on general research, he concluded he could wrap aluminum foil in copious amounts around his ankle, and that would likely make locating him enough of a challenge that his plan could work. He also figured he could take a hammer to the device, but he discarded that thought, realizing he would break his own leg. The aluminum foil would have to do. That and the time of his departure, when most of the police were still asleep, made him think his desperate gambit was worth the risk. Last, he needed a gun. When he was first arrested, he had been required to surrender all firearms, and he had not kept a handgun in the house anyway, just a hunting rifle, which the police had taken. He'd been leery of keeping a handgun in the house, since he'd become convinced that Nora might shoot him one day. He had hidden his hunting rifle in his study, and he hoped Nora did not know about it, but even that had made him slightly uneasy. Now he realized a gun was one more purchase he would need to find in Mexico.

After the police raided his home and discovered drugs, Justin had not returned. Tomaso knew his son was unlikely to escape and was going to have to face justice, but he doubted the boy would be incarcerated, and if so, only in a juvenile facility. Tomaso expected to be re-arrested rather soon once the police lab confirmed what was likely every type of illegal drug. This had led Tomaso to conclude that he had little time and had to leave immediately.

He'd hugged Jocelyn for a long time the evening before he planned on running, which she found strange. He had spent time talking with his son Billy, something he had rarely done because Billy's disability made it a challenge to have an extended conversation with him. But this night, Tomaso found a degree of patience for his son that he never had before. He listened to whatever Billy was willing to say to him. It was odd, Tomaso realized, that his best self was coming out now.

Dressed in hiking gear and with a backpack of food and water, at two-thirty a.m., Tomaso Ramirez, former West Coast president of RAM, proud member of Riv-aire Country Club, resident of Bel Air, owner of a twelve-million-dollar mansion, and father of three, went on the lam. He wrapped an entire box of aluminum foil tightly around his left ankle, put his full pack in the car along with hiking boots, and backed Nora's Mercedes with a full tank of gas out of his driveway.

Depending on one's point of view, Tomaso got lucky that night. There weren't enough people monitoring the ankle bracelets in the dead of night, so it was an hour before the weak signal from his bracelet set off the alarm. It took another half hour for someone to find a police officer willing to go after Tomaso, and by that time, four-thirty a.m., Tomaso had made it to the Orange County border and Camp Pendleton. For the next twenty miles as Tomaso sped through federal land, the signal was disrupted by the Marine Corps base technology. The California Highway Patrol motorcycle cops who had set off from Culver City received inconsistent information on where the runaway was heading, so they detoured off the 5 Freeway and drove east toward Escondido, while Tomaso continued south.

He made the car lot early, at five forty-five a.m., and concluded the transaction by six a.m. The manager looked quizzically at Tomaso's left ankle, since it was covered by a compression bandage to hide the aluminum foil. But the deal was too sweet to ask many questions, and Tomaso even persuaded the manager to call him a cab, since he'd left his cell phone behind, believing it could be traced. The cab ride was another thirty minutes eastward, past all the housing in South San Diego County, into the wastelands. The taxi reached the mouth of a hiking trail on his map by six forty-five a.m., at about the time that the highway patrol motorcycles were passing Encinitas. Tomaso paid the fare and started his hike, soon finding a Mexican teenager on the trail. He paid the young man eight hundred dollars to guide him, and they set off toward the border.

By the time the motorcycle cops made it to the trailhead, they were told Tomaso had crossed into Mexico, so they might as well return to headquarters; the federal police would contact the Mexican authorities in Tijuana and request them to pick up the escaping felon. They all presumed that Tomaso would be heading south toward Central America, perhaps Nicaragua, where there was no extradition.

But that did not happen. Tomaso made it to the chop shop before noon, all sweaty and grimy, and paid a thousand dollars to a fifty-year-old Tijuana mechanic to cut off his ankle bracelet. Then they took a sledgehammer and smashed the device to pieces. For another hundred dollars, the mechanic drove Tomaso to a used car lot and even helped him pick out and negotiate the price for a 2007 pickup truck. The brown vehicle had various dents and scratches in it, but it was solid, and Tomaso believed it could make the journey. No one was willing to sell him a gun, so he sped off unarmed.

Now Tomaso was driving, amazed that his plan had actually worked, that he was free, kind of—at least he felt that way—and that he was on his way. But Tomaso was not going to Central America, nor was he planning on staying in Mexico. Tomaso intended to re-enter the U.S. as soon as possible, and then drive all the way through the southwest to Florida. It was going to be a long, hard drive. Tomaso was on his way to find Miguel.

And he planned on killing his brother—with his bare hands if necessary.

Chapter Forty-Seven

Miami

BRIAN LOOKED OUT from the balcony of his hotel room at the spectacular view of Miami Beach and the blue of the Atlantic. He was wearing the hotel's complimentary bathrobe since he had not yet bought any pajamas, or more accurately, the Ramirez family had not bought him any. Maria figured he did not need those anyway—just some shirts, shorts, and sandals they picked up in the hotel shop.

They had traveled almost immediately from Jamaica back to Florida, on the first commercial flight available. No RAM planes were used since Miguel would have learned of it. Maria had insisted Brian go to the hospital emergency room on landing, so Aunt Francesca and Uncle Jamey arranged for hotel accommodations while Maria took him in for medical help. Eight stitches adorned his forehead, and he had a splint on his left leg. That and Tylenol plus a large glass of Scotch whisky had made Brian feel somewhat more comfortable.

The couple went to their hotel room and fell asleep almost immediately, even though it was just past noon. They woke up six hours later, had room service for dinner, then made love passionately, almost like it was their first time—or their last. They fell asleep again, exhausted, and this morning Maria would be leaving with Francesca to see her mother in New York. She kissed him goodbye, explaining that her company was in shambles, almost ruined by Miguel, and she had to do an intervention.

"You mean, contact the police and have him arrested for murder and attempted murder, conspiracy, and kidnapping, among many other crimes?" Brian asked her.

She shook her head. "No, my dearest," she answered somewhat sheepishly as she put on makeup from the hotel shop. They were both in the bathroom, Brian sitting on the bathtub edge, Maria standing at the makeup mirror. "First," she continued, "we have to take away his power, his position in RAM. My mother installed him with absolute authority while we were, uh, missing. My aunt gave me a thumbnail sketch of all the havoc he has wreaked, and now the whole company is teetering on complete disaster. I have to get control back, but I need to do it before Miguel is prosecuted. The Family Master Trust requires it, and I must do it in a very specific way."

Brian was nonplussed. "What are you talking about? The guy is a total criminal. After the police take him away, you can have the company's board of directors just vote to terminate him and reinstall you. I don't understand what the big deal is."

"It's not that simple. I'm sorry, but you don't understand. RAM was created by my grandfather, and he had law-yers draft a rather draconian trust document, and it holds all the assets of the company." She stopped looking at her-self in the mirror and turned to face Brian. He had always been awed by her beauty, but with just a bit of makeup, he was swept away by her. He wanted only to hold her. But he could tell now was not the right time.

"You look great," he simply said and smiled at her. "But that guy needs to go away, and for a long time, like for life."

She frowned at him. "Of course you're right—he is a total scoundrel. But if he is convicted of these horrible crimes, it could negatively affect RAM. That's what I need to find a way to avoid. That is why we came back without contact-ing the company, including my own mother. She does not even know that we are safe and back in the U.S. She prob-ably believes I'm dead and gone. I need to go see her with Francesca, to develop a plan, and to follow whatever I have to under the Family Master Trust to oust that evil brother of mine without hurting the company."

She reached out her arms to Brian, who quickly stood up and hugged her. But it was a short hug, since she pushed away to leave the bathroom and finish dressing in the simple green and white dress they had purchased in the hotel shop, along with brown sandals.

He followed her out of the bathroom. "But I'm not sure how his prosecution will hurt RAM if he's no longer run-ning things. He won't even be part of the company."

She turned to him with a serious expression, took his hand, and sat down with him on the bed. "We have relation-ships with lots of people, lenders, distributors, salespeo-ple. And of course, we are licensed by the government since we sell alcohol. Once everyone realizes a felon has been in charge of the company, there will be all kinds of repercussions. Fortunately, we are not a public company, but we are still subject to lots of regulations. The lenders will declare defaults and refuse to lend to us, our distributors will terminate their contracts, our salespeople will desert us, and the government will investigate us and likely pull our licenses, if not worse."

Brian looked down. "I guess you'll have to figure out how to right the ship," he said slowly.

She patted his hand and put her arm around his shoulder. "I need the help of my mother first, and my aunt too, and even my uncle—he's an invalid and we need to get him here from Mexico. We all have to work together. It will only be a day or two. You need to stay here to wait for me. Relax, read, call your friends, watch TV, just take a vacation."

Brian laughed. "Well, there's probably nothing left of my law practice, since I appear to have deserted all my clients for a couple of months."

Maria smiled at him. "I'm sure you can put it back together pretty quickly. You are so talented!" She smiled at him and kissed his cheek, leaving a red lipstick mark. "But give me a couple of days. Don't do anything, please. Just try to understand, I have to do things this way." She kissed him again and then left.

Brian tried to be understanding, but after she left, he realized he was not terribly sympathetic to RAM's plight. It had obviously been control of the company Miguel had sought, and it had motivated him to kill. And while Brian had only respect for Maria, she had obviously been blind to Miguel's actions. *Who knows what other evil he must have done?* Brian wondered. Brian knew Miguel had to be arrested, and a complete investigation into his activities had to be conducted. Yes, there would be some fallout for RAM, but frankly, the company deserved to pay the piper. Nefarious deeds had to be exposed and proper justice meted out to Miguel and whomever cooperated with him, which likely included his brother Tomaso.

With Maria gone, Brian began to seethe with indignation. He knew he could not be quiet while Maria conducted her company machinations. He knew she did not want it, but getting the authorities involved right now was, he believed, the only right thing to do. And he still had some loyalty to his client, Nora, who was a victim of both brothers' perfidy. He knew he had to act. The first question was where to start, who to talk to about what had happened. Who would actually listen to him? The first person he thought he should call was Detective Nate White. It was their investigation that had led him to fly to the Caymans. White could contact the Miami police with Brian and together they could provide the background for a warrant for Miguel's arrest. Perhaps the LAPD could be looped into the conversation as well.

Brian stared at the phone for a few minutes. He hesitated. He knew the call would be directly contrary to Maria's goals, that he would be disloyal to her, and that this would very likely cause a breach of trust between them—maybe end their relationship. He loved her and knew that he could never feel this way about anyone again. She was the one. She was the woman he wanted to spend the rest of his life with, every day of it. If he placed that call, his future with her was in jeopardy. What should he do? He went out on the balcony and looked at the expanse of the ocean for guidance. Or was it for solace? Or perhaps just to delay the inevitable? Brian knew he had to turn Miguel in; he could not wait like Maria requested—he had to have that murderer arrested. The man had killed his client and then tried to kill him and Maria. As an ex-prosecutor, he could not just stand by and wait around while corporate people put their papers in order and followed internal company protocols, whatever those were.

Brian went back into the room and picked up the phone. But he still delayed contacting the police. Instead, he first called his office, wondering if there was any tiny possibility that his secretary would answer. But she did not. Instead, he reached a recording of her voice: "The law offices of Brian Youngman have closed. We apologize for any inconvenience. If you are seeking legal representation, you may choose to contact the Los Angeles Bar Association, which can refer you to an appropriate attorney for your needs." Brian maintained his sense of humor and smiled at the recording. He really was out of business, he realized. *At least there was no forwarding information for any creditors whose bills had not been paid*, he thought.

Brian then realized he had not even called his own parents, who must be traumatized. Quickly he dialed that number and reached his mother, who began crying hysterically and called his father to the phone. After the weeping diminished and he assured them he was safe and well, he explained as briefly as he could that he'd been kidnapped but was able to get away, and now he was fine; he would come to see them as soon as he returned to Los Angeles. This call took longer than he had planned, as he could not get his parents off the phone. Finally, after promising to call again soon, he was able to hang up. But then, there was no further reason to delay. Quickly, so he could not think any more about whether to do so, he placed a call to the Houston police. He asked for Nate White.

"Hey, this is a surprise!" said Nate. "I figured you had forgotten about me."

"Not at all, Nate. I guess you didn't hear anything about me."

"That's true. I did hear some other things though, that the RAM company was taken over by Tomaso's brother, and also that Tomaso has been re-arrested—this time by the feds."

Brian proceeded to tell Nate the whole tale of what happened. Nate only interrupted to ask about several specifics. Brian left out many of the details of his magical island time with Maria, only acknowledging that they had become quite close. Nate did not ask any questions about that, clearly steering away from that subject. Nate did want a full description of the surprise ambush of the smugglers in Jamaica, marveling at the effectiveness of the police sting.

When Brian had finished, Nate whistled. "That is one amazing story, man. Almost too much to believe."

"I know. That's why you're my first call. I figured you'd be more likely to believe me than pretty much anyone else. Certainly, most other cops."

"Well, I'm having trouble buying it all, but I have no doubt that this Miguel fellow is one terrible dude. Let's take the next step."

"Call Miami police?"

"Nope. We need more info first, more evidence. We need to get the Miami cops' attention. Your story is pretty fantastic, and if I hear you correctly, your, uh, friend, his sister, may not be completely cooperative. We don't need her contradicting your story—they'd just laugh you out of their station. Let's start with the LAPD. They'll have a big file on this Tomaso—they've had weeks to investigate him, so your story may just fit with what they already know. If it all jives and they're on board, we will bring in the Miami guys. And then we'll get this bastard."

Brian was nodding. "He needs to be taken down."

"Yep, and we're going to do it. But we need to do it right, put together the case, begin the investigation in a proper way, get a warrant. You know the drill."

"Agree."

"So, are you ready to tell your story again to a bunch of other guys?"

Brian gritted his teeth. "Let's make the call."

And as luck would have it, they ended up speaking with a Sergeant Brewer, who was quite familiar with Tomaso and proceeded to loop in the federal authorities, who had already begun an investigation into Miguel based on Tomaso's lawyer's negotiations. And after hours of back and forth, Brian got dressed in his new tourist outfit and flip-flops and was picked up from his hotel by the Miami police, who drove him to their local station for his statement.

And it was quite a statement indeed.

Chapter Forty-Eight

Mexico / Miami

THE ROUTE FROM TIJUANA to Mexicali on the Mexican side along the United States border is not as fast as driving through Southern California on Interstate 8. In America, the highway is well-tended and collects tolls. I-8 extends from the Pacific Coast in San Diego County toward Texas and the I-10, and it is pretty much a straight shot through Arizona and New Mexico. On the Mexican side, Route 20 is not so well-maintained, and therefore not as efficient.

Tomaso knew he had stay in Mexico for this part of his ride, but he needed to drive quickly since he figured that it would not take much time for the federal police to release his photo to the border patrol. He needed to get back into the U.S. before the end of the first day. That was the other risky part of his plan since he was entering the U.S. "legally," being inspected by authorities, and using a fake ID. Once he did that, it would take about two days to drive to Miami if he drove hard and only stopped for gas, the bathroom, and to pick up whatever fast food he could eat in the car.

No one would expect him to do this, so he could make his way to Miami, to Miguel. He would go to Miguel's home—he had the address—and lie in wait for him. There had to be some type of weapon about, a shovel or a bat or a golf club. He hoped for the latter. It would be so satisfying to take his revenge. After that, he didn't care anymore. All he wanted to accomplish was murdering his brother, and then he would accept the inevitable, a lifelong jail term.

That is, unless he could get a boat to Cuba. Miguel had a speedboat—he had it moored at his own dock on the property.

Tomaso did not really hold out much hope of escaping on the water in Miguel's boat—he knew it was a fantasy. Besides, how would he live? Where would he get any money? He had no skill set and knew no trade. The only thing he could do passably well was play golf, and that was not going to provide him any income, although it might allow him to squarely hit Miguel in the head with a seven iron or a three wood, to bludgeon him repeatedly. Maybe his mother would send him something to live on, but that also seemed unlikely after he had just offed her other son in the most gruesome manner. What he really wanted from his mother was not support for himself, but for his three kids. They all needed her aid. Jocelyn would require funds for college now that he had used all of that money for his lawyer and for bail, which would now be forfeited. Justin had been expelled from school, had disappeared, and might be wanted by the police for his drug dealing at school. William desperately needed more effective treatment. Tomaso wondered what Jocelyn would think of her father when she learned he had run. He wondered where Justin had gone and what kind of punishment he was facing. He wondered if some new drug therapy could make the difference in Billy's ability to focus his attention and be less apathetic.

He drove with purpose to the border crossing, the Calexico East Port of Entry, which closed at ten p.m. He arrived at nine-thirty, and there was a line, a wait for the general public. He was in line when a uniformed border patrolman walked over, first stopping at the car in front of Tomaso, then at his vehicle. The officer was armed and also carried a taser on his belt. Tomaso watched the man approach, his heart racing. He quickly rolled down his window.

"Excuse me, sir," began the officer, "do you speak English? *Habla español?*"

Now Tomaso felt sweat rolling down his back. He shivered involuntarily. "English," he got out. Then more clearly, "I'm an American citizen."

"I'm sorry, sir, but we are going to be closing soon, and based on the vehicles in front of you, you won't be able to make it across the border tonight. You'll have to turn around and come back tomorrow. We open at six a.m."

Tomaso was downcast. "Are you sure, officer?" he asked in his politest tone. "It would be great if I could get back home tonight."

But the man shook his head. Tomaso wondered if he had been in his Porsche whether he would have been waived through. But in this beat-up old Ford pickup and his inexpensive jeans and work shirt, Tomaso expected no favors. And he got none. Instead, he had to turn around.

"There are several inexpensive motels nearby," the officer told him.

Instead, Tomaso headed to a nearby parking lot. He figured he needed sleep anyway before his long drive—he was utterly exhausted. He lay down in the back of the truck and fell fast asleep. The early morning sun woke him up, and he guzzled a bottle of water, urinated in the sagebrush near the lot, and drove to the gate. There was already a line of cars in front of him. It was five-thirty a.m.

By six-thirty, he found himself next up for inspection. He had combed his hair and used bottled water to wash his face. Looking in the mirror, he thought he was presentable. He pulled up to the gatehouse.

"ID please," said the curt border patrol woman at the gate.

"Good morning, ma'am," Tomaso said as brightly and clearly as possible, seeking to emphasize his American accent. He handed over his fake California license. The woman took the document, looking bored.

"Why were you in Mexico?" she asked.

"Just visiting some friends."

"You live in Los Angeles. Why are you crossing here?"

"My friends live near here. I thought it might be faster to come back to the U.S. here rather than wait in line in Tijuana." He tried to smile. The woman looked at him, looked at the photo, looked at the line of cars behind him, looked at her watch, looked at her computer. Tomaso held his breath.

"Okay, welcome back to the United States, Mr. Ramos. Drive safely."

She gave him back his fake ID. He drove slowly out of the gate and back into the country. No speeding, nothing to make him stand out. He headed to I-8. He had made it.

He was on his way to find Miguel.

Chapter Forty-Nine

Miami

MARIA sat at the large conference table in the RAM office that Miguel had rented. It was nine o'clock in the morning. She was dressed in a black Chanel business suit, her hair professionally done, her nails manicured. She looked like a consummate professional, a top CEO. Next to her sat her mother, Marta, and Francesca sat on her other side. Marta could not stop holding Maria's arm, almost as if making sure her daughter was in fact real and there. At the end of the table in a wheelchair sat her uncle Pedro. He had an oxygen tank with him. Jamey sat in the corner, a witness to the upcoming proceedings. They were all waiting.

The past two days had been a whirlwind of activity for Maria. After leaving Brian—and she had felt bad about that—she, Francesca, and Jamey went directly to the airport and flew up to JFK, then taken a limousine down to

Marta's Hamptons compound. Arriving intentionally unannounced, Maria removed the spare hidden key from behind a potted plant on the elegant white wraparound front porch with its loveseat swing. And when Marta saw her daughter, sister, and brother-in-law walk into her kitchen, she was so shocked yet overcome with joy that she fainted. Maria had to run to her mother to catch her and gently help her to a kitchen chair. When she recovered, Marta grabbed her daughter and could not stop crying. Ultimately, Francesca had to help gently pull Marta away from Maria, although from time to time as they talked, Marta would jump up from her seat and hug her daughter again. Slowly, Maria told the story of what had happened to her, with Francesca and Jamey chiming in when it came to their role in the saga. Her mother was aghast.

"Miguel did all that?" she cried out incredulously. "We all knew he was a bit wicked—I always thought he was tainted by the devil himself. He used to so relish causing pain to animals when he was young. But murder people? Especially members of his family? I can hardly believe it."

"But it's true, so true, so awful," Maria said.

"And this lawyer fellow, you've become close?" Marta stared tearfully into her daughter's eyes, and Maria herself then began to well up.

"Yes, very close. I know he was our enemy, but only because he was doing his job and representing Nora. That wasn't him, that was her. He is just very good at what he does."

Marta looked again at her daughter, who had looked down when she was answering.

"Do you love him?" Marta asked.

Francesca broke in. "Oh, you should see those two

together. They are like a couple of magnets. It reminds me of when I met Jamey." She looked at her husband, who started to laugh.

"You were a foxy lass back then—still are," he added. "And I still love you as much as the day we met, maybe more." He stood up and walked over to his wife sitting at the kitchen table, and laid a loud Scottish kiss on her lips. Maria smiled.

"But do you think you love him? Could you marry him?" her mother asked.

Now Maria was the one who started to cry. "I think so. Yes, I know so," she said through her tears.

"But how would that work?" her mother pressed. "He is in Los Angeles and you need to be here running RAM again. The company is in shambles, ever since I signed that document giving Miguel all the power irrevocably. I was a fool. I am so sorry. I thought we had lost you." Marta's tears began anew.

Francesca interrupted again. "That is why I am here and not back in Scotland. We need to oust Miguel. We need to do an intervention. Remember, that is expressly allowed under the Family Master Trust. We must be unanimous, of course, but that won't be hard. And we must have a hearing, remember."

Marta was nodding, her tears now wiped away. "Yes, that's right. But we need Pedro to be here, and he is so ill. Do you think we can get him here? I think it is mandatory that we do this in person together."

"I already spoke with him," Francesca responded. "He understands. He is making arrangements for a private flight to Miami. He is so sick, but he will come. You know, he doesn't have much longer with us."

Both Marta and Francesca had sober looks. Maria spoke up. "But why does he even have to travel? Can't he just get your legal proxy? He could sign a power of attorney for any documents, or we could send him a docu-sign for any formal papers he has to execute. I just don't understand."

Marta looked sympathetically at her daughter. "Your grandfather, whom you know founded RAM, had very specific requirements, and when I was in college, he hired a lawyer in San Francisco to draft a document. I think it was because of what happened to your grandmother, but he was quite inflexible about keeping the company in the family. So many people tried to take it away from him. He died trying to preserve it for us, for all of us. So, in the Trust, there is ironclad language about how RAM is to be passed down."

"It's also because he hated criminals, and they always tried to take advantage of him and steal from RAM," added Francesca. "That's why the Trust states that any member of the family who is found guilty of a crime is completely disinherited, has no rights to any part of the company, and is completely ousted."

"Miguel is clearly guilty of a crime, of many crimes," Jamey commented.

Maria nodded, but Marta answered. "Yes, but that's not enough—guilt of a crime is not enough by itself. Our family committed a lot of acts over the years that could be considered criminal. Sotero was aware of that. For this provision to apply, you have to actually be convicted. And we don't have time to allow the wheels of justice that grind so terribly slow and are sometimes so misguided to deal with Miguel. We have to act now to oust him and reinstall Maria and hope she can fix the disaster Miguel has created through his hubris and foolishness."

"What a mess he has caused," added Francesca. "He has no skill to run a company, even if he weren't a criminal. He is incompetent. He thinks that because he is CEO he can just get away with anything."

"Okay, so what do we do?" asked Maria.

Marta responded. "I know it sounds draconian, but we must have a family hearing, a live one with all three current trustees present, to set our grievances before Miguel and allow him to respond, to defend himself. We are like judges. And you, Maria, are like the prosecutor. Miguel can defend himself. And if we then all agree and are absolutely sure he must be ousted, then we formally eliminate him from RAM, from the family."

"What about his crimes?" asked Maria. "He tried to murder me and Brian, and he did kill Nora after abducting her. And I saw that he was doing other stuff with corporate property, laundering money and dealing drugs. I am sure I don't know all the evil he has done. He should be in jail."

"You are so right, lassie," commented Jamey. "Although in Scotland, sometimes when someone is that bad, we do take things into our own hands. Maybe that's what we should do here."

"No," said Marta. "We will not harm him. He will be excommunicated, out of RAM, but we are not going to take the law into our own hands."

"Then we need to have him arrested," said Francesca. "He needs to go to jail."

"That will just hurt the company," Marta said. "How will it look to our lenders and our partners? Things are bad enough with Tomaso under indictment. But with all this, the government will suddenly be involved, and you never know where that leads."

Maria began nodding in agreement. "Who said the most terrifying nine words are 'I'm from the government and I'm here to help'?"

"Ronald Reagan, I think," said Jamey.

"But he can't be allowed to get away with it," Francesca chimed in. "There must be a way for us to make sure he pays for his crimes."

"Perhaps," said Marta. "Perhaps after Maria has put the company back on track. We will see. But our priority must be RAM, not punishment for my son. I already have one son who is going to jail, then I will have two. What does that say about me?" Marta frowned. "I guess I made a mess of things."

They finally got down to logistics. Maria first needed to return to New York to see her son, who had been with Emilio all this time.

Marta, who had been checking in on Antonio, assured Maria that he was better than ever, that he had responded well to the treatment. Maria received this news with guilty relief—he was well, but she had not been there for him. *I am a failure as a mother,* she thought. After her day with Antonio, Maria planned to return to the Hamptons. The next day, a private jet would take Maria, Marta, Francesca, and Jamey to Miami early in the morning. They would take a limousine to RAM's headquarters and be ready to confront Miguel when he arrived, which, knowing Miguel, would not be very early. Marta would be careful not to use her phone, which had likely been bugged by Miguel, but Francesca and Jamey had cell phones, and they would coordinate with Pedro to get him to Miami.

Maria borrowed her mother's Toyota Highlander Hybrid to drive to Manhattan. Her mother was always thrifty and pragmatic—she could afford any vehicle, but she chose a reasonable option that had good gas mileage and lots of storage space. On her way to New York, Maria called the Miami Beach hotel to talk to Brian, but he was not in the room, so she left a message for him to call her on the new cell phone she had picked up on the drive.

After checking her apartment, which she learned had not been touched and desperately needed cleaning, she drove to Brooklyn to see her son. Her reunion with Antonio was joyful, and even Emilio was gracious and relieved to see her.

"I did not tell him that you were dead, or I should say presumed dead," he told her out of Antonio's earshot. "I just said you were on a long trip and could not be reached by phone. He did miss you."

It was hard for Maria to tear herself away from Antonio, but after a few hours she needed to leave. She promised her son she would never leave for so long again and would be back soon. Maria returned to her apartment after Antonio was in bed and spent an hour vacuuming and dusting. Exhausted, she immediately fell fast asleep in her own bed. It was late the next day when she awoke, jumped out of bed, collected her clothing and makeup, and started her drive back to Marta's compound. She called Brian again on the way, but again he was not in his room. *I wonder where he is*, she thought. *Probably sunning by the pool.* On her arrival at her mother's, she discovered both Marta and Francesca having their hair and nails done by two Korean women.

"You're next!" Marta declared, smiling at her daughter and hugging her.

"It was Marta's idea," exclaimed Francesca. "It was a good one."

Jamey was off on a beach run, so the women enjoyed the afternoon as a family, forgetting for a moment the traumas of the past and the daunting issues of the future.

Later, Jamey came in from his run smiling. "I just got confirmation—we recovered all of the stolen bitcoin!" he announced with a wide grin. "You know, they can do that these days. The dark web cannot hide from us anymore." This news was met with a huge family hug. They had dinner and went to bed early, rising early the next day and getting on a plane to Miami.

So now they were together, drinking coffee, waiting for the unsuspecting Miguel to come into the office. Wearing a bright blue business suit with no tie, he sauntered into RAM at ten-thirty a.m., yawning as he entered. The receptionist signaled to him.

"*Señor* Ramirez," she said. "You have visitors. They are in the conference room."

Miguel frowned. "I am not expecting anyone. Who are they?" he said with annoyance.

"Your mother is one," she said meekly. "There are some others. They are waiting for you."

"My mother? Marta?" Miguel was confused. "What could she want? Probably came to lecture me about the lenders, I suppose. Still, she could have called." He headed for the conference room. When he entered, he stopped in his tracks, his mouth open.

"Hello, Miguel," said Maria. "We are a long way from the Caymans now, and there is no boat here. Only all three trustees of RAM. And it is time for you to own up to the truth and face the consequences."

Chapter Fifty

Miami

BRIAN HAD SPENT eight hours at the Miami police station and only returned to the hotel after ten p.m., driven back in one of the squad cars. He was exhausted. He picked up the message from Maria from the front desk but decided it was too late to try to reach her, and he did not want to wake her. *She needs her rest,* he thought, *and so do I.* It had been a challenging day.

He was not surprised that the Miami officers looked at him with doubting eyes. What had happened was truly unbelievable, and the police had heard their fair share of tall tales before.

"So can we go over this again?" said Detective John O'Malley, one of three that were interviewing him.

When Brian arrived, after waiting for half an hour, only O'Malley was present. Brian had insisted that O'Malley first get Nate White of the Houston Police Department on the phone to bolster Brian's credibility. Nate was supportive and spoke in the lingo that police like to use with one another, describing the evidence he had obtained in a dispassionate monotone. After listening for a few moments, O'Malley called his partner over, a Cuban named Ricardo Perez. Both men listened to Nate's recitation, taking notes and asking questions about evidence, the witnesses, the spa visit, the Russian limo driver, the Goyard purse. Brian had explained that he was an ex-prosecutor and now a divorce lawyer—both Miami cops scowled at this—and that he was under court direction to find his client and report back. Nate also discussed the LAPD investigation and offered to loop in the sergeant in charge of the case against Tomaso, but the Miami officers indicated they would do that later. First, they needed to have a sense of the big picture: Nora was missing, her husband was under arrest for kidnapping her, and now there were accusations against the husband's brother who was here in Miami and may have been involved.

"What evidence do we have that this Miguel Ramirez participated in the abduction of, uh, Nora Ramirez?" asked Perez.

"Apparently, the lawyer for Tomaso fingered him to the LA prosecutors in trying to negotiate a better plea deal," Nate said.

"Any physical evidence?"

"No, just some cell phone records showing the two brothers were talking a lot at the time."

"But this guy, the husband, was at home with a bracelet on this morning, and you just heard he's running, he's a fugitive? So, he's not only pretty uncredible, he's not even available, right?"

"I am afraid so," Nate acknowledged.

Brian was listening. He piped in. "Miguel Ramirez admitted to me when I was in the Caymans that he killed Nora. He did that while he was in the process of attempting to murder both me and his own sister, Maria Ramirez."

Both investigators looked at Brian with cold but incredulous eyes. "We better get the lieutenant," said Perez.

They hung up with Nate, indicating they would call him back if necessary, and sat Brian down in the lobby on a torn gray sofa for an hour. Finally, he was approached by Lieutenant Vilma Rodriguez, who motioned him over to a conference room where Perez and O'Malley were already sitting, drinking coffee. Having introduced herself, Lieutenant Rodriguez took over the questioning.

"I understand you say someone tried to kill you. Can you tell us what happened?" she said in an understanding tone.

Brian proceeded to describe the entire experience again, leaving out his love affair with Maria.

"You say that this Miguel Ramirez was not actually on the boat during the voyage you went on," Rodriguez noted. "You acknowledge you boarded the boat willingly without any duress or force, and that this fellow you say killed Nora then disembarked. You were left on the boat with this Mexican man and black man from Panama, true?"

Brian knew where this was going. "True, but before he left us, he made it very clear that he had set all this up, that the Mexican fellow on the boat was from some gang acting under Miguel's direction—he tied us up and held us at gunpoint."

"Excuse me, who tied you up and held you at gunpoint? Was it Miguel or this fellow whose first name was Javier but you don't know the last name? Or was it the man who was called only Ricardo?"

Brian sighed. He continued with his description of events, but ultimately what made them start to take him more seriously was when he took off his tourist shirt and showed them the scars from the bullet wound, which were still quite red. O'Malley then asked to go through the facts one more time.

Brian described being found by drug smugglers who ransomed him and Maria, and how the Jamaican police had saved them. Upon hearing about the Jamaican authorities, all three of the detectives rolled their eyes.

"You know," said O'Malley, "Jamaica is not known for its great cops. I think the murder rate in that country is ten times the amount we have here in America. You mean the Jamaican police actually made a legit arrest?"

Later, they sat Brian down again on the torn grey sofa, and again he waited another hour, until an officer he had not seen before came out to him and offered him some dinner while he waited, which he thankfully accepted. This turned out to be nothing more than pizza that was brought into a break room, but Brian was not about to complain.

After another half hour, O'Malley came out to him. "Your story about Jamaica checks out," he said. "In fact, we had to listen to a whole bunch of bragging from those guys. I gather this was one of the biggest stings they ever ran and they wanted to go on and on about it. They did say you did some kind of karate move and threw one of the bad guys over or something like that."

"It was a judo throw, and yes, I was able to disarm him and get away. I still have some of the scratches on my face, you can see."

O'Malley studied Brian and nodded. "Better get a photo of those. And also of that nasty looking scar on your shoulder. Anyway, they're sending over their report and some pictures. We'll need everything they've got to support your story, you know. This Miguel fellow wasn't on that boat either. If we're going to get a judge to issue an arrest warrant, we'll need all the corroborating evidence to your testimony we can get. And what about the sister, who was with you the whole time and was an additional victim? You say she is out of town?" Brian nodded. "We'll need her statement as well. There is very little evidence tying Miguel Ramirez to much of anything—the abduction, the killing, the attempted killing. We have to rely mostly on your testimony at this point, and this is a tough sell. But with two victims both of whom state the same facts, that is a different story. Will there be any problem getting the sister's statement when she returns to Miami?"

This question gave Brian pause. He realized he did not know if Maria was ready to turn in Miguel. "I hope not," is all he could say. "But she won't be back for a couple of days."

"I think the lieutenant wants us to put this together right away. We contacted the LAPD, and they're sending us a statement and also whatever else they've found. Apparently, the brother escaped into Mexico—likely on his way down south to Central America, I bet. Your buddy Nate also sent us a statement and his evidence. Even those Jamaicans are cooperating—go figure. We have got to get it to the Miami prosecutor in the morning, all neat and tidy, then he'll want to talk to you as well. Plan on being here all day tomorrow. If we can, we are going to get a warrant of some kind—search or arrest or both—tomorrow afternoon or the next morning. Then we can move. Just be available, okay?"

Brian nodded. He really did not want to confess to Maria about all this, but he knew he would have to when he saw her in a day or two. He was unsure how she would react—he knew he was doing the right thing, but he did not know if Maria would think so, and even if she did, Miguel's arrest was not going to be good for her company.

———

Tomaso had been pushing himself to stay awake. The drive from Mexicali to Miami was over 2,500 miles. First, he was on I-8, which merged into I-10, which took him through Arizona, New Mexico, and Texas. He knew he could not risk being pulled over by the police, so he maintained a speed as close to sixty-five miles per hour as possible. This meant he would be on the road forty hours—with stops and a few hours of sleep here and there, a full two days. He was in Texas now, and it went on forever. He realized he would soon drive through Houston and laughed at the thought of stopping by the spa Nora had frequented and spent so much money at. He thought he could use a few days there, and he fantasized about beautiful women attending to his needs, all his needs. But mostly he thought about his family, how he had botched up pretty much everything in his life. He never should have married Nora, had been a terrible husband and a lousy father, had ignored his children, had not appreciated his sister or applied himself to his job, had foolishly trusted his older brother.

That is when the rage set in. He needed that anger to stay awake, to keep going, to stay on plan; the guilt was no help. Every once in a while, he would pass a highway patrol car, and the sweat would roll down his back again, but he kept a steady pace and tried to smile, even though the police could clearly not see the expression on his face as he drove sixty-five miles per hour past the speed trap. Then he would sigh in relief and remind himself, slow and steady wins the race, keep that speed low.

He continued to make progress. In fact, he drove through Louisiana and Alabama and reached Pensacola, Florida, the beginning of the panhandle, at about the same time in the morning that Maria's jet took off with his mother, aunt, and uncle, who he had no idea were also coming to Miami. *Just another ten hours,* he thought to himself. He turned off the I-10 south onto the I-110 toward Miami at the time Maria, Marta, Francesca, and Jamey arrived at the RAM conference room. *Just another four or five hours,* he thought. Tomaso was closing in on Orlando when Miguel walked into RAM's office.

————

Miguel stared dumbfounded around the conference room. He hardly knew his Uncle Jamey and barely recognized Francesca, but he was astonished to see his sister there, alive and healthy. He had seen his mother in person a month or so before, when he had convinced her to sign that irrevocable appointment of him as CEO, but she certainly looked older than he remembered. And then there was that old, sick-looking fellow in the wheelchair, wheezing. His uncle Pedro, he remembered. It took Miguel a moment, but then he realized they were all watching him closely, taking in his reaction, judging him, clearly because they knew what he had done; they knew he had tried to kill his sister, sadly unsuccessfully. How had she survived? He had even blown up his favorite boat. Javier had not come back, nor had Ricardo. He thought his plan had been foolproof. *Obviously, it was not,* he thought. He collected himself and regained his composure.

"Well, Maria, what a surprise to see you, but of course it is always a pleasure. It seems you have come back from wherever you were. I am so glad to see that our concerns about you being gone forever were misguided. Welcome home!" Miguel even managed a slight bow.

Maria scowled at him. "Please have a seat, Miguel," she said simply, pointing to an empty chair at the end of the conference room table opposite where the four of them sat.

"But why?" Miguel attempted to ask innocently. "What's this all about?"

"This is an intervention, Miguel. Sit down," said Marta sternly.

Miguel raised his eyebrows—his mother had not spoken to him in this manner since he was a child. He considered walking out, but then he thought better of it. *I can always leave,* he thought to himself. *I may even have to run.* He understood that Maria could sell him out to the police. But he decided there was no harm in playing this out—perhaps he could find a way to turn this little circus to his advantage. He walked over to the chair opposite his family and sat down.

"All right," he said. "Now explain yourself. Why are you all here and looking so serious?"

"As Marta said, this is an intervention," answered Francesca this time.

"Yes," said Pedro, speaking for the first time. "I have come a long way for this." And he coughed. "You have been bad, and so I had to come."

Miguel decided to engage. "Well, uncle, it is good to see you, and also you, Aunt Francesca, but I don't know what you mean. I have just been working, trying to make RAM the best it can be. This is all so unnecessary. And a bit of a subterfuge."

"No, it is an intervention," Marta answered.

"You keep saying that. What does that mean?" said Miguel, raising his voice a bit.

"You should take it from here, Maria," Marta responded.

Maria stood up. "You tried to kill me," she said, looking directly at Miguel.

"I did not!" he replied immediately. "That is preposterous. How dare you make such a scurrilous accusation?"

"You sent me out on that ship with that cartel criminal, who was armed. He tied us up, me and Brian Youngman, Nora's lawyer, and he attempted to execute both of us on the high seas. All of that was your doing."

"Nonsense," responded Miguel. "I did arrange for you and your lawyer friend to have a tour of the local areas of the Caribbean. I was giving you the opportunity to see what a beautiful place the Caymans are. I did not want to crowd the two of you, so I did not go along, that's all. I thought my time was better used working, you know, doing things to improve RAM. I am sorry you were lost at sea, but that is not my fault. I am glad you are back."

"You also admitted that you murdered Nora. That was just despicable on your part, Miguel."

"More lies! I don't think I need to sit here and be defamed by you in front of my family. I am glad you're back, but I'm running RAM now, and I need to get back to work." Miguel stood as if to leave.

"You are not going anywhere, laddie, so sit yourself back down," said Jamey, speaking for the first time, standing up and putting himself between Miguel and the door.

Jamey was older than Miguel, but beefy and brawny and at least five inches taller. The Scotsman crossed his arms and looked at Miguel with an expression which said, *I've been in plenty of tussles over the years, and you are no match for me.*

Miguel thought about it but figured if he was going to make it past the door, he had to choose a moment where there wasn't an imposing-looking man blocking his exit. He sat back down. "Okay, then what is this about? Why the star chamber with all of you here?"

"As you know, RAM is controlled by the Family Master Trust, created by our grandfather Sotero," Maria answered.

"Yes, so I've heard."

"This is a family business, which is why we both are officers and owners of RAM. The Trust gives us those rights. There are only a few provisions in it that allow for your complete expulsion from RAM and any of its wealth. For example, Sotero wanted the family to grow, so no one who did not have children could stay in RAM."

"Yes, sister dear, I know, but didn't you hear that I am now married and that my wife is pregnant?" Miguel looked around at his mother, aunt, and uncle. "I very much look forward to being a father. I cannot wait."

Maria rolled her eyes. "Perhaps," she continued, "but that is not pertinent today. Another provision of the Trust is that you are automatically expelled if you are a felon—by that I mean convicted of a crime. And you are clearly a felon, a deviant of the worst sort, seeking to kill your own family members for power. That is what you tried to do to me. That is why you killed Nora and set Tomaso up to take the fall for it. As a convicted kidnapper and killer, Tomaso would be expelled from the family, as would his children. Once out, none of your progeny are allowed into RAM and they are also disinherited—not a penny goes to them. So, your plot was not only to eliminate Tomaso, but also his three children."

"You have absolutely no proof of that," Miguel responded, shaking his head. "You think I am the devil, but I think you just want someone to blame for what happened to you. Anyway, Tomaso is obviously guilty, but that is not my fault. He will certainly be convicted at some point, although not yet I might add. He is suspended because he is under indictment, but the Trust does not expel you until there is an actual conviction. And I might add, I am not under indictment and certainly have not been convicted, so if you are trying to throw me out, you cannot. That provision does not apply to me. You cannot take RAM away from me. You never will. I will never be convicted of anything."

"You tried to kill me," shouted Maria, raising her voice for the first time.

"You have no proof of that," Miguel yelled back. He continued in a normal tone. "And let me remind everyone, in case you all forgot. Marta signed an irrevocable appointment of me as CEO. I am in charge legally and there is nothing you all can do about that."

Maria turned from him and walked around the conference table toward him. She did so slowly, not only to compose herself, but she hoped it would put Miguel on edge. She stepped toward him, and now she spoke softly. "You're right, Miguel. You have not been convicted in a court of law. That provision does not apply to you, at least not yet. But there is one more provision in the Trust. An ouster provision."

"A what?" he responded, now feeling less confident.

"It states that if all the trustees come together in person

with a claim against a member of the family they believe is working against the family interests, after listening to that family member's defense, if the trustees are certain that the family member has acted against the family, that member can be ousted from RAM, totally disinherited, and never allowed back into the company. And Miguel, all the trustees are here in person, and I accuse you of working against the family interests, and I demand that the trustees vote to oust you forever."

"But what about the irrevocable document? What about that?" Miguel started to turn pale.

"It is of no force or effect if you have been ousted," answered Marta simply. "Only a member of the family can be CEO. Once ousted, you are no longer a Ramirez. You can have the name—there are many people with that last name—but you are not a member of this family. You would be out, if we all so vote."

"You can't do that," Miguel protested.

"Oh yes we can," answered Pedro, speaking again.

"Not only have you sought to destroy your own sister and brother, but you have done serious damage to the company since you have been CEO," added Maria. "You have clearly acted against the family interests."

"You also forget," volunteered Francesca, "that you did not just try to kill Maria, but there was the lawyer too. We spent some time with him and Maria, Jamey and I did. He described the whole experience, and by the way, the hired killer you put on that boat told both Maria and that lawyer what you had done. It is clear you are guilty. You have acted against the family interest."

"You have acted against the family interest," echoed Pedro.

"We all agree, you have acted against the family interest, and I am so sad that my own son could be so cruel and foul," said Marta.

"Do you have anything to say for yourself?" Maria asked. "The Trust allows you to defend yourself, although you and I both know there is no defense. But you have the floor, Miguel."

Miguel looked down and said nothing. For a moment, there was silence.

Then suddenly, there were sirens ... loud police sirens, coming from below the large window of the conference room. A look of shock came over the faces of the three siblings. Both Maria and Jamey went to the window to look down on what was happening. They saw seven police cars, lights flashing, sirens wailing, all parked at the entrance of the office building. It appeared as if the police, many of whom were moving about, were cordoning off the area.

Jamey whistled. "Looks like they are coming for someone, and it might be you, boy," he said.

Suddenly Miguel bolted for the door, which Jamey had left unguarded. They all looked up and watched him flee. Jamey started after him.

"Let him go," said Marta, and Jamey stopped. "Our meeting was truly finished. All that is left is the paperwork for us to sign. Maria, can you see to that, please? And then I think we are done here."

Miguel ran past the front desk for the stairs. It was a long way to the ground floor, but he literally leaped down the flights of stairs, moving as fast as anyone could go. Five minutes after he left, the elevators opened, and six armed policemen entered. The receptionist was aghast. One of them came up to her and held out a paper.

"We have a warrant for the arrest of Miguel Ramirez," he said in a commanding voice. "We also have a search warrant for these premises."

"Yes, sir, officer," she answered, terrified.

"Is Miguel Ramirez here?" he demanded.

The young woman pointed at the stairwell door. "He was here," she said, "but I think he may have left."

"Where?" he said with authority.

"I don't know, sir."

At that moment, the CFO, Sammy Levine, came out into the front to see what the commotion was. "Can I help you, officers?" he asked.

The same cop held out a paper. "We have a search warrant to search these offices. We expect you to cooperate."

"Of course," said Sammy, who had turned white. "Whatever you need."

The officers then proceeded to spread out, executing their search warrant, looking for evidence.

The search began, with Sammy opening up every computer and supplying every password, quivering the whole time.

Chapter Fifty-One

Miami

BRIAN HAD COME to watch the police raid of RAM headquarters, and while he was watching the front door, Miguel reached the ground floor and snuck out one of the fire door exits in the back of the building. He had always considered he might have to run, and he first needed to get back to his home, if possible, to retrieve something secreted in his bedroom closet—and also to get the speedboat. Miguel had anticipated the need for a quick, surreptitious getaway, so he did not go to his Maserati MC20 that was parked below the building in the premier parking section. Instead, he kept a Ducati Monster motorcycle parked in a lot across the street from the rear of RAM's office building. He drove the bike right behind Brian, who was standing in the street with his attention on the main entry of the RAM office building. Brian was annoyed by the loud engine of the motorcycle that whizzed passed him, turning for a brief second to look at the noise polluter. All he saw was the back of a man in a blue business suit and a yellow helmet. *Asshole,* Brian thought.

At the same time Miguel loudly rocketed past Brian, Tomaso was approaching Fort Lauderdale. He had been speeding a bit since he entered Florida, so full of adrenaline in anticipation of reaching Miami and finding Miguel. He thought, *everyone speeds in Florida.*

His brother's house was in Miami Beach, slightly north and east of downtown Miami, so at this point the two brothers were driving toward one another. But Miguel reached his home well ahead of Tomaso. Surveying the area, he determined no police had arrived there, at least not yet, although he assumed it would not be long before the cops at his office came to his home. He knew he had little time—he figured he had to be gone in half an hour or less.

Throwing his bike aside, he did not stop to enter the house but instead raced out to the shed in back of the property on the Biscayne Bay. His first task was to load extra fuel onto his speedboat. He also needed to retrieve the briefcase with his emergency items. He wanted to change out of the blue suit into something low-key, but he did not know if he could take the time. It took him about ten minutes to load his boat with extra fuel and various supplies he would need for a longer journey. He owned a fifty-two-foot Cigarette Thunder, which had a 3,000-horsepower engine and had been specially outfitted to suit Miguel's needs. It boasted a full-service kitchen and full-size bed in the lower forward cabin. The boat had numerous holds for storage, state of the art technology, and a modern-day head that allowed the user to pump the waste into the ocean automatically. Simply put, Miguel could live on the vessel for an extended time, navigate throughout the Caribbean, and outrun almost any other craft.

When all was ready, Miguel checked his watch and felt he had perhaps a few minutes to dash inside his home and retrieve his briefcase. Hurrying through the back and into the kitchen, he rushed right by his pregnant wife, whom he ignored.

Angela called out to him. "Miguel, where are you going? Why are you running?"

"No time," was all he answered.

"But Miguel, I have something to tell you," she called out.

He paid no heed but instead raced up to his bedroom to recover his precious briefcase from a secret compartment in the back of his closet. He pushed aside a row of silk shirts, where there appeared simply a blank wall. Miguel bent over to the floorboard and pushed in a small part of the wood by the carpet. The wall slid aside, and Miguel grabbed the leather briefcase hidden inside. He did not bother to shut the door of the compartment since he did not expect to return. Pleased, he looked at his watch and felt he had just enough time to change his outfit. Ripping off the suit, he donned a pair of jeans, sneakers, and a polo shirt. He grabbed a double-breasted jacket as well, thinking he might want to have dinner at a nice restaurant along the coast. Then he raced back down the stairs, past his wife, who was trying to get his attention. He again ignored her, although she called after him, trying to tell him something. He slowed now to a confident walk and headed toward his boat. There were no sirens, no sound of any police at all. He had time. He had all the time in the world. He walked over to the dock and stopped in his tracks, utterly dumbfounded.

Tomaso stood there waiting for him. He had in his hands an oar he had taken from the wall of the shed. He had wanted a golf club, but there were none to be found, and he had only just arrived, looked about, and figured Miguel was about to flee by the looks of things. Not wanting to be unarmed, Tomaso simply grabbed the first item he saw that could act as a weapon. He swung the oar hard right at Miguel, hitting him square in the gut. Miguel dropped the case and the jacket and bent over. Tomaso followed that strike with another, directly on Miguel's back, knocking him to the ground.

"You lying traitor," Tomaso called to the prone Miguel. "You set me up. You framed me. And you killed my wife."

Miguel could only groan, but Tomaso was livid with rage. He hit Miguel again in the back with his oar.

Miguel cried out. "Wait," he gasped.

"For what? You are my brother and you destroyed my life. And my family. You are the most horrible human on the planet." Tomaso waved the oar over Miguel's head. "Now you will pay for it, all of it, you snake."

"You don't understand," Miguel whispered, blood now coming out of his mouth. "Let me explain," he begged, as he tried to turn over.

Tomaso held the oar above his head, menacingly. "What's there to explain? Nora was only supposed to be committed for a while, as discipline, to make her compliant, to make her agree to settling our divorce." He lowered the oar as he spoke. Miguel had turned over and was struggling to a sitting position while Tomaso went on. "But you killed her and now they blame me. You killed the mother of my children and sent me to jail. And now you are going to join her." Tomaso raised the oar to strike Miguel in the head.

"She's not dead," Miguel blurted out.

Tomaso froze. "What? What do you mean?"

"She's alive. I did not kill her. Yes, she is in a place hidden away. But she is safe and healthy and we can get her back."

Tomaso lowered the oar. "You are lying, Miguel. If she was still alive and you put her someplace, why haven't you brought her back? You know that I have been indicted for her kidnapping and murder. Where is she, if she really is alive?"

"Let me show you," Miguel responded. "I have all the information, all the records, even photos, so you can go get her and bring her home to your children. Just let me show you. Let me help."

Miguel began crawling toward the briefcase that had fallen from his hands a few feet away.

"But why?" continued Tomaso, raising the oar again to strike Miguel. "Why did you do this? Why are you not answering my calls? Why haven't you talked to me? You're my brother." Once again, Tomaso began to fill with rage. "Why did you do this to me and my family?" he yelled at Miguel, who continued to struggle toward his leather case.

"I can explain," Miguel said, a bit more clearly now, although blood still oozed from his mouth and his breath was labored. He reached the case and pulled it to him. "I will show you."

"You are just lying to me again, I know it," Tomaso cried out. "You always lie to me. You never really wanted to help me. All you wanted was to hurt me." He stepped toward

Miguel, brandishing the oar, thinking that he just wanted to hit him again.

Miguel sat up, opened the case, and reached inside. He looked at his brother standing above him, swinging the oar. "You're right, Tomaso."

At that moment, from his position seated on the wooden deck, Miguel pulled out a Glock G17 and fired three shots into Tomaso's chest.

Tomaso staggered back, blood spewing from the holes in his torso. Miguel shot again and again, emptying the rounds into his brother, whose body danced with the impact of each bullet before falling to the ground lifeless. Miguel kept pulling the trigger until he heard the clicking of no more ammunition. Blood was everywhere.

Miguel dropped the pistol and struggled, coughing, to get back to his feet. "You're right, Tomaso," he said, speaking to his brother's corpse. "I did set you up and I did kill Nora and I did ruin your family. And you were too stupid to kill me when you had the chance because you are a fool and a chump and were always a fool and a chump, even as a little boy. Well, now you don't have to worry about that anymore, do you?" Miguel reached for the oar that lay on the ground to help himself up.

"No, it looks like he has no more worries. But what about you, Miguel?" a voice from behind him spoke.

Miguel knew the voice, but it somehow sounded different than he remembered it, more confident, stronger, not whimpering or afraid. Using the oar, Miguel pulled himself to his feet and slowly turned around. There in front of him stood Manuel, a broad smile on his face. He was well-dressed in a white linen shirt and white pants, his hair was short and his beard well-trimmed, and he looked fit and tan. Behind him stood two men Miguel did not recognize. Both of them were Mexican and looked hard, unshaven, and grizzled, and they wore work pants and white T-shirts. One of them carried a small duffel bag.

"Manuel," Miguel spoke, but his voice was raspy and his breathing still labored. "This is a surprise. You've come back."

"Oh yes I have," said Manuel with enthusiasm. "I did not forget you or the things you did to me or all the things I heard. I also did not forget the things you did to others."

Miguel started to become nervous. He looked at the gun lying on the dock nearby, but it was empty.

Now Manuel laughed. "I heard the clicks. You used all your bullets, Miguel, your gun is empty. It is no more use to you. But if you had another round, I am sure you would shoot me too."

"Of course not," Miguel answered, turning away from the Glock as if it did not matter to him. "It is so nice to see you, Manuel. So who are your friends?"

Manuel smiled broadly. "I am glad you asked. In a way, they are your friends. Or I should say, they were your friends. But now they are mine." He pointed to the man on his right. "This man is Gustavo. He is very strong."

Gustavo stepped forward. Miguel could see that he was extremely muscular.

"Javier was my cousin," he said.

Pointing to the fellow on his left, Manuel continued, "And this man is Diego. He is not as strong as Gustavo, but he is a bit of a specialist. Let me explain. You see, they are both from Mexico and are working for the Mexican cartel. After I left you, I went to find the cartel's people here in

Miami. I knew they would want to talk to me because one of their people was missing. You may remember Javier."

"He was my cousin," said Gustavo again.

Manuel continued. "He was one of them, and you killed him. I thought they would want to know this, so I told them, and then I asked to work for them and they decided that I could do that, right here in Miami. I am a good salesman. So that is what I have been doing and it has been very good for me."

"No, that's not true," Miguel said. "I would never harm Javier. He died in an accident. Our boat exploded—I don't know how—but it wasn't me."

Manuel began to cackle loudly. Gustavo and Diego just looked on with stoic faces.

"I told them you would say that," Manuel said through his laughter. "I knew it. You see, all that time I spent with you, I was listening and watching. You thought I was just a fool, a plaything. But you see, my dear Miguel, I learned. I learned all about you and everything you were doing."

Gustavo and Diego walked toward Miguel, each grabbing one of his arms.

Miguel looked back at his briefcase, still on the dock.

Manuel continued. "I see you have readied your boat. You must be eager to get away, so I think we will help you a little."

Manuel walked over to the boat, while Gustavo and Diego hustled Miguel onto it. Miguel was still looking back at his briefcase. Manuel unhooked the lines and jumped in as well.

"Manuel ..." pleaded Miguel.

But Manuel interrupted him. "Did I tell you that Diego was a specialist? He is very talented in his way. He can make someone tell the truth—he has incredible techniques for that. He is going to show you, but we will take you out on the ocean first in your very expensive boat. Better to do it out there. This will be fun. I have been looking forward to it for a long time."

"No, Manuel," cried Miguel. "I was so good to you. How could you?"

"You beat me a lot, sometimes badly, too badly. Did you forget? I did not. I still have some scars."

"But the police are coming. They will be here any minute. You and your friends should get out of here."

"Well then, we better get moving. All of us."

Manuel started the engines and slowly edged the boat out into the Biscayne Bay. The Cigarette pulled away from the dock, then took up speed, and in a few minutes, it was on its voyage out to the Atlantic.

Fifteen minutes later, the police arrived.

Chapter Fifty-Two

The Gulf of Mexico

THEY FINALLY DROPPED ANCHOR in the Gulf of Mexico, having rounded the southern tip of Florida. Traveling at an average speed of thirty knots, they had covered about a hundred nautical miles from where the dead body of Tomaso lay on the dock. Manuel had thought it best for them to escape before dealing with Miguel, so the two cartel thugs sat on either side of Miguel on a bench at the stern of his boat during the over three-hour journey. Gustavo was on his right and Diego on his left.

The trip itself was torture to Miguel, even though the real torture had not yet begun. All he could think about was how badly he had planned everything—how he had not thought Maria and that annoying lawyer of Nora's could possibly have returned, not even conceived that Tomaso would come after him, and not in his wildest dreams viewed Manuel as any kind of threat.

I should have gone after Manuel and eliminated him when he deserted me, Miguel thought. His angry ruminations were occasionally interrupted by the comments of his two captors, one of whom kept reminding him that Javier was his cousin, while the other, the specialist, kept humming an odd tune and smiling at him in a strange manner. Miguel recognized the attitude of the specialist, since he was clearly a sadist as well, a kindred spirit. That fellow was obviously looking forward to all the pain and suffering he intended to inflict on Miguel's body and was reveling in his future torture plans. *He's probably thinking of different ways to do it*, Miguel realized, knowing that he would be thinking the same thoughts if their positions were reversed.

Oddly, although Miguel was angry—very angry in fact—he was not scared. He had felt fear at first, so surprised was he when he saw Manuel, but that had faded. Now he was just mad as hell.

The weather had turned in the late afternoon, and a stiff breeze rocked the boat. Manuel turned off the engines after dropping anchor, so except for the sound of the wind, all was fairly quiet. There was nothing in sight for miles around; they were alone in the Gulf.

"Now we can finally get down to business with you," Manuel said as he turned toward Miguel. "This is going to be fun, at least for me."

Diego stood up and went over to a table. When he did so, Gustavo put his left arm around Miguel's shoulder, squeezing him tightly, and held Miguel's right arm in a vice-like grip with his right hand. Diego had been holding his small duffel next to him on the other side of Miguel during their voyage, but now he placed it on the table in front of Miguel.

"These are my tools," Diego said, grinning. "I want to show them to you, all of them."

Miguel rolled his eyes. *Most would be terrified*, he thought, *but not me.*

Diego started laying out his instruments. There were two pliers of different sizes, a small hammer, brass knuckles, a sharp curved hook, a box of needles, a spool of wire, some rope, a small saw, a peeler, and a number of sharp knives of different sizes, some of which were smooth, others serrated. Each item was held up in front of Miguel, who stayed mute and expressionless. As he exhibited his tools, Diego explained some of their uses.

"This peeler is very useful in peeling off skin," he bragged. "I made some special adjustments to it. I am quite proud of it. I promise to show you how well it works." He continued his performance, clearly enjoying himself.

Although anchored, the Cigarette continued to bob up and down and back and forth in the water. Whitecaps surrounded the craft, and the wind became gusty. The weather was quickly turning for the worse.

"Now we are ready to start." Diego had finished his presentation.

"Excellent," said Manuel, who was relaxing on the other side of the table in a well-padded chair. Standing at this point required balance due to the wind and the waves, and he was happy to be sitting. Diego, who was not used to being on the ocean, had to work to keep his balance, and he was forced to sway back and forth. He first selected a short knife, similar to a paring knife. Diego liked to use this tool on the arm muscles of his victims. Having studied anatomy, his first task was to disable his subject by slicing various tendons and muscles in their arms, rendering them useless. Bleeding, these limbs would then be forced to hang motionless, unable to shield all the other horrible actions Diego would take. He approached Miguel, planning to sink the knife deep into his right arm, which was still held tightly by Gustavo.

"That knife looks pretty nasty, doesn't it," called out Manuel, watching with glee.

"We will start with your right arm," announced Diego. "That way, you won't be able to use it."

Diego came close to Miguel, wobbling from the boat's constant motion and trying to stay balanced. He quickly thrust, but just as he did so, the boat was hit hard by a sudden swell. The suddenness of the change caused by the strong waves sent Diego's thrust off target, and instead of piercing Miguel's right arm, the knife plunged deep into Gustavo's huge right bicep.

Gustavo screamed, letting go of his grip on Miguel. Red blood gushed forth from his arm as Diego, perplexed, withdrew his knife, which had sliced into an artery. Feeling himself freed and seeing that Diego was momentarily stunned and focused on Gustavo, Miguel quickly stood and kicked Diego squarely in the groin as hard as he could. Diego doubled over in agony. Stepping quickly past the incapacitated specialist, Miguel reached for the largest of the knives. He turned back to Gustavo and rushed at him with the blade. Gustavo, who had instinctively been holding his left hand to his bleeding right arm, attempted to ward off Miguel, but it was too late. Miguel stabbed Gustavo in his throat, pushing the knife all the way through the windpipe. Gustavo reached with both his arms to his throat and fell over from the bench onto the boat's deck, blood spurting everywhere.

Miguel now turned his attention to Diego, still recovering and doubled over. Returning to the instruments, Miguel grabbed the hammer, turned, and struck Diego squarely on the top of his head. Diego collapsed onto the deck. Miguel leaned over the prone man and quickly hit him three more times in the skull with the hammer. The sound of bone crushing and breaking was clearly audible above the wind and the waves, and blood and gray matter poured from Diego's head. Miguel turned and looked at Manuel, who had been astonished by this horrific turn of events and sat paralyzed, not moving.

"Manuel," said Miguel bitterly. "I think if you are so interested in this man's tools, perhaps we could experiment with them."

Now Manuel moved, lunging for the tools. He grabbed a knife with a serrated edge and the saw.

Miguel looked at him and laughed. "What are you going to do with those, Manuel? Saw off my arms? They are not the best weapons for hand-to-hand combat, my friend." Miguel advanced, and Manuel backed away, terrified. Miguel, who still had the hammer in his hand, scooped up the curved hook with his other. Manuel retreated in fear. Swinging his arms in windmill fashion, Miguel attacked Manuel, sinking the sharp end of the hook into his right eye. Manuel screamed. Using the hammer in his other hand, Miguel struck Manuel in the forehead, and he dropped to the deck, unconscious.

When Manuel came to, he was covered in his own blood and found himself tied with wire and rope to one of the deck chairs. Miguel sat opposite him, but Manuel could not see anything. He moaned in pain.

"You are awake," Miguel said. "Good. But you cannot see out of one eye. Perhaps the other eye still works. Let's find out." Miguel threw a bucket of sea water onto the helpless Manuel, and the salt burned his wounds, causing him to howl. Now he could see out of one eye. Miguel was standing over him, smiling.

"I have not used all of these tools. I think I must try them out."

"No, please, Miguel."

"I have gotten rid of your two friends from the cartel. I pushed them into the sea. I doubt they will ever be found. But unfortunately for me, you have fingered me to the cartel, so they will come looking for me. I will need to lay low for quite a while. I will certainly not be going back to Miami, that is for sure. I think I must find a new place."

"Miguel, I am sorry. Please. Remember all the times I have been good to you."

"Oh, I remember, Manuel." Miguel picked up the peeler and looked at it. "I wonder how this works. Your friend says it can peel away skin."

"No, Miguel, please."

"Come on, Manuel. You know I have got to try it out."

Miguel came close to Manuel and dug the peeler into his skin and started to peel. The screaming went on for some time. Afterwards, Miguel dumped Manuel's body into the Gulf.

Then, he set a course for New Orleans and began to plan how he would develop a new identity and a new life in the Big Easy.

Chapter Fifty-Three

Miami

BRIAN HAD ARRIVED at Miguel's house shortly after the police had cordoned off the area. An ambulance was already at the property preparing to take away the body of Tomaso, but that had not yet occurred since the police were still conducting forensic testing of the dock area. Angela had already been interviewed and confirmed Miguel had been there, that she had heard gunshots, and that the speed-boat was gone. Of course, Miguel's fingerprints were all over the dock location. Tomaso's prints were on the oar that lay nearby. Blood spatters were evaluated, spent shells were collected, and gunpowder was found present. The brief-case that Miguel had pulled the Glock from but left behind contained residue consistent with a firearm. It appeared an open and shut case: The brothers had argued, and Miguel had shot Tomaso and fled. The police ultimately put out a bulletin to the Coast Guard to be on the lookout for a Cigarette piloted by a single individual fitting Miguel's description; however, that alert went out hours after the boat had left, so by then, any craft of that nature could have been miles into the Atlantic in international waters in multiple directions, so no one expected to find it, and no one really tried.

The police allowed Brian to view the scene from a short distance, and he could see the body of Tomaso crumpled on the dock. It was a sad conclusion to his short-lived representation of Nora. Now both she and her husband were dead. The couple left behind three children with no parent. Shaking his head at the tragedy, he left for his hotel. When he arrived, although it was only midafternoon, he headed for the bar. He needed a drink. He sat down at the bar, and the man behind the counter asked Brian what he wanted.

"Something strong," he said. "No mixers."

"Well, if you're drinking it straight, I suggest either whisky or tequila," offered the bartender.

Brian looked at the man. "Definitely whisky. Anything but tequila."

Maria arrived at Miguel's house after Brian had left. Fortunately, Tomaso's corpse had already been taken away, so she was spared that horrible sight. She was interviewed by the police, and one of the officers brought her the briefcase Miguel left behind on the dock and asked her to examine its contents. She identified them as belonging to RAM and was promised they would be promptly returned to her after the investigation had been concluded. Then she returned to the hotel to look for Brian. He was not in his room, so she went searching and found him in the bar. He was on his second whisky.

"Where have you been?" she asked. "I've been trying to get hold of you."

Brian shrugged his shoulders. "You've been hard to get hold of as well." He was clearly in a dark mood.

Maria was not any better. "Were you the one who called the police? They raided the RAM offices."

"Yes, I know."

"Why did you call the police?" she demanded.

"He was a murderer," Brian responded, somewhat indignantly. "He killed my client, and he tried to kill both of us. Remember?"

"But we were in the process of dealing with Miguel and had not finished. We would have figured out what to do about him, like sending him to a different country where he could no longer do anyone harm. But instead, he ran, and now he's gone. How is that good? And if he hadn't fled, Tomaso might still be alive."

"Tomaso conspired with Miguel to abduct Nora. He is a murderer too, based on the felony murder rule."

"No, he's not, and don't quote me some stupid law. Half the laws in this country are just bad. Tomaso was merely an idiot, a fool. He did not intend any permanent harm to Nora. He was duped and manipulated by a very bad guy. And this scandal will be very bad for the company. No lender or partner is going to want to deal with us, and I have to try to put everything back together."

"That guy had to be stopped. He's a killer. You couldn't just hide him somewhere and ignore what he did," Brian responded emphatically.

"Yes, but you should have waited until I got back and we could have figured out how to deal with Miguel. We could have come to an agreement and worked together to bring him to justice. Instead, you had to do things your own way without considering the effect on RAM. You are so self-righteous."

"I don't think going to the police makes me self-righteous. It just makes me right," he said defensively.

Maria's eyes darkened. "Because you called the police, Miguel ran. Now Tomaso is dead and Miguel got away. If you hadn't acted precipitously, without me, we might have Miguel in custody and Tomaso might still be alive. And his children would still have at least one parent. I would say you weren't so right."

Maria turned and walked away from Brian, fuming. He shook his head as he watched her go. She did not return to their hotel room but stayed in her mother's suite that night.

Brian returned to Los Angeles the following day. He did not speak with Maria again for a week, until she called him to apologize for lashing out at him. He also told her he was sorry and offered to help with all of the California issues. But there was a gap between them now, as wide as the geographic gap between New York and Los Angeles. The love they found on the island seemed like a dream from the past. They started communicating primarily by email.

Brian's law practice had disintegrated; however, he had decided to change directions anyway. He was not going to be a divorce lawyer anymore. He found he had lost the patience to handle rich and needy clients who constantly craved attention and reassurance but had wildly unrealistic expectations. Divorce, after all, means both parties are losers, that they made bad decisions and failed at choosing a life partner and making it work. How could they expect to have everything go their way? It was just too taxing for Brian to deal with after what he had been through.

Instead, Brian decided to help people who were being mistreated by insurance companies. This made him feel like he was fighting the good fight in law and not getting too involved in the messes of family breakups. He also applied to teach law at a local community college and was preparing his syllabus. But he was ready to help Maria and RAM handle some of the legal challenges they had in California, including dealing with the Department of Child Services and negotiating with law enforcement over Justin's drug crimes.

It had not been entirely easy. Jocelyn had not yet graduated from high school, and Justin was in trouble with the law and had been hiding. Obviously, Billy would need new therapists. Then, there were the legal issues of adoption and custodianship in California that needed to be navigated. Fortunately, Brian was an expert and knew how to work the system. He still had a few friends in the police and the DA's office, so he was able to make a probation deal.

With the parents both dead and gone, the family conferred about Nora and Tomaso's three children and decided to bring them all to New York where they could be looked after properly. Maria knew she had to provide these children a solid upbringing—they were, after all, family. Maria agreed to take on the responsibility for all three of Tomaso's children, but Francesca volunteered to help, and Marta was pleased to see her sister stepping up for the family.

Francesca and Maria decided Justin should go to Scotland—Jamey would take the boy under his wing and have him work with their son Angus on the family farm—it would be like an Outward-Bound program for a wayward kid. Justin would work the fields and in the distillery like a common laborer for a year. Angus was a few years older and could be a role model and a friend and help put Justin on a better path. Brian arranged for Maria to be Justin's formal guardian, and she planned to visit Scotland more often to check on him and bring his siblings to visit. Family, of course, was paramount.

Maria became legally responsible for both Jocelyn and William as well, and she arranged for a battery of specialists to address Billy's issues. After only three or four months he began to show great progress. Even better was Antonio's recovery. Emilio took the laboring oar and brought Antonio to Europe to try a non-FDA-approved treatment, and it was like magic—all cancer gone. The boy's growth became supercharged. He gained weight and maturity and began playing soccer with a vengeance. The Ramirez family was healing.

So too was RAM Industries. Maria set about fixing the mess that Miguel had made. First thing, she rehired Colleen Stevens and all the other RAM employees who were willing to return, settling with all who did not come back and giving big bonuses to those who did. She paid the New York landlord all the rent due plus interest and penalties, and since he had not yet re-rented the RAM space, she resumed residence in her old offices. Initially, she was concerned about where the funds were going to come from, but as it turned out, Miguel had been siphoning off money from RAM for years and had been particularly aggressive in his weeks as CEO. When the briefcase that he had left behind on the dock was returned to RAM, Maria found twenty-five million dollars in bearer bonds. This was sufficient to get RAM's New York office back on its feet.

But it wasn't enough money to save the hotels or the boats or the planes or the plantation in the Caymans.

Maria's agreement was to allow them to be repossessed by the lenders; however, she was able to negotiate a compromise to the debt so that RAM had no further obligations after losing all these hard assets. All her forward progress had been destroyed by Miguel's negligent management. RAM was back to just being a producer and distributor of tequila and other alcohol products, but at least it had no more crushing debt. It was time to start anew at building a better company. Maria knew she had her work cut out for her. She also hoped the lenders would have trouble selling the hotels they took back and that in time she could rebuy them at a discount.

One day, a young Mexican woman came into the waiting room of RAM's New York headquarters holding a three-month-old baby boy. The child fussed a bit, so the mother decided to breastfeed the hungry child. The boy was healthy and had gained quite a bit of weight since birth. The woman had cleverly named him Carlos Ramirez. He was nothing like his father, Miguel. Instead, the baby was good-natured and smiled often, wanting to play and craving attention. *He will be very smart like his father*, Angela thought, *but not evil or cruel*. The receptionist in the room tried not to stare while the child was feeding, but since she was a young woman and had no children, she could not help but steal a glance and wonder if she would have the courage to breastfeed a baby in public.

The mother finished and was just burping Carlos when the door opened to the reception area, and Jocelyn Ramirez came out. She smiled on seeing the child. By then, Jocelyn had been in New York working at RAM for several months. This was to be a gap year for her, between high school and college.

"So, this is my little cousin," she said. "May I hold him?"

The mother smiled at Jocelyn and held out the child. Jocelyn took the baby into her arms and rocked him, and Carlos cooed and burped. Angela had no source of income, so Maria accepted another child and his mother to support. But this was family, and just like Tomaso's children, she took on the responsibility without question.

Brian and Maria did not see each other again until the funeral. Pedro passed away quietly in his home in Tequila. Days before he did, he began drinking a shot of his best tequila each day, wanting to savor his product in his last days, so proud was he of his many efforts. He left instructions that at his funeral everyone was to have a shot of RAM's top product in his honor.

The entire family came to Mexico for the sad event. Francesca and Jamey traveled all the way from Scotland with Justin and Angus. Marta chartered a private jet to bring the entire family contingent from New York, and even Emilio accompanied Antonio and Maria on the plane. Marta sat next to Maria on the flight, and it was only then that Marta realized her daughter's condition.

"Now I understand why you've been feeling sick for so long," she said to her daughter. Maria managed a smile. "What are you going to do about it?"

"I'm going to have the baby," Maria said. "What else is there to do? I guess it must have happened in Miami, that last night, our last time together. Ironic."

"Are you going to tell him?" Marta queried. "He deserves to know, at least. Maybe he will come to New York."

Maria shook her head. "I wouldn't want him to come because of that. Because of some moral obligation. He has to want to come. That is the only way it could work."

"Well, if you don't tell him now, someday he will find out, and then he will be very angry at you."

"I don't know what I'm going to do about all that. We'll see. Let's not talk about it now."

It was a much larger gathering at Pedro's funeral than at any others Marta had attended. She shed tears at the small church graveyard that also held her brother Carlos as well as Sotero and his wife, Xiomara, and her uncle. Even little Carlos attended, and his mother put a finger in the tequila and then into his mouth, in effect christening him as a Ramirez. The baby just frowned and cried.

Brian sat next to Maria during the church service, but the two did not speak. Maria wore a flowing black dress which hid her condition. It was not until after the ceremony and the burial that they talked.

"I want to thank you for everything you did," Maria began, breaking the ice.

"Of course," Brian replied. "I was happy to do it. I'm glad it worked out." For the first time, he smiled at her, noting that she had gained some weight since he had last seen her. "You look great, by the way. So glowing. Full of life. New York must really agree with you."

The two were silent for a moment, both looking down. Then, Maria spoke up again. "Are you happy to be back in LA?"

Brian looked thoughtful. "Well, I've retooled my law practice, and I'm back at the dojo training in judo. That's all going reasonably well."

"Your judo did come in handy—you threw that scoundrel to the ground at a pretty critical moment."

Now Brian laughed. "That seems like another life," he commented wistfully.

They were both quiet for a moment.

"They have judo places in New York, you know," Maria offered.

Brian looked at her. She had a hopeful expression on her face. "Perhaps someday, I'll try one of them."

Maria nodded, and Brian looked at her and thought she was more beautiful than ever. A powerful urge came upon him to take her in his arms again. But he did not do it. The moment became awkward.

Finally, Maria broke the silence. "Let me know if you do. You are always welcome at RAM."

Brian returned to Los Angeles. He fell into a state of depression.

He knew he still loved Maria.

Maria returned to New York. She did not tell Brian she was pregnant with his child. But she cried on the plane flight home. Seeing him, she realized she missed him more than ever.

The next day, she returned to work and tried not to think about it.

Chapter Fifty-Four

New York

ARIA WAS IN PAIN. The contractions were coming on more frequently. She had had been admitted to the hospital in New York and hooked up to monitors. The doctor and nurse had been in checking on her, but now it was just a matter of waiting.

She felt so many mixed emotions. She was alone and felt a sadness. She had not spoken with Brian for some time now, and she missed him terribly. She had not told him, and the guilt was unbearable.

But she was looking forward to her new baby. She had worked hard to get RAM back on its feet, and things seemed like they were getting better every day. She had also taken a liking to Jocelyn and was quite proud of how Billy had improved. Jocelyn would be off to college soon, and Maria realized she would miss her a lot.

A nurse entered the room. "It seems you have a visitor," she said.

Brian walked into the delivery room, a hospital gown over his blue suit, a mask on his face.

Maria cried out in surprise. "You're here," she said.

"Of course I'm here," he said, pulling off the mask. "Why didn't you tell me? I only found out because your mother called. I was on the first plane to New York." He rushed over to her and gently held her hand. "You should have told me. I could have been here a lot sooner."

"I didn't want to guilt you into coming," Maria said and then winced as another set of contractions began.

"Breathe. Let me help you. In, now out. In, now out."

When she was able to speak again, Maria sighed. "I'm sorry. So sorry. Will you forgive me? I'm so glad you're here. I was wrong not to tell you. I guess I thought you wouldn't want to come."

Brian shook his head. "Are you kidding? I've missed you so much. I thought you hadn't really forgiven me. I guess I was afraid that if I showed up, it wouldn't work out." He smiled at her. "You know, we're not on a deserted island in the Caribbean anymore."

"No, we're not," Maria said. "But I still love you just as much. Maybe more. I'm so happy you are here with me. Thank you."

"I wouldn't want to be anywhere else in the world. Or with anyone else."

The contractions began again. Brian did his best to coach Maria through them.

"They're getting closer," Maria said.

A nurse came into the room and examined her. "You're fully dilated. I will call the doctor. The baby's coming soon."

Half an hour later, Maria held her healthy baby girl, while the father, Brian, looked on adoringly.

"I will never leave you again," he said. "You or this baby."

"But what about your practice? How will you do business in LA?"

Brian smiled. "That's the good thing about technology," he said. "Now I can be anywhere in the world and appear remotely in LA court. Oh, I may need to fly back once in a while. Maybe you can come sometimes with the baby. We'll be bicoastal."

"As long as we're together, that's what matters," she said.

A nurse entered. "Let's get you cleaned up, Maria," she said. "And the baby too."

"I'll stay with our baby," said Brian to Maria. "I won't let her out of my sight."

And Brian gave his new baby daughter her first bath.

Acknowledgments

I want to thank my dear friend, Lindsay Conner, and my wife, Stephanie Blum Reuben, both of whom read my initial draft of *Tequila* and gave me invaluable comments and advice. My son, Danny Reuben, and my daughter, Becca Reuben, also read all or portions of the early version and gave me wonderful guidance from a younger point of view. I also want to acknowledge Sarah Conner, who introduced me to Bill Teitelbaum—Bill created an inspiring cover for *Tequila*, for which I will always be grateful. I thank Amy Cecil Holm for her exceptional editing skills—she taught me a lot. Nima Abtahi at my law office helped me through many technical challenges in writing and editing. Finally, I must acknowledge Meryl Moss and her team for guiding me through the process of publishing my first novel. Thanks to you all!

Tim Reuben is a graduate of Harvard College and Harvard Law School. A veteran trial lawyer, Reuben founded his own litigation firm in Los Angeles, where he also actively publishes articles on topics of law and society. Inspired by his legal experiences, Reuben presents his first wholly fictional "thriller-killer" novel, *Tequila*. When not practicing law or writing, Reuben plays tennis and golf, hikes with his wife and two big dogs, and enjoys imbibing aged spirits, *including tequila*.